**Also available from Adriana Herrera
and Carina Press**

American Dreamer

To survivors. Your strength and resilience humbles and inspires me every day.

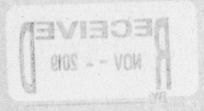

AMERICAN FAIRYTALE

———

Adriana Herrera

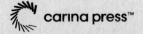

carina press™

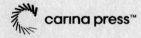

ISBN-13: 978-1-335-21596-3

American Fairytale

Recycling programs for this product may not exist in your area.

www.CarinaPress.com

Printed in U.S.A.

AMERICAN FAIRYTALE

Bring me all of your dreams,
You dreamer,
Bring me all your
Heart melodies
That I may wrap them
In a blue cloud-cloth
Away from the too-rough fingers
Of the world.

—Langston Hughes, *"The Dream Keeper"*

Chapter One

Camilo

"You better hurry up before I do too much damage at this open bar. Holy shit this thing is lit!"

I heard a tortured groan over the phone at my excitement. My coworker Ayako was running late.

"I'm on my way! Traffic is crazy. I don't know why I took a Lyft from Astoria during rush hour. It would've taken me half the time on the subway. Don't drink all the champagne, Camilo!"

I twisted my mouth to the side like she could see me, and gave her the real talk she clearly needed. "I can't make any promises. Imma let you go. I see the bar, and it's not too busy."

"Okay." With the way she sighed, you'd think this was a life-or-death situation, not that she was running late to get her open bar drinking on. "We just passed the Brooklyn Bridge. I should be there soon."

I ended the call with Ayako as I got to the complimentary alcohol distribution area. Once again, I was glad for my finely honed fashion sense. Stopping home after work to change into a suit was the right call, because this thing was fancy. I thanked my lucky stars for my job and my boss, as I glanced around the huge and beautifully decorated room where the Roi Green Center, a social services agency for homeless LGBT youth, was hosting its annual Fall Gala.

The event was at Cipriani Wall Street, which was as posh as you could get in New York City, and Ayako and I each had a seat at one of the tables. The room was decorated to look like Central Park in the fall. Lots of yellows, oranges and reds—it was stunning.

Melissa, the executive director of New Beginning, the agency Ayako and I worked for, bought two tickets for a thousand bucks a pop, but at the last minute had to stay home with a sick wife and kid. She'd sent an email offering the tickets to all the department directors and Ayako and I had jumped on them within seconds. Being a social worker didn't exactly pay enough to be able to do this kind of thing. So, after a very stressful week at work and some personal life fuckery, I was ready to pounce on the unlimited free alcoholic beverages.

After giving the bar offerings *and* the bartender an assessing look I leaned on the polished dark wood surface, raising my finger. "I'll have a glass of champagne please."

He winked at me in response and got busy pouring. Within a few seconds I had a glass of chilled Moët & Chandon in my hands. I lifted my glass to him while I put a couple of bills in the tip jar with my other hand. He gave me a big smile and went to serve another customer, as I followed his movements with my eyes.

He was hot.

Had a bit of a Jason Momoa flow going on, and I wasn't mad about it. I wondered how tacky it would be to pick up a guy at this thing. I'd only been here five minutes and had already gotten in some low-key, high-quality flirting and was sipping top-shelf champagne. I was musing on how the evening was already a success even if I went home right then, when I heard a deep and smoky voice from somewhere on my left.

"I like your suit." I lifted my eyes and saw a gorgeous man smiling down at me. I answered him without fully turning around.

"That's a pretty lame pick up line," I said, as I ran my free hand over the front of my jacket. "But I agree this suit looks amazing on me." He laughed, like I wasn't being one-hundred-percent serious.

I *was* rocking my Topman burgundy suit with a navy shirt and tie. I'd even gone for the messy man bun Ayako always said made me look extra fuckable.

I knew I was popping.

I turned so I was fully facing the guy and gave him a thorough once-over as I sipped my Moët. I had to admit there was a lot to like there. He must have been a few inches over six feet, because he was a full head over my five feet and eight inches.

He was big too.

Dark brown hair in a short-but-stylish cut and hazel eyes. His mouth was small, but perfectly shaped and, at the moment, the corners were tipped up into a tiny grin while he stood there letting me run my eyes all over him. I had an urge to push up and nip on that bottom lip, just to see what he would do.

Instead I kept looking further down his very large body, and barely withheld a sigh. He was a *very* good-looking man. His suit was navy blue and he had a boring white shirt and red tie on. It fit him well though, like it

was painted on. Once I was done with my inspection I
shrugged as he smiled at me.

"Your suit is pretty boring, but it's—" I cleared my
throat "—a pretty good fit. Although I have a feeling
you could wear a trash bag and you'd still look hot." I
went out on a limb on that one, assuming—given the
type of event—we were all family here.

Besides, he started it.

Another deep laugh burst out of him, his eyes crin-
kling as he shook his head. Like he couldn't believe I'd
just said that. He looked like he was about to say something else when Ayako barreled in between us.

"Oh my god! I saw bottles of Moët, this is fancay."
After she gave me a kiss on the cheek she leaned back
to get a good look at me. "Damn, you got your 'Come
Fuck Me' suit on, niiiiice." She stretched out the last
word as she leered at me, totally unaware she had interrupted something. Meanwhile Tall, Dark and Swole
behind her was turning purple from trying not to laugh.

Ayako was wearing a short magenta cocktail dress
which looked amazing on her and she kept shaking
her shoulders at me, clearly fishing for a compliment.
I rolled my eyes at her and complied. "You look stunning, friend."

She preened at that. "You're fucking right I do."

"You're so modest." I said, as she laughed and kept
blocking my view of Hot Guy in the Boring Suit.

Ayako and I went way back, were extra tight because
we both had Jamaican dads, and our moms were also
immigrants—hers Japanese while mine was Cuban. We
met in grad school and bonded over our sick love for
Golden Krust and hip hop classes. After school we'd
both ended up working at the same agencies. She was

a fucking riot and I loved her, but right now she was totally cock-blocking me.

I tilted my head to let her know where I wanted to be focusing. "Hey, hon, I was just about to ask the gentleman behind you for his name. Before you parked your luscious ass on the stool between us that is." She turned around and immediately did a double take.

She and I had done this particular routine too many times for her to miss a beat. As if on cue she spoke up, "Oh pardon me, kind sir." She extended her hand, those perfect teeth flashing. "I'm Ayako, and the lovely man you were just conversing with is my friend Milo." She pronounced it in Spanish, Mee-loh, like I preferred, as she waved a hand in my direction.

The guy looked at us like he was starting to suspect he was being punked, but he played along and extended his hand first to Ayako and then to me.

"I'm Thomas, nice to meet you both." He winked as we shook hands, then turned to Ayako. "Would you like a glass of champagne, miss?"

"Yes please! And its Ayako," she said, waving her hand at him. "It's an open bar. We'll be on a first name basis soon enough."

He chuckled at her and nodded. "Fair enough. Give me a minute." Then he looked at my empty flute and raised an eyebrow. I lifted my glass to let him know a refill would be much appreciated.

While he turned to get our drinks, Ayako tried to engage in a silent conversation with her eyeballs that I had no hope of understanding, even as sober as I was. So I just shook my head to indicate she needed to *play it cool.*

"Here you go." He passed around flutes and lifted his own glass. "To kind strangers."

We all lifted our glasses in a toast, and drank in silence. After a moment my mind started to wander. How was a man this hot and seemingly socially competent here by himself? He had to be waiting for someone to join him and just be killing time with me. Just as I was about to inquire, I heard a woman's voice call out.

"Tom! There you are. Please tell me there are mocktails, because I'm thirsty."

Figured.

The three of us turned in the direction of the voice, and I saw a very beautiful and very pregnant woman dressed in a stunning purple silk gown walking towards us, holding hands with an equally dashing man. I noticed the matching weddings bands they were wearing, and immediately felt annoyed at the butterflies fluttering in my stomach when I realized she probably wasn't carrying Thomas-who-I'd-only-met-five-minutes-ago's baby.

The man in question waved over the new arrivals. "Hey, guys! Thanks for saving me from sitting through dinner with boring rich people."

The woman came up to us and kissed him on the cheek, while the guy gave him the bro half hug/back slap combo. Thomas looked over at us and spoke to his friends. "Guys, these are my new friends, Ayako and Milo." He waved his hands in the direction of the new arrivals while looking at us. "This is my best friend Sanjay and his *much* better half, Priya."

We did the appropriate introductions and then proceeded to help Priya figure out what non-alcoholic drink she could have that, in her words, "wouldn't make her want to stab us in the neck for drinking champagne while she drank soda."

Ayako and I loved her immediately and I was about to ask her where she was sitting to see if our tables were close by when the MC announced that people should start heading to their tables. Thomas gave me a long look, as if he was struggling with whether or not to say whatever was on his mind.

I was disappointed when after a few seconds he just raised his hand.

"Have a good dinner, Milo." He said my name perfectly. Most people struggled with the Spanish pronunciation. I wondered where he'd learned it, but I never got to ask because after I nodded and waved back, Tom just walked away.

Ayako, who knew me a little too well and could probably tell I was disappointed, gave him some side-eye and mouthed "his loss." I finished up my drink and looked around to spot where Thomas and his friends were sitting. I almost choked when I saw them take their seats at a table right next to the stage. The tables I knew for a fact went for ten grand a plate. I heard a whistle from my side as I tried to pick my jaw off the floor.

I turned around to find Ayako looking very impressed by Tom's status at the very top of the gala food chain. "Damn he was pretty low-key for a dude dropping thirty grand on Friday night dinner. He's just like you like 'em too. Huge and looks like he could fuck your lights out."

"We don't even know he's gay," I offered, prompting an eye roll from Ayako.

"I'm going to point out the facts," she said, holding up two perfectly manicured pointy bright pink nails.

"We're at an LGBT benefit and the guy dropped ten grand a piece for three tickets. If that's not commitment to the cause I don't know what is. So there's at least a *slim* chance the dude's into dick. He was certainly eyeing your privates with interest." She gave my crotch area a pointed look, like there was some kind of indicator down there I was too dumb to notice.

I sighed and gestured to the other side of the room. "Fine, you *may* be on to something. Let's go find our seats, way back there." Ayako sipped the last of her champagne and signaled for another as I made my way to our table.

Just as I was sitting down I opened my Instagram app and saw a new post from my ex, which only worsened my sinking mood. It looked like the adoption he and his partner were working on finally went through. I scrolled through his recent posts and saw photo after photo of the tired but elated couple, looking adoringly at the bundled infant in their arms.

I didn't even know why seeing the photos made me feel like someone was squeezing my insides. Paul wasn't a guy I wanted to co-parent a kid with. At least not based on how he behaved while we were dating. It wasn't even about the baby though, it was about how fast he'd found someone who he wanted to make that kind of commitment with. Yet when we were together he could barely agree to keep a toothbrush at my place.

When would I find someone who saw me as their forever person? Who looked at me and saw exactly who they wanted? Not just a warm body to pass the time with until their soul mate came along.

And *that* was my other problem, despite all the firsthand knowledge I had of just how fucked up relationships could be, I was still holding out for some kind of fairytale. I always jumped in too fast, gave too much, put all of myself out there, and *every* time ended up getting my heart crushed. Why were these photos even bringing all of this up? I didn't have any feelings for Paul and we'd been barely speaking when we broke things off over two years ago.

Why do I care?

"Oh no you don't," Ayako whispered as she swiftly took my phone from my hand and put it in her clutch.

"Ayako, please give me my phone back."

"Why, so you can mope over that asshole and his stupid baby? Camilo, don't you remember how much of a jerk he was to you?" She sighed squeezing my hand. "Babe, Paul was not baby-daddy material. If you're going to feel sorry for someone, feel sorry for the poor bastard who's now stuck co-parenting with him for the next twenty years. He already looks like he wants out and that kid is only like three days old."

I chuckled at her attempt to make me feel better, but still felt annoyed with myself. Paul and I had been over and done with a million years ago. Why was I letting this ruin my night? A night at an amazing event for a cause I was passionate about, where I could drink as much as I wanted.

What the fuck is wrong with me?

I took a deep breath and tried to shake off my funk then turned around to give Ayako my best smile.

"You're one-hundred-percent right. Fuck Paul and his perfect baby. I have unlimited champagne at my disposal tonight, and two days to recover before work on Monday. So Imma put that open bar to good use."

"Attaboy!" she said enthusiastically then held up her

hand. "I solemnly swear to monitor your alcohol intake *and* phone use if you want to take your drinking to the next level. You held it down this summer when we went to that beach party in the Hamptons, and I owe you."

I saluted her, remembering the very wild night in question. "Anytime, babe. Let me finish this one and I'll go get myself another." I sipped from my glass, looking around the room. It really was beautifully decorated, with gorgeous centerpieces laden with lilies and roses in fall colors.

Each place setting had a menu printed on bloodred card stock and gold font. On one side we could read the courses we'd be enjoying during dinner, and on the other the story of one of the young people who benefited from the center's services. It was a smart and touching way to get people to pull out those checkbooks again before the end of the night.

After a few minutes the servers started coming around with bowls of delicious butternut squash and apple soup and to pour more champagne for us, and we got busy eating and moaning over how good everything was. Gorgeous courses kept coming as Ayako and I chatted with the other people at our table. Before long, dinner was over and the lights in the room were dimmed to begin the more formal part of the evening.

Between the couple of glasses of bubbly I'd had and the delicious meal, I was feeling pretty relaxed. As the speeches started to get on their way, I stood up and touched Ayako's shoulder to get her attention.

"Hey, do you want to go with me to the bar for one last glass of bubbly?"

She looked up at me smiling and pointed at her half-full glass. "No thanks, hon. I'll wait for you here." She turned around and went back to the conversation with a woman sitting next to her.

When I got to the bar I found it empty again, so I got the bartender's attention immediately. He poured me another glass of Moët without asking and pushed it toward me across the bar with a flirty smile. I thanked him but could not muster up the energy to flirt back. I stood by the bar sipping slowly and listening to the person speaking from the stage.

"Still enjoying the open bar, I see."

Thomas.

His voice was coming from behind me this time, and I felt a flutter in my belly. Suddenly my lack of enthusiasm was replaced by a burst of energy. I smiled to myself before turning around.

"Yes i am. How is your evening going so far?"

I gazed up at him and saw him lift a shoulder, as he asked the bartender for a Zacapa on the rocks. "It's another gala. This organization's mission is particularly important to me, so I try to push through. Once you've gone to enough of these, they all sort of blend together." He took a sip of the amber liquid in his glass, his eyes fixed on me. "Nothing terribly memorable ever happens at these things."

He paused then and tipped his glass at me, a very suggestive smile on his lips. "Although I must say, this year's attendants have been particularly impressive."

We stood there with a charged silence between us for a few breaths. Thomas looked me up and down with hungry eyes—like he wanted to rip all my clothes off and maul me where I stood—while I kept sipping from my glass and letting my own eyes look over whatever part of his body I wanted. I noticed a little bit of gray on his temples I hadn't seen earlier, which only made him that much hotter.

As Ayako pointed out earlier, he *was* one-hundred-percent my type.

Suddenly an insane urge took over me and I grabbed his hand, pulling him out of the ballroom and towards a sitting room I'd seen on an earlier trip to the men's room. To my surprise he let me lead him away without much resistance. Just as we crossed the threshold and turned in the direction of the restrooms, he asked off-handedly, "Where are we going?"

"To make this gala memorable for you." He didn't respond, just laughed quietly and squeezed my hand tighter.

When we got there I walked through the door, pulling him in with me. As soon as we were both inside, I locked the door, walked over to where he was standing by the wall on the far side of the room and went down on my knees.

Chapter Two

Tom

All the air left my body when I saw Milo gracefully kneel in front of me. From the first moment I'd seen him at the bar I'd wanted him. I couldn't remember the last time someone captured my attention the way he had.

He was so beautiful.

His mouth was broad and full, made for kissing. His body had the slim build of a dancer. Whenever he'd looked at me tonight, his gray eyes were intense, like he was trying to figure me out. Now he was staring up at me, with his lips parted, loose wisps of hair framing his face. Waiting for me to make the next move. I was not one to act on impulse, but the pull I felt toward Milo was undeniable. Before I could talk myself out of it, I lifted his chin with one hand and grabbed my cock through my pants with the other.

"You brought me in here because you want this cock?"

He nodded frantically, short pants escaping his lips. "Yes."

I put my thumb in his mouth, and he ran his tongue over it, sending a wave of lust through me so intense I had to lean against the wall for support. "What makes you think I want your mouth on me?" He didn't answer, just pushed his nose into my crotch, inhaling, then brought his hands up to undo my zipper, but I blocked his access. Emboldened by the heat in his eyes, I fisted his hair, pulling his face away, and asked into the silent room.

"What are you going to do with it, Milo?" I was growling more than talking, as I used a hand to frame my erection, so he could get a good look at what he was about to take in his mouth. "Do you think you can take all this?"

His breathing got heavier and he listed a bit trying to get at me again, before he finally spoke. "Let me have it."

His voice was reedy with need, and I found it irresistible. I made quick work of the zipper and pushed down my briefs. Milo licked his lips as I took out my cock and stroked it. When I pulled down the foreskin, he moaned and leaned forward, the tip of his tongue trying to lap up a bead of pre-come that leaked out.

"Oh shit. You're not cut. I wanna taste it." The urgency in his voice, the intensity of his need made me breathless.

I grabbed the back of his head and with one hand painted his lips with my cock. Milo moaned, trying to get at me again.

"Did I say you could put your mouth on me yet?" My voice sounded like someone else's, and I couldn't remember the last time I'd been this turned on, this caught up in a man.

"I'm going to push this cock down your throat," I said as I stroked myself.

He gasped and when he spoke, he sounded out of breath. "I want you to fuck my face, make me choke on it, so I can taste you for days."

I had to squeeze my balls hard then, because I was going to come just from the wanton look on his face.

I was burning up for him.

I wanted to take him right on this floor. Fuck him until we were both drenched in come and sweat. I ran shaky fingers over the loose curls around his face, as he licked my shaft. His eyes were so intent on me, the eyeliner around them a little smudged. He looked debauched and so fucking sexy.

"Open your mouth," I said as I tapped his cheek with my cock, and he opened for me. I pushed in slowly, taking in the sight he made. His mouth was red and swollen, lips stretched as he took me in. His pupils so blown out I could only see a ring of gray. I felt him shudder and then he started moving up and down my cock, his fingers making a tight circle around my shaft as he went. Between his mouth and tongue sucking on the head and the tight strokes, I was feeling lightheaded. I squeezed my ass hard hoping to stave off my orgasm for a little longer, as I ran my fingers along his hollowed cheeks. His hands were grabbing on to me so tightly I knew I'd have bruises tomorrow.

"Relax your throat, baby. Let me get in deeper." He breathed in through his nose and on the exhale I felt him open up for me again, and I pushed in further. He looked totally wrecked, his eyes watering as his throat pulsed around my cock.

I took a deep breath trying to get myself under control. "Are you ready? I'm going to fuck in now."

He tried nodding, his hands gripping me tighter.

"You look so hot right now, sweetheart, taking this fat cock." I moaned when my words prompted him to redouble his efforts.

I was so used to men who never showed their cards, there was always some subterfuge, an ace under the sleeve. Not Milo, he was completely open, no hiding.

I thrust in hard and his throat relaxed, pulsing around me. A liquid feeling pooled from my ass to my chest, and I knew I wouldn't last much longer. The only things you could hear in the room were our breathing and the wet sounds of my dick thrusting in and out of his mouth.

"Oh fuck, I'm so close. Get your cock out, baby. Make yourself come while you're sucking me so good."

He let out a long low tortured moan, and after a moment was stroking his cock as I pushed in again.

I thrust in a couple more times, white-hot pleasure blinding me for a moment, and then I was coming. I tried to pull out, but his strong hands kept me where I was. Milo took everything I had. I could feel the shiver run through his body when his orgasm hit, just a second after mine.

As my body started to come down, I slumped against the wall, glad I had it there for support. Milo had his face pushed against my thigh, his breathing harsh. I pulled him up so he was leaning against me, and put both my hands on his face.

"I can guarantee this is now the most memorable gala of my life."

The shy smile he gave me was completely devastating. "I don't go to a lot of these, but this is definitely the highlight of the evening."

I didn't respond, just bent down and kissed him. My tongue slipped into his mouth and I could taste myself there, mingling with the champagne and Milo. A crazy thought went through my head at that moment. I imagined myself doing this forever. Kissing this mouth, holding this body against mine, and it felt like everything I wanted.

I tried to chase away my ridiculous fantasies and focused on kissing Milo, on feeling him. He responded in kind getting closer to me and wrapping his arms around my neck as our tongues tangled together. Things were about to get heated again when someone knocked on the door.

We both startled and quickly separated. Milo started putting his clothes back in order, and I did the same. I looked up at him as he tucked in his shirt. His lips were red and his eyes a bit glassy. His hair was a mess. He looked freshly fucked, and it took all I had in me not to put him on his knees again.

I sighed with frustration about getting this moment cut short and I tried to smooth my clothes. Just to find something to do—now that it seemed like the moment with Milo had passed—I peered in the mirror to inspect how evident what we'd just done would be when I walked out of this room. I looked flushed and probably smelled like come, but we'd been gone long enough that the ceremony had to be almost done. Hopefully I could make a quick escape.

Milo's voice in the quiet room brought me back to the moment and him. "Why don't you stay here, and I'll walk out first," he said as he straightened his jacket.

My chest tightened when he said it, which was ridiculous, because what would we do? We couldn't stay in here all night.

"Okay," I whispered, feeling a little out of my depth.

I went to wash my hands, giving myself time to get my bearings. When I turned around, intending to ask him for his number, I saw him quietly slipping out of the room.

I was such an idiot.

Why did I have to make a big thing out of this? Okay, so I'd just gotten the best blow job of my life. That didn't mean the guy would want to see me again. It was just a little fun at a dull dinner.

I waited another minute and walked out of the room into an empty hallway. Apparently the asshole who'd knocked before found another place to sit.

I walked back into the ballroom and went straight to my table. I tried not to look to where I'd seen Milo sitting earlier and sank down next to Priya, who gave me a suspicious look and sniffed the air.

"Pregnant women have an elevated sense of smell, Thomas. What exactly took you so long?"

I tried not to smile at her undisguised curiosity. "I'm not going to answer that. Is this thing any closer to ending? Next year, I'm just going to send a check," I said, making a show of straightening out my collar and tie.

Priya shook her head and gave me some serious side-eye. "Surely you know I'm going to need details. Was it the guy from the bar? Because I'd do him too." She looked over at Sanjay who had the amused expression he usually sported whenever his wife was around.

He grinned and gave me an enthusiastic thumbs-up. "He was pretty hot, Tom."

"Shut up. I don't kiss and tell."

Priya's mouth twisted to the side as she assessed my demeanor. She wouldn't have to look very closely, I'd seen my face in the mirror before I left that sitting room.

"Uh you were doing a *lot* more than kissing if the scent I'm detecting is any indication. Did you get his number? Because any guy who makes you throw caution to the wind like that deserves a call back."

I cleared my throat trying to keep my tone light when I spoke. "He left before I could ask."

Priya narrowed her eyes at me like she was trying to figure out if that was a good or bad thing. "Maybe you'll see each other again?"

"I don't think so."

Despite my best effort, my tone was a bit regretful. I couldn't seem to shake the feeling that something important had just slipped through my fingers.

Camilo

"Damn, friend, you weren't joking when you said you were taking your gala enjoyment up a notch. Is that a post-coital glow I'm detecting?"

I didn't even try to deny it. From what I saw in the hallway mirror, I looked pretty fucked out.

I took a sip from my glass of water and answered Ayako while avoiding direct eye contact. "I might have gotten a bit up close and personal with Thomas in one of the sitting rooms outside."

Ayako widened her eyes, looking impressed. "Snap. I don't usually go for the big ones, but I'm feeling mad FOMO over here. That dude is smoking." She turned her head again, still trying to feel out if she was supposed to be happy for me or not. "How was it?"

I lifted a shoulder and this time I did look at her. "I'd take his ass to Red Lobster."

Ayako almost sprayed her drink all over the table

at the *Lemonade* reference, then cackled. "Oh my god, Camilo. How long have you been waiting for a chance to drop that one on me? So will there be a repeat? He seemed cool."

I shook my head at her suggestion, because, no. "Hell nah. Ayako, what the fuck am I going to do with a guy with enough money to drop thirty-grand on dinner? I'm a social worker! I can't fuck with people like that. It would be a betrayal to the profession."

"Speak for yourself, shawty. I'd get down with a millionaire."

"You're a disgrace to our guild."

"Whatever, Camilo. You always need to take everything to the extreme." She pursed her lips then, clearly not done telling me about myself. "You're too judgy sometimes, babe. Just because he's rich doesn't mean he's an asshole."

I didn't have the energy to get into an argument with Ayako about my bitchiness or anything else, so I just nodded and took another sip of my water. The thing with Thomas had gone from something impulsive and fun I did at a party, to incredibly intense and I was feeling out of sorts.

I'd expected him to be this uptight, shy or hesitant rich dude, but instead he just rolled with it. He was such a filthy fucker too. Just thinking of how he ran his mouth while he grabbed my hair and rammed his cock down my throat was making me a little short of breath. But what really messed with my head was how tender and sweet he'd been afterwards.

That *kiss*.

Thomas was not at all what I'd expected. I'd wanted more the second we were done and that's why I had to get out of there fast. A man like him just didn't fit in my life.

Ayako sighed at whatever face I was making.

"Okay." She raised her hands as if calling a truce. "We might want to call this night, babe. The champagne is making me verbally abrasive and you've already gotten off. I think it's safe to say we've peaked."

Ayako's superpower *was* diffusing my moodiness. I put my arm around her shoulder and nodded. "I think you're onto something, Ms. Russell. Let's blow this joint before we turn into pumpkins."

We stood up together and quickly made our way to the coat check after saying goodbye to the others at our table. I tried not to give any weight to the fact that at the very last second I turned around to see Thomas watching me walk out of the room.

Chapter Three

Camilo

"There's my favorite gala buddy!"

I grinned in response to Ayako's enthusiastic hello as I walked into the office Monday morning.

When I got to my desk I noticed a sticky note stuck to one of my desktop monitors. It was from our boss Melissa asking me to come see her as soon as I got in.

Not sure what the unusual request was about I stopped back at Ayako's in case she knew. "Hey, Melissa left me a note to go see her as soon as I got in. Do you know what it's about?"

She smiled big and then lifted a shoulder.

"I don't know exactly, but she did say it was potentially very good news."

I perked up at that, I could use some good news on this Monday. "Okay let me go see what's up."

I went to the floor above ours to Melissa's office, and popped my head in. She waved me in as soon as she saw me.

"Hey, Camilo! I've got some great news for you. You better sit down though, because this is *huge*."

I sat down bemused. "Wow I've never seen you this

happy, not even when Rita called to tell you she was pregnant."

She cackled like I'd said something hilarious. "I was too terrified about impending parenthood to be outwardly giddy. This, on the other hand, is literally a miracle."

"Okay, now you're just teasing. Tell me," I said, dying to know what had Melissa so damn happy.

She was smiling so hard I could see her molars. "So, I got a call late Friday afternoon from a private donor who wants to give two million dollars over the next two years to the agency. They want most of it to go to our residential program."

The room tilted a little and I shook my head, because surely I'd heard wrong. I wasn't even sure if I could come up with everything we could get done with that amount of money. We could renovate the Harlem shelter fully, and possibly do some updating on the other two safe houses.

I grabbed the edge of her desk and leaned in. "Don't play with me, Melissa. I haven't even had coffee yet."

She cackled again, which made it the second time I'd seen her do it in the five years I'd been at the agency. "I'm dead serious. The donor is coming today to meet with us. He said he chose us because we're a smaller grassroots agency, and we work in areas where there are predominantly immigrants and people of color. Which is the population he'd like to see benefit from the money." I bobbed my head up and down as she talked, so excited I could barely make words. "He also asked if we worked with LGBT clients. I told him absolutely *and* that part of our mission was to have the demographics of the clients we worked with well represented within our staff at all levels of the agency. He really loved that."

She smiled proudly at the last part, as well she should. Melissa fought our board hard to make sure they committed to having a leadership which was as diverse as our clientele. I respected her for it and had benefitted from her efforts.

She smiled at me again. "He was happy to hear you were bilingual as well."

"Uh that's good I guess." She stopped then and looked down, clearing her throat.

Fuck.

I *knew* there had to be a catch. Nothing this good could come with no strings attached.

"Don't get freaked out." She did "calm the angry bear" hands as she spoke and I started to get worried. "The donor asked to be loosely involved with the development of the project."

I had a rant about me not having time to babysit rich people ready, but Melissa held up her hand.

"He's a busy man and doesn't need day-to-day involvement. He just wants periodic meetings and to be kept in the loop. He's ready to give us the first million like today, Camilo, especially after I told him about the Harlem site and how much work it needs." She gave that last part some emphasis. "He even asked me to send the proposal we'd written for that last grant opportunity we didn't get. He read it over the weekend, and emailed last night saying he was interested in making it happen for us. That means by next year we could have a fully functioning job placement center and a wellness room on site at the shelter."

That last part actually made me a little lightheaded,

because those two things had been very improbable wish list items. "He wants the site named in memory of someone." She sighed and I felt like shit because this dude sounded like a really nice rich person.

She pressed on taking advantage of my obviously lowered defenses. "This is personal for him, he's not just a millionaire looking for a tax deduction. I doubt he'll want to meet more than a couple of times, and probably just in the early stages. Once things actually get going, I assume email updates will be as much as you'll need to do. Do you think you can do that?"

I glared at her because for that kind of money I'd throw in a blow job. How could I say no?

"Of course I can, Melissa. I'll meet with the guy every week for the next year if he wants. We need that money."

She nodded, looking relieved and smiled again like she could barely contain whatever it was she was going to say next, like this was like a game show... *Wait there's more!*

"He also said he's willing to commit to funding two full-time positions, like forever. He can arrange for an endowment." This guy was like a nonprofit world unicorn. "He asked that we think about what kind of positions those would be, and to send him a proposal."

Melissa's excitement was infectious and it was getting harder and harder to not start gulping the Kool-Aid. "He's interested in hearing about things we wish we could have. You know, something we need but can't get funding for through the usual channels."

So many thoughts were going through my head. A paid MSW internship? A therapist for the residential programs who would work exclusively with our clients? A housing advocate? The possibilities were literally endless.

"You said he's coming *today*? I have to be at the Harlem site this morning, but I can move it around."

"Will you be back by one?"

"Yes, definitely. I'm walking over there right now. I'll be back in time."

"Excellent," she said, clapping her hands with glee. "I'll call you when he's here. This is exciting!"

At this point even my surly ass couldn't help but be a little giddy. "This is like a dream come true, Melissa. We can do so much with that money."

She nodded, her face open and happy. "It *is* a dream come true." Then her eyes widened like she remembered something. "Oh I forgot to ask. How did it go Friday?"

Oh god. I thanked the saints for my minimally blushing brown face and nodded tightly. "Good," I squeaked out. "Very fun."

"Great, I'm so glad you guys could make it. It would've been a shame for the tickets to go to waste."

"Oh no, we sucked the marrow out of the evening."

She gave that indulgent laugh she'd use sometimes with me and Ayako. "I wouldn't expect any less from you two."

If you only knew how literal I just got with you, boss.

"How are Rita and Theo? All better?"

She nodded a big smile on her face when I mentioned her wife and son. "They're much better, thanks for asking."

I nodded and pointed towards the door. "Okay, I'm heading to the shelter. I'll see you at one."

As I walked out of her office I realized I never asked her for the donor's name.

Tom

"Are you fully recovered from Friday, Thomas? Because even I'm still thinking about that guy's mouth." I didn't answer, hurrying to take Priya off the speaker.

I was still thinking about that mouth too. In fact, I hadn't been able to get anything about Milo out of my mind all weekend. Remembering how hot it had been with him for those few moments, to succumb to a desire so strong I forgot where and who I was.

"I know what you are up to, Priya Raghunathan," I said unable to hide the humor in my voice. Priya had been on a mission to get me to "get out more" for years now, so I was not surprised she was not letting this one go. "I'm on my way to my meeting and I'm running late." I looked out the window of my Rover.

"Well if you ask me—"

I did laugh this time interrupting her. "But, I *didn't* ask."

She went on unbothered. "You're so cute, acting as if I'm not going to tell you what to do regardless. *Anyway,* I just wanted to say that I thought it was great that you did something a little impulsive, Tom."

Her tone shifted and I knew we would get into the "you've changed" conversation that came up every few months since my divorce. I put my head back on the warm leather headrest and sighed. "Priya, that was more than a little impulsive. I could've really embarrassed myself."

"So fucking what? You *relaxed* for once. The way

you were looking at him, I hadn't seen that glint in your eyes since the Boston days." She clicked her tongue before she spoke. "You've always been serious and measured, but since things ended with Maxwell it's like you've been dead set on denying yourself of anything that's just for you. I just wanted to tell you how good it was to see you cut loose a bit, that's all. Even if you could've been arrested for public indecency, I feel like it was totally worth it."

I laughed again as we reached the Harlem address where I had my next meeting.

"Priya, I gotta go. I'm almost at the New Beginning offices."

"Oh! I forgot you were going to that. Can't wait to hear about it this afternoon. See you later."

"See you later. And Priya?" One thing I'd vowed after that whole mess with my ex was that I would tell the people in my life how grateful I was for them.

"Yes?"

"Thanks."

"Don't get too emo on me. You know I love you and everything, but that I'm also nosy as fuck!" We both laughed at that truth.

We ended the call as my driver pulled up in front of the building. As the director of New Beginning had explained, there was a very discreet sign in the front indicating this was the right place.

"Manny, this meeting shouldn't take long. Go find a spot and let me know where you are, I'll walk over to you."

My driver turned around with the annoyed face he always made when I tried to do too much for myself, like walking a few blocks to meet him. "You sure, boss? It's wet out there."

I looked out the window. The rain had mostly stopped.

"I'm good, really."

I stepped out before he could fight me some more. As I walked into the offices of New Beginning, I realized I was almost twenty minutes late. You'd think someone who was semi-retired could manage to arrive on time to meetings *he* requested, but no.

I stepped up to the receptionist who had just finished talking with someone, mindful not to make any sudden moves, hyper aware of all the space I was taking up. There were a few women in the waiting area, and I didn't want to scare or intimidate them by being too loud. This was a place which provided services for people who had experienced domestic violence after all. In the gentlest voice I could manage I said to the receptionist, "Hi, my name is Thomas Hughes. I'm here to meet with Melissa."

The receptionist, who had perked up as soon as she saw me walk in, beamed when I told her my name. "Yes, Mr. Hughes, she's expecting you. She asked me to call her when you arrived so she can come down."

I waved my hand at the suggestion. "She doesn't need to come down. I'll go up there."

She looked a little frazzled at this change of plans, so I tried for the smile that usually smoothed things over. "You can let her know I'm on my way, so I don't surprise her." Then I whispered. "I just don't want to make anyone uncomfortable with the tall guy looming in the waiting room."

She smiled at that and nodded. "Right. I'll buzz the

door open and you can just take the elevator up to the third floor. That's where Melissa's office is. She'll be waiting for you when you get there."

"Excellent. Thanks so much, what's your name?"

"Miosotis."

"Gracias, Miosotis." I grinned at the surprise on her face when she heard my Spanish. It always threw people off when the white guy busted out the Dominican. I waved at her, then walked through the door when she buzzed me in.

As I went up to meet Melissa I thought about how glad I was to be finally doing this. Being able to help an agency like this had been years in the making. Of all the places I'd reviewed, New Beginning had by far been the closest to what I'd had in mind when I started looking for an agency to fund. I hoped the people I was meeting today were as impressive in person as they'd been on paper.

The elevator opened and a short woman with a pixie haircut and a huge smile was waiting on the other side. She looked exactly like the idea I had of a social worker. Warm, friendly and seemed like she gave amazing hugs.

She extended her hand out to me. "Hi, Mr. Hughes, I'm Melissa Stein-Campos. Thank you so much for coming today."

"Hi, Melissa, please call me Tom."

Her smile got bigger as we shook hands. "Of course, Tom. My office is over there." She pointed to a door at the back of the floor. Once we were in the office, she quickly walked to her desk and got on the phone, holding a finger up.

"Hey." She smiled at whatever the person on the phone said.

"Yep, he's here. Okay see you in a minute." She winked at me as she hung up the phone.

"That was Camilo, our residential programs director, he'll be right down. Would you like me to get you something to drink before we start, Tom?"

"Some water would be great actually."

"Of course, I'll be right back."

While she went to get the water I glanced around the room. There were some posters of what looked like old events the agency had hosted, and a couple of prints with inspirational quotes. She also had some photos on the ledge behind her desk.

One was of her and a beautiful woman who looked Latina holding a little boy between them. They were all smiling brightly at the camera, a lovely family photo. I was about to look closer at what looked like a group of people at a New Beginning event when the door opened. I turned around expecting to see Melissa, but instead I saw Milo from the gala walk in looking very serious. Having spent over a decade doing business at some of the highest echelons of the tech-world there was not much that could put me off my game in a meeting, but when I saw him, I actually stumbled.

This must be the *Camilo* who would be in charge of the project. I was not one to wax poetic about fate, but this was a pretty spectacular coincidence.

Because regardless of what I told Priya, I'd felt pangs of regret all weekend at letting him slip away at the gala. Now he was *here*.

In my surprise I moved abruptly and bumped into a chair. The noise startled Camilo, making him look up. When he saw me all the blood seemed to drain from his face. The flutter of happiness in my chest at seeing him again didn't go unnoticed, but I had to think fast. He was probably freaking out and thinking this would somehow affect the project I was here to talk about.

I walked up to him and extended my hand. "It's nice to see you again, Camilo. This is a very pleasant surprise. Are you the shelter director?"

He nodded slowly like he was trying not to make any sudden movements.

"Hi. Yes, I manage all the housing related programs for the agency. It's nice to see you again as well." I could see red creeping up his neck. The impulse to touch him and get closer was intense. He had his hair in a half knot today and was wearing skinny jeans, with a very slim fitting dark green corduroy jacket over a purple button-down shirt. His style was so different than what usually caught my attention. It didn't make a difference though. To me, everything about Camilo shined.

"Excellent, I'm excited to hear your ideas on how I can help with the great work you're doing here." I sounded a bit more enthusiastic than necessary, but I really wanted to put him at ease. He swallowed visibly and then exhaled like he was realizing I wasn't going to make what happened on Friday a thing.

"Okay, yeah, I'm excited too." He still looked a little startled, but seemed to be coming around. "What you're doing is incredibly generous, so thank you."

"Not necessary but you're welcome."

As we stood there in an awkward silence the door opened again and we both turned to see Melissa walking into the room with some water bottles in her hands.

"Camilo, you're here. I see you met Mr. Hughes. Excellent." She extended a hand towards a small table near the door. "Let's sit at the table where we can talk more comfortably. Tom, I didn't know what you liked so I brought flat water and seltzer."

"Flat is fine." She passed me a bottle, gave Camilo a seltzer, and took another for herself. Once we were all seated, Melissa passed me a packet of papers and we got to the business at hand.

She gestured towards Camilo and smiled. "So this is Camilo Briggs, our residential programs director. He's been with New Beginning for almost five years. He started as the program coordinator for residential. Working with advocates who support our clients in preparing for the job market and securing permanent housing among many other things. He did such an amazing job and developed such wonderful initiatives there, we had to give him a raise and *a lot* more work!" Melissa and I chuckled at Camilo's mortified face. "He's been in the position for two years and he's been killing it there too."

She waved a hand over the folder in front of me. "As I mentioned when we spoke on the phone. Our agency has a strengths-based, client-centered approach. We meet our clients where they're at in every way, and walk with them as they figure out how they want to move forward after finding safety. Camilo is an amazing advocate and leader, and his programs have thrived because of it. I couldn't have wished for a better person to head the renovation of our Harlem site." Melissa stopped talking suddenly and gave Camilo a funny look.

He lifted his eyebrows and she laughed. "I'm sorry, it's just you're so quiet! You're usually a lot more opinionated than this." The look of astonishment on her face was so genuine I almost laughed too.

"Maybe it's me." I winked at Camilo, hoping I didn't

scare him if I mentioned we'd met. "Camilo and I actually met at a gala on Friday. We were both kind of surprised at the coincidence."

"Really?" Poor Melissa sounded like this meeting was turning out to be a lot more of a roller coaster than she'd planned for. "That's wild! New York City can be like a small town sometimes, huh?"

I laughed with her, but just nodded silently, hoping Camilo could tell I had no intention of divulging any more information about our first encounter. After a moment his shoulders seemed to relax, but not by much. I looked from Camilo to Melissa, hoping I looked harmless enough to get them to relax a bit. "Thanks for the introductions, Melissa. Camilo sounds like the perfect person to lead this project." I turned around so I could speak to him directly and on impulse I decided to switch to Spanish. "Me dice Melissa que tú hablas español. Eso será de mucha ayuda para mí."

At this Camilo's eyebrows shot up and he blurted out, "Wait, why's your accent Dominican?" The suspicious look on his face was so endearing, I almost had to sit on my hands to keep from touching him.

Melissa's eyes widened like she hoped Camilo would not open his mouth again and I chuckled before answering.

"I'm Dominican. Born and raised."

Chapter Four

Camilo

I knew I hadn't fallen into some bizarre parallel universe, because Melissa's office was stifling hot as usual and those corny affirmation posters she had all over the place were still hanging on the walls. But something or someone was definitely fucking with me today. First, the random I decided to give a blow job on Friday turns out to be the mysterious billionaire donor for the shelter project. *Then* the guy—whose name is *Thomas Hughes*—breaks out into Dominican Spanish. I mean both these things were possible, *obviously*, but it was all just too fucking weird.

I looked over at Tom, who was staring at me again with an amused expression, like I was the most adorable thing he'd ever seen. He was dressed down today, just gray slacks and a burgundy cashmere sweater. The red made the sexy salt and pepper at his temples stand out even more. It was a challenge not to stare, to be honest.

"So you're Dominican?" I didn't mean to sound like I thought he was shady, but I was barely hanging on to my sanity by this point.

More rich and velvety laughter escaped his lips. The

husky sound reminded me of being on my knees and him asking me if I wanted his cock down my throat. I coughed to cover the moan that almost came out of my mouth.

Tom's eyes widened like he knew exactly what I was thinking.

Shit.

He cleared his throat and leaned in to answer my question. "Well my father's American, but he's lived in the DR since the seventies. He was a marine during the '65 occupation. He fell in love with the island and the people while he was there." His lips turned up on a lopsided smile.

Working with this guy was going to be torture.

"When he left he vowed to return someday. He served two tours in Vietnam, and only returned to the U.S. long enough to get his GI Bill degree. In '74, he moved to Santo Domingo and took a job as a high school math teacher at the international school. He met my mom about six months later and that was all she wrote." He smiled fondly at that. "I came to the States for college and stayed. My family are all in DR though, so I go back a few times a year."

Melissa was the first one to react to his story. "You rarely hear stories of Americans immigrating and settling in other countries, even though there are so many living as expats all over the world. Thanks for sharing that, Tom."

I knew I should say something, but Tom's whole vibe was really throwing me off my game.

He was so...*unlikely.*

"One of my best friends is Dominican. He came

from DR with his mom when he was six. We grew up together in the Bronx."

His smiled turned just a tiny bit mischievous then. "Is that how you recognized the accent?"

I shrugged and tried hard not to moon over the sexy dimple on his right cheek. "Well you do sound like Nesto, but there are *a lot* of Dominicans in New York City, as you probably know."

He dipped his head before he answered. "I do. I've lived here for most of the last twenty years. With the exception of two years of grad school in Boston and short-term stints overseas for business."

This conversation felt too intimate, like it was almost wrong to have Melissa here to witness it, still I kept talking. "I was born here but my mom's Cuban, so we made the mandatory pilgrimage through Miami. We came up here when I was thirteen."

I had no fucking clue why I was giving him my bio in detail, but I didn't seem to be able to keep my mouth shut. It was the look he was giving me. Like he wanted to throw me on the floor and order me to have another go at his dick.

Between trying to keep my tone professional and managing all the feelings being this close to Tom were inducing, my body was trying to do too much, and my mouth was taking the hit.

I needed to get this conversation back to the actual project before I offended this guy. I regrouped quickly and put my game face on. "I'm fluent in Spanish, so if that's how you prefer to communicate, I'm happy to do so." I flashed him my best Becky smile and tried to bring this motherfucking meeting back on track. "Melissa tells me that you'd like to be kept abreast on how the project progresses. Is there anything in particular you'd like me to be aware of? I'd be happy to send you updates." Rambling, I was rambling.

"That sounds great, Camilo."

I clenched my fists under the table before I said more. Because I knew this was where I would be doomed. "Or we could meet periodically. Just say the word."

Tom kept looking at me with an amused expression and it was fucking unnerving. Was he mocking me or did he think I was funny?

What the hell?

My face must have started to show how anxious I was because he broke eye contact and when he looked at me again his face was softer. No more smirking. He leaned in a little like he was going for more approachable body language. The problem was him getting closer only got me more worked up.

"I'm not sure if Melissa told you, but the reason I requested someone bilingual is because I'd like my mother to get some updates too." At the mention of his mother his face lit up. A Dominican boy who loved his mother.

Like I needed one more reason for my ill-advised crush to grow.

"Mom doesn't speak a lot of English and I may bring her to a meeting when she's in town for a visit." His face changed for an instant, and it was clear whatever he was remembering was painful. I wondered if his dad had been an abusive asshole, but he smiled when talking about his parents, so maybe it was something else. Whatever was on his mind must've had to do with his reason for doing this project. I wanted to ask, but I managed to keep my prying to myself.

I nodded, already so invested in making sure things with Thomas went smoothly. "That's absolutely fine. How would you prefer that we communicate?"

I hated myself for hoping he said face-to-face, because how could that have any sort of good outcome?

Tom's face turned serious again, like he was also struggling with how far we were going to take this farce. A few seconds passed and I sat there with my hands gripping the edge of the chair, waiting, because I knew. I fucking *knew* this was it. If Tom said he'd be fine with getting updates by email it meant whatever it was we'd shared at the gala had just been a bit of fun for him.

Usually being in a situation where someone else clearly held the upper hand, would send me running in the other direction. But as I sat there all I could think was, *please say you want to see me again.*

He glanced at Melissa who just sat there beaming, blissfully ignorant of the unfolding drama, then back to me. "If it's alright with Melissa and it doesn't interfere too much with your responsibilities, I'd like for us to meet once a week, Camilo." My heart thumped so hard I almost pressed a hand to my chest. "Just during the initial stages, after things start moving we can adjust."

Melissa piped up then and I was surprised she could get a word out, with how hard she was grinning. "That sounds totally fine, Tom. Camilo and I already spoke and he will be able to meet with you as needed."

I tipped my head in agreement, as I tried hard not to show how much his answer was affecting me. The feeling of utter elation at his words should have tipped me off to just how inappropriate this all was, but I ignored all that shit and just sat there nodding. I looked over and smiled at Melissa whose head was also bobbing up and down. "That should be fine, Mr. Hughes—"

"Tom. Please, call me Tom." His face looked so earnest, like he was trying to do everything he could to make himself non-intimidating.

I assented and when I spoke again there was a warmth in my voice that had no place at a work meeting. "Once a week sounds good. My schedule is pretty full, so if it works for you I'd prefer if we set a day and time to meet on a weekly basis. That way I can have it in my calendar as an ongoing thing."

He smiled again, and this time Thomas from Friday night creeped out a little.

He was so fucking sexy.

"That's fine. My schedule is relatively flexible right now," he said, pulling out his wallet, then passed me a business card.

"Why don't you email me some times that work for you, and we can go from there." He stood up then, our meeting was over, apparently. Melissa and I got our asses in gear and stood up as well.

I extended my hand to him as I got up. "I'll be in touch before the end of the day."

When he took my hand in his I was sure I saw sparks. "Looking forward to it, Camilo."

Melissa's grin was still in full force as we walked out of her office. "Tom, thanks so much for coming today, we're incredibly excited and grateful for this project. It's a game changer for us."

He seemed happy and genuinely pleased at her excitement. Keeping my shit together with this man was going to be an uphill battle.

"I'm glad we can move forward. I'll have my finance person contact you regarding some information we need." He turned to me again. "Thank you both."

With that he walked out to the elevators with Melissa as I stood there stunned. I knew I was in over my head with this whole situation. This could cost me my job, or worse, could cost the agency a once in a lifetime donation. I should have been worried.

I should have come clean to Melissa.

Instead I power walked down to my office and my calendar, so I could email Tom with a time and place to see him again.

Tom

"Daddy!" I opened my arms and smiled as my daughter, Libertad, ran down the steps of her preschool towards me.

"Hola, mi amor," I said, crouching down to meet her. "Did you have a nice time with Papa Maxwell?" She bobbed her little head, making her brown curls bounce around. She turned to point at a group of kids on the playground behind the school. "Can I keep playing with Bella and Anouk?"

I grinned as I saw the two little girls waving her over. "Sure, baby, but then I want to hear about your weekend." She screamed an "okay, Daddy" as she ran back to her friends, while I stayed behind. My ex, Maxwell, and I shared custody of Libe, and she'd been with him since Friday after school.

Maxwell and I had been married for a year and not in a great place in our relationship when we started the surrogacy process to have Libertad. I was reluctant about the timing, especially since I'd wanted to adopt, but Maxwell pushed so hard for it I eventually relented. In hindsight I could see the baby was his attempt at saving our relationship, doing something that forced us to be together.

To make me pay attention.

I'd been working and traveling nonstop back then, first running my company which was expanding at breakneck speed, and then preparing to go public with it. I agreed because I wanted a child too, but I didn't stop my work pace at all. Eventually Maxwell's loneliness turned into an affair that broke our marriage. We divorced a month after Libe was born.

As I looked at her now, talking to her friends, so carefree, it was hard to imagine my life without her. Things with Maxwell and I were much better now, but they'd been rocky for a while. He went into a bit of a tailspin after we split up and it was almost a year before he was in a place where he could be a parent to Libe. I blamed myself for his state of mind at the time, so I took care of the baby until he could be more present.

It was a hard year for all of us. If it hadn't been for the help of my mom, Priya and Maxwell's mom I don't know what I would have done. Having Libertad was worth it though, she was the greatest joy in my life. I bit back a smile as I saw her twirling around and laughing with her friends.

I checked the time and waved Libe over. "Come on, sweetheart."

She begrudgingly started walking to me as I checked in with her teacher. I grabbed Libe's little hand, and we started the walk towards our house just a few blocks away right in the heart of East Harlem.

I loved my neighborhood, there was so much energy

everywhere. Three years ago, after my two business partners and I sold our company for more money than we knew what to do with, I bought a renovated brownstone here. Sanjay and Priya bought the house next door to mine, which had been on the market at the same time. Heni, the third one in our trio from grad school, got a condo just a few blocks away.

I fell in love with Harlem and its history as a Columbia college student, and when I had the chance to settle anywhere in New York City I wanted, Harlem was the spot I picked. My friends and I were all committed to the neighborhood and being part of the revitalization happening here. We were also invested in preserving the culture, and helping the people who already had roots in Harlem stay in their homes. To not let gentrification erode the heritage of this part of New York City, which had given this country, this world, so much brilliance.

We were getting close to our street when Libe finally let me know my attention needed to be on her. "Daddy, you didn't even ask me how my day was at school."

"Sorry, baby, I got distracted. How was your day?" I asked as I picked her up and hoisted her on my hip.

"It was good, except for the boys being so mean to us." I tried not to laugh at how aggravated she looked. There was a full-on turf war going on at that preschool. Every day it was like the Bloods and the Crips over there.

"What happened?" Libe scrunched her face as she shook her head in disgust at whatever the boys had done.

"Well Mauro was pushing Bella and me on the playground. We told him to stop, but he just got meaner and told us we were dumb." At this she rolled her eyes, and she could have been my mother in that moment. She had very fair skin and Maxwell's green eyes, but her hair was a mass of tight curls. My mom always said, "Esa cabecita es Dominicana."

That personality was definitely from the Dominican side of the family. "I told him he was the dumb one. Everyone knows girls are smarter than boys." Priya and my mother had indoctrinated Libe in girl power and feminism since birth. She was not about to let any boy call her anything.

"Mi amor, you know the rule about name calling." I tried hard to keep a straight face, but her outraged expression made it very hard. "Just because he said it to you doesn't make it okay for you to do it to him."

Her dramatic slump was almost too much.

"But, Daddy, he doesn't even know how to write his name yet!"

"It's still not okay to call him names, honey, people learn in different ways."

"Okay, but I don't like him." She pouted and again I almost burst out laughing.

"You don't have to like him, but you *do* have to be kind."

"Can I have a cookie when we get home?" She could have a future in politics with those pivoting skills.

"We were talking about name calling. What are you going to do the next time Mauro calls you a name?"

Another eye roll. "I will stand up for myself wespeckfully."

I gave her a big kiss and she giggled. "Exactly. And yes we can do snack and play when we get home and then Tia Priya and Tio Sanjay are coming over. You'll hang out with Tia, and Tio and I will work for a bit."

"Yes!" She pumped her little fist in the air at the mention of time with Priya. "Are they staying for dinner?"

"We can ask them, I'm sure they'd love to."

"Okay good." With that she put her little head against my shoulder and stuck her thumb in her mouth. I held her tight as we walked up to our house. Suddenly a random thought popped into my head.

How would Camilo get along with Libe? Would he be turned off by me having a kid?

An image of Camilo and Libe sitting down in my living room playing and laughing came into my mind with such clarity it felt like a memory. The idea of sharing moments like this with someone, exchanging a look at Libe's antics, was a yearning I'd not indulged in since the divorce. I could see it now though, and Camilo's face was right there, front and center.

This infatuation was getting ridiculous.

As I walked up the stoop to my door I thought about my earlier meeting with Camilo and Melissa. He held himself so tightly, like he was bracing for the world to fuck with him. I knew I'd freaked him out when I'd asked for weekly face-to-face meetings. I wondered if he could tell I was full of shit.

Obviously, I didn't need that level of involvement in the project. It was just an excuse to see him again. I wasn't even sure what my endgame was with any of it, but when I saw a chance to get more time with Camilo—who I thought had disappeared from my life forever last Friday—all I could do was find a way to lock it down.

Chapter Five

Camilo

"Last time I take your advice at a fancy gala!" I yelled as I barged into Ayako's office, firmly closing the door behind me. I paced the space in front of her desk a couple of times, then slumped into a chair while she stared at me like I'd lost my mind.

"Could you please start by telling me what the hell you're talking about? I thought you were with Melissa and that donor."

I pulled hard on my hair when she said the word *donor* and covered my face with my hands. "It's the same guy."

"Who's the same guy?" Ayako asked sounding exasperated.

I took my hands off my face and put my head back, staring at the ceiling, before facing her again.

"Tom, the guy from the gala, is the fucking mystery donor!"

Ayako's face went from confusion, to realization and then horror.

"Oh shit."

I hung my head sighing. "Exactly."

"Oh my God, did he say something at the meeting? Was he an asshole about it? He seemed like a nice guy, but we know *that* counts for nothing."

I tried to collect my thoughts and tamp down the panic, which had returned with a vengeance. I was going to give my brain whiplash from the hot and cold. One moment I'm elated about getting to see Tom again, and the next I'm having a meltdown because I have to see him again.

"No he was fine, actually went out of his way to make me feel comfortable. He didn't mention anything."

Ayako relaxed her shoulders. "That's good then, right?"

I shook my head again, struggling to come up with everything that was going through my mind at the moment. "It's good he didn't spill the beans on me choking down his cock at the party, sure, but that doesn't mean I'm free and clear. He wants to be closely involved in the initial stages of the project, Ayako!" I stood up and started pacing again as I talked. "Apparently he's giving the money for personal reasons. The plan is for us to meet once a week, so I can keep him updated on the project."

Ayako burst out laughing.

"Oh shit, Camilo. This could only happen to you! Of course the guy you decide to suck off at a party turns out to be the millionaire who wants to fix the shelter. You can't make this shit up!" She cackled some more while I glared at her, hating my life.

"What am I going to do, Ayako? I can't jeopardize this project and I honestly have no clue how to handle this. What if this guy wants to turn me into his sex toy? Or tries to fuck with me because he has all the leverage?"

Ayako's face got serious then. "Melissa would *never* let that happen, she'd tell him to take his money and fuck off if he tried anything like that." She held up her hand. "But we're getting a little ahead of ourselves. Let's not jump to conclusions. He didn't say anything about Friday at the meeting, and you said he tried to put you at ease. I mean you're both adults, these things happen. You can work together, it's not like you were involved with him or anything. It was a onetime thing."

A lot of what she was saying made sense, but I was still coiled up in knots. Tom Hughes was too much of a temptation to underestimate the possibility of disaster.

"From what we know from this guy so far, he seems to be a decent person, who's extremely invested in giving away *a lot* of money to causes you care about."

That was true.

So far, the one thing I knew for sure about Tom was that he was a very generous man who cared about things which were very important to me. He also had an enormous cock I'd been dreaming about since the party on Friday, but I digressed.

"We need to take this whole thing to Dr. Google," Ayako snapped, bringing me out of my thoughts.

"Here," she said as she pivoted her desktop monitor so I could see it. "Let's look him up."

I gave her his full name, and as soon as she typed it in we saw there was a *ton* of information about Tom on the internet. Ayako clicked on a link to a *Forbes* magazine article and we both started to read in silence. After a couple of minutes Ayako whistled.

"Damn, Camilo, this dude is a legit zillionaire. Holy fuck."

Apparently, Thomas Hughes, age forty-one, was a legend in the entrepreneurial world. Thirteen years ago, when he was twenty-eight, he'd started his company, Nuntius, while attending business school at MIT. Tom and his two best friends from the program created a service through which immigrants living overseas could pay their families' bills back home.

If you lived in New York City and needed to pay your mom's rent and electric bill in the Dominican Republic you could go to the Nuntius website and for a fee, have a messenger service go take care of the payments without wiring money or having a relative lift a finger on the other side. You could do anything, pay for school or medical fees, even pay their groceries. It was like Postmates, but for bills, and it worked all over the world.

It was *brilliant*.

They initially piloted the model in the trio's hometowns: Santo Domingo, New Delhi and Addis Ababa. Within five years of them starting the company, smartphones made their way around the world and the Nuntius app blew up. By year six, they were operating in more than sixty countries and booming. The article Ayako and I read was written three years ago when Tom and his partners sold Nuntius to PayPal for *just* over a billion dollars.

I let out the long breath I'd been holding after reading the sum of money for the third time, still unable to make words. Ayako looked up from the screen and flinched when she saw my face.

"Okay this is pretty intense, and I can tell from how stiff you are right now that you're freaking out. *But* I just want to point out a couple of things before you do or say something over the top." I just stared at her in silence, because the screaming inside my head was too loud for me to speak.

She held up a finger. "One. Even on Friday when we knew nothing about him, we both thought he was charming and very low-key." Another finger joined the first one. "Two. It seems this guy made his money *working*. Also I don't know about you, but I think this whole story is amazing. Three immigrant kids starting a company in grad school and selling it for hundreds of millions. You have to admit it's pretty great." I nodded slowly at that because she was right, this was the kind of story I loved. I couldn't believe I hadn't heard of this guy before.

My mom didn't really have any family left in Cuba, so we didn't send money there. But I was sure my best friends Nesto and Patrice who had family back in DR and Haiti had probably heard of Nuntius.

I held up my hands in defeat. "Okay fine, he's a gorgeous, smart and generous guy who started a billion dollar company in his twenties." I covered my face with my hands. "I should just tell Melissa, so she can deal with him herself."

I heard teeth sucking from the direction where Ayako was sitting and even though I couldn't see her, I could tell she was losing her patience with my whining.

"I'm not going to tell you what to do, Camilo, but I would at least give him the benefit of the doubt and go to the first meeting." Exasperation was quickly edging the sympathetic tone from earlier. "You already said you would do it. If he ends up getting an email from Melissa saying you're bailing, it's *really* going to get awkward.

Especially since even if you don't meet with him regularly, you'll still have to be in touch. It's *your* project."

She was right, making a thing out of it was just going to make it worse. Tom had handled things like an adult, and I could too.

I exhaled and stared at the ceiling again.

"Fine. I'll just have to make sure to stay off his cock the next time."

Ayako gave me her best "I have faith in you" face and squeezed my hand.

"You got this, babe."

I was glad at least one of us thought so.

Tom

"How was the meeting?" Priya asked with enthusiasm as she munched on a graham cracker. After her snack, we'd sat Libe down for thirty minutes of TV, so Sanjay, Priya and I finally had a moment to chat.

"I'm so excited to hear about it! I was telling my colleague Anne at the hospital what you were doing and she raved about New Beginning. She said her friend volunteered for them and they do amazing work."

I nodded, desperate to give them the news about running into Camilo.

"Yes, they're great." I swallowed. "Something funny happened at the meeting though."

"Oh?" Sanjay looked skeptical and Priya gave me a worried look.

"Nothing bad, it's just today I was supposed to meet with the director of the residential program. Since he'll be my point person at the agency once the project gets going. And um, it turns out he's the guy from the party on Friday." I broke eye contact then, knowing I had to be turning red. "You know Milo? The guy I was talking to before you guys got there."

Priya's cackle was epic and Sanjay just shook his head.

"Oh my god, Tom. The one time you cut loose a little at a party. What did you do?" This was from Sanjay, who I knew was feeling my pain.

"Did he freak out? You made sure he knew you weren't going to make a big deal out of it, right?" Priya the advocate.

I moved to grab a cracker and tried to reassure her I had not acted like a clueless ass. "As much as I could, given the situation. I mean there wasn't any time to have a conversation about it, because the executive director of the agency was there too. But I tried to make it clear I wouldn't be bringing it up. He looked pretty spooked though." I covered my face with my hands. "I sort of requested he and I meet weekly for the foreseeable future to discuss the progress, which is completely unnecessary."

Both Priya and Sanjay looked at me with amusement.

"I just couldn't resist. Was that a horrible abuse of power?"

I was mostly asking Priya. She entertained no bullshit, and she would give it to me straight.

Priya is as tough as they come.

She came from India on her own at eighteen on a full scholarship to Yale and was from a family without the financial means to support her while she was in school. She worked multiple jobs under the table all four years of college. She met Sanjay there in their sophomore year, when she was working as a server at one of the local Indian restaurants. I had enormous respect for her and also knew she would not let me get away with being a creepy asshole.

She raised an eyebrow at me like she could read my mind. "Wow, this is a big deal, huh? Normally I would've reamed you out for being a manipulative jerk, *but* I know you too well to dismiss that you going this far means something." She held up a finger at me. "What I will say is this, please be respectful and careful. He is in a *very* precarious position. You have *all* the power, and I'm sure he's nervous. So when you meet him make sure you clear the air and let him know how aware you are of your position."

I nodded in agreement, feeling relieved that she didn't think I'd crossed a line. "I was planning to, I don't want him to think I'd take advantage. But when I had the chance to see him again, I just took it."

Priya's face softened again. "He's certainly made an impression. It's time to take some chances with your heart again." Her smile was genuine and I'd bet anything she was thinking about our conversation this morning. "I think you should see where it goes."

I was about to say something to the effect of, "I hope all of this doesn't end blowing up in my face," when the email alert on my phone pinged. I looked at the screen and saw I had an email from Camilo S. Briggs. I quickly opened it to see what he'd said, my heart fluttering all over my chest. After a second I looked up at Priya and Sanjay.

"Looks like Camilo is available to meet next Wednesday afternoon."

Priya laughed and looked over at where Libe was zoned out watching *Peppa Pig*.

"How convenient that he can meet on the night you have the house to yourself."

She was giving me and my prowess way too much credit, but I'd be lying if I said I didn't get a small thrill at the possibility of having some alone time with Camilo.

Chapter Six

Camilo

I shook my head as the smell of stale cigarettes hit me in the hallway of my mother's apartment. I rang the bell before I pushed my key in to open her door, so I didn't startle her, and braced myself for whatever mood I'd find her in. I suspected it wouldn't be good if she was feeling so out of sorts she was smoking inside the apartment.

As I walked in, I felt a wave of relief when I saw she was up, dressed in jeans and a sweater, and pulling something out the fridge in her tiny kitchen. "Mama. ¿Como estas?" I greeted her as I put down the bagels and lox I'd brought on her breakfast counter.

"Milito, hijo." She turned around and walked to me with her arms wide-open to give me a tight hug and kiss. As she enveloped me in her slender arms I smelled the peppermint castile soap and the almond oil lotion she used. She'd showered too, so things couldn't be that bad.

She leaned back and the lines on the corners of her eyes pulled up as she smiled at me. "Hola, mi corazon." I squeezed her hand, grateful to find her in a good mood.

My mother struggled with depression. It was tough but manageable most of the time. But every once in a while she'd hit a rough patch and get leveled by it. It was just her and me, so I made sure I paid attention when I came to see her.

"Hey, Ma, you're looking good today. How was the hospital this week?" She shrugged as she got out the stuff to make the coffee. She turned around, holding up the old stovetop espresso maker she'd had ever since I could remember.

"¿Quieres café?"

I nodded enthusiastically in response. My mother's Cortadito was the best Cuban coffee in New York City, full stop. "Si, por favor." She came over to the stool I was perched on and kissed my forehead.

"Okay, mi amor."

I watched as she efficiently worked on the coffee, scooping out heaping spoonfuls of Bustelo from the yellow can and pressing them into the metal funnel before setting the coffee on the stove. When she was done, she turned around, sighing heavily.

"The hospital is all right. You know how it is, now with all this uncertainty with health care, every week it's something different. We keep working and taking care of the patients, but it's stressful right now, and you know the nurses' aides aren't exactly a part of the conversations when decisions are made."

She shook her head again and went for her pack of cigarettes, looked at me and put it back down. She knew I worried when she started smoking, but she was an adult and I was not going to tell her how to live. Besides I knew it was a sign she wasn't doing great and I didn't want to push.

"How are you feeling, Mama?" I asked as I glanced at the pack.

She leaned against the counter and looked at me with tired gray eyes exactly like mine. My mother was very fair skinned with fine light brown hair she'd let go gray. I was a complete mix between her and my dad. He'd been tall and strapping while she was petite and slim. I had her body type and her eyes, but my skin was brown and my hair a mess of dark brown curls. She smiled sadly as she reached for one, tucking it behind my ear.

"It was our anniversary Thursday."

Fuck.

I forgot to call her. My father passed away twenty-four years ago, and my mom still mourned for him on significant dates like it happened six months ago. I knew it was because he'd been the only person in her life to ever give her refuge, but seeing her still be brought so low by the past was hard to watch at times.

"Mama, I'm sorry, I forgot to call you. This week has been so busy."

"You don't have to apologize, papi. I know you've got a lot going on. Besides, it's not a big deal. I just remembered that's all. I lit a candle for him." She smiled sadly and turned around to fix my coffee.

I felt like an ass. "Did you go to Mass?"

She lifted a shoulder. "I didn't feel like going out. I just came home after work."

I worried about my mom. She'd never really wanted to deal with all the traumatic shit she'd been through and I knew eventually it would wear her down. She was a Marielita. One of the thousands of Cuban refugees who'd left from Mariel harbor in 1980 to come to the U.S. That year Fidel Castro lifted all restrictions to leaving the island and told the Cuban people that anyone who wanted to leave was free to go. Within days, hundreds of makeshift boats filled with people looking for asylum had arrived in Miami, and my mother had been in one of them.

As I watched her fiddle around making our breakfast in her little South Bronx kitchen it was still hard to imagine my mother, at twenty-two years old, getting on one of those boats on her own. She'd told me once she'd left Cuba with only the clothes on her back, a roll of old twenty dollar bills her father had given her before he died and a few family photos.

Once she arrived she'd been held in a detainment camp for months before settling in Miami. I knew very little about what that experience had been like for her, because she rarely mentioned it. She would always jump right over all of it and talked about how her life had changed when she met my dad.

As a teen I'd read about the Marielitos obsessively trying to get a sense of what she'd gone through to make it to the States. Everything I'd read suggested she'd probably experienced unthinkable trauma to come to this country. On top of whatever pushed her to get on a makeshift boat alone and cross the ocean to get here. As much as I tried, I could not imagine how terrified and how desperate I'd have to be to do that. But my mother had done it and she'd survived.

"M'ijo ¿A donde te fuiste?" My mother's concerned voice pulled me back from my errant thoughts.

I stood up and went over to kiss her on the cheek. "I didn't go anywhere, Ma. Just thinking," I said as I pointed at the old photo of my dad, my mom and me at Disney World she kept on a little table in the living room. "Just thinking about the story of how you guys met."

My mom smiled at that and put down the bread knife she'd been using to slice our bagels. My dad had come to the States from Jamaica with his mom as a little boy. Back then there were lots of jobs for nurses and my grandmother came over to work at a hospital. Like my mom and I, it had just been the two of them for a long time, until my mom joined their little family.

"He was so handsome." My mom's eyes always sparkled when she talked about my dad. It made me sad that my memories of him were fuzzy at best. "Every day I would get on the bus to go from my little efficiency to the English classes at the church, and he'd be sitting at the driver's seat, so tall and strong in his uniform, and I could barely breathe." She actually blushed, still, after all these years. "I practiced for weeks before I worked up the courage to talk to him, because I wanted him to understand me when I spoke to him. I didn't want to embarrass myself."

She lifted a shoulder then, a soft smile on her lips. "I didn't have to worry. We didn't need English, from the first moment your father and I had a connection that was…undeniable."

"I love hearing about you and Dad," I said trying hard not to sound too maudlin.

She sighed and started working on our brunch again. I leaned on the counter and watched her preparing our bagels. She was slicing avocado to put on top of mine, just how I liked it.

I thought about what she'd said about the connection she and my dad had, and it made me think about Thomas Hughes. How drawn I was to him, how no matter how much I knew I shouldn't, I kept going back to that first night we'd met and the pull I'd felt for him. How incredible it had been to be completely myself. How hot it was to know that everything I'd done that night turned Tom on that much more. Too bad getting involved with him was ill-advised in every way possible.

She gave me a funny look as she handed me my plate.

"How's work? Anything new going on over there?" I immediately stiffened, unsure of how to explain just how much *was* going on at work. I sat down, picked up my bagel and took a big bite before getting into it.

"We got pretty big news this week actually. We have a donor for the renovation. It's this rich business guy, he wants to give two million dollars to the agency." I tried to school my expression and sound neutral, because I knew if there was anything in my tone that sounded even remotely like drama, my mom would pick up on it. The way she raised her eyebrow told me my attempt at being coy had completely failed.

"Oh, so what's wrong with him? Because your eyelid's doing something funny." I slumped and laughed in defeat.

"I sort of know the guy. Like, *in that way*." I was the only child of a woman who grew up in the Cuban revolution. Sex had never been taboo in this house.

"Who is he? You hadn't mentioned you were seeing a millionaire, Milito!" She widened her eyes like she did when something particularly juicy happened in one of her telenovelas.

"We weren't seeing each other, Ma. It was a onetime thing." I took another bite of my bagel, just to have something to do. I felt so exposed and weird talking about Tom, even with my mother.

She looked confused now, like she couldn't understand why I was making a big deal out of it, then a worried expression settled on her face.

"Did he say something disrespectful to you? Is he trying to force you to do anything?"

I help up my hands, concerned I'd scared her.

"Not at all, it's nothing like that. It's just awkward."

And here was the part that was hard to admit. "I'm just a little worried I'll do something stupid. I'm so attracted to him and the more I learn about him, the more amazing he seems." I slid a hand over my face, before I continued, feeling a little mortified. "I don't want to be unprofessional, and I *know* he should be off-limits, but I'm not sure if I'll be able to keep it together if he pushes for something."

"And what would be so bad about being swept off your feet by a handsome and generous millionaire, Milito?" she asked, genuinely baffled by my dilemma.

Aaaaaand there it was. My friends always teased me about being a closeted Disney princess, secretly waiting for Prince Charming to whisk me away on a white horse, and maybe I was. But I'd come by it honestly.

My mother was a hopeless romantic, fanatical about watching her telenovelas, hooked on those happy endings. Even though she'd given up on love for herself, she still held out hope I'd find the perfect partner. In my dad she'd found *her* prince charming, and she fervently believed there was someone out there who was made just for me. I doubted it would be the guy I'd given a blow job one hour after meeting him though.

"Mama, I can't get involved with this guy. It would be inappropriate, and it could mess up the project or get me fired. I have to meet with him on my own Wednesday and I have no clue how it's going to go. I'm nervous." I knew I was being overly dramatic, but I was completely at a loss on how things would go once I was on my own with Tom.

My mom shook her head like I was being ridiculous. "Camilo, you'll be fine. No one knows how to handle himself better than you. Especially when it comes to a man who wants to take advantage." Suddenly her face looked sad and she turned around to pour herself another coffee. "You learned that lesson from what I let that man do to us."

I frowned and walked up to where she was cursing her ex Ramon for the millionth time.

"Mami, you're the bravest woman in the world. Everything I know about standing up for myself I learned from you. Please don't be so hard on yourself."

She let me walk into her arms again, and held on to me tight. She was a few inches shorter than me, but she was *so* strong. With her arms wrapped around me I finally started feeling like I could handle this meeting with Tom.

Tom

"¿Cómo están mis viejos?" I asked around the grin I was sure I was flashing my parents with. They loved to act like they hated being called old.

"M'ijo. You look tired. Are you sleeping all right?" my mother said, ignoring my "viejos" comment and doing her usual assessment of my face. Getting in as

close as the FaceTime screen allowed. I shook my head
and shared a look with my dad.

"Mami, I'm fine. I'm just forty-one and don't look
like your baby anymore." She flipped a hand at me
like what I was saying was ridiculous, then bumped
my dad's shoulder.

"You may be light skinned, but you got the Dominican genes for sure, you don't look a day older than
thirty," she said in a teasing tone as my dad rolled his
eyes. "Where's my niña?" she asked tilting her head
from side to side as if I was hiding Libe behind me or
something.

It was late on Sunday and I usually called them when
Libe was around, but today I was feeling like I wanted
to check in with them on my own. My dad must have
suspected there was something going on with me, because he leaned in for his own close inspection of my
face.

"Is everything alright, son?" He'd let his beard grow
in the last few years, so his weathered face was covered
with salt-and-pepper hair.

I nodded quickly, not wanting to worry them. "Yeah,
we're good. She's in bed already. We had a busy day
at the zoo."

My mother's face relaxed and my dad smiled as he
reached for her hand. They still did that, held hands
when they were sitting together or walking. After so
many years they sought each other's touch for comfort.

Theirs had been such an unlikely love story.

My dad the ex-Marine who'd come to the Dominican Republic as part of the occupation forces, and my
mother one of the young activists who fiercely stood
up against them. They never crossed paths then, but

when my dad returned almost ten years later, hoping to find the same magic he'd felt on his first visit, he found love too.

Camilo once again came to my foolish mind, and I surprised myself by wanting to tell my parents about him. It was too soon to tell my parents, so I veered in another direction, which of course took me right back to Camilo.

"We finally got the domestic violence project going, Mamí. I met with the director of the agency last week."

My mother's face lit up immediately. I'd been talking about doing something to honor my aunt's memory for years and I finally had the time to do it.

"Ay m'ijo." Her eyes filled with tears. "I'm so proud of you."

My dad put his arms around her shoulders and kissed the side of her face, before he spoke too. "That's great, son. Tell us about the agency. You told us about a few the last time we got an update, which one did you finally decide on?"

He was such a contrast to my mother. Measured and not overly emotional, but he was never shy about showing his affection. He told my mother he loved her every day of my childhood. From my mother I learned how to be bold about what I wanted, to go for my dreams, and my dad taught me how to be a man his family could rely on for everything.

Once again Camilo popped into my head and I wondered what my parents would think of him. I couldn't help the smile that appeared on my face as soon as I started talking about New Beginning.

"The agency is exactly what we wanted, a grass-roots organization working with immigrant women.

They have a solid reputation, and things got off to a great start."

The urge to say something about Camilo was almost overwhelming, with every word it felt increasingly important to tell my parents about him. To let them know I'd met someone. I wasn't one to share things until they were basically a done deal, but I wanted to tell them all the things I was feeling. That I had hardly been able to get Camilo out of my mind since the moment I met him.

"I'm meeting with the manager for their residential programs this week. He, uh." Talking about Camilo made me feel clumsy, unprepared. After so many years at the helm of a company that took me to the highest levels of business, I'd forgotten what it was like to feel out of my depth.

"What about him?" my mother asked, startling me.

"He's Cuban, so he speaks Spanish," I said, sure that I was blushing.

My parents gave me matching puzzled looks and I sat there debating if I should tell them or not. All of this was new for me. I was not one to harp about my feelings until it was absolutely necessary, but my usual playbook had been completely gone from the moment I'd seen those gray eyes at the gala.

After things ended with Maxwell I'd taken my time about going back out there, dating. My carelessness in my marriage, my lack of attention to how bad things really were with Maxwell until it was too late, left me feeling scared of my own judgment. I wasn't sure if I could be a good partner, and Libe needed me so much, I just poured myself into being a parent. So this thing with Camilo, this urgency, it was like waking up to myself after a long sleep.

"¿Ay Tommy, m'ijo, que te pasa?" My mom's voice was a mix of worry and exasperation.

She did not like brooding.

My mother needed every feeling aired out immediately. No holding back. She always said the universe gave her two "reserved" children as a test to her patience.

I looked at my parents, and the way they were together. The love that was always palpable between them. They'd been good models to me, and yet, when the time came I hadn't been able to live up to it.

"Did I let you guys down with the way I treated Maxwell? That I didn't take better care of him?"

My mother clicked her tongue at my question and my father's face contorted as if the questioned pained him, but my mother spoke first.

"Mi amor, I couldn't have dreamed for a better son. Look at what you've done, Tommy." She waved her hand around the apartment. I'd built the building after my dad retired, so now they lived on the beach like they always dreamed of.

"You went to New York *solito*, all on your own, son, what you've done with your life is remarkable. Your brother too, he could've stayed in the States after medical school, but he came back to his country and is doing so many wonderful things with the border communities that need so much. My sons are such good men, but I wish I would've been better at letting you know you don't have to be perfect I—"

"We," my dad added, earning a kiss and sad smile from my mother. He looked at her with that adoring expression he always had for her. "Raising these boys was never just on you, Esperanza."

I smiled at my dad's still thick accent when he spoke in Spanish and how jumbled it got when he got emotional.

He turned to me, and his face was so serious. "Son, you've always been so good, so noble, but you're not perfect. You were building a business, and doing things that your mother and I are still amazed by. But accomplishing something like you have, at such a young age, it comes at a cost." He lifted a shoulder then. "That doesn't mean you don't know how to love, that you don't deserve a second chance. Things didn't work with Maxwell, but you're raising a great kid together."

My mom interjected again. "It's true. Don't doubt yourself, Tommy, when the right person comes along you will know exactly what to do."

"I would argue, but we both know that you won't let me off FaceTime until I agree with you," I said teasing.

That got me a laugh from my parents.

"Mi muchachito." I could be a hundred years old and my mother would never stop calling me her little boy.

We were all silent for a few breaths, but the conversation had lost its heaviness as we veered into talking about my brother's work before ending the call. I sat for a moment with the fact the first thing that came to mind after my mother's last comments was that I was seeing Camilo Briggs in two days.

Chapter Seven

Camilo

I'd been feeling pretty good about my ability to get through this first meeting with Thomas Hughes, *until* I saw his name like a beacon in my inbox.

Hours away from our first meeting I was sitting at my desk squinting at my computer monitor, a hesitant finger hovering over the keyboard like I was about to disable a ticking bomb.

I assumed it was just a confirmation the meeting was happening, but given my current emotional state, you'd think my computer was going to blow up the moment I opened the fucking thing.

After spending Sunday with my mother, I'd arrived at the office on Monday feeling like I could handle being around Tom without putting myself in a precarious position. That lasted a total of three hours, until Melissa asked me to read over the other philanthropic efforts Tom had been a part of over the last ten years.

Thomas Hughes, on paper at least, was not only ridiculously wealthy, gorgeous and smart, he was a *good* man. Which was why opening the email where he had probably typed perfectly charming and lovely words about our meeting today was going to blast the last of my already very vulnerable defenses.

"There you are!" I almost fell out of my chair when I heard Melissa's voice. "Sorry. I didn't mean to scare you."

"Hi, Melissa," I said with a lot less enthusiasm than she seemed to have today. The extra pep in her step could only mean she was here to talk about the renovation project, namely my meeting with Tom.

"Are you ready for this afternoon?" The inflection in her tone made it clear that she was well aware I was dreading this meeting. She had no clue it was because I'd had Mr. Hughes's dick in my mouth nary a week ago. But she knew me well enough to know a welfare check was in order.

"Yes, I just got an email from him. I think it's just confirming the time and place."

"Oh great!" She grinned, her eyes lasered in on the back of my monitor. "Check to see what he said." I reluctantly clicked on the message and quickly read the few lines he'd sent under Melissa's scrutiny. As I suspected it was a perfectly worded message. I took a deep breath and tightened my leg muscles as I stared blankly at the screen, trying, but failing, to not get taken in by the giddiness I felt about seeing him again.

I glanced at Melissa and almost laughed at her expectant expression.

"We're on for three o' clock today. He said he'll let me know where soon, because he's got stuff going this morning and not sure where he'll be, but that it'll be around here."

I tried not to sound annoyed with the whole "mystery location" drama.

Melissa didn't seem too perturbed by the fact I might be lured into some seedy situation though, she just smiled and gave me a thumbs-up.

"Excellent. I'm sure he'll come up with something convenient. He is such a considerate man." She legit sighed. Tom's juju had gotten to Melissa too.

"So, I wanted to check in with you, because I just heard about a couple of potential developments that could put us on track to start this renovation even faster than we thought."

"Oh?"

She leaned in before answering and she was smiling wide, so I expected this was more good news. "Sounds like Suarez Construction is available after all."

I perked up at that. They'd worked for us in the past and had been incredibly professional, going out of their way to make sure our clients felt safe around their staff.

"That's great, I thought they were working on that big health and wellness center for trauma survivors in Brooklyn though. Are they done already?" I asked handing Melissa the small bowl of candy on my desk she'd been eyeing. After she popped a Jolly Rancher into her mouth she leaned in closer.

"Bueno, apparently there was some *escandalo*."

The gossipy tone in her voice almost made me laugh. I knew it was going to be some good chisme if Melissa was speaking in Spanish. Melissa was a self-proclaimed Jersey Girl, but her wife, Rita, was a gorgeous Puerto Rican woman. They'd been together for like twenty years, and married for ten. At this point Melissa could roll into any Latinx cookout and own the tíos in a Dominoes game without breaking a sweat.

"This gossip must be good, boss. You pulled that

chair so close, you're almost on my side of the desk."
She waved my shade off as she got to it.

"Well sounds like the project is not happening, at
least not for now." It was adorable how she whispered
even though it was just the two of us in the office, *and*
the door was closed.

It was interesting news though. That wellness center
had been the talk of the NYC nonprofit crowd all of last
year. A wealthy family had offered to fund the project
completely in partnership with an agency in Brooklyn.

"So what happened?"

Melissa got even closer. This shit must be real scan-
dalous, because she was now practically sitting on my
desk.

"Apparently the donor pulled out. It was a woman
who used the services from the agency decades ago.
She's from a very wealthy family and through the years
has been a big funder." Melissa's face hardened before
she went on. "The word is that she found out one of the
agency people working closely with the family started
seeing the woman's granddaughter. Who apparently is
very young, like barely eighteen."

The skin on my face heated as Melissa's words sunk
in, and a bubble of dread settled in my stomach. Melissa
was not the type of person to be passive-aggressive, but
this was way too close to home for me not to notice…
or panic.

Shit. Shit. *Shit.*

I couldn't even come up with a response, so I just
nodded, hoping she didn't notice the twitching in my
eye. But Melissa went on unbothered.

"When she found out about it, she shut down the
whole thing." She shook her head, her face mutinous.

"Can you imagine throwing away a project of that size that would help so many people?"

I moved my head from side to side, my eyes focused on her, trying to figure out if this was a test or just the worst coincidence ever. My heart was beating so hard I could feel it in my throat. These were the stakes if I fucked up and blurred boundaries with Tom. *Losing our project.*

I had to remember that.

I made myself speak before things got weird, since Melissa was clearly expecting a reaction. "That's in super bad form. I can't imagine how that guy thought it would be a good idea to get involved with a donor."

I was sure my face was showing genuine horror, because that was exactly what I was feeling. "Not his best moment, that is for sure."

I knew that most likely Melissa hadn't come in here to terrify me, she was not that type of person. Regardless, I *would* take this story as a cautionary tale in how I conducted myself with Thomas Hughes.

"I need to get to that meeting with our immigration lawyers. There's a lot to cover today." Melissa stood up from her chair then, angling her head towards the door.

"Okay, and no worries. I'll make sure to let Tom know we have contractors lined up."

"Great. I feel like we should run it by him, since he wants to be kept in the loop. Make sure you show him the proposal Suarez Construction gave us. If he wants more than that let me know, and I'll get you in touch with them."

She was at the door when she turned around again, her hand on the doorknob.

"Actually it may be easier to just put you in contact

with them anyway. You're the one in charge of the project, and the contact person for the donor. We might as well get you in communication with everyone." My stomach sank again at her words.

It was all riding on me. This project, the agency's relationship with Tom. All of it. On me.

I just lifted a hand to her as she slipped out of the room and sat at my desk quietly freaking out for a few minutes.

"This dude is deliberately trying to mess with my head," I muttered as I walked into the place where I was meeting Tom. Of course he'd pick my favorite fucking restaurant in New York City, which I could only afford like twice a year. Red Rooster on Lenox Avenue was a Harlem jewel.

Owned by an Ethiopian chef who'd been adopted by a Swedish family as a child and blended those two worlds with the food culture of Harlem. This place evoked the golden age of the Harlem Renaissance. Amazing food, great music and a fantastic vibe. It was the coolest spot in town, in my opinion, and of course Tom had to know about it. Because he wasn't happy with being, rich, nice and gorgeous, he also had to have great taste.

Why the hell did he even want to meet here? It wasn't exactly a business atmosphere, even at four in the afternoon.

I walked up to the hostess and gave her Tom's name, and she immediately led me to the dine-in area where he was sitting in a booth by himself. The restaurant area was half empty, so at least we'd be able to have a conversation. I quickly slumped into the red leather booth opposite from Tom, before he did something ridiculous like stand up and pull out a chair for me. Without saying hello, I pulled papers out of my messenger bag with my eyes trained anywhere but on him.

I knew I was being rude, but it seemed like Tom Hughes's sole purpose in life was to throw me off my game by being fucking perfect. After tugging out what I needed to show him and setting it on the table, I pushed my back against the booth and glared at him. When I saw the amused smile on his face, like he'd caught me being adorable again, I finally lost it and let whatever fly out of my mouth.

"Who picks Red Rooster as a place to meet about a domestic violence shelter renovation? Don't you have an office where we could do this?" I waved my arm around, signaling the beautiful bar area and even more beautiful servers buzzing around us. "Isn't this a bit much? I could have come downtown or wherever your office is, you know?"

The bastard laughed.

He literally put his gorgeous fucking head back and laughed at my tantrum. I sat there waiting him out, trying *very* hard to keep my mouth shut. I was on the verge of losing my temper and, given the conversation I'd had with Melissa just this morning, I knew that was *not* advisable.

He drove me *crazy*.

"Hi, Camilo. It's nice to see you again. Thanks for coming to meet with me. I know you're very busy."

And now I felt like an asshole, because I hadn't even said hello. What was wrong with me? Was I actively trying to get fired? This was next-level self-destructive, even for me.

I gritted my teeth and tried to smile. "Hi, Tom."

He sat there with a happy grin on his stupid beautiful face and kept talking. "I picked Red Rooster because I thought meeting alone in my office might be awkward for you. At the moment, my office is just me and my assistants and since—"

He stopped talking then, cleared his throat and looked down at the table. That bit of shyness, like he was also a little nervous about our meeting totally disarmed me. I felt my shoulders relax as I focused on what he was saying. "Anyway I thought a public space for our first meeting would be better. I also live just around the corner, on 126th," he said, pointing at the busy street outside. "And since your office is close too, I figured it would be a good spot."

Now I felt like an even bigger asshole.

I cleared my throat and tried to cool down. "That makes sense actually, and thanks for considering my comfort. I appreciate it." I managed to keep a begrudging tone out of my voice, but barely.

He waved his hand like it was nothing, then started talking again. "I just want to clear the air a bit. I realize this could be a very uncomfortable situation for you, given—"

Another embarrassed pause. Tom the gazillionaire was sort of precious.

I angled my head and asked innocently, "How I sucked you off in a bathroom the first time we met?"

He shot me a pleading look and a sound that was a mix between a groan and a laugh escaped his throat.

"Right." He grabbed the glass of water that was sitting in front of him and took a couple of nervous gulps. When he set it down he seemed a little less flustered. "I just wanted to reassure you I would never use what

happened to make you uncomfortable in any way. I'm
not going to pretend that the coincidence didn't throw
me for a second."

Yeah you and me both, pa.

He put an actual hand to his heart before saying, "If
at any moment I say or do *anything* to make you un-
easy, please just say the word. I mean that." His face
looked so earnest.

God he was a really decent guy.

I nodded feeling mollified by how much he was
doing to make sure things went smoothly between us
and tried to get my head back in the game. We were
here to talk about the shelter renovation project not re-
hash how we knew each other.

"Okay. Thanks for saying that. You didn't have to,
so I appreciate you doing it *and* I can guarantee I will
say something if you make me feel uncomfortable. I'm
sure you've already noticed I don't have any issues with
saying what's on my mind."

He was legit beaming at me now. "Good. I'm glad
to hear that." His hazel eyes twinkled like me telling
him I'd have no problem cursing him out was the best
part of his day.

Tom Hughes did not make it easy for a guy to hate
him.

I couldn't help myself and leaned in, getting closer.
We sat there in silence as the energy changed between
us, suddenly the air felt charged. The spell broke when
a server came to refill our water. We both pulled back
and I cleared my throat again.

"So what do you have for me?" Tom asked. His voice
sounded a little breathless and it made my mind go
somewhere totally not safe for work. I closed my eyes

and tried to regroup, again. I'd been at this meeting for five minutes and I was already picturing us fucking on this table.

I swallowed hard and shoved the folder with the estimates at him. "So those are the estimates we got from the contractors. They built our child therapy center a few years ago and they've worked with other agencies like ours in the Tri-State area. They're very mindful of confidentiality and that we work with trauma survivors. Their workers are also really great about being respectful with the clients, and have even been trained on domestic violence." I tipped my chin in the direction of the papers he was holding. "Anyways they're ready to go anytime, so if you approve them, our finance manager and I can start setting up a timeline with them."

As Tom looked through the papers, a server came by and asked if I wanted anything.

He looked up from what he was reading and told the server offhandedly, "Another seltzer for me. He'll have a glass of the prosecco."

My hackles immediately went up. Was he *ordering* for me?

I was about to tell Thomas Hughes what I thought about people making decisions for me, when I remembered he was a donor for my agency, not my date, and even though he had told me to speak my mind, I still needed to be diplomatic.

I cleared my throat again to get his attention, and made sure I pasted on a smile when he looked up.

I held my hand up for the server who was about to walk off. "Actually, I'm good with water." I kept my tone light, but just then I wasn't feeling too concerned about my inability to stay away from Tom. Nothing turned me off faster than a man with a Daddy complex.

Tom looked up and I could see that despite my efforts to appear neutral, he could tell I was not amused. I pointed at the menu.

"I'm not really comfortable ordering alcohol, since this is a business lunch." I made sure I really emphasized *comfortable*, given his request I point out my discomfort. He reddened and looked at me contritely. I didn't want to make things too awkward so, I ventured into a territory I usually avoided. I compromised.

I stared up at the server who was patiently waiting by our table, then at Tom.

"I haven't had lunch though. So, I'll take the chicken and waffles. They're so good here." I made sure I looked extra hyped about the food to lighten the mood a bit.

He seemed pretty pleased with the fact that he would be paying for *some* of my nourishment during this business meeting. To be fair, I didn't really have to fake my enthusiasm. I loved the food here and could rarely afford it. If Tom the gazillionaire wanted to have meetings at my favorite restaurant, then the least he could do was pay for my meal.

"Chicken and waffles and waters then." Tom's tone was a mixture of relief and surrender.

After the server walked away Tom put his hands over the papers on the table, winked at me and went back to reading as I sat there assessing the situation. Tom Hughes had an unnerving effect on my body. Not just my body, my *person*. I felt out of sorts around him, like I wanted to perform for him. Make him see I was likable and sexy and smart. That I wasn't just some random who sucked off guys at parties. And *that* line of thinking did make me uncomfortable.

I didn't care about what people thought of me or how or who I fucked. If Tom was making a judgment on my character over a blow job we both participated in and enjoyed, then he wasn't the kind of man I wanted to be involved with. But it *wasn't* Tom judging me. Hell, everything he'd done so far made it pretty clear he wasn't a judgmental asshole, and yet here I was feeling self-conscious.

This was my MO.

Anytime a lover tried to be kind, or surprised me by not fulfilling my expectations of being a fuckboy, I mined every word or action for the true meaning, the hidden subtext or falsehood. I filled in the blanks with my own self-doubts and baggage. Then I tried to smother my own neurosis by throwing myself into the relationship too hard and too fast, until I either ran out of steam and walked away or scared the other guy off with my clinginess.

And where the fuck was I going with any of this? Tom wasn't my lover, Tom wasn't my *anything*. He was a guy I was working with, so I needed to get my shit together. My face must have been doing something particularly distressing because when Tom finally looked up, he did a double take at whatever he saw. I tried to smile it away and pointed at the estimate. "Any questions?"

He gave me a worried look, but in the end just shook his head. "This all looks good to me. Honestly, I'm not looking to be this closely involved in the decision making for the project, Camilo. I chose New Beginning because you're doing important work in my community, and have a great track record. I trust you," he said, earnestly. "My expectation is to get an update and maybe hear about how things are going when we meet. I don't think it's my place to pick who you use as contractors or anything else."

He could have said that from the beginning, but I wasn't going to make a thing out of it.

"All right." I nodded as he handed me the papers, trying not to get distracted by how hot he looked in that sapphire blue cashmere sweater. "Well then, I guess the update is we have a contractor. I'll talk to Melissa tomorrow morning and let her know we're good to go. We'll do the renovations in stages, so it doesn't affect operations too much. The whole thing should be done within six months give or take. We should have a fully renovated shelter by March."

I couldn't keep the excitement out of my voice for the last part. We'd been wanting to do some work on the shelter ever since I'd started five years ago and our goals for what we could do never got close to all the changes Tom's generous donation would allow.

"Thank you, Tom, really, from all of us at New Beginning. This project is life-changing for the residential program."

He shook his head again, as if trying to push away the compliment.

"Like I said in the first meeting, I'm very happy and honored to be able to do this. This is something very close to my heart. I'm just glad I have the means to make it happen."

This should have been a great moment to wind things down and get the hell out of there, instead I blurted out, "Who are you doing this for?"

It seemed like whenever he was around me Tom's

face only had two settings, amusement and disbelief. We sat there quietly for a second and after a moment, he leaned in closer.

"I guess it's time for us to get to know each other then."

Chapter Eight

Tom

Camilo looked a little spooked at my suggestion we get to know each other, but since he asked the question I was going to go with it. I wanted to know everything about him. Who he loved. Where all the prickliness came from.

So, before he could take it back, I went in. "I wanted to do something in honor of my tía's memory. My mother's youngest sister." I cleared my throat because suddenly I was feeling choked up. "She died when I was sixteen. She was living here then. She'd been in a very abusive relationship for a long time. Her husband had convinced her to leave the DR, claiming they needed to be away from our family and all the meddling."

I closed my eyes, remembering how my mom and my grandmother begged her not to go. Telling her they were scared something would happen to her when she was all on her own with him.

Camilo's face changed then, and all I could see was concern, his entire body totally focused on what I was saying. Those gray eyes flashing. All the abrasiveness gone now.

"That's typical abuser behavior, to isolate." He angled his head, as if assessing how this conversation was affecting me. "Sounds like your family tried their best to be supportive."

I pursed my lips, remembering how awful that time was. "They tried, but in the end they weren't able to help her. Things got so bad when they got here, she decided to leave him. But when she called shelters for help, she couldn't find anyone who spoke Spanish. She eventually tried to leave by going to a neighbor, but he found her."

Camilo put his hand over mine, his eyes grim. "That's why you're donating the money to our shelter, so we can help women like your aunt."

I nodded and he squeezed my hand. "It's a wonderful way to honor her. A lot of survivors will benefit from your kindness."

I exhaled, feeling heavy from the conversation, but also like Camilo would be here with me for as long as I needed it. After a moment he leaned in and said, "Tell me about your family. Are they all still in the DR or just your parents?"

I smiled at him, grateful he was steering the conversation in another direction. "Yes, they're all there pretty much. I think I'm the only Dominican without at least one relative in New York City."

Camilo laughed at that. "I was wondering if you at least had one primo or something. My friend Nesto seems to have family all over New York State."

I wondered if this Nesto was more than a friend, since he'd mentioned him a couple of times already.

I had to calm down.

"Not me. My brother came here for medical school, but he went back as soon as he was done. My parents and him come visit and I go back a few times a year, but they like it there, they won't leave that island." I smiled, thinking about my dad's devotion to the "homeland of his heart." "My dad never really had any interest in coming back to the States. He wasn't very close to his parents and he loves life in the DR."

I lifted a shoulder before I spoke. "Family was always my mom's side, and there *were* a lot of them." Camilo grinned at that. "My grandma lived with us too, so the family always came together at our house. We always had a ton of people at our place."

Camilo's face turned wistful when I said that, and it made me want to know all about him. Know all the reasons that made that heart-stopping smile escape his lips, so I could do away with them one by one.

He quietly waited for me to continue. "My mom is a sociology professor at the public university, so in addition to our relatives, we always had students and other faculty using our living room to have political meetings or for planning protests. It was an interesting household to grow up in. How about you? Do you have a big family?"

He shook his head at my question, the wistfulness still there in his eyes. "It's just me and my mom." He pursed his mouth and then smiled. "Well that's not completely true. I also have my three best friends, Nesto, Patrice and Juanpa, and their families."

So a best friend, not a boyfriend. I could live with that.

"But my mom came from Cuba on her own. She was a Marielita." His voice grew stronger when he said that, and I nodded, letting him know I understood what he meant.

"She must be a hell of a woman." He smiled at me again. I was already addicted to pulling those out of him. That could be my new full-time job: making Camilo Briggs smile.

"She really is. My dad passed away from cancer when I was ten. He was Jamaican and other than my grandma, who passed when I was still a baby, he didn't have any close family here. So it was just the two of us for a while."

He paused there, like he was deciding on whether he should say whatever went next in the story, then he squared his shoulder and kept talking. "My mom started seeing this man, Ramon, who turned out to be very abusive a couple of years after my dad died. He was nice at first, but once he started helping her out financially, he got violent. Things were bad for a while, but the summer before eighth grade I came out to her and that lit a fire under her." His face grew more serious then.

"I think her fear of how he'd react to me being gay, or the possibility he'd hurt me, was the last straw for her." His brows dipped and I could tell whatever he was thinking of was not a good memory, but from one breath to the next he smiled again. "My friend Patrice's mom helped us get settled in the Bronx where they lived, and the rest is history."

"Sounds like you're both survivors." He shrugged trying to dismiss the compliment. The more I learned about Camilo Briggs, the more I wanted to know.

"Was that experience with your mom the reason you got into this work?"

At my question his face went serious again, not sad, just like he wanted to take his time with his answer. He leaned back and put his hand under his chin before finally responding. "Partly. It certainly had an impact on me, but I do this work because I love it and because I'm good at it." His certainty and passion was intoxicating. I just sat there in silence, getting my fill of all the energy Camilo exuded.

"Thank you for sharing all that with me," I said sincerely.

He broke eye contact then and looked down for a moment.

"I sort of Google stalked you."

I laughed at how embarrassed he sounded. "You did?" I asked, surprised.

He widened his eyes at my question, a look of complete disbelief on his face. "Of course I did! I needed to know what to expect. You have to admit the circumstances around our meeting were a bit unusual."

An image of him on his knees with his mouth stretched out from my cock flashed in my mind. The effect was like lightning, every nerve in my body lit up at once. I wondered if Camilo could tell what I was thinking.

I cleared my throat and tried to bring us back to the conversation, before I broke my promise to not make him uncomfortable.

"So what did you find out about me?"

He shrugged and took another bite of the plate he'd been working on. "Mostly stuff about your business, which was very impressive by the way," he said raising an eyebrow. "I resisted the urge to go into Page Six or other gossipy sites. I just wanted some background and to make sure you didn't get all your money running sweatshops or something."

I laughed at that. "Fair enough." As I was about to

ask if he'd like to order something else, just so I could keep him with me a little longer, my phone went off. When I looked at the screen I saw it was Maxwell asking me to call him about something regarding Libe. I tried not to huff, but it was a close thing.

Camilo was staring between me and my phone when I looked up.

"You need to take that?"

I grimaced. "Yes, I'm sorry." I'd promised myself I'd ask him if he was comfortable with continuing to meet, even if it gave him an out, so I made myself follow through. "Are you up for meeting again next week? Only if you're comfortable, of course."

He was already gathering his things, so he wasn't looking at me when he answered. "Sure, this was a lot less painful than I anticipated."

I laughed again, surprising myself. I was not usually this excitable, but Camilo's presence was like oxygen in my blood, and I hadn't gotten nearly enough. "Excellent. I'll see you next week, Camilo." I lifted my hand to ask for the check as he gathered his things and slipped out of the booth.

He looked at me as he got his messenger bag on and winked. "Next week then, Tom. This wasn't much of a business meeting, but this is my favorite restaurant, and eating here is a rare treat. If you want to buy me chicken and waffles on the regular, I'm here for it. No wine though."

I assented to his request. "No wine."

For a moment we stood by the table. Closer than the purpose of our meeting warranted. All I wanted was to be able to kiss him. I looked at his mouth and he leaned in just a bit, like he could feel the pull too. We just stood there, wanting. Then the server came with the check, breaking the spell. We pulled back, both looking a little dazed, like we'd been caught off guard by the moment.

I lifted a hand again as he moved away from me.

"Take care, Camilo."

He waved goodbye and walked out the door to Lenox Avenue. I stared after him mulling over the fact that this meeting had only increased my desire to get to know Camilo better.

But I wouldn't rush it. I was in for the long game. Week by week we'd get to know each other, until I could tell him I wanted a lot more with him than just business.

Camilo

I stomped out of the Metro-North station in Yonkers musing over the events of the day. The meeting with Tom would've been a total success *if* the goal had been for me to go from solid attraction to full-on infatuation.

Every new thing I learned about him made him more human and intriguing. My heart had hurt for him when he talked about his aunt.

It was funny, with Tom, I'd imagined his money and position would put him at arm's length, but every time I saw him it seemed like he wanted to move closer. I knew he was trying to get personal, and if I was smart I'd put a brake on it, but who was I kidding?

I wanted him.

My plan to heed Melissa's cautionary tale and keep things professional for as long as this project was going went completely out the window the moment I set eyes on him. Which was ridiculous because Tom was a multi-millionaire, and I was a social worker living in a studio in Harlem. This could never work, our lives were too different. That reminded me about living right by Red Rooster. Harlem *was* booming these days, but it was still not the fashionable part of town for the rich and famous. Someone with Tom's money only lived in Harlem if he made a very intentional choice.

Dammit.

I so wanted to dismiss him as just another rich asshole, but everything about Tom so far was wreaking havoc on my plans to hate him.

I was brought back from my thoughts when I walked into my best friend Juanpa's condo and smelled the homemade pizza he'd promised for dinner. I was trying to tug my shoes off when I noticed lit scented candles on the coffee table and smiled. He bought this place in Yonkers last spring, and he'd been surprising us with his domestic side since then.

I called out since he was nowhere in sight, "I'm putting these bottles of wine I brought down and then I'm going to go look in every closet to see where you hid the boxes, Juan Pablo. You're not fooling me into believing you made pizza from scratch."

Patrice, our other best friend, was on the couch texting on his phone. He just smiled and shook his head at my teasing. Juanpa hollered from the kitchen.

"Fuck you, Camilo! You ingrate. Here I am killing myself to make you a nice meal and you start disrespecting me as soon as you walk into my crib. Did you take your shoes off, motherfucker? I don't want you tracking your subway filth on my hardwood floors."

He was ridiculous.

"Oh my god! You're so fucking annoying with this floor obsession. I came on the Metro-North, thank you very much, and I'm not wearing those stupid slippers you put by the door either." I stopped in front of the couch where Patrice was still tapping on his phone. "Patrice! Get off the damn phone. I haven't seen you in weeks and you can't stop texting dick pics to Easton long enough to say hello."

Patrice, as always, was completely unbothered by my ranting and finished whatever he was doing before getting up and coming to where I was to give me a double kiss and hug hello. He had his locs coiled up in a big bun today. He was wearing a Cornell sweatshirt, loose jeans and had his Malcolm X glasses on. I'd missed his face so much. I pulled him in for another hug before letting him go.

"I missed you, P."

His usually unexpressive faced softened. "I missed you too. I was texting Odette about tomorrow." I smiled at the mention of his mom. He always called her by her name, never Mom, they were so formal with each other. "Are you and Dinorah still coming to her place for dinner Friday?"

I rolled my eyes at the question. He knew that was a given. My mom and Patrice's were still very close. Odette was the only one who could get her out of the house these days.

"We'll be there. No way am I missing the annual Joumou night." Patrice smiled at that.

"Good. I'll have someone to back me up when she starts getting on me about not wearing 'proper clothes.'"

I laughed at his annoyance and shook my head. "You need to get over that. You two have been having that argument since middle school." He just glared in answer and I shrugged. "You know I have your back, but I'm not pushing, because that soup is too fucking delicious to mess with my standing invitation."

Patrice smirked as he pulled his phone out of his pocket. I noticed the way his eyes widened at whatever he saw and I wondered if my teasing about the dick pics was more on point than I thought. But before I could ask, he shoved his phone in his pocket without responding to whomever had messaged him. "You know that Joumou night invitation will always be there."

I nodded, because he was right, I knew that.

Every year his mom would make a traditional Haitian pumpkin and beef stew and invite our group over. Traditionally the soup was part of the New Year's Day celebration our families always did together, but after we got out of college and were busy doing our own things, Odette started making it in the fall, when "we could all make it." This year only Nesto, the fourth guy in our little crew from the Bronx, would be missing it.

Nesto moved to Ithaca the year before to try his luck in getting his Caribbean food truck to take off. He'd had massive success up there and this past spring opened his restaurant. Along the way he'd also met Jude, the love of his life, and they were happy as fucking clams up there in the boonies. I missed having him around but was so thrilled for him and all he'd achieved in the past year. He'd worked his ass off to make his dream happen and deserved everything he'd gotten.

Now Patrice was up there too. He'd finally finished his PhD at Columbia in May and taken a position as an assistant professor for the economics department at Cornell University. Although he assured us there was nothing going on, it didn't escape any of us that from all the offers he had, and he'd gotten plenty, he chose the school in the town where a certain assistant district attorney he'd gotten tangled up with last year lived.

"What are you glaring at?" Juanpa walked out of the kitchen with a wine opener and three glasses, looking like Drake's skinnier little brother.

"He's been sexting with Hudson or whatever the fuck his name is since he got here," he said, angling his head in Patrice's direction. Juanpa refused to call Easton by his name just to get a rise out of Patrice.

"He thinks I can't tell, but his eyebrows get mad twitchy when he's up to something. You're not fooling anyone, pa." He cut his eyes at Patrice and we all laughed. I noticed Patrice didn't even try to deny what Juanpa was saying though.

Juanpa turned to me after a minute as he poured us all some wine. "How was your meeting with the millionaire? Did he get creepy on you?"

I shook my head and sighed. "Nope, not at all. He cleared the air as soon as I got there, assured me he would be respectful and then we proceeded to have an hour of polite conversation. If anything now I'm more attracted to him."

I took a big gulp from the glass Juanpa had just handed to me and slumped on the couch. "I'm such a hypocrite too, because I was actually disappointed. I was hoping he'd be all flirty, and suggestive and then I could just say he was the one who started it. But instead he was real and respectful and basically gave me no excuses to do anything stupid. Isn't that fucked up?"

Neither of them answered, they knew me well enough to know I had to process all this to death and that I probably had more to say. "I don't even know why I'm so worked up about this guy. What could possibly happen between us? He's a rich dude with all kinds of privilege, it's only a matter of time before all that rears its ugly head." Even as I said it I felt like shit, because so far all I'd seen from Tom was that he was generous and incredibly down to earth.

The eye roll I got from Juanpa was so intense, his eyelids actually popped. Patrice just looked at me and shook his head like I was an idiot.

"Why do you need to take everything to the extreme, Camilo? Why can't you just chill and see what happens?" Juanpa rarely chimed in when it came to relationships, so the fact that he was so fired up about this gave me pause. "Not everything needs to be decided and done with after two minutes."

Not that I was going to admit to that to him just yet. "Like I'm taking advice from you. You've been in love with Priscilla for eighteen years and you still can't make yourself say it."

"We're not talking about me right now though." He jerked his thumb at Patrice. "And we're not talking about how this one is upstate now, literally fucking with the Po-Po—

"He's not a cop!" All three of us looked stunned at Patrice's very out of character outburst and then Juanpa busted up, pointing a finger at him.

"Eeeey! Made you say it!" His glee at Patrice's slip up was hilarious.

Patrice just glared and muttered. "Asshole."

Juanpa just kept shaking his head with a huge grin on his face. "Can't take it back, my guy."

The interlude was fun, but we were supposed to be focusing on my fucking man problems. So I got up and waved my hands in between J and Patrice.

"Back to me, assholes!"

Did that shut Juanpa up? Nope, he jumped right back into his lecture.

"Nah. That's where your shit gets problematic, Camilo." He pointed his glass of rosé at me to press his point. It was really hard to take this asshole seriously sometimes.

"You're too judgmental, pa. You create a whole fucking situation in your head. God forbid a dude says or does something differently than how you deem it should be done, then they're dead to you. You don't leave any room for people to be human, mi hermano. Under those conditions you will always be disappointed. Full stop."

I was about to respond with something defensive, but before I spoke all the air went out of me. Because he was right. I was always anticipating disaster or predicting all the ways in which people would let me down before we even got started. There was nothing about Tom to dislike or judge. I knew he wasn't perfect, no one was, but so far all he'd been to me was decent.

"Fine. I'll try to keep an open mind."

Juanpa and Patrice both widened their eyes after I said that.

"Wow. This guy *must* be something," Patrice said in a rare display of emotion.

Juan Pablo, who thought he was fucking hilarious, got up and put his palm on my forehead pretending to feel for a fever. I slapped it away and took another sip of my wine.

"Leave me alone, you idiot."

He took his phone out of his pocket.

"We're calling Nesto, because he needs to know there's some molecular level shit happening with you.

I mean you almost admitted to me being right about something, and if that's not an indication we need to keep you under close observation, I don't know what is."

I just ignored him as Patrice laughed on the other side of the couch. Pretty soon I could hear Nesto.

"Yo, is that the new couch? It looks fly, man." I immediately stood up and yelled at the phone before J could get a word in.

"Don't believe anything Juan Pablo says, Ernesto, you know how he lies."

Our best friend's amused voice sounded through Juanpa's apartment. "Oh shit, are you all drunk already, it's like seven! How come you're not at the stadium, J?"

Juanpa was a physical therapist for the Yankees and this time of year he was usually working all the time. He shook his head as he looked at the phone.

"I'm off tonight, working six days straight next week."

Patrice stood up and calmly took the phone from J, which meant he was about to bring the conversation back to me.

Great.

He winked at me before smiling at Nesto's face on the screen. "We're not drunk. We're just trying to gently tell Camilo he's occasionally judgmental and impulsive."

J and I sat down on either side of Patrice as he held the phone out, so we could all get a look at Nesto. I bit my tongue as our friend cackled. "Damn and he hasn't slashed your faces with a rusty razor yet? Camilo, you're losing your edge, pa."

I grumbled under my breath but stayed quiet as Patrice relayed my woes to Nesto. As he talked, Jude,

Nesto's partner, came into the room, put his head on his shoulder and joined the conversation.

By the time Patrice finished, Jude's pretty face had broken into a grin and his bright blue eyes were looking in my direction.

"Camilo, this guy sounds great." He gave me a sympathetic look, an adorable pout forming on his lips. "And like he'll keep you on your toes. I can't wait to hear how you guys get on."

I crossed my arms over my chest and huffed. "I'm not dating this guy, people! He's a donor for the agency."

Nesto shot me some side-eye before chiming in with his hot take on the matter. "First of all, it feels amazing to be giving you relationship advice. Second, bitch, please. This man asked to meet with you every week so he can get a random update you could send him in a two line email, and you don't think it's because he's looking for an excuse to see you? Come on, Milo."

"Fine. Okay," I answered a little wildly. "But it's really not that deep."

Various protests resulted from my very obvious lie, and I finally conceded.

"Okay, maybe he does want more, but I really don't want to go there, because I'm *really* attracted to him and so far, he's been very much sticking to business." I sighed feeling like I needed to let this out. If only to admit it to myself, and if I couldn't say it to these people, then who could I say it to?

"And I'm kind of freaked, because he's amazing, not just because he's gorgeous, and rich and really does have a magnificent cock." That broke the tension a bit at least. "He's nice and down to earth. He talked about his family in DR when we met today, and about the aunt he's honoring with the shelter renovation."

I pressed my fingers to my eyes as I talked. "I get carried away when I like someone this much, and then ruin everything by running my mouth or acting jealous. I just don't want to get my hopes up, that's all. I don't want to end up brokenhearted *and* jobless over this. I mean that seriously too, my boss will not be okay with me fucking around with a donor. Hell, *I'm* not okay with it. It's inappropriate and...fuck it's just not a good idea," I said, feeling miserable.

When I stopped talking I saw they were all looking at me with worried faces. Patrice put his arms around my shoulder.

"Camilo, you're not going to lose your job. You're amazing at it, and you will run that renovation like the pro you are. As far as Tom is concerned, just see where things go. You're being too hard on yourself right now, nothing has happened yet." He tugged on my ear then, like we usually did to each other when one of us was being particularly dense. "And for the record, whether it's with Tom or anyone else, just let go a bit. Be yourself, don't try to be who you think you *should* be. The person you are." He gently tapped my chest with his finger. "The guy we get all the time is wonderful. No one who gets to see the real you would ever walk away."

I looked around at my friends and their faces were so full of affection, so certain I deserved to be happy I felt the tightness in my chest loosen a bit. Maybe if I could not trust myself, I could trust what my friends believed about me and what I deserved.

"Thank you, but now we have to stop talking about this. *Please?*" I pleaded then turned my attention to Patrice. "Nesto, give us the real report on what Patrice is up to with Easton. Are they fucking or what?"

Juanpa muttered, "Dayum, you're just gonna drag him like that, huh? Ruthless little fucker."

I preened at what was clearly a compliment, and let the conversation steer off me and onto Patrice's new job.

As I sat there hearing my friends chatter, I thought about Tom, and wondered if he was thinking about our talk today. If like me, he was anxious and eager for next Wednesday.

Chapter Nine

Camilo

"Hola, Camilo." Tom's voice was like a caress in my ear, and I had to squeeze my eyes to focus and not do something ludicrous like sigh, or whimper.

This was a professional call. Tom was not my lover.

"Hi. So, I hate to do this so last minute, but could we move our meeting tomorrow to 4:00 p.m.? I have something I can't get out of and need time to get back to Harlem."

He made a rumbling sound, and it was like thunder crackling through my nerves. It'd been a week since our first meeting, and I really wanted to see him again.

"Sure, no problem." His voice was lower when he spoke again. "I thought you were going to have to cancel. Like I said before, my schedule is fairly flexible. Do you need more time? I can meet later than that."

The way Tom spoke to me, like he cared about my needs, or like making things easier for me was a priority to him, was intoxicating. It was most likely because he was a decent person and didn't act like a diva because he had money, but deep down in a little corner of my heart where no one else was invited, I imagined this was only for me.

"No, 4:00 p.m. should work, I just need to drop my mom off—"

I stopped talking, horrified that I'd shared information about a personal appointment with Tom. My lack of professional boundaries were going to get me in a serious bind before this renovation even got off the ground.

I sighed internally and tried again. "I need to get back to Harlem from the Bronx. I shouldn't need more than an hour."

The silence on Tom's end was making me squirm. I felt exposed and weirded out by the possibility that he'd ask what I was doing.

"Camilo." The way he said my name, in that perfect inflection, like it was *supposed* to sound, got me every time. "If you need to take care of your mom, we can reschedule. Your family is the priority."

I hesitated before I spoke, but soon I was saying more than I probably should. "It's fine. I'm just going with her to an appointment." *To do an intake for a domestic violence support group, which she's finally agreed to do after years of trying to convince her and I don't want to miss the chance to get her there.* "The place is right by Fordham Plaza. We should be done by three. I can take the Metro-North from there, it won't even take thirty minutes. I just want to give myself enough time, so you don't have to end up waiting for me if I get delayed."

Again his response took some time and when he spoke, he was the hesitant one. "Why don't I meet you up there?" I actually had to suppress a gasp at the question. "We can have our meeting at the botanical garden." His voice suddenly rose with excitement. "I've been wanting to see the Georgia O'Keeffe exhibit, and it's supposed to be beautiful out tomorrow."

There went my pulse again, threatening to jump out of my chest. This was not a good idea. This was the opposite of sensible. The botanical garden was not a place for business meetings, it was a place for dates. I could *not* date Thomas Hughes.

I opened my mouth to put a brake on this course of action, but when I spoke I heard my stupid mouth say, "I've been wanting to see that too."

This time there was no pause and I got a firsthand glimpse of the tenacious businessman Tom was rumored to be. "Excellent. I'll meet you at the conservatory. I'll leave a ticket for you at the front."

"Tom, you don't have to do that," I protested, feeling already like this was getting closer and closer to a date by the second.

"Of course I do, I keep changing meeting locations and it's the least I could do given how easygoing you've been." I wasn't even sure what he was talking about. I was the one who'd changed the time of the appointment and he had come up with the gardens because I was going to be in the Bronx. Somehow Tom had made me feel like I was making *his* day easier by changing our entire plan for the meeting.

I wanted to be contrary, to tell him that he was changing the rules and making it harder for me to keep myself at bay, *but* I also wanted to see him. I wanted to see the exhibit with *him*. I wanted.

Tom.

I heard the sound of his throat clearing and I wondered if he was as fucked up about the pull between us as I was, but when I spoke I could do nothing to mask the anticipation in my voice. "All right. I'll see you then."

"Until tomorrow, Camilo."

I ended the call and sat there wondering if there was any chance I could realistically stick to my "stay off Tom's dick" plan for much longer, until Ayako's voice mercifully yanked me out of my fretting.

"Yoooooo… Is all that frowning about Mr. BDE?"

Ayako thought she was fucking hilarious.

"I'm not frowning and calling a major donor 'Mr. Big Dick Energy' is super unprofessional," I said primly.

She laughed at my very weak attempt at outrage and planted her ass on my desk. "I have sources who can confirm that the dick is indeed big." She widened her eyes and put a finger over her lips, then aimed it at me.

The smile threatening to break out of my face was very hard to hold back. "I'm sorry. I can't confirm or deny any knowledge concerning Mr. Hughes's dick, or any other body parts."

She twisted her bright red lips to the side as she rolled her eyes. "Uh huh, so what's the deal, why are you sitting here looking spooked? Did he cancel on you?"

I sighed as I tried to extract what was appropriate to say about everything I was feeling at the moment. "No, I just called to let him know that I needed to push back the meeting an hour."

A spark of cautious optimism warmed my chest as I thought of the reason for the time change. "I finally convinced my mom to do the intake for that support group for Spanish speakers the DV center from the Bronx is doing." Ayako's face lit up at that. She was well aware how much I'd struggled to get my mom to do anything related to her trauma history.

"I'm so happy to hear that. It'll be so good for her to talk to other women." She sounded genuinely excited. Ayako knew how long I'd been trying to cajole my mom to do a group.

I nodded, still not wanting to call this development with my mom a victory. "I'm a little bit worried that she seemed to say yes too easily. Maybe she's doing worse than she's letting on."

Ayako leaned and smiled in that way she did when I was getting "too pessimistic."

"Maybe she's just ready. We talk about meeting people where they're at until our tongues fall out around here. If it's good enough for our clients, it should be good enough for us."

I exhaled, conceding her point. "You're right. I just worry."

"Take this as a win, friend. This a good step toward Dinorah starting to believe that what happened to her isn't who she is. I've heard really great things about that program, they use a good model."

I dipped my head in agreement. "I *will* take it as a win, and yes, I've only heard positive things." I glanced at my office door, as if checking for eavesdroppers. "I ended up blabbing to Tom about it and by the time we were done talking, we'd arranged to meet at the botanical garden tomorrow." Ayako widened her eyes at this development. "These meetings sound more and more like dates, and I'm pretty sure I do *not* have the self-control it takes to resist Tom Hughes if he even hints at a repeat from the night at the gala."

I stared up at Ayako, hoping she would give me the talking to I needed. Instead she got up and walked over to the door, shut it and walked back to my desk.

"I'm not going to tell you to have a torrid affair with a donor, because that would be *terrible* advice."

Awesome I was about to get another "just go with the flow" pep talk. I needed a fucking reckoning, before I ruined my career and this project, not one more person telling me this was *not* a terrible idea.

"Don't think I don't know you're internally rolling your eyes at me." She leaned over to smack my shoulder playfully. "Camilo, I know that despite your insistence that you have terrible judgment and can't be trusted to be sensible when you have feelings for someone." She leaned in close, so she was looking straight at me. "You are an *excellent* judge of character—" she held up her finger and waved it in the air "—*and* you have very good self-preservation instincts. I also know that your mother has always been sacred ground for you. If your gut is telling you this guy is trustworthy, then fucking go with it, babe. I've seen shit go down in flames between you and some of the clueless assholes you've dated."

She hooked her thumb over her shoulder as she talked. "But that was on them, *not* you."

After a moment of me just staring at her, she threw her arms up as if recalling a particularly compelling piece of evidence. "Fuck, I don't think you ever even told that dickbag Paul Dinorah's *name*, and you dated for almost two years. Yet from one meeting Tom already knows how she came to the States. It took you three years to tell me, motherfucker!"

I broke as soon as *dickbag* came out of her mouth. "Fine," I said, too amused by her to keep arguing. "But if I end up getting fired for this shit, I'm moving in with you."

She laughed and got up from the spot on my desk where she'd perched. "I would not mind splitting Astoria rent prices, but I don't think you're going anywhere. Just chill out and go on your meeting/date with the Dominican billionaire with the BDE."

"*Stop*," I pleaded as she back walked out of my office with a huge grin on her face.

Why did I think I could go to Ayako for sensible advice?

I was completely sure that doing this with Tom was the road to perdition, but it seemed like I'd at least have some friends with me when I got there.

Tom

I sensed him before I saw him coming up the path to the conservatory.

He had his hair in a bun again, but this time he was wearing dark red slacks and a gray sweater under a leather bomber jacket. A messenger bag slung across his chest. There was nothing particularly remarkable about the outfit, but to me he looked perfect.

He glanced up as he started walking towards the steps where I was standing. As soon as he saw me, his face broke into an easy smile, and he lifted a hand in greeting. Before I knew what I was doing I started walking to meet him halfway.

"Hi," I said holding myself back. The need to kiss him felt like a gravitational force, every part of my body wanted to get closer, to touch him.

Camilo looked up at me, and I could see just a slight tremor go through him. I wondered if he was having the same reaction. After a moment he blinked and pointed to the glass doors of the conservatory.

"Shall we?"

I realized that we were standing in the middle of the steps and people were having to walk around us. I felt a little embarrassed but nodded and turned toward the glass doors.

Once inside, Camilo stopped to look around. "I haven't been here in ages," he said, inspecting the glass-encased building. "My mom used to love to come see the orchid show in the spring." His smile faded a bit then. "We haven't come in a while."

I stepped closer to him, looking up at the glass dome above us. "It's quite a building. I didn't come here until I'd been in New York for a few years and was pretty blown away by it when I did."

We looked at the tropical plants as we talked. "And a little homesick."

Camilo lifted and eyebrow at that. "Homesick?"

I gestured towards the doors that led to another greenhouse. "They have a lot of trees that are indigenous to the DR here."

He perked up at that, nodding at all the plants I was pointing to. "That makes sense, my mom loved tearing off pieces of the Bay Rum leaves whenever we came here. She said it reminded her of her mom."

I smiled at that, because that smell also brought up memories for me. "My grandma always had a bottle of rubbing alcohol with Bay Rum leaves in it. Anytime any of us fell down, she would soak a cloth with it and make us press it to the bruise."

Camilo sighed wistfully at my memory. He curled into himself a little bit as if he was getting chilled, and the impulse to put my arm around him had me almost vibrating. We walked a bit more, looking around the trees and plants of my childhood, and it felt like the most natural thing in the world to be here with him.

"How did it go with your mom?" I asked while he inspected a cacao tree.

His shoulders tensed at the question, but after a moment he answered in a low voice. "It was fine. It wasn't anything major, she just didn't want to go alone."

"I'm glad to hear that." I didn't want to pry or ask for more details, since it was clear to me this was not an easy topic for him. I was going to leave it there, when Camilo spoke again.

"My mom has depression and anxiety. She knows she needs help with it, but the stigma around mental illness she grew up with is still an issue. She feels embarrassed to seek out help." His face was a study in frustration, his lush full lips flattened as we started walking again. "I mean if it were me, she'd be begging me to do whatever it took to feel okay, but since it's for her, she finds every reason not to do it."

I nodded in understanding. "My dad struggled with depression a lot."

"From the war?" Camilo's voice was gentle and so understanding. In the last ten years my life had changed so much that I rarely met anyone new who I didn't approach with caution. The men that came into my life were usually the ones doing the pursuing and I rarely ever took them up on it. And yet here I was with this man who I barely knew, but could feel already getting into my blood.

I wanted to tell Camilo all my secrets.

When I spoke he turned from what he'd been looking at and focused completely on me. "Yeah. My mom talked my dad into seeing someone and taking what he needed in order to feel better. He has his ups and downs, but he's been able to cope. Going to a therapist isn't exactly considered 'normal' in the DR, but my mom has always been a bit counterculture."

"She sounds awesome." A warmth spread to my chest when he said that and I remembered my mom's words from the other night. Was this feeling the certainty she told me about?

"She is." I stopped then, noticing a tree I hadn't seen before.

Camilo stood next to me and bent over to look at it more closely. "What is it?"

I lifted a shoulder as I pointed to a cluster of green fruits that looked like tiny pickles hanging from the trunks.

"I'm not sure what they're called in other countries, but in the DR they're called vinagrillos. We had one in our backyard growing up. They're really sour, thus the vinegar related name," I said, my lips almost puckering from the memory of biting into one. "We used to do contests to see who could eat the most without puking." I grinned at his horrified look. "I haven't eaten one in at least fifteen years, but I can totally remember the taste."

Camilo was focused on what I was saying, his eyes wide, listening to my story.

"I like hearing your DR stories."

"I like sharing them with you." I sounded winded. So many feelings that I thought no longer applied to me.

We were quiet for a second looking around before starting for the next part of the exhibit. After a few steps I noticed that Camilo had stayed behind. When

I turned around I saw him hurrying toward me with something in his hand. When he got to me he gestured behind an enormous palm tree, extending his hand once we were hidden.

"Here."

When he opened it I saw a green vinagrillo in his palm, and my face broke into another grin.

"I didn't steal it. This one fell to the ground," he said in a tight voice.

I tried to lighten the mood and teased him a bit. "Those looked pretty green," I said, lifting an eyebrow in question.

"Okay, maybe I gave it a little nudge." He looked so flustered, like he had no idea why he'd done it.

I put my palm over his, touching him for the first time in what felt like forever. Our hands brushed as I took the fruit and we both shivered from the contact. Here, hidden from view, the moment felt wildly intimate.

"Thank you."

He shrugged again, but I could see the tension in his shoulders. This mattered. "Try it."

I brought it up to my mouth and bit into it, it was too sour, and familiar. I closed my eyes as I chewed.

I laughed when I was done. "Wow that is so sour, and delicious." I extended the bitten fruit to him in offer. He immediately leaned in, and for a second it seemed like he would take a bite from the fruit in my hands. But at the last second he reconsidered and plucked it out of my hand.

Looking more than a little harried, he brought it to his mouth, and took a big bite.

Immediately his eyes widened and he turned his head to spit it out.

"Oh my god. That's crazy sour."

I did not dare laugh as he gulped water from a bottle he grabbed from his bag. When he was done he took a deep breath and narrowed his eyes at me.

"Were you fucking with me?"

I held up my hands, still holding in a laugh. "No, I really *did* love those. We almost never took more than one bite out of them though, and never one so big." I smiled ruefully. "It was a pretty lame contest."

He cut his eyes at me as we stepped around the palm tree back to the exhibition. "You could've told me." His grumbling was adorable, and I would've given almost anything to be able to grab him and kiss that grumpiness out of him.

I dipped my head and tried to sound contrite. "Sorry. Next time we are revisiting my childhood in the Dominican Republic, I will provide disclaimers."

"You're not cute." He scoffed as we walked and again I felt like being here with him was exactly where I was supposed to be.

All of a sudden he piped up. "Can I ask you something?"

He looked so serious I was almost afraid to say yes, but I nodded.

"Do you see yourself as Dominican?" He gestured at my face, as if presenting me with the evidence. "I mean, you look…white. Your name is *Thomas Hughes*. But it sounds like so much of who you are is tied to your DR roots. How do you negotiate those parts of yourself?"

Damn. He didn't beat around the bush. Sanjay and Henock waited years before they'd asked me that.

Not Camilo.

"That's a pretty loaded question, Camilo. Are you sure you want to get to know me this well?"

He dipped his head, those gray eyes certain and locked with mine. "Yes I do."

"All right," I said, once again surprised at how eager I was to open myself up to Camilo. "Well the short answer is yes. I don't just see myself as Dominican, I *am* Dominican. That's where I was born and lived my entire childhood. I came to the U.S. as an adult. Well a legal adult anyway. I'm American too, of course, but I consider myself an immigrant in this country in a lot of ways. When I came to New York for college—I won a scholarship for Columbia."

He nodded, impressed, and mouthed "fancy."

"Thank you." His reactions were always so genuine, I felt like I was always just on the cusp of smiling whenever I was around Camilo.

"It was an amazing opportunity, but at first I was lost. I'd only been to the States for visits a few times, and always with my parents. It was so intimidating to come here on my own. Just me and my two suitcases. It was daunting and so lonely. I didn't know where I fit. In the DR I'd been Dominican like everyone else. Here I looked white and with my name the Latinx students weren't sure what to make of me. The white students just assumed I was some kid from the suburbs." I held up my hand then, because I wasn't trying to imply I didn't have all kinds of advantages. "Don't get me wrong. I was very privileged. I'd gone to the international school where my dad taught in the DR, so I was fully bilingual and had a scholarship to one of the most prestigious universities in the world, and through my dad was a U.S.

citizen. I was living the Dominican boy dream, but it was still a hard adjustment. College was tough."

I smiled thinking about Heni and Sanjay, and how meeting them was like finally finding my people.

"I didn't really come into my own until grad school. There I met my two best friends who ended up becoming my business partners and my U.S. family in many ways. Sanjay's family emigrated from India when he was a boy, he grew up in the Midwest where his dad was a physics professor. And Heni came here for grad school from Ethiopia."

Camilo was still intent on me, he'd made affirmative sounds as I spoke, but he hadn't said a word yet.

"The guys and I had very different backgrounds, but we hit it off from day one and became each other's support system. Well and Priya too. I don't know what I would have done without them. As for how I negotiate those sides, I'm still figuring it out. I think in many ways I chose the path of least resistance. I just let people assume what they want."

He seemed to be struggling with the last part or whatever he wanted to say in response. Then he looked up and took a sip from his water.

"Thanks for sharing that."

I knew he was holding something back, but I didn't want to push. I had a feeling whatever was floating around in his head was not going to be something I wanted to hear.

"You seem like you have something on your mind?"

I felt like Camilo could see into those parts no one else noticed. I'd always been cautious about who I let in. Depending on the people I was with or the situation, I could be Tom Hughes, successful American businessman or Thomas Caonabo Hughes Gomez, son of Esperanza and grandson of Libertad. Those two people were very different and they almost always stamped each other out.

He shook his head and smiled. "I was just thinking. My mom's really light skinned, and in many ways she could pass. But her name is Dinorah Santiago and she didn't speak a word of English when she came here. So there was always a line there for her. Even for me. I was born here, but I'm brown and it puts me in the 'other' category."

He paused then and his eyes were trained on something in the distance, like he was making sure he got whatever he was going to say right. That was something I was beginning to learn about Camilo, he didn't shy away from talking about the uncomfortable things, but he was careful with his words. It wasn't oversharing or flippant prying; Camilo asked about the hard stuff because he wasn't afraid to grapple with the answers.

When he was ready to say more he turned those gray eyes back on me. "It must be challenging to have what gives you an advantage also erase you. That the Tom people see doesn't fit with who you actually are."

I dipped my head in agreement. Camilo saw too much.

"It's something I think about all the time. I always wonder, would I have been able to have the success I had with my business if I would've looked more like my mom or if my name was Juan Perez? I wonder if I would've been able to get into the rooms I did. Or if I did, would I have been taken seriously?"

After a moment, I spoke again. Wanting to share with Camilo these things I rarely ever spoke about out loud. "When we started our company Henock and Sanjay asked that I be the face of the business during our initial talks with investors." I fiddled with a little branch on the tree in front on us, recalling the discomfort of that conversation.

"They thought it would give us a better chance of securing the funds we needed for the startup. It hurt so much to hear it, and I debated with the decision of going along with it. Not just because I knew they were right and it made the world so fucked up, but by how matter of fact they'd been about it." I shook my head remembering how awful I felt for them, for us.

"I try not to take things for granted, but I forget sometimes." I sighed feeling like I'd said too much. "I overshared."

He was looking at me with such kindness, like he really was trying to understand.

"Don't apologize. Thank you for telling me a bit more about your story and being so honest. Sounds like you *don't* take any of this lightly." The smile he gave me was the one I got when something I said had caught him off guard. "You keep surprising me, Tom."

I turned so that I could look at him when I spoke. "Is that a good thing or a bad thing?"

He lifted his eyes to the ceiling as if he was searching for an answer.

"I'm not sure yet." His eyes looked unsure when he focused them back on me. "But the more I know about you, the harder it is to remember it's not a good idea to get involved with you." After that he walked off too fast for me to respond. As I went after him, I realized I probably wasn't supposed to. But I hadn't made it as far as I had in business by missing opportunities, and this was one opening I was not going to miss.

Chapter Ten

Tom

"I can't go to the movies with you guys tonight. I'm meeting someone. This is my night to myself and I made plans." I could hear my ex sigh over the phone. We usually did well with the shared custody, but every once in a while Maxwell would get on a kick of doing something as "co-parents." I was usually all for it, but not with eight hours' notice.

"You're usually free on Wednesdays." His tone was casual, but I knew he was fishing. "What are you doing?"

This was not a conversation I was having with Maxwell.

"I'm sorry, but I have to go. I'm about to start a meeting. I'll see you on Friday when I drop off Libe. Have fun at the movies tonight." I ended the call and turned around to find Henock and Sanjay staring at me.

"How's Maxwell doing?" Sanjay asked with a hint of amusement. He knew how annoyed I got when Maxwell got pushy like this.

"He's just great."

"Sounded like he was trying to guilt you into one of

those co-dads outings." I didn't even answer, because what was the point? But it seemed Sanjay wasn't done.

"Have you told Henock about that thing you're doing, Tom?" The amusement was clear on his face.

"You're just getting away with this because Priya isn't here. I'll tell her you were shaming me as soon as she gets back from the hospital." Sanjay just laughed me off, but Heni was already on it.

"What thing? Did I miss something?"

He was still getting stuff sorted out in the kitchen, so I just ignored them both. Sanjay, Heni and I were having a business brunch to discuss a new business investment at Heni's place. He'd been home in Ethiopia for a few weeks and had missed the news about Camilo. Today would be the fourth time Camilo and I met to discuss the project, and things were going slow but well. Ever since that day in the Bronx, something had changed for me. I was more myself with Camilo than I'd ever been with anyone.

Our little weekly ritual had become one of the things I looked forward to the most, and if I was being honest with myself I was dying to touch him. The desire to kiss him during those meetings was so strong at times I had to remind myself to breathe. I couldn't keep this going forever, pretty soon I'd have to come clean and ask Camilo if he would have dinner with me.

I just hoped we were on the same page. Today we'd see each other at Red Rooster again only a little later than usual because he was doing something with clients first.

The eagerness for five to arrive, so I could see him was intense and new for me. I craved Camilo's company, and couldn't get enough of his energy when I was with him. There was nothing filtered or curated about him. He was who he was and he thought what he thought, and *he said it*. If you didn't like it, that was your problem to figure out.

"Wow. I don't think I've ever seen that expression on his face." I straightened up on Heni's couch and looked over at him and Sanjay standing by the dining table.

"What?" I glanced up to find matching bemused expressions trained in my direction. I knew they were about to get on my case for daydreaming while we were supposed to be discussing business, so I stayed silent.

Heni walked over and passed me a cup of the coffee he'd brewed with the beans he'd brought back from Ethiopia. I inhaled the aroma as he sat down next to me.

"Well it's our duty as your best friends to inquire about this young man's situation. Sanjay informed me of what's been going on and we're doing our due diligence." I shot some side-eye in Sanjay's direction. "Uh, that's really not necessary."

"We failed the last time, and you ended up married to Maxwell." He held up his hand, anticipating my protest. "Who is a nice guy, but who we knew was not right for you. So we're being proactive this time. When can we meet him so we can assess?"

They were ridiculous.

"You're not meeting Camilo any time soon, because he and I aren't dating."

Yet.

"So far we've been discussing the project I'm funding at his place of work." I got two variations of very over-the-top eye rolls, at my stuffy answer. "Also, who says either of you had any business telling me who to marry? I admit things moved fast with Maxwell, but

I have no regrets. I have Libertad and even though he and I weren't right for each other, I think we're doing a pretty good job raising her."

This last statement seemed to mollify them both. They were on this new kick of being more in touch with their straight man feelings, and it was getting old.

I pointed at Sanjay, knowing exactly how to end this line of questioning. "Sanjay, Priya would tear your balls off if she knew you're ganging up on me with Heni." This time he actually looked scared at the mention of his wife.

I laughed again and shrugged. "I really like Camilo. He's been…surprising. Being with him reminds me of how much fun the three of us had building Nuntius, the pride we felt in that, you know? When we thought our ideals would help us take the business world by storm. Even the hard parts had joy. Same with Maxwell and Libertad. There was a lot of pain, but there was joy in that struggle too. I don't know, I guess he's just made me think about things differently."

When I finished Sanjay and Heni were both staring at me slack-jawed.

"I don't think I've ever heard you get this deep about anything, even when we were running the business." Sanjay's amazed look again matched the one on Heni's face. The comment about not remembering me being deep about anything before stung, but it was a fair one. I was cautious with my feelings, of showing too much. Camilo was teaching me by example that to find some-one's love I had to be bolder.

Heni lifted his hands in defeat. "We take back what we said. You do you, take your time."

"I do hope you guys can meet him soon. Believe me,

I'd love for him to take pity on me and let me take him on an actual date. Not these made-up meetings we've been doing for the last month."

They both nodded but didn't say anything. So I didn't volunteer the fact that I was thinking of asking Camilo out to dinner tonight. I wasn't sure I could wait anymore. Thankfully it seemed like we were done talking about our feelings for the day. I clapped my hands and moved to the table.

"Now can we please switch the conversation to tech startups in Tanzania?"

Camilo

"Well don't you have a pep in your step? Headed home, Mr. Briggs?"

I rolled my eyes at Ayako's teasing tone as I put my scarf back on and grabbed my bag from the corner on the floor where I'd left it. "You know exactly where I'm going."

"Remind me again." I ignored her and her smartass tone as I walked out of the old computer lab at the shelter where we'd had our dance therapy class. Our residents had already gone up to their rooms, but Ayako and I stayed behind to put everything back in order. I'd been rushing, so I wasn't late to my meeting with Tom.

I also didn't want to risk running into Melissa and getting another one of her "I know I can trust you, Camilo" pep talks.

"Wow, what's happening in there?" Ayako asked, swirling a finger in the vicinity of my ear. I was about to answer when one of our clients walked by and waved at us, a smile on her face. "Another great class, except no one can ever keep up with Camilo."

I grinned at how happy she looked, and felt glad we could do something here where she could take a break from everything she had going on. I called after her in a teasing tone, "I don't know about that, Yesenia, you were giving me a run for my money today."

She laughed as she took the stairs to her room. "Well I try."

I turned to Ayako who was still standing there, waiting for my answer, and pointed to my office at the bottom of the stairs. "Come on, I need to get my keys and then head out. I told Tom I'd be there by five thirty p.m. and it's almost five p.m."

She rolled her eyes as she walked in and closed the door behind her. "It takes five minutes to walk to Red Rooster from here. You're rushing because Tom Hughes has you in a bad way." Her smirk was fucking annoying.

I almost deflected or did my usual "deny, deny" routine, but today felt different. From the moment I opened my eyes this morning my skin was buzzing, and I knew the reason for it had a first and last name. It's not like I didn't usually feel good, I loved my job and I had a lot to be happy for, but I could not remember the last time I'd felt this *exhilaration* with someone. Like I could show up and be exactly who I was, and it would not only be okay, it would be exactly right.

I sighed and looked at Ayako—or, as I thought of her lately, my No.1 Enabler. "I'm excited to see Tom. I'd deny it, but your pushy ass probably wouldn't let me leave until I admitted it." I grabbed my keys from my desk as I glared at her. I turned to the window and looked at myself. I didn't exactly look like I was going

to a business meeting with the billionaire who was donating money to my agency. But I did look like I could
be meeting my boyfriend for an after work drink.

Ayako's whistle jerked me out of my spell just as
it was getting good. "Wow, you're legit daydreaming
about Big Dicked Tom."

I had to laugh. "You're a piece of work, Ayako Russell."

"I don't know why you don't just go for it. You've
been meeting with this guy for like a month and every
single week you're more into him than the last."

I widened my eyes and waved my hand up and down
indicating she was raising her voice. "Shhhh. Also," I
whispered furiously, "go for what? Tom has not made
a single move in the direction of taking things further."

"Ah-ha!" She grimaced at her loudness, and continued in a lower tone. "So you *would* be up for it."

"Maybe." I cocked my head genuinely mystified. "I
don't want to disappoint Melissa or ruin things for this
project. I—"

Ayako walked up to me shaking her head. "A. He
probably hasn't come on to you because he doesn't want
to abuse his position. B. You're both adults and he has
given no indication he'll be the type of asshole who
would refuse to finish the domestic violence shelter renovation he's funding if things between you guys don't
work out. C. You fucking *glow* every time you see that
guy. I've known you for way too long not to know that
a man who has not tried your patience after a month is
a fucking keeper."

I nodded to the door. "I'm aware of the fact that Tom
Hughes is fucking perfect. It's just not that simple."

She nudged me as we walked out of the shelter and

into the lobby of the building. "Just don't talk yourself out of something that could be great."

"When have I ever denied myself something that could potentially feel good?"

People always said my eyerolls were over the top, but Ayako's were next level. "I'll tell you when, if it involves your mother or your job, your own needs automatically drop to the very bottom of the list."

I could deny it, but what would be the point?

We parted ways then and as I walked the couple of blocks to meet with Tom, I kept thinking about what Ayako said. I knew she was right. By this point I had a very good idea about the type of man Tom was.

As I was about to walk up to the restaurant my phone buzzed with a call from my mom, as if Tom needed any more women in my life rooting for him. "Hey, Mama."

"Milito, are you off work?"

"No, I'm about to go meet with the donor."

"Ooooh." Dinorah perked up immediately, the recaps from my meetings with the "Handsome Billionaire" were her new favorite telenovela. "Well I don't want to keep you then. Don't be too grumpy with him, Milito. He sounds like such a nice man."

For fuck's sake, like Tom was some kind of helpless kitten. If anyone needed help it was *me*. The struggle to keep my clothes on whenever I was around him was no fucking joke. *I* was the one in need of assistance.

"I won't be grumpy, Ma, but I have to go, I'm already late. Love you."

I slid my phone back in my bag and stood just on the corner before the Red Rooster for a moment. Maybe I needed to, for once, take romantic advice from my loved ones and see where Tom Hughes and I could go.

Chapter Eleven

Tom

The buzzing on my phone from Priya's text gave me the jolt I needed to get myself together.

Priya: Are you going to do it?

I looked around before responding, then tapped a message on my phone.

Tom: I think so.

Priya: Good luck! I feel really positive about this. *heart eyes emoji*

I had to laugh at Priya's close monitoring of my love life.

I put my phone on the table and looked up. I noticed him as soon as he walked in, and when I saw what he was wearing, every nerve in my body lit up.

Today he had his hair up in a bun and he wasn't in his usual business casual. It'd been an unseasonably warm October day, and he was wearing leather Vans

without socks and tight black yoga pants looking things.
A loose black tank top under an oversized denim shirt
and a patterned gray scarf wrapped around his neck.
He had black leather cuffs on his wrists and I could see
black nail polish on his finger nails.

He looked edgy and a little flushed, his gray eyes
bright, like he was glowing from the inside. More than
one head turned as he made his way to the table. When
he saw me, he smiled wide and waved as he came toward me. At that moment, I wanted him to be mine so
badly. I wanted to stand up and meet him halfway, so
everyone could see the most beautiful man in this place
belonged to me.

He was still smiling as he sat down and it took everything in me not to lean over and kiss his mouth.

"Hey, sorry I'm late and showed up dressed like
this." He apologized, gesturing at his shirt. "But we had
a thing at the shelter and I didn't have time to change
before coming to meet you."

"It's fine. I was running late myself. So what were
you doing? If it's okay for me to know." He waved his
hand, indicating it was okay to ask. I could tell he was
happy I wanted to know what he'd been doing. I would
never get enough of seeing Camilo's passion for his
work.

"Well it's this really cool thing we've been doing for
oh—" he put his finger under his chin and looked up
"—a year or so now. We've been partnering with this
dance group called New York Bodies, they do these choreography classes. Like each session is just one song,
and we practice a set of moves as a group and then do
the whole thing at the end. It's so much fun. Ayako and
I have been taking classes at their studio downtown for

years. So we talked to them about coming to the shelter and doing a sort of dance therapy class twice a month."

I nodded, a smile already forming as I was infected by his enthusiasm. "That sounds great."

"It is. Their whole mission is to offer classes in a shame-free body-positive environment. So any person of any shape or ability can come and do a group class. The instructors are fantastic too, and will modify the lessons so everyone can participate. I always make sure I can make it, because it's amazing to see how much our clients love the classes. They also get to pick which song we'll do each time." He laughed and shook his head. "Most weeks it's either Rihanna, Ariana or Beyoncé."

I wanted to say something about how great the classes sounded, but my mind was stuck picturing Camilo in those tights and tank top dancing until he was sweaty and flushed. My cock got so hard I had to adjust my trousers. I swallowed a few times before I could speak, while he looked at me like he was well aware of where my mind had gone.

I regrouped and tried to say something at least somewhat coherent. "It's great you offer some programs that aren't just the typical financial literacy class or job training."

He nodded again and gave me a funny look, like he'd expected me to say something different.

"Those things are very important, of course, and we have them too. But part of our mission at New Beginning is try to dismantle all these destructive constructs our clients are steeped in."

I leaned closer as he talked, once again amazed at how effortlessly Camilo commanded my full attention. "Tell me more about that."

"Like, if you're poor, or black or brown you have no right to do something just for fun. That if you spend money on yourself or on something you enjoy you're being careless and deserve to be victimized. Part of our work is to walk with our clients as they begin to see there's *nothing* wrong with them. That the issues they're dealing with aren't there because they made them happen, but because they're trying to navigate a system literally built to *not work* for them."

By now he was leaning into the table and talking with his hands.

"It's consciousness raising you know? We have to *make* spaces for them to do things they don't feel entitled to, like take an art class or dance for an hour. We work from a perspective of understanding the intersectionality of oppression. Gender, race, sexuality, ability, socioeconomic status, country of origin—" he went on excitedly, ticking things off his fingers "—each one of those things cut across our clients' lives and hold them back."

Turning, he pointed in the direction of the street. "What they hear out there is, 'If you're black or brown, poor and a single mom, you have no right to joy, you haven't earned it.' *We* say, 'Fuck that because neither has anyone else.' So we make a point of doing stuff like the New York City Bodies classes. To reinforce they have the right to moments that are just theirs, that no matter what good or bad decisions they've made or how hard things are, they still get joy."

He stopped talking then and widened his eyes like he realized he'd been going for too long. I was going to say something smart and neutral, but my heart was faster than my head.

"You're magnificent. Did you know that?"

This time his smile was shy and small, and he looked down as if he was a little embarrassed.

"I get a bit carried away sometimes. I don't mean to lecture people all the time."

This shyness was so unlike him. I went out on a limb, reached out across the table and grabbed his hand. He jumped when our hands met, but didn't pull away.

"It wasn't a lecture. I love hearing you talk about your work. Seriously, you amaze me, Camilo. I'm so grateful our paths crossed." This time it was my turn to look down. "I was talking to my friends about you today."

"Oh?" That was all he said, but his eyes were wide with expectation, and I knew this was the moment. My chance to say what we'd been tiptoeing around for weeks.

"I was telling them how much I loved our conversations, how much you challenged me." His face looked a little disappointed at my words, so before I lost my nerve I said it.

"I told them I wanted to ask you to dinner."

He quickly pulled his hand away like I'd shocked him. The hesitation on his face made all the breath leave my body. Maybe I *was* in this alone. Maybe Camilo wasn't interested in me like that. I'd forgotten what this was like, the breathless expectation of waiting to hear if the person you wanted felt the same way about you.

Finally he placed the hand he'd pulled away on top of mine and spoke. "I'd love to have dinner with you, Tom."

The fluttering in my chest was so intense I was sure Camilo could hear it across the table. I knew I was grinning hard too. I was so glad to hear him say yes though. I couldn't help it.

"Can we do it now?"

He laughed at my eagerness and shook his head like I was ridiculous. "Well I'm all sweaty and gross from the dance class and this is definitely not what I'd wear for a first date with *the* Thomas Hughes, but yeah, we can have dinner now."

I gave him an astonished look, because he had no idea the effect what he was wearing had on me when he walked in. "I think you look hot, exactly how you are. And so do a lot of the people here, if all the stares you were getting as you walked in were any indication." He laughed and rolled his eyes.

"Okay, if it works for you, who am I to argue? But what do we even talk about? I feel like we've had all the first date conversation already?"

"Tell me about the dance classes. I have to say the idea of you in those tights, dancing to Beyoncé got me overheated very quickly." The smile he gave me at that was dirty enough to make me blush. This was the Camilo from the gala. The sexy and confident man who grabbed me by the hand and gave me the best blow job of my life.

He tipped his head to the side and put his finger under his chin as though he was thinking about an answer. "Well let's see, today we did 'Formation' which is kind of fierce but also sexy. There was a lot of hip gyration and hair flipping. We've done it a few times before. The clients love it."

"When you say hip gyrations—"

That husky laugh was going to be the end of me. Under the table Camilo moved his legs so they were brushing against mine, and leaned in to me, "Well it's hard to explain it. It's more the kind of thing you have to see. I'd have to *show* you."

I gulped and ran my hands on my thighs, trying to calm myself down. I needed to get out of here before I did something crazy in this restaurant full of people.

"So I was thinking maybe we could do a drink at my place before dinner." Then closed my mouth and thought about what I'd just said. Why would we leave a restaurant to go and eat somewhere else? I'd been at meetings discussing billion dollar deals and felt less out of sorts than I was right now.

I shook my head as Camilo looked at me from under long thick eyelashes. "That's sort of stupid isn't it? We're already at a restaurant. We could just get dinner here."

I laughed a little hysterically and all I could think of was finally getting to touch him after weeks of holding back. But before I opened my mouth again Camilo took control of the situation. He grabbed my hand and ran his thumb over it, as if trying to put me at ease, then he squared his shoulders and looked at me full of certainty.

"But if by drinks you mean go back to your place for sex, then yes. We can absolutely go to your house for a pre-dinner drink."

It felt like someone zapped my balls with a charge of electricity and I immediately stood up. I left way more money on the table than necessary to pay for the water we'd gotten, and for the second time since we'd met I let Camilo pull me by the hand and lead me away.

Chapter Twelve

Camilo

I was doing this.

I was walking to Tom Hughes's house with the intention of getting my hands, mouth and everything else I could come up with on him as soon as we walked through the door.

I'd tried my best, I really had, but this man was irresistible. The way he looked at me, like I was a rare and precious thing he'd just discovered...it undid me. And the way his face lit up as I told him about our clients and the dancing, as if I was telling him something incredible, it was the last straw.

We were adults and there was no rule saying I couldn't date (fuck) a donor. I'd actually looked at the agency policy manual the day Melissa gave me that boundaries lecture, because I knew if he pursued me, it was only a matter of time before I gave in.

As we walked up Lenox Avenue Tom looked a little shy, but full of anticipation. He glanced down at me with a question in his eyes, then extended his hand as if asking to hold mine. We were in Harlem and the streets were busy at 6:00 p.m. on a Friday. I usually would not go for any display of affection just as a precaution. But with Tom, in this moment, I felt bold. So I hooked my index finger around his and smiled at him.

"So where are we going? You said your house was close, right?"

He nodded and pointed further up. "Yes, I live in a brownstone on the next block. I've only been in it a couple of years. My friends Sanjay and Priya, who you met at the party, bought the one right next door. It's nice to have them close by. We love the neighborhood."

I nodded distractedly feeling a little intimidated. Living in the area myself, I was very aware of the prices that brownstones went for these days.

What was I doing with a guy living in a house that cost millions of dollars? I could barely afford my little studio in Hamilton Heights. As we got to 126th street and turned left, Tom squeezed my hand, beaming. I tried to push aside my nervousness and come back to the moment, to Tom. Then I remembered what my friends told me. I didn't need to make a judgment based on things I perceived as problematic. I could rely on what Tom had *shown* me so far.

Everything Tom had done since I'd met him was more than enough evidence he was the kind of man I wanted to get to know better.

To be with.

"Why did you buy a place here in Harlem? I mean it's not the typical spot for millionaires to move to."

He nodded and his face got serious. "Harlem was the first place I lived in when I came to the States. I arrived like three months before I started my first year at Columbia, and I stayed with an old friend of my mom's on 122nd and Park. She's Dominican, but she's been here

since the sixties. That whole summer she would take
me on walks around Harlem and talk to me about the
history. She told me about the Caribbean diaspora who
settled here over the last hundred years. I got hungry
to learn more. I read about queer authors like Langston
Hughes and James Baldwin who came up here. I learned
about Latinx civil rights movements like the Young
Lords which all happened in these streets. Learning
about those who'd come through this same place made
me feel connected to New York City, like I wasn't so
far from home."

Dammit. Of course, he couldn't just be a douchebag
buying up property mindlessly.

"So when I decided to buy a place in the city, I got
one here. I'm also invested in trying to keep this community from being erased by gentrification. I try to
be mindful of the footprint I'm leaving, of course, but
also help families who've been here for generations
keep their homes. My friend Henock and I have been
working with a few advocacy groups that serve families who're being pushed out of their homes by devel-
opers. So far we've just helped with funding agencies
that do housing advocacy in the community, but we'd
like to do more if we can."

I looked up at him and tugged at the finger I was
holding. "You know I'm already planning to have sex
with you right? You don't need to try and convince me
with all this 'good guy' stuff."

He barked out a laugh and bumped me with his hip,
which was almost up to my shoulder.

"Most people wouldn't find my views on gentrification sexually arousing. I think that just works on you,

Camilo. Not that I'm complaining." He slowed down then and pointed at the stoop in front of us.

"That's me."

We walked up the steps and he quickly opened the door for us. I stepped inside cautiously, not sure what I'd find. I wasn't exactly going to billionaires' houses for afternoon sex on the regular.

The little bit of the house I could see from the foyer looked expensive and elegant though. But before I could freak out, Tom put both his hands on my face and bent down so our foreheads were touching.

"I've been dying to kiss you for weeks."

His voice was gravelly and his eyes were so intent on me, like he could barely contain how much he wanted me.

My own desire crashed into me like a swell. I couldn't deny this any more than I could stop breathing. All reservation flew out of my mind and I pushed up to kiss him. We both let out long exhales when our mouths finally touched. The inevitability of the moment tightened around me; everything felt right. This was always going to happen.

It was just a matter of time.

Tom groaned and ran his tongue across the seam of my mouth. I opened for him and as my tongue touched his I felt a shiver run all the way through my body. I tried to get closer, with my arms around his neck, pressing forward. He brought his hands down to my ass and pulled me up, and I wrapped my legs around his waist as he began to walk us up the steps.

"Are you okay with taking this to my bedroom?" The uncertainty in his voice just got me more turned on.

"Yes," I answered wildly and he laughed at my eagerness. As he got to the second floor I saw what looked like a dining room/kitchen combo, but he kept going to a third floor. When we got there, he walked us into the first room off the hallway. As he lowered me to the floor our eyes locked and for the first time ever, I felt like a man was looking at me as if I was everything he wanted.

"I can't describe what it's doing to me to have you in my bedroom right now." He was panting a little bit. I assumed it was from the exertion of carrying me up the stairs, but his eyes were smoldering. He bent down to kiss me again, and I opened up for him, already wanting to get to the fucking part. I pulled at his sweater as he ran his teeth down my neck, making me shudder.

"You're wearing too many clothes," I said, tugging on them as he laughed. He pulled back from our kiss to pull his sweater off. Once his chest was bare, I stepped back to take a good look at him. A curse escaped my mouth when I saw him in all his shirtless glory. His chest was strong and sculpted with a salt-and-pepper pelt covering his pecs. He had a thin trail of hair that went down the center of his flat stomach. When he finally bent down to peel his pants off I got a glimpse at that fucking glorious cock I'd been fantasizing about for weeks, barely restrained by his briefs. All I wanted was to get down on my knees and worship him with my mouth.

"Dajame verte, Camilo," he said, in a throaty whisper. He wanted to see me too. I started taking pieces of clothes off as he watched, palming his crotch.

When I took my tank off he sucked in his teeth and came forward to run his fingers over the tattoo on my chest. It was a piece I'd gotten when I turned twenty-one. Patrice, Nesto and Juanpa all had the same one. It was a forearm stretching up from my ribs, ending in a hand holding a beating heart right over where the real one was. The heart was covered with the American, Jamaican and Cuban flags, all blending together. One couldn't tell where one ended and the other ones began.

Just like me, like all four of us.

"That's beautiful," he said, his voice full of awe.

I ran my fingers over it, feeling the familiar roughness right over my heart. I looked down at it and then at him. "Thanks, I got it a long time ago. The guys, my best friends, each have one. But theirs have their own flags."

I grabbed the hand he'd been using to trace his fingers over the tattoo and brought it to my mouth, then sucked on them as his eyes scorched me.

He cupped the back of my neck, pulling me close. "¿Que quieres, Camilo?"

What *did* I want?

Him. Inside me, over me. Tom, everywhere.

I met his gaze and told him. "I want to ride you." I ran my hands up his chest and then brought one down to that dick I was so thirsty for. He sucked his teeth again, shivering as my hand tightened around him, then bent down to nip at my mouth.

I looked up at him and said all the things I wanted.

"I want to look at your face while I fuck myself on this cock. I haven't been able to stop thinking about it since that first night." I tried to go down on my knees, but before I could he went down on his.

I swayed at the image he made.

He was so big, so powerful and he was down on his knees, for me. It was heady and intoxicating as hell.

I'd known once I went down this road with Tom things would complicate. He was *everything* I'd ever thought I wanted, and *every single thing* I could never see myself with. He threw all my assumptions out the window. I wanted him so much, and the way he was looking at me right now. I wanted to believe in that desire. That it was really all for me.

He pulled down my tights and when he saw there was nothing underneath he let out a long exhale. He pressed his face to my crotch as he pulled the clingy material further down and off. I was so hot for him and the touch of his tongue, his warm breath on me was making my head pound.

"Tom, babe. Let's go to the bed." He didn't answer, just grabbed my ass, pushing me closer and licked again, then took the head of my cock into his mouth.

I moaned at the sensation, it felt so good. "Oh god. I'm gonna come, and I really don't want to until you're inside. Please, baby."

"Te quiero comer, Camilo."

I wanted to be devoured. I nodded furiously at his words and tried to pull him up. He still had his briefs on, and I made quick work of them as soon as he stood up. We fell on his huge bed with our hands and mouths all over each other. I ran my fingers over his strong shoulders and back, feeling so hungry for his skin. After a moment he moved us around so I was on my stomach and he started kissing down my spine. Nipping and licking as he went.

The only sounds in the room were of our ragged breaths, as his tongue and lips brushed over my skin.

I felt every touch from Tom so intensely. The world had fallen away in the last few minutes and everything I needed was this bed and this man.

After a moment he paused and traced a finger over

the spot where I had my other tattoo. "'Oleo de Mujer Con Sombrero,'" he breathed out. It was the title of a song, from which I'd had a line tattooed.

I just nodded still resting on my arms. "My mom has a complicated relationship with the music of the Cuban trovadores, but that's one of her favorite songs."

The tattoo went up my left side, from my waist up to my armpit.

Tom read the line in Spanish in a husky voice, and when he was done he leaned, so his lips brushed my ears when he spoke. "You're amazing."

"I'm not sure how to feel about you making me get turned on by my mother's favorite song," I said, with a laugh turning my face to nip on his lower lip, before he went back to exploring my backside.

My mom and I had always loved the song and that line in particular, so I'd gotten it for her. Tom was the first man I'd been in bed with who'd known what it meant.

In that moment I knew there would be no simple walking away from Tom Hughes.

He leaned down again and kissed my cheek before he spoke. "My mom loved it too. She played it all the time when I was growing up. I haven't heard that song in so long. Everything I discover about you makes me want to worship at your feet."

I turned my head to look up at him, my eyes narrowed. "That's just the Dominican going to your head."

He shook his head, a grin forming on his lips, but his eyes were very serious. "It's you. This is all you." His skin was flushed and he looked ravenous. I felt like prey lying there as he ran his hands over me.

"Stop saying stuff like that, Tom."

"Why? It's true." He bent down to kiss me again.

I opened for him, as our tongues mingled together he grabbed me tight, his fingers digging into me, like he was afraid I'd vanish if he let go. As the kiss deepened I felt his hard cock bumping into my back and ass.

Without speaking he pulled back and effortlessly flipped me around so he was on his back and I was straddling his thighs.

"I'm not sure about this manhandling." I sounded breathless and probably would've been more convincing if I hadn't been bending down to kiss his neck and shoulders as I delivered my grievance.

"Sorry. I won't do it again." He was smug as fuck, and it was clear he knew exactly how much it turned me on.

"Well I wouldn't say I hate it," I said running my hands over his massive chest. "It's just a new thing for me."

"How about if I let you know when the manhandling is about to happen." That lopsided smile and little bit of gray around his temples was going to be the end of me.

I bent down for another kiss. "Sounds good."

He let me admire and touch as much as I wanted, and I *wanted*. He was so strong. His legs thick and hard. Such a contrast from my own lean build. I ran my hands over his chest again and leaned in to bite his nipple.

"From the moment I saw you I wanted to go to bed with you," I whispered as I slid down his body, licking and tasting, until I had my mouth against his cock. I ran the tip of my tongue up the vein.

Tom answered with a sigh as I took him in my mouth. "The feeling was mutual."

I took him deep and swallowed around him, making him shudder. "Baby, I'm going to come if you keep doing that." He ran his finger over my forehead as I looked up, my mouth full of cock.

"I want to be inside you." Tom no longer talked, he growled.

I wanted him inside too. It had been a while since I'd been with anyone, certainly not since the night at the party, and I couldn't wait any longer.

I pulled off and looked around the room. "Where are the lube and condoms?"

In response, he stretched his arm towards the table by the bed and felt around the drawer until he pulled out a condom and a tube of lube and handed them to me.

I popped open the tube and got a little bit on my fingers. I used one hand to lean on his chest and with the other I reached to get myself ready, but Tom quickly pulled my hand away and grabbed my hips. In a voice that sounded like gravel, he gasped, "Let me, please."

I nodded then turned around and pushed my ass back onto his chest. The lyrics to a song came into my head as I did, making me laugh.

He ran slick fingers over my hole; the lube felt silky against my skin. I sighed, holding myself up with my elbows.

"What's so funny?" Tom asked with humor in his voice.

"Not a thing. You've got me so hot and bothered right now, Tom Hughes, I've got Beyoncé in my head for background music."

He chuckled and began opening me up slowly. Every so often he'd run a hand up my back, his fingertips brushing along softly. He worked his fingers inside me so good. He nudged and pushed in, all the while telling me how much he wanted to be inside already. How good I'd feel around him.

"The way your spine dips right here," he said while grabbing on to the top of my ass. "So fucking beautiful. Siento que me quemo por ti, Camilo."

I was burning for him too. I was so turned on. I was grinding into him, needing more friction. I took a deep breath and pushed up, turning my head to look at him.

"Now, Tom."

He nodded and I turned around, quickly sliding the condom onto his cock. I pushed up on my knees as he grabbed his dick and I slid down on to it agonizingly slow. I felt that wide head pushing, opening me up.

It burned, but fuck, it was *so good*.

I wanted to shove myself down, and get on with it, but I made myself take my time. With one hand Tom kept me steady as I rocked my hips until he was all the way in.

I planted both hands on his chest as I breathed out. I could feel him vibrating with the need to push up, but he held himself back until I was ready. I was so full of him, I could feel him in my throat.

"Tom." I sounded so needy and Tom did not make me wait. He grabbed me with both hands, tipped me forward and moved those hips exactly right.

"Oh god." He was hitting me right in the place that drove me crazy. My cock was leaking as he pushed up and I rocked down, meeting him with every thrust. The slapping of our skin and our harsh breaths echoed around us. I ran my hands down his chest, and then grabbed my dick.

Tom shook his head. "Todavia, hold on, baby. Just a little bit longer." He was gritting his teeth hard as he thrust into me. After a moment he sat up and turned us around so I was on my back. He hovered on top, leaning on one hand, as he used the other to guide himself inside again. He kissed me hard and I gasped into his mouth as he slid back in.

"Agarrate, Camilo." I nodded and grabbed my cock as he pounded into me, getting me *right fucking there*. Pretty soon I could feel the orgasm coming. That tingling sensation building at my groin and spreading up my spine.

"I'm so close." I moaned.

"Ungh." I heard Tom grunt as I came so hard my head felt fuzzy. After a few more thrusts he slumped on top of me. He was careful not to land too hard and squeezed me tight as we both tried to get our breathing back to normal.

"Is there anything you don't do perfectly?" I tried for feigned annoyance but a trace of genuine amazement was clear in my voice.

He chuckled and kissed me again. "We can do it again later, so you can compare." I pinched him and he yelped while I cracked up. After another kiss he got up and went to the bathroom. I stayed in his humongous and comfortable bed with my eyes closed, enjoying the moment, feeling utterly sated.

He came back with a washcloth and cleaned us both up. After he got back in the bed and got us both under the covers, tangled together. I couldn't remember feeling this at ease with anyone.

After our breathing finally slowed down, Tom spoke into our comfortable silence. "I'd like to see you again, Camilo. Maybe even actually take you out on a date." My heart thumped against my chest at his words.

I wanted that so much.

But still, the idea of having this man in my life was overwhelming. I looked around his room. The beautiful dark furniture, the paintings on the walls. Everything looked expensive and elegant. It was such a different world than the one I lived in.

I leaned over and kissed him, not ready to answer. But as soon as our mouths touched our connection gave me certainty. I wasn't sure if I could reconcile Tom's world with mine, but I wanted to try.

When we pulled apart, I nodded. "I'd like that." His smile was so big, like I'd given him the greatest gift.

"Good." Right then his stomach grumbled and we both laughed as he sat up. "I should go see what I can do about getting some food. Would you stay and eat with me?"

I was about to give him an enthusiastic nod, when I heard feet running up the stairs. Before I could process what that meant, or ask Tom who it was, a little girl's voice called from the hallway.

"Daddy! We're home!" I sat up, clutching the sheets to my chest like that would help any, and Tom bolted up, hurrying to close the bedroom door.

"I'll be right out, Libe, honey," he called out, then turned to me. His face looked startled and confused, as he put on his pants. I was already up looking for my clothes.

"Who's that?" There was no hiding the panic in my voice and the pause before Tom answered felt like it lasted for hours. When he finally spoke, his voice was crystal clear though.

"That's my daughter, Libertad."

Chapter Thirteen

Tom

"Your daughter? You never mentioned a kid!" Camilo's face went from surprise to panic in a surprisingly short time when I said the word *daughter*.

I tried to speak calmly as I got dressed, because I knew I was on very thin ice right now. I didn't want him to think I'd intentionally not told him about Libe. I'd thought about it, of course, but decided to wait on it until things were on more solid ground. For when he finally agreed to go out on an actual date with me. Except when he did, I'd immediately brought him to my house and fucked him, instead of having a conversation.

I looked up and saw him struggling into his tights and cursed Maxwell for totally destroying my evening.

"She's four and I co-parent her with my ex-husband." His eyes, which were already pretty big, got huge at the mention of an ex-husband.

I put my hands up in an attempt to de-escalate the situation, knowing I had about thirty seconds before Libe got fed up of waiting and barged into the room.

"We got divorced when Libe was just a baby. We've been sharing custody since. She's with me most of the time, but he has her on Wednesday nights and every other weekend." I sighed, trying to control my annoyance at the situation. "This was supposed to be my night to myself."

Camilo looked frazzled and very close to running out of the house. I tried to get closer, to touch him. But in the same moment, he bent down to grab his tank top, which had ended up tossed over the back of a chair.

"I didn't intentionally not tell you," I pleaded, hoping he could see I was being sincere. "Telling someone I'm seeing about Libe is a big deal for me, and I was hoping we'd get to a place where it made sense to talk to you about her."

He stood on the other end of the room, looking like he regretted every decision he'd made in the last hour.

"Please don't think I was keeping things from you, Camilo. I wasn't." He seemed to soften at this, and let me grab his hand. I pulled him closer for a kiss, but just as our mouths met, Libe yelled from the hallway again.

"Daddy, what are you *doing* in there? Were you sleeping? It's not even *my* bedtime yet!"

At least Camilo found her funny. He shook his head, laughing, and pulled away.

"You should go to her. I'm just going to finish getting dressed."

I shook my head, not happy with that idea at all, and spoke in a much whinier tone than I intended. "But I don't want you to get dressed. I want you to get back in my bed. Naked."

He just pointed at the door and whispered, "Go."

I pulled on a t-shirt and stepped out into the hallway. Libe had clearly dressed herself before the movies. She was wearing her "The Future is Female" t-shirt under a My Little Pony hoodie and leggings with unicorns on them. Her curls were all over the place too. Seeing her melted away all my annoyance. She had her little hands on her hips, and looked like she was about to give me a piece of her mind for keeping her waiting.

"Hey, muchachita, what are you doing here?"

I knelt down in front of her after giving Maxwell a withering look. I knew he'd come over to see what I was up to. I hadn't dated anyone seriously since the divorce, so managing a relationship hadn't come up so far. I was not going to lose Camilo this early just because Maxwell couldn't resist snooping around my life. "I thought you guys were going to the movies?" My tone was not exactly friendly and Maxwell knew me well enough to know this pop-in was not going to go over well.

Libertad on the other hand dished out one of her meme worthy eye rolls.

"We did! We came to the one close to this home. Papa said I could come and get my book if I wanted after." Of course, it wasn't like she didn't have a bookshelf with a hundred books at Maxwell's place. This was just a bullshit excuse to come and see what I was doing.

I sent another glare in his direction. "That's a lot of running around on a school night."

He lifted a shoulder like he had no clue why I was so annoyed. "We were close. I parked in the garage across the street. We'll head out soon. Libe, honey, go get your book."

She nodded and started heading to her room which was next to mine. But at the last minute she turned and went into my room. I thought of stopping her, but figured it might as well happen now. As I walked over I heard her introducing herself to Camilo.

"Hi, I'm Libertad."

As I stepped into the room I saw Camilo kneeling in front of her with a big smile on his face. He extended his hand to shake her little one.

"Hi, Libertad. I'm Camilo. It's nice to meet you. I love your outfit."

She preened and twirled around to give him the full effect. Camilo chuckled and looked at me. I just lifted a shoulder. She was something, I agreed.

"I dressed myself."

He nodded solemnly. "You did a great job."

Libe looked like she was about to sit down for a "getting to know you" session with Camilo, but I scooped her up before my night really did go up in flames.

"Hey, señorita, *you* were here for a book and then going home to Papa's house. Say goodbye to Camilo and we'll go get it, so you can go to bed. It's a school night."

She didn't look happy, but she waved goodbye to Camilo. Before I walked out, I mouthed, "I'll be right back." He didn't look too sure about my request, so I tried to hurry and get Libe sorted out.

By the time Libe and I got her book and went downstairs Maxwell was by the door and it looked like Camilo was down there too, putting on his shoes and looking ready to leave.

"Camilo, this is my ex-husband, Maxwell." I put extra emphasis on the *ex* part. Maxwell just stood there looking at me placidly like he had no clue why I was so annoyed.

After it seemed like Camilo was too spooked to react, Maxwell extended his hand to him and smiled. "Nice to meet you."

Camilo thrust his own hand out and gave him a very short handshake, barely making eye contact.

"Same." He looked up, where Libe was perched on my hip and smiled. "It was nice to meet you, Libe." Then he turned and gave me a look I couldn't read. "Thanks for everything, Tom."

"I'll call you." I didn't even try to hide the urgency in my voice.

He nodded, but his blank expression gave no indication on whether the call would be welcome.

"Sure." With that he muttered a goodbye in Maxwell's direction and walked out.

I turned to Maxwell, trying my best not to yell in front of Libe. He at least had the decency to look remorseful.

"I'm sorry! I just thought I'd catch you before you left for whatever you were doing. I didn't know you'd have company. That's never happened before." He threw his hands up like it was a real shock to find out I had a life. "I never thought I'd actually find you here…entertaining."

He let out an awkward laugh. "I didn't think you knew people could do that sort of thing at six p.m. on a Wednesday." Okay he went for a low blow, but I guess I deserved it. He looked a little hurt about it, which was insane, because things between Maxwell and I were more than over and done with. When I didn't answer he deflated and angled his head toward the door. "Next time I'll call if we have to come over."

"Thank you," I said tersely, then looked at Libe who was sucking her thumb as we talked. "And you better get to bed, young lady."

"Okay, Daddy." She gave me a kiss and went to Maxwell's waiting arms. Soon after they walked out of the house and across the street to the parking garage. As soon as I saw them off, I ran up the stairs to get my phone.

I was going to call Camilo, grovel and hopefully repair any damage done in the last twenty minutes.

Camilo

"Help me!" I yelled into my phone as I walked into my apartment. I'd been so out of sorts when I left Tom's house I'd actually sprung for a Lyft instead of taking the subway. The encounter with the adorable kid and the tall, blond ex who looked like a runway model had left me too unsettled to deal with the New York City subway system.

I heard some shuffling on the phone and after a few seconds Patrice finally spoke. "Okay, but can you tell me what you need help with?"

He sounded short of breath, and I immediately got annoyed. "Are you at Easton's? Do you even go to work, or is fucking with that guy your full-time job now?"

I heard the kind of exhale that meant Patrice was already on his last nerve with me. *Too fucking bad*, this was an emergency.

"Camilo, I don't have to tell you what I was doing, but for your information I was at the gym. I've been coming with Ted, Carmen's husband."

"Oh." I felt bad for being bitchy and judgmental. Carmen was Jude's best friend and I knew they hung out all the time now. A pang of nostalgia hit me. We would never be together like that again. Now Patrice and Nesto were upstate and it was just Juanpa and me here. Our lives were changing so fast, and now I had to grapple with the fact that Tom came with quite the package.

Fuck.

"What's going on, Camilo?"

I hesitated for a second on how much to say, but I needed help figuring this out, and Patrice was the only one who would tell me exactly what I had to hear. No matter how much I didn't want to.

"Well I fucked Tom and it was even more amazing than I could've ever imagined." I sighed. "Then five minutes after we were done, his secret baby and husband showed up at his house!" I slumped on my little love seat, trying not to be too dramatic, but I was having a very hard time regulating my emotions.

Usually I was not the guy calling for advice. I was the one who *gave* advice. Tom had me all over the place. The worst part was I knew I would be back for more. Fucking him had done nothing to slake my thirst for him, it was worse now.

Way worse.

Patrice's voice was so steady when he answered, it was like he'd barely registered my revelation of a secret husband and baby. "Please explain in detail what you mean. Is he actually married, Camilo?"

"No." I grumbled. "He's divorced. And it's not actually a baby, she's like four. He said he and his ex got divorced when she was still a baby, and now they share custody. The guy didn't seem jealous or anything, but he did look like he'd dropped by looking for something." I knew I sounded childish, but I couldn't help it. "Things were going so well too. Fuck, I knew this would happen. As soon as I let myself go for it, everything gets complicated. So much for perfect Tom Hughes."

I could tell Patrice was trying hard not to sound exasperated.

"Camilo, you know better than anyone life is never that simple, especially when it comes to relationships. I also know you wouldn't want someone perfect, or even near perfect. You'd want someone kind and with his head on straight. Sounds to me like this was just bad timing, and that considering the situation it went pretty well. Did Tom ask you to leave?"

I pursed my lips at his question, because now we were getting at the fact that I'd acted like a hot mess. "No, he asked me to stay, but I felt weird, so I just went home while Libertad and the ex were still there. He named his kid *Freedom* in Spanish, Patrice. It's like the universe hates me."

Patrice chuckled at my whining. "It sounds like the universe is telling you *something*. Please, Milo, don't let your doubts cheat you of someone that could be great. Give it a chance. You have a lot of information showing you he's a good guy. Maybe there's more to him than you originally thought, but so what? We all have our shit." He paused then, and when he spoke again he sounded so serious. "We're all struggling to figure out how to negotiate what we thought were our absolutes with the people life puts in our paths. None of this shit is easy. We at least learned *that* lesson well, Milo."

I sighed and felt such yearning to have him here. I also wondered if he was talking about himself and Easton. I knew merging those two worlds wouldn't be easy.

"Are things okay with you and Easton? I'm sorry I haven't asked, you've just been so secretive about it."

"I'm not ready to talk about it yet." Patrice's voice

sounded tired but firm, and I knew pushing would get me nowhere.

"Alright, but you know—"

"*I know*, Milo, but we were talking about you. So, what are you going to do? Are you going to let a little girl and some ex scare you away?"

I didn't *want* to be scared away.

Just as I was about to say so, I heard my phone ping with another call. I pulled it from my ear to look at the screen and saw it was Tom. I let the warmth I felt in my chest make the decision about taking the call for me. Sure, feelings in my body parts had steered me wrong in relationships countless times, but I could still *smell* him on me. I wasn't strong enough to close that door yet.

"P, it's him on the other line."

"Okay don't jump down his throat. Let him *talk*."

"Fine! Thanks, friend. I love you."

"Love you too."

I ended the call and picked up the one from Tom. As I said hello, I couldn't ignore my racing heart or how much I hoped this call put us back where we'd been an hour ago.

Chapter Fourteen

Tom

"Hi." There was so much uncertainty in that one word. Camilo's voice sounded small, so different from the man I'd had in my bed. The one who'd walked into the restaurant this afternoon.

"Camilo. I'm so sorry about earlier. Please believe me, I wasn't trying to hide anything about Libertad. It's just I'm cautious, you know? Even if you hadn't agreed to go out with me, I would have told you about her. But it hadn't come up and well, I'm sorry."

He was quiet for a moment and I held my breath hoping his next words weren't to tell me to go to hell. "I get it. I was just surprised. Things were going so great, and it just all sort of went up in flames."

I groaned feeling like a total heel.

"That won't happen again. I have Libe a lot, but I will talk to Maxwell about respecting my space." Camilo's silence was not exactly reassuring, but I had called ready to grovel, and I would continue to do so as long as he let me. "Listen, I don't want to be a pushy asshole, and I'm completely fine with you being done for the night. But before we were interrupted I was hoping to order something to eat and spend more time with you. I'd still like to do that."

Camilo started to say something, hesitated, then tried again.

"I'm already home, Tom."

My usual tactic when I encountered resistance was to retreat and try again later when the odds were more in my favor, but when it came to Camilo Briggs I had zero chill. The only thing I wanted right now was to see him, touch him, get back the connection we'd had this afternoon.

"I can come to you. I'll pick something up on the way over there. If you're up for it, of course."

More silence.

I was starting to think it really might be best to give up before I made him uncomfortable, when I heard him speak in a very low voice.

"My place is *really* small. Like your bedroom might be bigger than my whole apartment."

Shit.

I hadn't even thought of that. God my head was so far up my ass sometimes.

"That's fine." I went out on a limb and tried to get us back to flirting. "I'm hoping to get all up in your grill while I'm there."

He chuckled at that. "Your street is pretty corny, but I appreciate the effort." He let out a long breath and when he spoke again he sounded a little more at ease. "I'm trying to not second-guess myself anymore tonight. Dinner would be nice. I'll text you my address."

The relief I felt was almost debilitating.

"Okay, I'm going to head out right now."

"Just buzz when you get here and I'll let you in." As

soon as we hung up I got my ass in gear. I ran down-stairs and walked over to the Ethiopian place down the street to pick up some food. We ate there all the time, so I could get them to rush my order. Camilo only lived like twenty blocks from me, so I would be able to get there fast. I had the food and was in a Lyft within twenty minutes.

As the driver navigated the busy streets of Harlem, I tried to think about what I was feeling. I couldn't re-member this much urgency to be with someone, to make things right. With Maxwell, I had just let the current pull me. Let him decide for us what the next step was. When he said it made sense to get married I went with it, same with the surrogacy. So much of my personal life felt like that.

In business, I wasn't afraid to work hard or be com-petitive. But with my personal life I never felt the urge to get in there, to push.

Not with Camilo. With him, I wanted everything, *right now.*

Once again I thought of my mother's words. That once I found the right person, I would know what to do. I really hoped she was right.

I stepped out of the Lyft and rang the bell for Ca-milo's apartment. It was a red brick building with a bo-dega next door. People on the sidewalk were speaking in Spanish, bodies moving in every direction.

Such a New York City corner.

He let me in without asking who it was, and I walked up to his second floor apartment. I got up to the land-ing, and saw him standing in the doorway. His hair was in a thick braid and he looked like he'd taken a shower. He was wearing an oversized Fordham sweatshirt and seemingly nothing else. My dick throbbed from the sight and I wanted to drop the food on the floor and just go right back to where we'd been when our night got derailed. Instead I tried to keep my shit together before I scared him off.

"I hope you like Ethiopian," I said, holding up the bag. "I should have texted to ask."

He shook his head and pushed up for a kiss when I bent down for one. I couldn't help running my hand over his ass, which was clad in very small briefs.

"How am I supposed to keep it together when you're waiting for me like this?"

His laugh was hoarse and just on this side of filthy, there was just enough brattiness in there that I had to grit my teeth so I didn't maul him.

"Thank you for bringing dinner. I love Ethiopian." I nuzzled his neck as he pulled me into the apartment and closed the door. He smelled like coconut and limes.

"Not fair, you had time to shower. I smell like come, sweat and the patchouli from the Lyft I took up here." He grinned as he took the bag from me and started pulling containers onto his small counter.

"You smell fine, but you're welcome to take a shower if you can squeeze into my tiny bathroom. I don't think my clothes would fit you, but you'd at least wash the sweat off."

I looked around his place. It *was* small, like a big-gish studio. Right by the door was a little kitchen area with a tall table and two chairs. He had a small love seat against one wall, next to a bookshelf packed with books. His bed was tucked behind a sliding door. It was open right now so I could see into his private space.

His entire place was an explosion of colors.

There were prints on the walls, the couch was a bright green with red and blue cushions on it. His bed had all kinds of patterns and colors. This was exactly what I'd expected Camilo's apartment to be like— vibrant, just like him.

I turned around and saw he was leaning against the counter quietly, letting me explore.

"I told you it was small."

I walked up to him and put my hands around his waist. "You have no idea how happy I am to be here right now. I thought our evening was doomed." I kissed his cheek and he tightened his arms around me. "Thanks for letting me come over."

He shrugged, but his eyes shone. "Thanks for calling."

"I'll always call, Camilo." He nodded, and even though he didn't respond, it felt comfortable, like we were back in sync. After another minute, I decided to go for that shower after all.

"If you were serious I'll take a shower while you warm up the food. I'll be quick." He nodded and pointed to a door next to the bathroom.

"There are towels on the shelf in there."

I grabbed one and stepped into his bathroom. Thinking once again that I couldn't remember the last time I'd wanted anyone this much.

Camilo

Tom was *everywhere*.

His body, his smell, all of him had taken over my apartment. I was feeling so many things just from having him in my space. I couldn't believe how at ease he was. I'd been nervous he'd walk in and look down on my tiny apartment. But of course he hadn't.

I took him in as he walked out of the bathroom in nothing but his jeans. His biceps bulged as he dried his hair off with my towel, and I had to dig my nails into my hands to keep from jumping him.

He must have noticed that my breathing got a little faster looking at all those muscles and tanned skin, because the fucker winked at me.

Smug bastard.

The effect his naked chest and sexy wet hair were having on me was significant. I waved my hand at my little table to indicate we could eat, to see if I could maybe distract myself with food.

He groaned when he saw everything laid out and walked over. "I'm starving. Thanks for letting me shower, I needed that," he said as he yanked his t-shirt back on, mercifully shielding me from his lust inducing torso.

"No problem, do you want a beer?"

"Sure," he answered while pulling out a chair.

I grabbed a couple of bottles from the fridge and sat across from him. When I put the bottles on the table he beamed at me after looking at the brand.

"You drink Presidente?" he asked delighted. The imported Dominican beer was pretty easy to find in Harlem these days, but I'd only bought it because when I'd seen it at the bodega it had reminded me of Tom. I was corny as hell these days.

I lifted a shoulder trying to act like it was no big deal, but Tom's presence was like truth serum. "When I saw them I thought of you, and I got them because I'm now

a walking cliché." He laughed at my words, like I was
being adorable, and leaned in to kiss me.

When he pulled back he had the confident grin he
sported every once in a while, like he knew I was a
goner for him. "You were thinking about me."

"I can't *stop* thinking about you, that's my problem,
Tom," I said, unable to mask my exasperation.

I pointed at the food. "It's going to get cold," I said
ready to be done with this sudden exploration of my
thirstiness.

I'd arranged the stuff he'd brought on a big platter.
With the *injera*, the sour crepe-looking bread used to
scoop up the sauces and stews in Ethiopian meals, on
a plate to the side so we could both eat off the platter.

Before digging in he grinned at me again, like he
knew what I was doing, but was letting me get away
with it. "This looks great."

I lifted a shoulder. "Hey, you brought the food, I just
arranged it."

The corner of his eyes crinkled. He seemed to find
my grumpiness endlessly delightful.

"It's great to be here with you, Camilo."

I felt faint sometimes from the things he said to me.
In my past relationships most of the feedback I got was
that I needed to tone it down. I was too salty, too intense…too much. With Tom, me being me was not only
okay, it was like he couldn't get enough of it.

"Stop, you already got in my pants once today. Let's
eat already."

Those grins of his were addictive.

We tore off pieces of *injera* at the same time and
started digging into the food. It was delicious and I was
hungry, so we ate in silence for a bit. Bumping hands

and smiling every once in a while as we both reached for the same things. After a few moments we slowed down and Tom took a sip from his beer. I noticed the hand he was holding the bottle with was pristine, while both of mine were a mess.

"How come you can do this with one hand?"

He laughed as I sat there baffled.

"Practice," he said waving said clean hand around. "Henock taught me how to eat like a proper Ethiopian." He smiled and put down his beer. "Here, I'll show you something."

He tore off some *injera* and picked up some bits of meat and greens from the platter, then extended his hand, offering it to me. I reached for it and he pulled it back, a very predatory smile on his lips.

"You have to eat it from my hand."

The way he looked at me made the whole thing feel incredibly intimate. I opened my mouth and took the bite of food from him and chewed slowly as he watched me eat.

His voice was low when he spoke. "That's a *gursha*. In Ethiopia, when you're eating a meal with friends or family it's customary for people around the table to offer each other bites of food, as a sign of love or friendship." He cleared his throat then, looking a little self-conscious.

"That's lovely. Thank you."

He nodded again. "It is."

"I like hearing you talk about your friends. It makes me think of mine. I—"

I shut my mouth then because I was about to go overboard. Feeling self-conscious, I went back to eating.

Tom put his hand under my chin.

"What were you going to say?" I shook my head trying to avoid the subject, but I looked up at him and his eyes were so focused on me, I just said it.

"I was going to say, I can't wait for you to meet my friends. But then thought better of it, because we've been on like a quarter of an actual date, so it seemed just a *tad* desperate—" I help up my hand, the tips of my index finger and thumb pressed together "—to talk about meeting each other's people."

He smiled in that way that made me feel like there were a million butterflies fluttering inside me, and shook his head leaning in. "If you only knew how ready I am to take this—" he waved the hand holding the beer between us "—a lot further than just a casual thing."

I looked down, not knowing what to say, but he kept going.

"I'm ready to meet your friends and have you meet mine, Camilo. I'm ready for whatever you're ready for." Then he took my hand and kissed my palm, because my life was a Jane Austen novel now.

"Okay then. Duly noted," I said with a sharp nod.

We kept eating for a little bit and after we were done he helped me clean up. Once we finished in the kitchen I turned off the lights, and pulled him into the bed with me. I helped him out of his jeans and we got under the covers. We fit together in my queen-size bed, but just barely. It all felt so normal though, like we'd done this a million times before.

It was tempting to just go with the feeling, and avoid discussing the reason why we were in my apartment instead of his house. But I needed to know about the situation with his daughter and his ex before I agreed to take things any further. This whole thing with Tom was already a big fucking risk to take, and I needed to know just how badly I could get burned.

"So this is amazing, and I basically want to order a body pillow shaped exactly like you, because you feel incredible," I said, resting my head on his chest to take the edge off the conversation a bit. "But we need to talk about your daughter, and your ex. I need information, Tom."

He sighed and held me tighter before answering, "Well there's not too much to tell. I was with Maxwell for about five years. We got married right as things with my company were getting really hot, so I worked all the time. Like *all* the time." He bit his lips then, in a way that I'd noticed happened when he was talking about something sad or upsetting.

"Maxwell got lonely and I wanted a baby, so we started the surrogacy process right after we got married. I would have preferred an adoption, but Maxwell really wanted a biological child. His cousin offered to be our egg donor, so we decided to do it. It took so long to get everything in order that by the time the surrogate was pregnant, our marriage was completely in shambles. I take a lot of blame for it, because I didn't pay attention."

I had to bite my tongue then, the impulse to take his side, to tell him I couldn't imagine him ever letting anyone down had me practically vibrating. In the short time I'd known Tom I already saw how much he took on, how driven he was to fix things. I ran my hand over his chest and waited for him to keep talking, because no matter how much I wanted to soothe, I needed to know more.

"I have Libe most of the time and Maxwell gets her on Wednesday nights and every other weekend."

"Ah." So it really was his night off.

He exhaled and shook his head. "We split holidays too, we switch between Thanksgiving and Christmas. The arrangement mostly works for us. Since I sold Nuntius I've been on a semi-hiatus from work. I wanted to be home more, at least until Libe was a bit older. I didn't want to fail her."

He stopped talking and pulled me up to press his face to my neck. I let him. The pain and remorse I felt coming off him made me feel protective. "Tom, it can't all be on you." He shook his head and his hand moved up to pull me in for a kiss. He tasted me, as if he needed comfort before he went on.

When he pulled back he continued in a sober, regretful tone. "I was so focused on Nuntius and how fast it was growing, I didn't take care of our relationship. In hindsight we shouldn't have gotten married. Too many things weren't right. But I also got Libertad out of it and I could never ever regret having her."

His voice was so full of love when he talked about his daughter. "I love her name. Gutsy to name a little kid *Freedom* in Spanish."

He nodded and when I looked up to see his face, it was serious and sad.

"It was my grandmother's name. My mom's mom. She died just a few months before Libe was born. It's one of the greatest pains of my life she never got to meet her." He smiled then, but it was so broken. "My grandmother helped raise me. When she died I hadn't seen her in almost a year. I'd been too busy to go home for a visit. *That* I will always regret."

He was quiet for a moment, but when he spoke again he sounded better. "It's kind of a thing in my mom's family. Names with meaning. My mother's name is Esperanza. My mom *hope*, Libe and abuela *freedom* and my aunt Patria *homeland*." His voice was sad, but full of pride.

"And they named you Tom?!" I blurted out without thinking. He barked out a laugh and kissed my forehead. The smile that I realized only appeared when I did something over the top—which he thought was adorable—was out in full force.

"Tom was my dad's best friend and my *full* name is Thomas *Caonabo* Hughes *Gomez*. My mother named me after a Carib chief because she's badass like that."

I had to give him a kiss for that.

Tom was a constant source of wonder. Every time I thought I had him figured out, he did or said something to make me think I wasn't even close. "That's a *lot* better than regular Tom."

He chuckled quietly and then said, "Would you be open to getting to know Libertad?"

I stiffened at his request. Not because I didn't want to, I was just surprised by the question.

Probably sensing my discomfort, he quickly added, "Not right now, just sometime in the future. I'd really like to keep seeing you and if things go well, it just makes sense."

There was so much I needed to unpack about his situation. Taking things with Tom to the level of meeting his kid felt like a deep dive.

It sounded scary, but in Tom's arms after hearing more of his story, of seeing the lengths that he went to tonight to show me what was happening between us mattered, I had to step up too.

I could be messy, but I was not a coward.

If Tom Hughes was hell-bent on sweeping me off my feet, I was going to be fucking in it with him.

When I answered I looked him right in the eyes. "Sure, I'd love to meet her sometime."

"Whenever you're ready. I don't want to rush you."

I pushed up to give him a kiss. "She seemed pretty awesome just from the minute I spent with her, and I love hanging out with kids."

And I really did.

I loved kids, I *wanted* kids. I wanted my own little family. That was the dream I'd never dared to dream. Of course perfect Tom would stroll up to my life with an adorable kid as part of the deal.

"Tom, I like you. I mean I *really* like you a lot, and with me that sometimes means going overboard and twisting myself into knots for the person I'm with. Almost every time it ends with me getting my heart stomped on. I'm not saying you'd do that. I just need to protect myself. Your life seems to have a lot of working parts, and I may be up for that. But I need to make sure I do it without losing myself in the process. It's happened before and gone badly for me."

Tom's silence freaked me out a little, because I wasn't trying to make a judgment on his life. "I'm not being judgy or anything."

After a moment he nodded and his voice was serious but understanding. "I know, I'm glad you feel comfortable enough to tell me, and please do so anytime I overstep."

"You didn't overstep, and thank you for understanding. I'd love to meet Libe when we're both ready for it."

He nodded and kissed me again.

I wanted to be done talking and focus on the fact I

had Tom in my bed in just his underwear and running his hands under my clothes. I sat up and pulled my sweatshirt off as he ran his hands over my chest, then I moved so I was straddling him again. I stroked his arms and neck. Loving how his big body filled my bed.

"I like this view."

He pushed up with his hips so his cock brushed my ass, reminding me how good it felt when he'd been there before.

"View is not bad from where I am either." His voice was low and so fucking sexy. Everything he did set my blood on fire.

I bent down and kissed him as I ground up hard against him.

"Chat time is over, Thomas Caonabo."

Chapter Fifteen

Camilo

"What do you get to bribe a four year old so you can get full-time access to her daddy's privates?" i asked Ayako, who was walking into my office with our daily mid-afternoon caffeine fix.

She laughed as she passed me my coffee. "Wow, you're all the way in on this one, huh? Doing the dirty to a preschooler to get at her dad. Damn, Camilo."

I rolled my eyes as I blew on the piping cup of coffee. "Okay I admit it's shameless, but I'm nervous and I really want her to like me! The time I met her she was wearing a 'The Future is Female' t-shirt and unicorn leggings, Ayako. This kid does not fuck around. I don't want to lose access to Tom's dick because I mess up with her."

I was shrieking a little, but this was an emergency. Tom and I had been solid for over a month. After that first time at his house things had gone pretty smoothly. He had Libe a lot, but whenever he wasn't with her, we'd been together.

When Libe was at Maxwell's house for the weekend, I essentially moved into his house from the end of the day on Friday until I had to go over to my mom's on Sunday. We'd had a couple of weekends like that so far, and they'd been amazing. Seriously like toe curling, "how is this even my life" incredible. We'd cook, go to the farmer's market or go to Priya and Sanjay's for a drink. But mostly it was just the two of us.

I'd never had a connection with anyone like the one I had with Tom. It wasn't even the sex or the chemistry, which was pretty intense in its own right. Or how easy it was to be with him. What made it all feel so monumental was the reciprocity. I never felt like I wasn't getting as much as I put in with Tom. It wasn't even tit for tat or that I was keeping track. I just felt *balanced.* Like he wanted exactly what I gave, and I got as much as I needed. Attention, time, sex, space. Everything just right.

I felt Ayako tapping the side of my coffee mug with her sharp fingernails bringing me back from my Tom musings. When I turned, she was looking at me with concerned eyes.

"Whatever's going on in your head, stop it. Things are going well with you guys. Why are you so worried about this?"

"That's exactly why I'm nervous. Meeting his daughter means change. Our relationship is going to expand, and I'm not sure I want to give up the fairy-tale weekends yet. There is so much that could go wrong if we take things further than this." I lowered my voice and looked at my open office door. "You know I'm walking a very thin line here."

Ayako twisted her mouth to the side as if she was trying to figure out how to say something to interrupt my mental hand-wringing. "Camilo, look at me."

I reluctantly met her gaze.

"So far, you've managed to keep the renovation project and the thing with Tom completely separate. I don't see why that has to change, why are you inviting trouble?"

Because I was scared that taking things further with Tom would bring it all tumbling down. That if I kept things a bit more casual then I could hold on for longer. But I also wanted to feel like we were solid parts of each other's lives, and the biggest thing in his was Libertad.

Meeting her also meant the next step was introducing Tom to my mom.

My mother, like Ayako always said, was sacred ground for me. None of the guys I'd dated had ever had patience for my taking off on Sundays to go see her, or that I would drop everything if she ever needed me. So far Tom had been nothing but understanding, but I didn't know if he still would if my mom hit a rough spot and demanded all my attention.

"I'm just a little anxious. Things are moving so fast."

Ayako was about to protest, but I held a hand up acknowledging that wasn't completely accurate. "I shouldn't say that. Because it's not true. I want to meet Libe. I'm just worried. I mean, do I need to introduce him to my mom? Because she's not in the best place right now. I've told him about it a little, but I don't know how much I want to go down that road just yet."

Ayako's face softened finally understanding where my worry was coming from. "Camilo, you don't need to do anything you don't want to do. Go and meet Libe, bring her a My Little Pony plushie or a book or something. You'll be fine. Hell, I've seen you talk down kids who were practically feral, you can handle a well-adjusted four year old." She sighed then squeezed my shoulder. "As for Dinorah, take your time, babe. If she's not at her best right now, you don't need to rush it. If Tom asked you to meet Libe, and you're okay with that, then meet the kid. That doesn't mean you need to bring your mom into the picture." I exhaled and she smiled, knowing she was probably wearing me down.

"Although I have a feeling her hearing about how well things are going with Tom would make her happy. Is she really that bad?"

I shook my head. "It's not a crisis, but you know how it is. I can tell she's starting to go into herself more and more. She doesn't want to go out as much, she's been going from work to home for months, and she's been really inconsistent with her support group." Ayako grimaced at that.

"Odette can barely get her to come over, and I'm not sure she's been taking her meds regularly." I ran my hand over my eyes, feeling the worry weighing down on me. "I don't want to push her too much, but it scares me when she gets like this." I sighed forcing myself to be more positive. "Thankfully she's going to the Poconos with Odette this weekend and the plan is for her to go again for Thanksgiving. I *have* been keeping her up to date about Tom, but I also don't want to get her hopes up too much. Because if things don't work out, she'll end up more devastated than me. I don't need to give her more reasons for her anxiety to spiral."

Ayako nodded in understanding. "You're a good son, and you worry too much." She gave me a rueful smile. "But I'm glad to hear she's going on the annual Thanksgiving trip. That'll be good for her. Speaking of which, I know it's still a couple of weeks away but are we still on for Chinese and TV show binging?"

I nodded at that, grateful to go in a less stressful direction with the conversation. "Absolutely." I held up my hand for a high five. "On-call buddies." Ayako and I signed up to be on-call supervisors for the New Beginning hotline almost every Thanksgiving. We got paid extra, and since we didn't really do big family celebrations it was nice to let the other supervisors who did have the weekend off.

"We're good. You still staying at my place?" Astoria wasn't super far, but when she was on call, she sometimes crashed at my place. Since I was only a couple of subway stops away from the shelter.

She nodded. "Yeah, I might go home Friday night though. My brother's coming down from Boston on Saturday."

"Okay, I think Tom won't have Libe, so I can always stay at his place."

"Niiiiice." She waggled her eyebrows at me and we both laughed.

I sighed, feeling better about the meeting with Libe. "Thanks for talking me off the ledge, *again*," I said rolling my eyes. "I'm going to go with your advice and get the kid a My Little Pony toy of some kind and hope for the best."

"You can't go wrong with MLP. Not that I'm worried, she's going to love you."

I hoped she was right.

Who knew a person could see animals dancing hip hop in the middle of Central Park?

I'd lived in New York City since I was thirteen years old, unaware this had been going on all along. And yet here I was, less than two months after meeting Tom, at the Central Park Zoo, looking at what seemed to be sea lions busting out moves for fish.

I was making my way through the crowds out on this sunny November day to meet Libertad and Tom. I'd been so nervous about meeting Libe, I'd texted Tom like ten times asking questions the night before. He thought my nervousness was adorable and was no help at all. His big piece of advice had been to be prepared to get a million questions, and to be bossed around the entire time. I could certainly handle a bossy four year old, but I was still dying from nerves.

The zoo was sort of tucked away in the park, covered by trees and canopies. Despite that, it was packed with people. I spotted Libe before I saw Tom. They were standing by one of the columns surrounding the sea lion pool. He had her perched on his shoulders so she could see the show. They were close enough to have a clear view, but not so close they'd block anyone else's. I hurried towards them clutching the stuffed animal I'd gotten her in a small shopping bag.

When Tom saw me walking in their direction his face immediately lit up, and he pointed toward me to let Libe know I was there. I walked up, unsure on how to greet him, but he quickly put the question to rest when he pulled me in for a quick but very firm kiss on the lips. The entire situation was unnerving and felt so very grown-up.

Just as I was about to panic, not sure what to do with myself, my social worker training kicked in. I reminded myself that as far as difficult first meetings went, this one was nowhere near the scariest one I'd experienced. I could do this. I looked up to where Libe was perched on Tom's shoulders, got the pony out of the bag, and showed it to her.

"I found this lost pony on the way here. I was hoping you could take her home with you, Libe."

She squealed and reached out for it as Tom put her back on the ground.

"Pinkie Pie! I'll take good care of her. I have lots of other ponies in my homes. She can come and live with me." She took the pink toy and squeezed it tight.

She was so fucking cute. She had this mass of tight brown curls that sprung out of her head in a big fluffy halo. She was light skinned, but still had a little bit of a summer tan left. Today she was wearing a bright purple puffy coat, a pointy wool hat with lots of hearts on it and tights with multicolored stripes. Her boots were so stylish I almost asked where she got them.

"What do you say to Camilo, honey?"

She hugged the toy again. "Thank you, Camilo." It sounded more like "Mamilo."

"You know, Libe, I have a nickname just like you."

"What is it?" she asked, as if I was withholding vital information from her. I smiled, and veered my eyes toward Tom who was completely focused on the conversation Libe and I were having. "It's Milo. My friends all call me that. My mom too."

Libe glanced up at Tom at the mention of my mother. "I don't have a mom, but I have two dads." She held up two gloved little fingers at me.

"I know. You're a lucky girl to have such good daddies who love you so much." She nodded and went back to doing things to the pony's mane, then pulled what looked like a lemur out of her little backpack and was introducing them to each other.

I looked at Tom who was giving me an amused look and went back to my chat with Libe. "So, Libe, I was hoping you could help me today." Her head immediately popped up from playing with the pony when she heard my request for assistance.

"Help with what?"

I sat down on the bench next to where we were standing and waved her over. She immediately climbed up without asking for help and sat next to me. "Well I've never been to the Central Park Zoo before. So I don't know what I should see first. What's your favorite animal here?" She immediately gave me a look that was all Tom, eyebrows scrunched, her finger under her chin, like she was working on a perfect answer. Before she said anything she turned to her dad, who was now on the bench next to me.

"Oh we can help you with that. We come to the zoo *a lot*. Right, Daddy?" Tom very solemnly dipped his head.

"Yes we do."

I almost laughed at Tom's extremely weary answer, but Libe went right back to giving me the rundown on the best of the zoo.

"My favorites are the penguins and the puffins and second favorites the goats and the donkeys because we can feed and pet them."

She turned around and pointed towards an indoor exhibit. "The penguins are there. It's a little smelly, but you just have to power through it." I burst out laughing at that, and she stared at me like she had no idea what was so damn funny. Then she gave her dad a look that said, "This one may be too regular to get another invitation to the zoo."

After a moment she climbed down from the bench,

gave me her little hand and started tugging me in the direction of the penguins.

As we walked over to the exhibit, I glanced up and found Tom watching me with laughter in his eyes. I was holding Libe's hand and in the other had the lemur, who she'd informed me was named Bobby.

"What?" I asked feeling self-conscious.

He shook his head. "Nothing, I'm just glad you're here." He bent down and kissed my head.

"I'm glad I'm here too."

"Me too!" Libe piped in, not about to be left out of the conversation.

Libe had me in stitches as we moved around the exhibit. She was a riot, offering me some facts about the animals, and just being generally sassy and amazing. At the moment she had Bobby and Pinkie Pie shoved against the glass and was giving them a lesson on puffin eating habits.

Tom and I were standing there listening to her hilarious monologue when an older woman approached us and bent down to talk to Libe.

"Oh that's so cute, are those your little friends? A horsey and a monkey."

Libe's head swiveled up to look at the lady and her stank face was so fucking epic I almost died. She held up her arms, showing the lady the stuffed animals. "This is a ring-tailed lemur and his name is Bobby." Then she extended the arm with the pony. "And this is Pinkie Pie. She's a magical pony. I don't like monkeys." With that she was done with the woman's foolishness. When she turned around she gave Tom and I a look that said, "Can you believe I'm out here dealing with these basic bitches while i'm tryna talk to these

damn puffins?" Then walked off to the next exhibit.
The lady just stared after her as Tom tried to offer an
apology without losing his shit.

This kid was my soul mate.

The day at the zoo was great. It was a pleasure to see
Tom with Libertad. He was a fantastic father, engaged
without being overprotective. He spoke to her like a
human being and it was beautiful to watch. I knew I
was half in love with him at the end of the day, when
he picked her up as we were leaving the zoo and then
grabbed my hand. Like it was the most natural thing
in the world.

As we got close to the sea lion exhibit Libe lifted her
head up, popping her thumb out of her mouth. "Daddy,
we need a selfie!" I let go of Tom's hand so I could
cover the grin that broke out on my face. This kid did
the most.

Tom shook his head as he tried very hard to keep a
straight face. "Libertad, you don't even have a phone.
What are you going to do with a selfie?"

She cut her eyes at him like the tiny savage she was,
and turned to me. "We always take selfies so my daddy
can send them to my abue and my nana." She said the
last words like she knew Tom was playing with fire by
not documenting every precious moment with Libe for
the grandparents.

Tom straightened up then, barely holding it together
from his kid's antics. He seemed like he was going
to say something when Libe spoke up again. "I want
a photo with Milo and Pinkie. I want to put it on my
smiles walls."

I raised an eyebrow at that and Tom's eyes widened,
before launching into an explanation. "Because Libe

has two bedrooms, in each one she has lots of photos of all her favorite things. So she can be with them every night."

The looks Tom kept sending me were making my knees weak. For all I knew Libe had everyone under the sun on that smiles wall, but this all felt so fucking huge.

"I'd love to take a selfie," I said, sounding completely breathless, but Libe immediately took charge of the situation. She got Tom's phone out of his coat pocket and within seconds we were trying to find a spot for the photo. I moved closer to Tom as Libe put her little arm around my head. "Take the selfie, Daddy!"

We both laughed at her bossy tone and big grin. Tom held his arm out and we all looked up, smiling at the camera. After a few tries Tom brought the phone down and when he looked at it his face shone.

"Let me see it, Daddy," Libe said, reaching for the phone.

"Libertad, paciencia por favor. What do you say?"

"Please," she said grudgingly, her little hands twitching to grab the phone.

When Tom handed her the phone she turned so I could see it too, I could barely speak through the wave of emotion that crashed into me. "I like it."

That was a picture I never imagined myself being a part of.

Tom glanced down at me like he knew exactly what was going through my head. When he spoke I heard the emotion in his voice too. "It's great." With that he grabbed my hand again and started making our way out of the zoo.

Chapter Sixteen

Tom

I couldn't stop smiling, at how great this day had gone. Libe, like me, was smitten with Camilo. He was so good with her too. Right now we were in her bedroom about to do the nighttime reading routine, and she was not at all interested in me.

She scrunched her face as she shook her head at my attempt to read her a book. "No, Daddy, you're going to watch today. Pinkie and I want Milo to read us the story." She was in bed with her usual array of stuffed animals, but the place of honor right in the crook of her arm went to the little pink pony Camilo had brought her. I was about to go and ask Camilo if he'd like to join us, but because she *was* half Dominican, Libe just yelled.

"Milo! You have to come here. Pinkie is waiting for you!"

I heard a chuckle from the TV room and soon Camilo was walking into the room.

"Hi, Miss Libe, you said Pinkie needed something?"

She nodded hard and signaled for me to pass her the book. I handed it to her and she gave me a distracted thank-you. All her focus on her new favorite person.

"Thanks, Daddy. Milo, could you read me my bed-time story?"

"What do you say, Libe?"

"Please."

Camilo gave me an amused look and sat down by the bed. He grabbed the book and read the title on the cover. "'Tango Makes Three.'"

Libe nodded again. "Tango lives in the Central Park Zoo and has two daddies like me."

Camilo gave me a look as he leafed through the book. "Gay penguins? Really?"

I laughed and put my hands up. "Hey, Priya was the one who got it for her, and besides, representation *is* important. Even if the dads and child in question are not of the same species as you."

His face softened at that and then he leaned over to run his hand over Libe's forehead. She nuzzled her head against it.

After a moment Camilo opened the book and started reading while Libe and I listened. The peace and con-tentment I felt in that moment was utterly complete.

I knew Camilo had been nervous about meeting Libe, but just like I suspected she'd warmed up to him immediately.

With each passing day Camilo's presence in my life was becoming more necessary. I just had to convince him that to me he was not just a temporary thing.

"Thank you for today. I had so much fun. Libe's a trip," Camilo whispered to me as we lay on my couch watching TV. I felt overwhelmed by this day and the things it was making me want. I tightened my arms around him and kissed the top of his head.

"Thank *you*. I loved having you with us all day. And yes, she's a trip and you were wonderful with her. She usually gets on with people fast, but not this fast, and a dinner invitation is a pretty big deal. You were a hit."

He gave me a shy smile as I mentioned the invitation. After we'd taken the selfie Libe requested, she casually asked if Milo could come home with us. I had never had Libe meet anyone I'd dated before, so my plan had been to part ways after the park. But like me, my kid didn't seem to want to let go of Camilo.

I was about to say more but I got distracted when he turned his head so he could kiss me. He slid his tongue into my mouth and I felt the stir that took hold whenever I was with Camilo. We shared some quiet kisses, our tongues tangling together, and our arms tight around each other. After a few minutes Camilo pulled away with a satisfied sigh and laid his head on my chest. It felt so good and right, to have him in my arms like this.

Eventually Camilo spoke into the silence. "Can I ask you a question?"

"Uh oh. Should I brace myself?" He looked up and stuck his tongue out at me before asking.

"Seriously though, how are you this low-key? I mean you have all this money." He raised a hand and waved it toward the lit fireplace, presumably to illustrate his point. "Yet you seem to do all your own stuff and watch your kid yourself. Like where's the army of servants and nannies and shit?"

I chuckled because Camilo *had* a way with words. I thought about my answer for a minute, certain there was another question hidden in there.

"Well to be honest that's partly why I love living in New York. I can be completely anonymous here. I'm just another guy on the subway. And I *do* have people who help me. I have a cleaning service, a property management company, and there's someone who comes and cooks for me a few times a week. I have a driver on weekdays and a couple of assistants too," I said lifting a shoulder. "They're just not in my space all the time. I like my privacy. And when Libe was smaller I had a live-in nanny. I still have someone who watches her regularly, she just doesn't live here. No one's here on the weekends for the most part, unless I'm hosting a dinner party or something."

I exhaled, trying to get to what I thought he was really asking: why I wanted things this way. "After the divorce I promised myself I wouldn't let money or business steal me away from my life. I think that was part of the reason the three of us decided to sell Nuntius. As much as we loved it, it was running our lives. I guess I'm still recovering from that. I'm enjoying the freedom not having to worry about money gives me, and all the time I get with Libe. I try to be mindful of it, and most of the time I succeed. Although it can be tempting to just throw money at things that come up."

He stayed silent for a while, digesting what I'd said, then turned around with a look of genuine annoyance on his face.

"Someday soon," he said, pressing a finger to my chest. "You're going to have to do something completely asinine and enraging. Because it's not fucking possible for anyone to be this well-adjusted and thoughtful all the time. It's annoying, Thomas!"

I barked out a laugh. "You probably won't be waiting too long. Believe me."

He huffed in answer but gave me a kiss before settling against me again.

After a minute I decided to ask something I'd been waiting on for a while. After the day we had, it felt like the right time. "What are you doing for Thanksgiving?"

He shrugged in my arms. "Nothing, I'm on call."

I knew he had weekends when he had to be available to respond to emergencies in the shelter, but it hadn't really come up since we started seeing each other. "Do you have to be at home? What about your mom?"

He shook his head and shifted a bit so his back was flush against my chest. "No it's not so strict. I just need to be available on the phone in case one of the advocates has a question or something happens. My mom is going to the Poconos with Patrice's mom. She's actually there this weekend. We were finally able to convince her to go out of town for a bit."

At the mention of his mom his brow furrowed and I wondered if there was something going on. He hadn't said much about her lately, but I knew her well-being was a major priority in his life. "Anyways, Ayako will be on call too, so we're planning to hang out at my place. Get some takeout and binge-watch cooking competitions. The parents will be back on Saturday, so I'll see my mom Sunday."

I nodded at his answer, figuring out how to ask my real question.

"Why don't you come here? Ayako's welcome too. I promise you'll finally get a glimpse of my obnoxious rich-guy side then."

He lifted his head and narrowed his eyes at me. "Will there be turkey? Because my people don't do turkey."

I couldn't resist that mouth. I kissed him again, smiling against his face.

"There will literally be everything *but* turkey."

"Go on," he said, sounding intrigued.

"It's sort of a tradition at this point. We started in grad school. Heni, Sanjay and I were roommates and stayed in Boston for Thanksgiving since none of us had family close by. Priya was in medical school at Yale and came up too. We invited all the international students who stayed in town and asked whoever wanted to bring a traditional special occasion dish from their country." By this point I had his complete attention. "We ended up with this amazing meal and decided we'd do it again the next year, and we've been doing it together ever since. We used to take turns hosting, but in the last few years it's been here. The group has grown too, now that people are married and have kids. A lot of our friends are in the area, so we get a crowd. I think there are about thirty coming this year. I have some of it catered, but people still bring some dishes from home. It's always a nice evening."

Camilo had turned around while I talked and was now looking at me slack-jawed. "It's not fair that you can be this geeky and cool at once."

I grinned at how pissed he looked and went in for another kiss.

"It sounds like an amazing way to celebrate. I'm totally in. Ayako will love it too, she'll probably want to bring something."

I smiled, pleased with myself for impressing him. "Good. Priya will be here, so you can see the baby. She's been asking about you." He nodded and settled back into my arms again. It was time for Camilo to get to know my people.

Camilo

"I wish we could stay like this forever," Tom whispered and I nodded, thinking again how good he made me feel. We'd been watching a movie and dozing off after our talk about Thanksgiving plans. I had my head on his chest and was falling asleep when my phone rang. When I held it up I saw Odette's number on the screen and my heart immediately sank. If she was calling this late something was probably going on with my mom.

"Hey, Odette. Is something wrong?"

"Hi, Milo. I'm just calling to ask how Dinorah's doing. I tried to call her this morning and she didn't pick up."

It took me a moment to process her words. When I realized what she was saying I stiffened in Tom's arms and scrambled to sit up. This whole time I thought my mom was with Odette. I'd even texted with her this afternoon and she'd said she was fine. What the hell was going on?

"What do you mean? I thought she'd gone up to the house with you?" I sounded scared and Tom immediately sat up on the couch, his face alert.

I heard Odette click her tongue. "No, when we went to pick her up last night she said she wasn't feeling well and was going to stay home. I tried to convince her, but you know how she gets. I told her I'd check on her today, but she's not answering her phone. I didn't want to worry you, dear, but you know she's been down lately."

I was in a full panic by now, because this meant my mom had been alone and so depressed she couldn't even leave her house while I'd been out with Tom all day. The guilt slashed through me. I'd barely checked in with her this week, I'd been so preoccupied with meeting Libe. I knew she wasn't doing well, but I was so caught in this thing I had with Tom, I'd totally dropped the ball.

"I haven't talked to her since yesterday, Odette. I've been at my—"

I looked over at Tom.

"I've been busy. I texted her today and she said she was good. It was short, but I figured she was distracted doing stuff with you." I got up and started walking downstairs with Tom right on my heels. "Thanks for calling. I'll go over to her place now and see how she's doing."

"Okay, sweetheart, and please don't feel guilty. You didn't know and your mother is an *adult*. Please, don't blame yourself okay?" She sounded worried. If anyone knew how hard I took things with my mother, it was Odette.

"I won't. I'll check in with you once I see her." I ended the call before she could even say goodbye and started looking for my stuff. I got my shoes and jacket on then grabbed my backpack on the way to the door, without saying a word to Tom. The happiness I'd been feeling all day had completely evaporated. If anything happened to my mother I would never forgive myself.

I was in my head and feeling too fucked up for explanations. He might as well see me like this, in one of my "ugly moods," like Paul used to call them.

Tom followed me to the door, and I stood there holding the doorknob with my back to him. I didn't want to look at him. I didn't want to have to explain why I needed to go to check on my mom. I could already see his puzzled expression when he heard why I had to go. The questions, the implication about my "co-dependent" relationship with my mother, or my using her as an excuse for running out. I didn't have the energy to do it tonight.

I felt Tom's gentle hand on my shoulder. "¿Que paso? Is your mom okay?"

I took a couple of deep breaths, then turned around slowly, trying not to glare at him. This wasn't his fault.

"That was Odette, Patrice's mother. Sounds like my mom didn't go up to the Poconos with them. She's not answering her phone either. She's been down lately and I'm worried. I was so distracted—"

I paused because I didn't want to lash out at Tom, even though I really wanted to find a reason to yell at *somebody.*

I pulled on the strap of my backpack feeling restless at the fact that I was still here talking and not on the way to see my mother already. "We only texted once today. I figured she was around people and wouldn't want me pestering her. But she's been home this whole time, and I'm sure she probably hasn't left her house. I have to go and check on her. I'm just going to get a Lyft and go up there."

The concern on his face did a lot to soften the edges of the panic I was feeling.

"I can drive you there," he offered. "I'll just ask Sanjay to come and stay with Libe. They're home right now. It'll take him a minute to get here. I'll get my car from the garage. It's just across the street. Let me help, please."

My instinct was to say no. To tell him I didn't need anyone to do anything for me and could handle this on my own. That I couldn't start relying on him when it came to my mother. I was feeling fragile though, so I nodded, and I saw his shoulders immediately relax. "Okay, I'll wait for you outside."

I don't know how he did it, but within ten minutes he'd gotten Sanjay to come over, retrieved his car from the garage and was taking me up to the Bronx. We drove in silence as I tried again and again to call my mom, but her phone was shut off. Tom was tense and I knew I was being rude by not talking, but I was so worried, I was incapable of making conversation.

As we pulled up to my mom's building I started unbuckling my seat belt, so I could jump out of the car as soon as we stopped.

"Thanks for driving me, Tom. I really appreciate it." I was about to step out of the car when he pulled me by my arm.

"Can I at least get a kiss?"

I was about to snap at him that I didn't have time to kiss him, then reminded myself once again none of this was his fault.

I sagged and turned to give him a peck on the lips. "I'll call you later. Okay?"

His mouth was pursed and he looked worried, but he nodded. "I hope everything's alright with your mom."

"Me too." I appreciated Tom not attempting to make me feel better or minimizing things, but I had no time to talk. I jumped out of the car, a copy of my mom's keys in hand, and rushed into the building as he drove away.

Chapter Seventeen

Camilo

I turned the doorknob to my mom's apartment with my stomach in knots, unsure of what I'd find on the other side of the door. I couldn't keep at bay the images of those months after my dad died, when her depression got so bad she'd spend weeks in bed with all the curtains drawn, in total darkness. When I stepped in I saw the lights were on, and heard the TV on in her bedroom, I felt dizzy with relief.

I called out so I didn't startle her as I walked down the hallway to her room.

"Mama. ¿Dónde estás?"

No answer.

I walked in and saw her asleep in her bed, with a book on her chest. She'd fallen asleep reading. The house wasn't disheveled and the kitchen looked like it had seen some action in the last few days. All good signs. I was still worried, because even if she wasn't in full-on crisis, the fact that she opted out of the Poconos, which she usually loved, was a red flag.

I called her again, not wanting to scare her.

"Mama." She opened her eyes and smiled when she saw me.

"Milito, what are you doing here, papi? I thought you were at Tom's house."

I walked over so I could stand by the side of the bed, trying hard not to let her see how worried I'd been.

"Mama, Odette called worried about you. She said you'd skipped out on the trip to the Poconos. Why didn't you tell me? I would've come here and kept you company."

She waved me off as she sat up on the bed.

"I just didn't feel like being around people, baby. I'm fine. You know I like my alone time. Work's been crazy and I just wanted to spend my time off in peace. That's all. Everything's okay." She looked at me and must have noticed how stressed I was. "Come here."

I went over and she gave me a hug. "You worry too much, papi. I'm always worrying you."

I shook my head, my face pressed to hers. "That's not even remotely true. I just want to make sure you're all right. That's all."

"I know, and I'm fine." She moved over and patted the spot next to her on the bed. "Come, tell me about Tom's daughter. I'm sure she loved you. You're so good with children."

I knew she was trying to deflect, but I was just so glad to find her doing okay. I let her get away with it this time. I sat down and grabbed her hand.

"It was good." I smiled remembering all of Libe's antics at the zoo. "It was great actually. You'd love Libe, she's so sassy and smart. Tom is so good with her too."

She smiled wistfully at that. "I'd love to meet them some time." Right then I thought about how much fun I had with Libe and Tom, and how good it felt to be part of their little unit.

My mom was the most important person in my life and things with Tom were getting more serious every day. Despite my hang-ups and the very real complications, that fact was undeniable. He'd been so gentle and strong with me tonight. He'd given me exactly what I needed without smothering or taking charge. But the most important thing was that he hadn't tried to minimize or tell me I was overreacting about my mom. I decided then I wanted them to meet.

Ayako was right, seeing me with Tom *would* make her happy.

"Mama, what do you think about inviting Tom to come to the Juan Luis concert with us?"

She perked up instantly at my suggestion. "You should. I'm sure he's a fan." I already knew he was. Juan Luis Guerra was practically a deity in the Dominican Republic. Really, he was a big deal for the entire Spanish speaking world, but he was *from* the DR. I doubted Tom didn't know he'd be performing in town next weekend.

I put my arm around her, smiling at how excited she looked. "I'll ask him if he wants to join us."

She gave me a cheeky smile. "You've been hiding him from me, Milito." I laughed at her glee. We both knew this was a big deal.

"I haven't been hiding him, I talk to you about him all the time. I'll let him know."

I didn't know if there were tickets left, but for all I knew he was already planning to go. I'd bought ours a while ago and they'd been pricey, but my mom and I decided they could be our Christmas gift to each other. It had been a long time since we did something like that

and we'd been looking forward to it. It was a good idea
to invite Tom.

"I can't wait to meet him. So what did you do at the
zoo?"

We chatted for a while about the day and I told her of
Libe's run-in with the lady at the puffin exhibit which
my mom thought was hilarious.

After a while she stood up. "Do you want me to get
you something? I'm going to make some tea and then
we can watch a movie."

"I'll have some tea." She nodded and walked out of
the room. I exhaled heavily, trying to not whip myself
up too much. My mom seemed fine, she just hadn't been
in the mood to be around people. I had to take her word
for it, and not put my stuff on her.

I took my phone out and quickly texted Odette. Then
I called Tom, who picked up after one ring.

"Hey, is everything okay?" He sounded breathless
and tense.

"Why do you sound out of breath?"

He grunted and I could hear him gulping down
something. "I was a little on-edge when I got back to
the house. I just put the car in the garage and went out
for a run to clear my head."

Now I felt like shit.

"Sorry I worried you."

"You don't have to apologize or make me feel better. You were concerned for your mom. I get that. We're
fine." Those last two words I felt in my gut.

I exhaled again, feeling emotional. How did he know
exactly what to say, every time? Whenever he fucked up—
and I knew the time would come, because as far as I could
tell he *was* a human being—it was going to *rock my world*.

"She's okay, just didn't feel up to being with people.

She asked me to invite you to come and see Juan Luis Guerra with us. He's playing at the United Palace next weekend." I was a little self-conscious asking, but it wasn't presumptuous to invite him. I'd already met his kid.

He answered almost immediately. "I'd love to. I'd forgotten about that, I'd seen it announced somewhere. Libe's with Maxwell next weekend, and I'm sure I can find a ticket. Thanks for inviting me."

"Well I don't know if you can get tickets by us this late in the game, but we could still go together."

"I'll find something." The delight in his voice made warmth spread to my chest. "Thanks for checking in too. I'm sorry our night got cut short, but I'm glad your mom's okay."

"Thanks for driving me and being wonderful, again. I had an amazing time today, Tom." I wanted to say more. That tonight for the first time I'd felt like I was with someone I could trust enough to let in to my life, all of it.

"I had an amazing day too." He paused then and I held my breath, wondering if like me this day had changed things for him, but after a few breaths we signed off, both sounding relieved.

I ended the call as my mom walked back into the room with two steaming mugs of tea.

"He's in for Juan Luis."

She beamed at me as she passed me my cup. "Que bueno. I can't wait to meet him."

She sat down and started flicking through Netflix looking for something to watch and I tried to let the stress of the last hour wash away and focus on the positive. My mom was okay, things with Tom were good and soon they'd meet.

Our worlds were coming together.

Chapter Eighteen

Tom

Tonight felt like a big deal.

I was driving up to Camilo's mom's place in the Bronx to pick them up and then we'd go to the Juan Luis Guerra show together. I had a hell of a time finding tickets but managed to get three together for a steep price. They were aisle seats about three rows from the stage. I wasn't sure what seats Camilo had, but was certain we could turn them in at the box office or even sell them outside without much issue. Tickets for a Juan Luis Guerra show in the heart of Washington Heights were not going to be hard to get rid of.

Camilo had been excited about the show whenever we'd talked in the last few days, and said his mom had been in a great mood all week.

I hoped the great seats and the dinner reservations I'd made would go over well. Priya warned me I was trying too hard, but once I'd started it was hard to stop. Camilo mentioned how this was a rare treat for him and his mom, and I just wanted to make the night as special as possible for both of them. His mother was obviously the most important thing in his life, and I was feeling the pressure to make a good impression.

I pulled up in front of the building and saw them standing on the sidewalk waiting for me. It wasn't too cold for November, but it was still chilly, so I hurried to get them inside. Camilo's mom was shorter than him by a couple of inches and she was very slender. Her skin was fair and her hair was streaked with gray. She had it done in a fancy braid coiled around her head, and she was wearing a festive red coat. When I came around to them, she gave me a big hug and kiss.

"Tom, encantada. I'm so glad you can come with us tonight. Milito has been keeping you all to himself." She gave Camilo a fond look as he protested.

He rolled his eyes, but that slight edge that was usually present in Camilo was just not there when it came to his mother. "Mama, please don't start. We're here. We're all going to see the show together."

She laughed at him and let me help her into the car.

After she was inside I turned to Camilo. He was in a very well fitting navy blue peacoat with a soft red cashmere scarf around his neck. I lifted his chin and went in for a kiss.

"Hola, Milito." I teased. He narrowed his eyes at me, but his mouth was twitching like he was barely able to hold back a smile.

"I refuse to respond to that name from anyone but my mother. So don't even try it." I laughed and opened the passenger-side door so he could get in.

"So salty, mi amor."

Those gray eyes flashed with humor. "Oh, Tom, if you only knew how little of my salty side you've seen.

It's almost a miracle how little you've managed to piss me off since we started dating."

I laughed again but suspected he was being completely serious. "Don't jinx me. I don't want to end my streak."

He shook his head at me as I closed the door to the car.

As we got on the road back to Manhattan Dinorah started talking excitedly. "I'm so thrilled for this show. This is my first time seeing Juan Luis in concert. I've been wanting to for so long. Have you ever seen him, Tom?"

I nodded from the front seat. "Yes, I have, but not in a really long time. He gave a free concert in Santo Domingo my last year of high school. That was the first time I saw him. Then maybe ten years ago I saw him with my parents and my brother in the DR. He's great live. It should be a good night. Especially with the venue. There are going to be a lot of excited people in that theater tonight."

Dinorah clapped her hands at that. "It's going to be wonderful to have him right there in front of us. I love going to live music shows, there's so much amazing energy. Too bad we won't be able to dance."

I smiled at that, and winked at Camilo, who was busy rolling his eyes again. "Don't count the Dominicans out, we're not above dancing in the aisles once things get going." Dinorah giggled from the back.

Camilo chuckled too and shook his head.

"Don't get too excited about how close he'll be, Mama. Our seats are in the balcony. We will be in the same building, but it won't be up close and personal with Juan Luis or anything."

I stiffened when he mentioned the seats and figured this was probably the right moment to mention I'd gotten them tickets to sit with me down by the stage.

"So when I was looking for my tickets I found a group of three together." I looked over at Camilo whose eyebrow was already higher on his forehead than I necessarily wanted to see. His voice was a little chilly when he answered me, but not fully pissed off.

"But we already have tickets, Tom."

I tried to go for a conciliatory tone. I should have anticipated Camilo was not going to be into me buying him expensive concert tickets without telling him.

"I know, babe." I flashed a pleading look in the mirror hoping to get some help from Dinorah. "I knew you had tickets, but I thought it would be more fun to sit together. I'll make sure your tickets don't go to waste. I'm sure we can return them at the box office. If not there'll be people outside needing tickets."

Dinorah threw me a bone from the back seat.

"I'm glad we'll be able to sit together. I think you're right, someone will take those tickets off our hands. Juan Luis is so popular. Right, Milito?"

Camilo was still looking at me with narrowed eyes, but he nodded at his mom and gave me a tight smile.

"Sure, that's fine. It'll be nice to sit together."

I let out a breath and tried to distract us out of the tense moment by putting on some music. I hoped our night wasn't spoiled by my going overboard.

The tickets *were* pretty easy to get rid of. As soon as we got to the theater, we ran into multiple people outside asking if we had extras. Within minutes Camilo handed them off to a group who were extremely grateful to get them at face value. After some curbside money exchange, we walked into the theater.

Camilo and Dinorah had never been to a show at the United Palace, so they moved slowly, their heads turning as they took in the place. The United Palace was an institution in New York City. It was right in the heart of Washington Heights, which had one of the largest Dominican communities in the city. In addition to being a music venue, it was also a functioning church and a cultural arts center.

It was a place with a lot of history and had hosted some of the greatest Latinx musicians of the last century. I'd been here a few times for shows, but it'd been a while. I'd forgotten how beautiful the architecture was, and about the elaborate woodwork all over the building. It was also amazing to be in a venue full of Latinx. Everyone was dressed to the nines and walking around excitedly as they filed into the building.

As we got up to the entrance of the theater I felt a little nervous. These seats were a lot closer to the stage, and likely much more expensive, than the ones Camilo bought. As I handed the tickets to the usher, I started to feel like I may have seriously misjudged his reaction to my gesture. The woman scanned them and waved her hand toward the orchestra, "You're on the third row from the stage. Orchestra Right. Enjoy the show."

Camilo's eyes got so big when he heard the location of our seats, I was sure he would say something. But he just gave me another icy look and walked in. Dinorah, on the other hand, was having a moment.

"Tom, you got us seats down by the stage!" She put her arm in the crook of her son's elbow as they made their way down the aisle. "Milito, we're going to be so close." Camilo smiled tightly and I could tell he was trying to be excited for her. When we got to our seats, Dinorah let out a bona fide squeal. The seats *were* amazing, only feet away from the center of the stage. I attempted to lighten the mood with Camilo and put my hand around his waist, pulling him close to me. He was a little stiff, but he still managed to give me a lopsided smile.

"Are you going to dance with me tonight, Camilo?"

He shook his head, bemused. "In a theater?"

"Right here," I said gesturing to the aisle we were standing in. He laughed and I kissed him on the cheek before pulling away.

He looked around. "I'll admit these are pretty good seats, even if someone got them without asking first." His tone wasn't exactly friendly, but then he looked at his mom, who was chatting with the couple sitting next to her. "But my mom is in heaven right now, so thank you."

I bent down and kissed him again.

"So you're not pissed at me for getting the tickets?"

He narrowed his eyes at me again so that they were almost slits but this time the humor there was obvious. "You're hard to resist, especially when you're clearly doing it to impress my mom. Just chill out next time okay? You don't need to do any of that."

I nodded, a bit mollified. "I know. I just wanted to make this night amazing for you. I know how much your mom was looking forward to it."

He gave a weary sigh as he wrapped his arms around my waist.

"You do the most sometimes, Tom Hughes, but I'll be damned if I can stay pissed at you."

I grinned at him and then followed him to our seats, thinking about our plans for the rest of the night. The show would be over around nine and I'd made a nine-thirty reservation at a place in Little Italy in the Bronx close to Dinorah's apartment where we could have a late dinner. I turned to Camilo who had joined the conversation between his mom and the couple next to us.

"You guys are still up for a late dinner, right?"

He looked inquiringly at his mom who nodded. "Yes, that way we can get a chance to talk."

I smiled at how happy she looked. "Great, I'm looking forward to it."

Camilo had so much of his mother in his face, his eyes an exact copy of hers. He looked at her with such tenderness too.

He was such a good son, such a good man.

Soon the lights in the theater were turned down, and immediately we felt a buzz build around the room. It was a packed house and the anticipation for the show was palpable. After a moment the band stepped out and we could see the trio of backup singers also getting in place. The cheering as they set up was already deafening. But when the tall, lanky man in his trademark beard and fedora walked out onstage and got in front of the microphone every person in the theater was on their feet at once, yelling at the top of their lungs.

Without much of a preamble the first notes of a fast and furious merengue sounded across the theater. Accordion, percussions and every instrument on the stage fired off at once and the entire place lost it. Within seconds we were all dancing and singing along. I looked over at Camilo and his mom and saw they were both swaying to the music with huge smiles on their faces.

By the fourth or fifth song the aisles were packed with people dancing. I turned to Camilo and winked at him, cupping my hand around my mouth so I could talk to him over the music.

"Los Dominicanos no juegan, Camilo."

He laughed at my suggestive tone. "I know you fuckers don't play. Get ready Thomas Caonabo, because Dinorah is looking like she wants to step out onto that aisle with you."

I didn't hesitate and extended my hand to her as the first notes of "Visa Para un Sueño" sounded around the theater.

Visa for a dream. A song about people risking everything to come to the States to make their dreams come true, just like Dinorah and I had done. She and I got to the aisle by our seats and danced with the other couples who were singing and moving as Juan Luis serenaded us. This theater could have been lit with a match just from the energy in the room.

I noticed Camilo glancing at Dinorah and me dancing. Dinorah blew him a kiss as we spun around, and he threw his head back laughing.

Suddenly what I felt for Camilo slammed against me like a brick wall. The way that his eyes followed Dinorah and me as we danced. The softness there I knew only a precious few ever got to see, directed at me.

I felt so in love with him in that moment. I never wanted to let this man go.

Chapter Nineteen

Camilo

The show had been amazing. The music, the crowd, everything had been complete magic. I couldn't remember the last time I'd seen my mother so happy. Granted Tom had pissed me off by getting tickets I knew must have cost him over a thousand bucks a piece without asking, but it was hard to stay mad when what he'd done made my mom's whole year.

We were waiting for the valet service outside the theater to bring Tom's SUV around, and the plan was to eat at a restaurant on Arthur Avenue where he'd reserved a table. I hoped he hadn't done anything over the top. But it seemed that was the theme for the evening.

Once we were on the road, my mom immediately started gushing about the show.

"Juan Luis was so good and I can't believe how much we danced." She cackled. "Only Latinos can get away with that. I'm glad the show was at United Palace. We wouldn't be able to do that in Carnegie Hall." Tom and I both laughed at how giddy she sounded.

I teased Tom, who was focused on driving. "I don't know about that, Mama. Dominicans would at least try."

He nodded with a smug smile on his face. "That is correct."

From behind my mom piped up. "Cubans too. We can't stay sitting when there's good music playing." She sounded so damn happy. I saw her lean in from the back seat, her face turned toward Tom. "Thanks again for the amazing tickets, Tom. This has been one of the best nights I've had in a long time."

Tom gave me one of those looks that made my heart want to jump out of my chest before answering. "It's been a great night for me too, Dinorah. Thank you both so much for inviting me."

He reached for my hand, and I took it without hesitation.

We chatted about the songs and how great the band sounded as we drove the fifteen minutes to the restaurant. Before I knew it, Tom was pulling up to a place I'd never been to before. My mom, on the other hand was cooing in the backseat, apparently impressed with the location. I'd grown up pretty close to Little Italy, so we ate here all the time. Most of those places were family owned and low-key, but this restaurant looked high-end. I didn't even know you could do valet parking on Arthur Avenue.

We got out of the car and Tom handed off his keys before leading us into the restaurant. It was still pretty full for a 9:30 p.m. reservation, and it smelled great. My mom looked around with a big smile on her face.

"I'm so excited for this dinner, Tom. I've heard this place is really good and reservations are impossible to get," she said, beaming at him. "One of the doctors at the hospital was saying he brought his wife here for their anniversary and they had an amazing meal."

Tom nodded, looking a little too pleased with himself.
"I've been here a few times for business dinners,
and it's always been very good. Camilo said you liked
Italian, so I thought it would be a nice way to end the
evening." My mom nodded some more and kept looking at Tom like he was a real-life superhero. I, on the
other hand, was quietly trying to assess the situation.
The place was very fancy, but I reminded myself Tom
had a lot of money. The expensive restaurant wasn't
exactly surprising, so I tried to roll with it.

Tom gave the hostess his name and she walked us to
a table hidden away in a little alcove. It wasn't exactly a
private room, but we were definitely tucked away. My
hackles were going up a little, but I was determined to
keep an open mind.

Once we were seated a server came up to ask what
we'd like to drink. He passed around wine lists, but before we could even read them, Tom opened his mouth.
"We'll have a bottle of the Krug, the antipasti and the
grilled octopus."

The server took down the order and left without my
mom or I having a chance to even look at a menu. I was
really starting to get annoyed now, but kept my mouth
shut for the moment. Tom turned around and spoke to
my mom.

"The antipasto here is amazing and I love the octopus. I also ordered some champagne so we can toast
to our first night out." My mom was beaming, while I
tried to keep my temper in check. Where the fuck did
Tom get off ordering my food for me like I was a five
year old?

I glanced down at the wine list and looked for the
bottle he'd ordered. It was a three hundred dollar bot-

tle of wine. I lifted my face towards him and he must have seen through the pleasant smile I was trying for.

"Everything okay?"

"Fine, you didn't give me time to look through the menu though."

He at least seemed a little sheepish after my comment.

"Sorry, I just thought you guys would like to try everything. It's all delicious," he said reassuringly. And it probably was and I'd love it, but it wasn't the point. The point *was* that for the second time this evening Tom decided he was going to do whatever, without asking if I was okay with it. I just nodded without answering, as he gave me one of the smiles that usually made my knees weak, but just then it didn't quite take.

I really hoped I could get through this meal without letting my temper get the best of me.

Once the wine and the food came we all dug in, and like he promised everything *was* excellent. The grilled octopus was tender and there were these zucchini blossoms stuffed with mozzarella which were so good I almost swooned. My mom was having some kind of religious experience with whatever *she* was putting in her mouth, so again, I tried to roll with it.

When the server came back and announced more food was on its way, I was a little confused, since we still hadn't looked at a menu.

Tom must have seen the expression on my face. He cleared his throat, looking like he was about to give me another explanation I didn't want to hear. "So I prearranged to have the Chef's Table menu for the rest of the meal. I hope that's okay."

My face must have been more pissed off looking

than I thought, because his eyebrows dipped and his face blanched a bit. He seemed worried, and he fucking should be too.

Nothing pisses me off more than people making decisions for me. And today Tom seemed to be hell-bent on making even the most trivial ones for me tonight.

I looked at my mom, who was totally clueless and having the best time ever sipping three hundred dollar champagne, before giving him a very chilly answer.

"That's fine." I turned around and fished the wine from the ice bucket thing it was in and topped off my glass.

The rest of the food started coming soon. Everything smelled and look great, but I was so annoyed at Tom I could barely taste what I was eating. He tried multiple times to engage me in conversation, but all I gave were one or two word answers. My mom seemed a little worried about my silence, but I had zero fucks to give at this point.

Tom wanted to hijack the night so he could show off all his money? Then he could deal with me not being happy about it.

I kept pouring wine in my glass and staring at the wall until dinner ended. I knew I was acting like a brat, but I could not for the life of me turn my mood around. So, of course I drank too much, which made me feel messy and stupid.

Did I stop? No.

At this point I was committed to being shitty to Tom, no matter how badly things ended. I felt reckless and resentful as I watched him chatting with my mom. He was sitting there in his Tom Ford suit looking like Mr. "I Have Life by the Balls 24/7," meanwhile I was the hot mess getting wasted on the wine he was paying for. The only thing keeping me from telling him off and leaving was the fact that my mom was there, and she'd raised me better than that.

Once dinner was over we all walked out together, and it was clear the earlier mood was long gone. We got in the car and drove the short distance to my mom's building in complete silence. Before she got out she went around to give Tom a hug and big thank-you for the amazing night. I thawed a bit at this, but not nearly enough to take Tom off my shit list. As I walked my mom to her door she took my hand and looked up at me with worry.

"Camilo, why are you so upset?"

I looked up at the sky, hoping I'd find a fresh batch of patience there, because I was all out. I was a little drunk and upset, but I really didn't want to completely mess up this night for my mother.

I shrugged, as she stood there waiting for an answer. "Nada, Ma. I'm just tired and I'm a little annoyed at how Tom made all the decisions for us at dinner. I felt handled and I don't like that."

She nodded, knowing all too well how that type of shit went over with me. "I know, papi. I think he was just trying to show us a nice night out. Give him the benefit of the doubt, Milito. He may have gone a little overboard, but we still had a good evening."

I exhaled, still struggling with how frustrated I felt. "You're right. It was nice and I'm glad you enjoyed yourself."

"I did. I'm going up now, so we don't keep him waiting too long. Go easy on him okay, papi?"

I smiled at that. "Okay, Mama, I'll see you tomorrow."

I went back to the car once she was in the building, trying to let go of some of my bad mood. My mother was right. Tom had been trying to be nice. Even though he pissed me off, I could at least acknowledge he was coming from a good place.

We drove off and were on the road for a while before Tom flashed me a worried look.

"Camilo, did I do something wrong?"

I looked out the window and tried to organize my thoughts, so I didn't jump down his throat. The alcohol from dinner *had* gone to my head, and I knew how nasty I could get when I was drunk and pissed.

I sighed, trying to center myself, afraid I'd cross the line and say something I could not take back. "I understand you were trying to show my mom a nice evening, and she did have a lovely time, so thank you for that. However, I don't appreciate what you did tonight."

He didn't respond right away and I could tell he was trying to figure out where he'd fucked up.

"You mean the tickets? I'm sorry I got those without asking, but I figured it would be nice for all of us to sit together. In the end it turned out to be such a great show."

Okay. He was missing the point, so I was just going to have to explain it.

"The seats were great and the food was delicious. What I didn't like was the fact you made decisions *for me* all night long," I said in the calmest tone I could manage. "You even decided what I was going to eat and drink for fuck's sake. I know how to read a menu and order my own damn meal, Tom."

His face got serious, like he was getting pissed off too. This wasn't going to end well.

"I'm sorry, but I don't know what is so bad about me planning a nice evening for us." He was careful to use a neutral tone, but I could hear the frustration beneath it. "Sure, I did make some decisions without consulting you, but it worked out in the end. Right? Dinorah had a nice time."

I gripped my hands together on my lap, so I wouldn't start waving them all over the car.

"That's not the point though," I said leaning into the space between our seats. "The issue is that all of it could have *still* been amazing, if you'd asked me whether I wanted whatever fucking meal that isn't even on the menu you decided we would eat."

His face was stony, but I was on a roll and there was no stopping me now. "I don't like people making decisions for me, Tom. I don't like people taking away *my choices*." I tapped my chest as I spoke. "That is my problem, not the fucking grilled octopus you ordered."

"Okay." He said it like he was trying to talk down a raging tiger. "I understand. In the future I'll try to be mindful of that."

Tom stayed quiet for a minute like he was deciding whether or not he should say whatever he was thinking. We stayed like that for a few minutes until we were at the garage by his house. We parked and got out of the car with a heavy silence between us. Neither of us had spoken a word by the time we came up to his house.

"You could have said something at the restaurant, Camilo."

I stopped so I could look at him. Because if he wasn't

done, if he wanted to do this here, on the sidewalk...
okay we'd do it here.

"Said what?" I snarled at him, "Don't order my food
for me because I'm an adult and I can read? I thought
that was pretty fucking obvious."

He put his hands up, exasperation clear on his face.
"Okay I think we should probably have this conversa-
tion at another time when we're both in a better place.
I'm tired and we had some wine—"

Oh he did *not* just fucking imply this was about me
being a drunken mess. That "we" sounded a lot like
he meant to say "you" and I was so close to losing my
patience. I forced myself to stay where I was instead
of getting right up on his damn face like I wanted to.

"So now you're gaslighting me and making it about
me being a shitty drunk? You know what, Tom? I think
you're right. I think we just need to call this a night.
Nothing good is going to come out of this conversation." I turned to go get myself a cab home.

"Camilo, that's not what I meant." He sounded so
desperate I stopped to look at him, the panic on his
face making it seem like he finally realized how bad
he was fucking up with me. "I wanted this night to be
perfect and I clearly missed the mark. I'm sorry I didn't
consider how you'd feel about me making all these ar-
rangements without asking."

The genuine concern in his voice and the way he
cautiously held back from touching me diffused my
anger a little bit. I was still frustrated, but at least I felt
like he was finally hearing me. I was about to suggest
we go in when his phone rang with Maxwell's ringtone.

He looked annoyed as he pulled it out of his suit
jacket.

"I'm sorry but it could be about Libe."

I just waved my hand and turned to go up the steps to his house.

"Is something wrong, Maxwell?" he snapped out, his face looking more pissed by the second as he heard the answer.

"Then we can talk about it tomorrow, good night." He ended the call without another word and quickly ran up the steps to meet me at the front door. I could tell he wasn't sure if I was going to go in or not, but I glanced up at him and then nodded. He let go of a long breath that was pure relief as he went to open the door.

As soon as we stepped inside he grabbed me by the waist and bent his head so his mouth was against my neck. My body immediately softened to his touch, like the traitorous bitch it was when it came to Tom Hughes.

"I'm sorry, mi vida." He lifted his mouth to kiss me, and I let him because he was my kryptonite. How the fuck was I supposed to stay mad when he was calling me *his life*? Also after feeling pissed and scared things would blow up between us, I was feeling needy as fuck.

I pulled back after a moment, already pliable as putty in his hands. "I'm still pissed at you, and I'm dead tired of Maxwell interrupting shit for no good reason."

I could tell he was trying not to laugh as he nodded and nuzzled my neck. "I'll talk to him. He needs to know things are different now. I have someone in my life. I'm not available all the time like I used to be." He shook his head then, and I could see how spooked he was about our fight. "I don't want to do anything to mess with this, Camilo. I'm crazy about you. Even though I was off base by a mile tonight, what I wanted was for you and your mom to be able to enjoy your-selves without worrying about anything."

He grimaced at that, his eyes full of regret. "I hate that instead I made you feel uncomfortable." He looked so fucked up, like the fact that he'd done anything to upset me was physically paining him, and with that the last little bit of annoyance I was holding on to went completely out the window.

"You don't ever need to use your money to show me you care, Tom." I put my hand on his face, trying to smooth out the worry lines there. "I don't need that. What I want is you and your company, your presence and support. I can take care of myself. And even if I can't afford orchestra seats or the chef's table at a fancy restaurant, I'm still capable of going to a show and hav-ing a nice dinner." He hung his head then.

"I'm so sorry, mi vida."

"I know." I shook my head again, trying to gently press my point one last time. "I'm just not impressed by stuff like that." I hugged him tight and pushed up for a kiss. "This, you and me, is what I'm here for. Noth-ing else."

He nodded and gave me that rueful smile I knew only happened for me.

"Me too. This is all I want."

I tightened my arms around his neck and put my mouth close to his ear. "Let's get to bed then, but first I need water and some ibuprofen. Because I did have too much wine and don't want to wake up with a headache."

He laughed but at least had enough of a self-preser-vation instinct to refrain from saying "I told you so" as he followed me up the stairs.

"Water and Advil first, then maybe we could make up properly?"

I looked over my shoulder, trying and failing to give him a serious expression.

"Don't push your luck, Tom Hughes, you're still on thin ice."

The look he gave me let me know he was one-hundred-percent sure how solid the ground he stood on with me was.

Damn if I had it in me to argue.

Chapter Twenty

Tom

"How bad did you piss him off?"

I looked down at Priya, who was sitting like the Madonna with her new baby in her arms, before turning to roll my eyes at Sanjay.

"How did you already tell her about last night? I told you three minutes ago."

I'd come over to Sanjay and Priya's for lunch after Camilo went over to his mom's house. I'd only been here for ten minutes, and in that time Sanjay had somehow ratted me out to Priya.

He held his hands up in defeat. "She asked how the show went, when I brought her the tea."

"So you told her how I fucked up with Camilo instead? You were up here for like thirty seconds!"

Priya just looked on quietly, seemingly having a hell of a time watching us argue. When she finally spoke I could tell she was barely containing a laugh. "He didn't need to say anything. He told me with his eyes."

I rolled mine at this bald-faced lie, then spilled my guts anyways because she had the same effect on all three of us. "For your information we resolved the issue last night. He was upset because I bought tickets for him and his mom, so they could sit with me. And I get they already had tickets and it was a bit presumptuous of me to just get other ones." I felt like I wanted to hang my head for the next part, but resisted. I hadn't built a billion dollar company from nothing by cowering under pressure. "Then at dinner I pre-ordered the chef's table and he didn't like that either. Which now that I think about it, may have been a little heavy-handed, but I really didn't expect him to be that pissed."

All three of them gave me varying versions of exasperated sighs.

Henock was the first one to speak. "I don't think you're actually this clueless. You *must* know it can be a bit much when you do that."

Do what?

They must have seen the confusion on my face. Heni opened his mouth then closed it again like he wasn't sure where to start. When he did speak he was holding up both hands in a "calming down the angry lion" gesture. "It's just sometimes you forget to ask for people's opinions when you decide on a course of action. It's been useful when we needed to push hard in business, but in relationships it can be problematic." He averted his eyes as he finished that last part.

"How is this only coming up now?" I asked, flustered.

Since when was taking care of the people I loved an issue?

Heni pressed the palm of his hand on his forehead like he was trying to figure out why he even brought it up.

"Because so far, in business it was fine, and with Maxwell—"

Three throats cleared at once, and now I was sure I

was going to hear something that would make me feel like an ass.

"What?" I hissed as they all avoided eye contact. "What happened with Maxwell?"

I was feeling self-conscious and that usually led to me overthinking and overdoing. Heni and Sanjay were looking a little panicked probably afraid I was going to get into my feelings a*gain* and they would have to deal with it. Priya on the other hand looked ready to read me for filth.

"Tom, I expect this level of emotional mediocrity from these two." She flipped her hand towards Heni and Sanjay without even looking at them. They both balked, but she ignored them and kept talking. "But you're not this hopeless. You know you can be overbearing, especially when you get all protective."

"Well thanks for pointing out this major character flaw," I said in an aggrieved tone. "We've known each other for fifteen years, it could have come up sooner."

Priya rolled her eyes at my dramatic response. "Honestly for the most part, it's not an issue. You're such a level-headed and utterly decent human it rarely comes up." She smiled at me and then at Sanjay. "You're a protector. You take care of the people you love, and sometimes you can go a bit overboard. With Maxwell it wasn't a problem. He loved being taken care of."

She smiled again and this time there was a hint of pity in there, and it made me squirm.

"You guys worked longer than you should have, because you like to be the savior and Maxwell loved to be saved." She said this as if stating a well-known fact. The other two just nodded, so I guess this was common knowledge. "It sounds like with Camilo, you've met your match."

Despite the many levels of discomfort this conversation was bringing on I had to smile at the impressed way she said that.

"You need to give him space and not come on too strong. He wants to *want* you, not need you."

Both Sanjay and Henock nodded in agreement, but Henock spoke first.

"Just make sure you don't steamroll Camilo, even if your intentions are good."

I tried to laugh it off, but I still felt like an ass. "Okay I'll try and refrain from acting like too much of an overbearing asshole."

"We didn't say you were an asshole." Sanjay thought he was a fucking riot.

I leveled a finger in his direction. "You're not funny. But thanks for the advice. It *is* true I get carried away. I will try to dial it down when it comes to Camilo."

Priya stood up then, put the sleeping bundle in the bassinet by her bed and came over to squeeze my shoulder. "You're fine."

"Am I though?" I asked, genuinely worried that so far I'd completely misjudged what Camilo wanted from me. "I mean, this is my problem. This is how my marriage ended. I don't pay attention." I sat down on one of the armchairs in the room and Priya sat next to me. Sanjay and Henock sat on the small loveseat across from us.

"I'm doing it again. Seems like being selfish had less to do with Nuntius and more to do with me being a clueless pendejo."

"Thomas, stop," Sanjay said angling his head, his eyes trained on me. I knew that expression and it was the one I usually saw at work when he was done letting Heni and I set the trap and he came in for the kill. "You're not listening. You're letting your fragility—"

This got him a whispered "See how he listens to me?" from Priya, and I had to bite my lip not to smile, when he turned around to look at her then said, "Like I'd still be in one piece if I didn't."

"Tom. We are telling you we love you, and that we want to see you happy, for the long run. That means you may need to approach things a little differently. Will you get it right every time?"

Priya answered that question with a scoff. "None of you will."

Sanjay dipped his head, because that man knew how to keep himself in check when it counted.

I threw my arms up in defeat and leaned against the chair. "Okay. I will try to keep the entitled asshole side of me in check."

"If you don't, I'm sure Priya will get you back in working order," Heni quipped in a completely serious voice.

But Priya just laughed him off. "Oh no. I am pretty certain that Camilo has this situation handled."

I shook my head at her knowing grin and when I spoke it was the honest truth. "I'd protest, but from where I'm sitting, that sounds about right."

Camilo

"Well I'm certainly glad I dressed up for this," Ayako whispered as we walked up the street to Tom's house for his No-Turkey Thanksgiving dinner. Ayako was more than dressed up in a gorgeous green coat, underneath which she was wearing a purple sweater dress that hugged every one of her curves.

"You look great and you know it, stop shamelessly fishing for compliments."

She preened as we got to Tom's stoop, then hip checked me. "You don't look too bad yourself. Those pants are fire."

I ran a hand over my coat as we made our way up the steps. I did dress up a bit with my very tight burnt orange sweater, some slim trousers and ankle boots. "Tom pays extra attention the tighter my pants are, so I didn't want to disappoint the host."

Ayako just cackled at my shamelessness as we ascended the steps.

It'd been a couple of weeks since the day of the concert and things were going really well between us. Tom had been on his best behavior and going out of his way to show me he'd learned his lesson after that night, but it wasn't like I'd tried to stay mad at him or anything.

Now I was here to celebrate Thanksgiving Day with him and his friends, and I felt nervous, worried they wouldn't like me. Ayako bumped my hip again, yanking me out of my thoughts.

"Chicken's gonna get cold, babe." She pointed at the doorbell. "I also want to see this place on the inside," she said eagerly. "You so fancy with your millionaire. Give me the food, so he doesn't think I'm a total scrub." She gestured for me to hand over the Jerk Chicken we'd brought as a contribution. Store bought because we were tacky and bad planners.

I turned away so she couldn't reach the pan, clicking my tongue. "Stop, you don't need to show up with chicken, you're an invited guest."

She ignored my protest and leaned to hear what was going on inside the house. "How many people are at this thing? It sounds like a party!" We could hear music and a lot of people talking on the other side of the door.

"Tom said it would be like thirty or so. Most of the guests are his friends from grad school, so expect geeky snobs from MIT."

Ayako just rolled her eyes at my insult. "Right, like the snob you've been thirsting after for the last month and a half. You've lost all credibility with me when it comes to salty judgmental bullshit."

I was about to argue when the door opened and a very handsome, tall and slender man opened the door.

"Hi, you must be Camilo. I'm Henock." He looked at Ayako and gave her a subtle, but very appreciative look which she returned in kind. I cleared my throat and looked up at him.

"Hi, Henock, it's nice to meet you. This is my friend Ayako."

He extended his arms to take the chicken from me, but I shook my head and gestured for Ayako to say hello.

"Hi." All of a sudden she was shy.

"Nice to meet you both, please come in." He stepped aside to let us into the big study/den room right by the entrance. I hadn't been in here much since Tom and I usually hung out upstairs when I came over.

It was a huge room with lots of gorgeous furniture in grays and dark blues. I turned to Ayako and pointed at a huge painting on the far wall. It had to be eight feet by ten and it was an explosion of color. It was a street scene with lots of brown bodies in colorful clothing huddled together, walking along a wide street. It was a little chaotic and vibrant. Blue and white vans, donkeys and motorcycles all fought for space on the road alongside the people in the image. At this time of the day, with the sun rays slashing across the canvas, it seemed to come to life.

"Isn't it amazing?" I asked her. Ayako took it in, and nodded as we walked over to it to take a closer look. Henock came up with us, and explained.

"This is a scene from Addis Ababa. Tom got it a few years ago when he came on a trip home with me. I have one from the same artist at my place."

Ayako kept her eyes fixed on it and smiled. "It's beautiful."

Henock beamed at her. "Tom has amazing taste, and he's always on the lookout for good art when we travel. Well that and the art scene in Addis is pretty spectacular." He flashed us both with a million dollar smile that I know had to be having an effect on Ayako. "He's gotten Sanjay and me into buying art as well. We're going to run out of wall space soon."

Ayako twisted her mouth to the side and I could tell she was working hard to keep from teasing him. I should've known better than to expect her to bite her tongue. "I don't know about that, there's *a lot* of space here."

We all laughed as Henock got us moving again, and introduced us to a few of the people in the room. There had to be about twenty of them, all in their late thirties to early forties, and it was a very mixed crowd. Tom's friends were a very diverse group of people. After we walked further into the room where there was a huge sideboard laden with food.

"Servers are coming around with some snacks and the drinks are on the other side." Henock gestured at a bar area where an actual bartender was mixing drinks for people, and there were servers moving around the room carrying trays laden with food. Ayako and I gave each other a look when we realized we were at a Thanksgiving dinner with an entire serving staff. "They'll bring out the meal at around four. Tom is upstairs right now. I'll go let him know you're here."

He extended his hand to take the container Ayako was now holding. "Is this your dinner offering?" he asked, giving her a cheeky smile. He really was handsome. His eyes were huge and soulful with thick and incredibly long eyelashes. He had a thin face with sharp features, and a smile which would be very hard to resist. Ayako looked like she was liking all of it.

I cleared my throat, trying to break the eye-fucking happening between those two, when I saw Tom.

God, he looked so good, and the smile on his face when he saw me was like the sun. I ran my eyes over him as he made his way toward us. Repressing sighs was a real struggle when Tom was around. He was wearing another one of his cashmere sweaters, this one in a forest green. He had on jeans that looked amazing on his long legs and Ferragamo loafers.

When I got to his face our eyes locked and I felt that mildly sickening dip in my belly that only happened when Tom was close.

"Hey, you're here," he said, gathering me in his strong arms. Before I could respond he gave me a scorching kiss.

"Hi." I knew I sounded breathless, but who could blame me?

He squeezed me tight again, then turned around to give Ayako a hug and kiss combo. "Ayako, thanks for coming. It's good to see you again."

"Thank you for letting me come to your fancy party. I approve of everything happening here right now."

Tom chuckled at her giddy expression. "You're most welcome."

He looked at Henock then at me. "I see you've met the third member of our trio."

"I have."

Henock smiled at me and then lifted his arms, which were full of chicken. "We've been getting acquainted, and I have some questions for Camilo. I want to hear how it's been for him putting up with you all these weeks. Poor man," he teased. "First I'm going to go put this upstairs. Ayako, you want to come up to put away your coat and bag?"

She nodded with a little more enthusiasm than was warranted for what he'd suggested and hurried behind him. I called after her, "Hey, speedy! Could you take my damn coat too since you're already going up there?" She stopped and extended her arm without looking back. I shrugged it off and passed it to her before she walked away.

Tom and I stood there watching them leave. "How loose is Henock? Because this could end with people fucking in your coat closet," I asked completely serious.

Tom barked out a laugh. "He's pretty loose, and it wouldn't be the first time people have gotten up to something at this party. As a matter of fact," he said putting his arms around my waist and his mouth right up to my ear. "I could go and show you that thing in my room."

The only *thing* I could think of was his dick, and at the moment, seeing it sounded like a great idea. Tom nuzzled my neck and I put my arms around his. I wasn't about PDA all the time, but I wasn't against it either.

And hey, it was his house. If he wanted to get handsy while the place was full of people, I was totally here for it.

We pulled apart and he whispered in my ear again. "I don't know what it is, but when I'm with you I just can't stop touching." I playfully tugged on his ear and tried for some humor before I went up in flames from everything he was making me feel.

"Duh, because I'm irresistible, that's why."

His chuckle was completely dirty and this time he put his mouth so close to my ear his lips brushed my skin as he talked. "You have no idea how bad I want to drag you to my room right now."

I was a little breathless and about to suggest we go for it, when I heard some people walking up to us. A man's voice I didn't recognize came from somewhere next to us.

"Wow, you weren't kidding."

We pulled apart and found Priya smiling at us while she rocked a tiny baby in her arms. Next to her were two men I hadn't seen before.

Tom smiled at the trio and waved his hand between us as if he was about to make introductions. But before he had a chance to say anything the man who'd spoken earlier extended his hand to me.

"Nice to meet you, Camilo, I'm Teevrat. I'd heard about your magical powers, but this is beyond what even I could imagine."

I shook his hand and smiled, bemused. Teevrat was shorter than me and had lovely dark brown eyes. The man he was holding hands with was slightly taller and very blond.

"Nice to meet you, Teevrat. I'm not certain which

one of my magical powers you're referring to, but I'm sure you're right."

They all laughed and Teevrat wagged his finger at Tom. "Tom, I didn't even know you were aware hugging and kissing was allowed in public."

Tom blushed but didn't say anything. Just grabbed my hand looking happy as hell.

Interesting, so Tom wasn't usually like this with past lovers. I would need to digest that piece of information later, for now I turned my attention to the baby and Priya. She had her dressed up in an outfit in fall colors and she had tiny diamond studs in her ears. Priya was looking majestic with her long black hair falling around her shoulders, wearing a yellow and burgundy long sleeve maxi dress that looked striking against her dark brown skin.

"Priya, you look amazing and this little person is adorable."

She preened in that way only a new mother could. "Thank you." She turned the baby so I could see her better. "This is Kalyani, she's been pretty mellow so far. I'm not sure if I want to do this a second time though." We all laughed at her flustered expression.

After a second Priya pointed at Teevrat and the guy who hadn't said a word yet.

"Teevrat is my best friend from undergrad and the very quiet man with him is Marc. They're one of our No-Turkey Thanksgiving success stories. They met at the very first one."

Marc extended his hand to me, while Tom explained. "Marc was our classmate at MIT."

"I'm Austrian, so was one of the lucky few who got invited to the first No-Turkey day." He extended his hand to Teevrat who gripped it tight. The way they

looked at each other made me ache. I wanted that, someone that would look at me like I was the only one in the
room, even after years and years together.

Tom tightened his arm around my waist and I
glanced up to find him looking at me in a way that
made my maudlin thoughts evaporate. I *had* someone
that was looking at me like that right now, and I needed
to let myself enjoy it.

"This party is notorious for getting people together,"
he told me proudly.

"Sounds like this potluck is quite the scene."

Priya smiled mischievously. "Oh it's the salsa dancing afterwards when things usually get interesting."

"Salsa dancing?" I swiveled my head and stared at Tom.

He winked, obviously proud of himself for keeping me on my toes. "Oh did I forget to mention? After
people sleep off the food we usually put music on and
dance a bit."

Priya and Teevrat protested in unison. "A bit?"

"It's a major part of the event," Priya explained. "It
started with Tom and Enrique, over there." She pointed
at a Latinx looking guy at the other end of the room.
"Trying to teach us all salsa and merengue."

I turned to Tom again and smiled. "So am I finally
going to get a chance to dance with you since my mom
got you all to herself last time?"

The way he ran his eyes up and down my body made
it feel like the temperature in the room went up by
twenty degrees.

"I'm dancing with you all night, mi amor."

Chapter Twenty-One

Camilo

Once again Tom managed to make something that should have been regular, like Thanksgiving dinner, and made it a totally special and moving experience. When the food was finally brought out, it was like having dinner at the UN. There were dishes from all over the world either catered by different restaurants around the city or contributed by the guests. Everyone chatted about what they brought and shared memories about eating it with their families back home. It was a beautiful way to celebrate Thanksgiving.

Almost everyone in the room had either been born somewhere else or were the children of immigrants. It felt really special to be celebrating the most American of holidays hearing about different cultures and taking time to be thankful for the lives we had made here in the States. Ayako and I spent the meal exchanging looks as people offered their stories. Right now she was on the other side of the room talking to Priya, while picking desserts from the vast array set out on a table.

I was sitting on one of the sofas waiting for Tom who had offered to get some for us to share. I tried not to look too ridiculous as I stared at him, a plate full of desserts in one hand and two forks in the other. I smiled and patted the spot next to me on the couch. "Are you letting me have any of that?"

He sat down and pecked me on the cheek before handing me one of the forks.

"Of course. Here." He pressed closer and moved the plate so it was right between us. "Which one do you want to try first?"

Everything on the plate looked delicious and delicate. There was a cake I recognized from Lady M's. It was layered chocolate cake with a hazelnut filling.

I pointed to it with my fork. "That one."

He immediately cut a piece of it, and lifted it up to my mouth. "May I?"

As I chewed I cut a piece of cake and offered it to him.

Tom kissed my temple and then accepted a bite of the cake from me.

"Mmm that's pretty good," he said appreciatively, and because my mind was in the gutter all the time when I was with Tom, I immediately thought of the last time I'd heard him moaning like that.

"You're looking flustered, mi amor."

"Don't even think about it. I am not acting all skanky and letting you have your way with me with the house full of people."

He actually pouted. "But you were up for it before. We have time before the dancing, no one will even notice we're gone."

My clothes were going to burn right off my body if he kept looking at me like that. "Stop it, Tom," I pleaded. "That was before I actually *met* your friends, and was practically in tears with that speech Marc gave before we ate."

I sighed, putting the plate on the table, as he looked at me intently. I didn't even know where I was going with this. "I just don't want to ruin tonight."

He immediately got closer and put his arms around me. "That's impossible."

"You just say that because you want me to put out later."

Without answering he pressed a kiss to my mouth, his tongue curling into mine making me want to shove the damn cake plate out of the way and let him fuck me right here. When he pulled away that dirty grin of his made an appearance. "I think that part of the evening has been secured."

"Smug toppy bastard." My attempt to sound put off failed miserably.

"You know you like it." There it was again, that thing that Tom did where he made me feel that being exactly me, would never ever be anything other than perfect.

The dancing part of the evening was getting on its way.

About an hour ago Priya stood up and announced it was time to make space for dancing, and people started moving furniture to clear the area. It was a trip to see all these grown ass people excitedly moving furniture so they could dance at a house party. At the moment, Sanjay, who was the official DJ and took his role so seriously it was hysterical, was playing some soft merengue from the little booth he'd set up for himself by the bar.

Ayako and I were standing on the periphery of the designated dance area people watching and sipping from wineglasses when she leaned down to whisper in my ear, "Thanks for inviting me today, friend."

I gave her some side-eye and teased her a little. "I didn't send Henock after you. You can take full credit for that."

She laughed and waved me off, but I could see a flush creeping across her cheeks. "That was just playing, and stop it, let me express my gratitude on this day of thanks, asshole. Today has been amazing and special. So, *thank you*."

"Fine, you're welcome." I grumbled.

"You're such an ass." Her amusement at my crankiness was a sign that she was either tipsy or really having a good time. When her face went all soft, I braced for it. "It's also been incredible to see you and Tom together. You look so happy with him, Milo, and the way he looks at you." She actually clutched at her chest, she was so corny. "I'm so happy for you. No one deserves it more."

Ayako's words made me emotional again. No matter how much I griped, it *had* been special to spend the day around the family Tom had made for himself since he'd come to the States. The life he'd built.

It was a life to be proud of.

He was a man to be proud of, and being a part of it made me feel so fortunate. Still I had to pivot this conversation or tears were going to happen. "Calm your tits, woman. We've barely been dating for six weeks, ain't nobody getting married."

She rolled her eyes at me and took another sip of her wine. "Whatever, but if I'm not a bridesmaid, there will be blood."

I stuck my tongue out at her as I looked around, hoping Tom was not within earshot of this conversation. "You're ridiculous."

She was about to say something when Juanpa strolled up, holding a drink in his hand with a huge grin on his face. He's shown up a half hour ago after sending like ten texts saying he needed an excuse to get out of his parents' house.

He was tricked out in his BX best tonight. Huge studs on his ears, a black sweatshirt which looked totally regular, but probably cost three hundred dollars, and tight camo pants with brand new black Tims on his feet. All topped with the ever present fitted Yankees hat on his head.

Who cared we were inside and it was dark out?

"Yoooo, your man's the GOAT." He took a sip of whatever he was holding and smacked his lips like a total jackass. "They're pouring Zacapa Centenario like it's water at the bar." He gave me a playful grin, leaned down to fake whisper by my head, "If you're having second thoughts about what you got going on here, let me know, son. Because I *will* hit that." He paused for emphasis in between each of the last four words.

Instead of answering I just narrowed my eyes and stretched my hand to pinch him hard on the arm. He yelped and jumped back.

"Ow, damn. Why you so aggressive, Camilo?"

I just rolled my eyes at him. So fucking extra. "Like anyone who has access to all this," I said, running my hands over the front of my very well fitting sweater, "would fuck with your whiny ass, Juan Pablo."

Juanpa just glared at us while he switched the glass to his other hand so he could keep drinking *and* rub where I'd pinched him at the same time.

I could barely control my laughter, and Ayako was literally clutching her side behind J.

Suddenly I felt arms wrap around my waist from behind. Tom kissed my ear and I could feel the smile on his face, pressing against it.

He looked up at Juanpa and shook his head. "Sorry, man." He tightened his arms, as he spoke. "I got all I need right here."

Juan Pablo's face softened at that and he lifted his glass to Tom before taking another sip of his Zacapa.

All he needed.

My heart.

Chapter Twenty-Two

Camilo

How was this my life? It was the Saturday morning after Thanksgiving and I was in Tom's bed still panting from what had been the most epic morning sex of my life and waiting for him to bring me breakfast.

After Thanksgiving I'd just…stayed. We'd spent Friday eating leftovers, watching movies, talking and making love. We'd ventured out in the afternoon and gone down to Central Park for a walk, but mostly we'd been content in our cocoon. I felt so utterly and completely happy, it scared me.

I sat there wondering when the other shoe would drop, because I knew it was a matter of time before one of us fucked up somehow. Nothing could be this perfect. I didn't want to be pessimistic or dramatic, but I had enough of a frame of reference to know this wouldn't last. And it was terrifying, because I knew losing Tom would hurt more than anything had before.

I tried to shake my negative thoughts off and enjoy the fact I was in this incredibly huge and comfortable bed, freshly fucked and waiting for my millionaire boyfriend to bring me coffee, but the anxiousness still crept in.

I was still fretting when Tom walked in with a tray laden with coffee mugs and toast, like the embodiment of fucking perfection. I started to get up so I could help, but he shook his head.

"No, corazón, don't get up." He was calling me his heart now. Low-key like, he was calling me *his heart*. I wasn't going to make a thing out of it and swoon or anything, but I almost wanted to take out my phone and record him.

I obediently stayed in bed as he handed me a cup of steaming coffee. I took a sip then groaned because it was delicious. "Is there anything you don't do perfectly?"

He grimaced as he grabbed his own cup. "Too many to name."

He got in bed and reached over for the plate full of buttered toast he'd brought up. I took a piece and shook my head before taking a bite.

"I don't believe it, give me one example."

"Well since we've already had our first fight, I know you're very aware of some of my shortcomings." I nodded once, conceding him the point, but didn't interrupt. "I also don't exactly have the best track record when it comes to relationships. I *am* divorced."

I picked at my toast as I answered him. "Neither do I. My relationships tend to have very disappointing endings."

He stared at me in genuine disbelief. "I can't imagine you disappointing anyone."

I wasn't going to swoon.

"You're just riding the high from the blow job I just gave you." I went for levity, because I knew we were about to get deep, and I had to pace myself on this before I confessed every single one of my many, *many* feelings for him. "I mean I know I have mad skills, but I'm not *that* good."

His response was a gentle bite on my shoulder. When he was done, he licked the spot where his teeth had been. I shivered so hard I had to hold out my coffee so I didn't spill it. We just sat there in silence, waiting for the heat of the last few seconds to diffuse.

Tom eventually broke the silence. "I beg to differ. But what I mean is you're so honest and real, Camilo." He turned so we were facing each other, and I almost wanted to hide from the awe in his voice. "You don't hide what you feel or say something you don't mean. You're so open. When I'm with you I feel known. Like you see *all* of me." He shook his head like he was getting his thoughts in order, while I drank my coffee worried I was nowhere ready for where this conversation seemed to be going.

"I don't mean Maxwell didn't know me, he did. In some ways." He pushed a knee against his chest as he talked, his eyes full of whatever he was remembering. "Maxwell's parents are wealthy. Even though they're great people, their perception of the world is still filtered through all of that." His face got serious, obviously still struggling to articulate his thoughts. "I look like them," he said lifting a shoulder. "I walked in and I was this person who belonged to their world. But I didn't, not really, and instead of saying that, of letting them know who I was, I just went with it. For them I was just Tom Hughes—no Gomez." He pursed his lips and I could feel the frustration coming off him.

"I don't think I'm explaining myself very well."

I took our coffee mugs and put them on the table by

the bed, then moved so I was sitting up and he had his back against me. He was so big, his torso covered me completely and it felt perfect.

I ran my hands over his chest as I spoke. "I get what you're saying. They only knew the part of you they could see."

He dipped his head to kiss my hand. "I think that's part of the reason I pulled away from Maxwell in the end. I lost myself in those years. I was so immersed in the business, and so much of that world required I be this guy. It was exhausting and when I came home, the mask had to stay on for Maxwell too. That's why the ease I feel with you means so much. You make me want to stop compromising and just *be*."

I turned his face so I could kiss him and thought of all the ways in which I'd tried so hard to be someone else in my relationships. In college the guys would tease me and say I did this "oasis" thing whenever I was into a guy, let him only see the parts that I thought would go over well, and then hid everything else. I tried to refrain from ever making waves. Never giving my opinion to the person I was dating to avoid conflict, to the point where I was almost an inanimate object. It was horrible and I ended up hating myself and everyone I dated the entire four years.

"That's the funny thing with you, Tom. You're the first guy I've ever really been *me* with. I always try to smooth my edges, not be so intense all the time." I grimaced, thinking of some of those relationships and how hard I tried to please people who weren't worth it. "I had a guy tell me once I would be the perfect boyfriend if I kept my answers to just yes or no."

Tom just shook his head then muttered, "Asshole."

I chuckled, kissing the top of his head. "Thanks. But to be fair, I am too much sometimes, too opinionated. I get worked up and angry about things I feel are unfair, and I need to be okay with not everyone being the same level of outraged as me all the time. It's not fair to expect that."

The expression on his face when he looked up at me was one of genuine confusion. "I get that, but it doesn't mean you need to repress who you are. I love hearing you fired up and pissed. Other than Libe, I'd forgotten what it was like to have someone in my life who made me want to try and be better to myself, so I could be good for them."

That was the moment. *Those* were the words.

I felt my heart in my temples from the swell of emotion. From the minute Tom and I had started this, I'd wondered what could I possibly do or add to this man's life. He seemed to have everything, what value could I add to someone who already had so much? And now I knew.

I gave him what he gave me, the freedom to be seen exactly as I was and be loved for it, not *in spite* of it.

I moved again so that I could sit in front of him, be face-to-face. "I never thought it would be being myself." He looked at me like he couldn't understand what I was saying and I laughed. "I'm too abrasive, even with my best friends, who love me unconditionally, who would do *anything for me*."

He shook his head like that was the most absurd thing he'd ever heard and I loved him so much for it. "You don't need to do anything, mi vida, just keep being you, that's all I need."

The look on his face in that moment was everything.

I moved closer. He ended up sitting with his back to the headboard, legs spread open under the sheets. We were in our underwear, but I could see he was starting to harden, and as I ran a hand over my cock he licked his lips, very much on the same page.

"So this conversation has been incredible and I totally want to get back to it, but I really want to fuck. Like now."

Tom's hand was already pushing down my briefs and I was working my way up his neck with my tongue when he panted, "But I thought we were making heart-felt confessions on how we're perfect for each other."

I nodded frantically as I tried very hard to come up with an answer. "Yes we were, and I'm *very* moved and really restraining myself from saying all kinds of shit that's entirely too early to say. For now, just know I am very grateful to be here with you."

He didn't answer, just held me tight as we sank down onto his bed, tangled in each other.

Tom

"M'ijo?" I smiled at my mom's question and everything she could say in one word.

"Is everything okay? Where's Libe? This is a surprise."

"Everything's good, Ma. I got you on Bluetooth. I just dropped off Libe at Max's for the weekend."

She clicked her tongue before answering. "Ay, Tommy, why didn't you call me when my baby was in the car?"

I grinned at her reproachful tone. Libe was the only

grandchild on both sides and she was a hot commodity for her abuelos.

"Sorry, Mami. We'll give you a call on Sunday night when she's back home." I cleared my throat then, a little stumped on how to proceed. It would be Christmas in two weeks and since I'd been going home to the DR religiously for the past ten years I figured I needed to actually give my mother a call to let her know that was not happening this year.

"¿Que pasa, Tommy? Are you sure everything's okay?"

I needed to get it out, because she was one more awkward silence away from freaking out on me.

"Everything's good, Mami," I said placatingly. "Actually that's why I'm calling." I smiled, thinking of Camilo's face when I told him I wasn't going to the DR for Christmas and tried to act like it was no big deal. He pinned me with those gorgeous gray eyes and said, "I did tell you my best friend's Dominican, right? I know for a fact they start planning the trip to the DR for next Christmas on the plane home in January. So get off that 'no big' bullshit you're on, Thomas Caonabo."

After I'd grabbed him and kissed the saltiness out of him, I'd had to 'fess up to the fact that I wanted to be here with him. He didn't fawn all over me for it, but I did notice a lot of secret smiles coming my way for the rest of that day.

"Tommy." My mom's genuinely confused tone finally got me out of my daydreaming and I blurted it out.

"Libe and I won't make it this Navidad. We're going to spend it here in New York."

My mother almost said something then stopped. When she finally spoke, it was straight to the point.

"So things are going well with your new man, then?" I could hear the smile in her voice and I shook my head, because my mother never changed. She wanted her children "fairy-tale happy"—nothing less would do.

"Things are very good, Mami, and I'd like to be here for the holidays so I can spend time with him."

She made an "mmhm" sound, like she had my number. "Well you've been holding that card close to your chest, querido. Then again I can't remember you ever calling me to tell me about someone. You usually just fall into things and let us know after the fact." Her tone wasn't even disapproving, just matter of fact. And she was right, in my relationships things happened almost by osmosis. Not Camilo, he demanded my attention at every step. There was no playbook for him, he was like no one else and he wasn't trying to be.

When my mother spoke again her tone told me that she knew I was in unknown territory. "I'm happy that you've finally met someone you're willing to do things differently for."

That was an interesting choice of words and very similar to the lecture I'd gotten from Priya and the guys.

"He isn't like anyone I've ever been with."

She laughed then and it was that sound that usually came before a loving but firm "I told you so."

"Well some people come to your life to change it, baby. Just ask that gringo I've had on the right side of my bed for forty-two years."

I shook my head at that and grinned as I answered. "When you're right, you're right, Mami."

"Of course, I'm right." The "as always" went unsaid. "So tell me, when can I meet him?"

This time the throat clearing was legitimate. "Most

likely when you come and see the shelter renovation. He's um, he's with the agency we decided on."

"Ay m'ijo, this man must really be something because you never mix business with your personal life. What's his name?"

"Camilo." Even I could hear the adoration in my voice.

"Tommy, Tommy, te agarro el Camilo," she said brimming with humor. "I think you finally got caught, son."

"I know I did." There wasn't a hint of reservation or trepidation in that answer.

Chapter Twenty-Three

Camilo

I ended the call with my mom feeling real worry for the first time since she'd started this rough patch with her depression. I was at Tom's, and it was early afternoon on Christmas Eve. I'd stopped in to hang out with him and Libe before I went to pick her up. We had plans to be at Juanpa's place for Nochebuena dinner, but when I'd called her to let her know I was heading to her place, she said she wasn't feeling well and wanted to stay home.

As I sat there thinking about what to do, Tom walked into the living room from putting Libe down for a nap.

"Something wrong with Dinorah?"

I glanced up at him, smiling despite my worry. Tom never resented my checking on my mom, or the time I spent with her. On the contrary, he told me again and again how much he loved how close we were. By now, he also knew me well enough to realize if there was anything amiss.

"My mom isn't feeling up to going to Juanpa's for dinner." I ran my hands over my face, trying to shake off some of the worry. "She was doing so well for the couple weeks after the concert, but since Thanksgiving she's been down again. She keeps saying she just needs to rest, but she's depressed. It's a real thing and she can't just snap out of it." The frustration of watching my mother get worse and worse without being able to do anything for her, was starting to get to me.

"I wish she would *see* someone, but it's like pulling teeth talking to her about this stuff. I thought we were getting somewhere in October with that group, but she stopped going after two or three sessions." I closed my eyes and tried to calm down. Going to see my mom while I was upset too was not going to help matters.

Tom sat down next to me and just his proximity did a lot to ease my nerves. "Maybe she'd do better with a one-on-one therapist. It's hard opening up to strangers like that."

I lifted a shoulder at a loss of what if anything could help. "She was the one that said the group would be better, but when it came time to go she said she couldn't make the times work with her schedule. She's so fucking smart and strong, but so stubborn when it comes to admitting she needs help."

"Sounds like someone I know." He said it in a teasing tone, which I knew was his way of diffusing the situation.

"Shut up. I ask for help all the time," I said, grateful for his attempt at humor.

He put his arm around my shoulder and pulled me to him. "Next time you do it take a video so I can see it for myself."

"Very funny. Seriously though, I don't know what to do with her. It's not good for her to be cooped up in her apartment all the time. I told her we could stay in tonight, but we have to go out and do *something* for Christmas."

Tom widened his eyes and gave me a hopeful smile, like he had just come up with the best idea ever.

"Why don't you bring her when you come tomorrow? It'll just be us. Priya and Sanjay will come for a bit, but they're flying out in the afternoon to visit his parents in Ohio. I would tell you to come tonight, I'm going to Teevrat and Marc's, but there will be a lot of people so it might not work if she's not up for being in a big crowd. I didn't exactly plan ahead this year, otherwise I would have hosted something myself."

His tone was casual, but I knew it had nothing to do with him being a bad planner. He usually went to the DR for Christmas with Libe, but decided to stay here at the last minute. For me. Tom was here for me, and maybe I could let him help for a change.

"I could suggest that." The more I thought about it, the more it seemed like a great idea. My mom would love meeting Libe, and it would be nice to have her with me instead of home alone.

After a minute I moved over a little so I could rest my head on his shoulder. He kissed my forehead before scooping me up so I was practically on his lap.

"Good." His stepping up like this was making me weak with relief and gratitude.

"Libe will have even more people to give her undivided attention, and I'll get to see Dinorah again. I actually got a little gift for her."

I narrowed my eyes at him at the mention of a gift, and he held up his hands. "I stayed within your price limit for her gift too!" I'd put my foot down on gift giving limits, because my budget was not huge, and I knew how extra he could get.

"Thank you."

"It'll be nice to be together tomorrow. I hope it helps your mom to come and share the day with us." He pulled me even tighter, brushing kisses on my brow, and all I wanted was to stay right there. I closed my eyes, hoping to rest a few minutes before going over to my mom's. "Me too."

"Feliz Navidad, Camilo!" I was about to take the stairs up to the apartment when I saw Antonio, the super of my mom's building, walking towards me. I liked Antonio, he'd been working here for like fifteen years and was the most helpful guy in the world, especially when it came to my mom. I'd always suspected he had a bit of a crush on her.

"Hey, Antonio. Feliz Navidad," I said, genuinely happy to see him. He playfully slapped my attempt at a handshake away and gave me a one-armed hug and a pat on the back.

"Are you here to spend Nochebuena with Dinorah?" he asked glancing up the stairs as if he expected to see her there. I nodded and looked up at my mom's door, which I immediately noticed didn't have the usual wreath this year.

"Yeah, I am."

He made a sound of approval and then stepped a little closer to me, his voice barely above a whisper when he spoke. "Good. Listen, Camilo. I don't want to worry you or anything, but have you guys figured out what you're going to do about the rent increase?"

Rent increase?

I shook my head in confusion. "Mama hasn't said anything about her rent going up."

Antonio grimaced and muttered a curse. "Your mother is a stubborn woman." He held up his hands, like he knew he was about to jump deep into chisme territory, but was going in anyway. "You know how much I care about Dinorah, and I don't want her to lose her apartment to this mess."

Lose her apartment?

I opened my mouth to ask some questions, but before I could say anything, Antonio finished filling me in. "She's always been a great tenant. If the owners heard I'm even talking about this I would have problems."

"Okay now, you're really worrying me," I said, already feeling the tension settle on my shoulders and neck.

He looked around again and started talking again in a really low voice. "About ten months ago the owners sent out a letter saying they were going to increase the rent because of some of the 'capital improvements' they'd done to the building." He made air quotes for the *improvements* part.

"You know all the stuff they did in the common areas and the new elevator."

I nodded, still too stunned to talk.

"The increase wasn't the same for everyone, but for some people it got up to a few hundred dollars more per month. The tenants were pissed, and said they weren't going to pay it. So the management backed off and said they'd give people a year to get it together and pay it back. The deadline is coming up soon." His brows dipped then, and I could tell he was worried about my mom. "Make sure Dinorah gets up to date on it."

He lowered his head for this part and his voice was so low I could barely hear him. "What they want is for people to start leaving those rent stabilized apartments, so they can lease them out for twice as much. You didn't hear any of this from me, of course."

It was just like my mother to "forget" to tell something like this.

"I had no idea any of this was going on. Thanks for telling me, Antonio. I'll talk to her about it today."

I was so fucking tired of this gentrification shit. Where were people supposed to go? My mother had been in this apartment for twenty years, and now she was supposed to leave and go where? My head was pounding just thinking of how much back rent she'd let accumulate for an entire year.

"No problem, I know she's going to be pissed at me." He gave me a rueful smile. "But this is some bullshit they're pulling here. Since the old owner died and his kids took over, this place has gone to hell." He shoved his hands into his pockets, looking disgusted. I didn't even know what to say. I gave him a last wave as I walked up the stairs to my mom's place.

I had no clue how much her increase had been, but it was probably adding up fast.

I got to the apartment and opened the door, and found my mom sitting in her dark living room smoking a cigarette. I noticed she was still wearing her pajamas. My mom sitting in the dark in her pajamas at 2:00 p.m. on Christmas Eve was not good.

"Hey, Mama. How are we doing today?"

She'd put out her cigarette when I walked through the door and stood up as I got to the couch.

"Hola, papi." At least she sounded glad to see me. I went over and hugged her. She felt thinner.

I pulled back to get a good look at her. "Did you eat? I got some stuff to make us some sandwiches," I said lifting the bag of food I'd brought with me. She shook her head and made like she was heading to the kitchen.

"I'll make them."

I stopped her and pulled her to the stools by the counter.

"Why don't you sit here and keep me company while I fix them?" Without a word she sat down. That, more than anything else, put me on high alert. My mom letting me wait on her without putting up a fight was a red flag.

I was thinking of a way to bring up the thing about the rent increase without getting her worked up. I figured I could start with the bad news, and then throw in the invite to Tom's to get her back in a good place. Since the night at the concert she hadn't stopped going on and on about how much she liked him and how perfect he was for me.

I started getting stuff out to make the sandwiches. I was going to make "Cubans" which had roasted pork, ham, Gouda cheese and pickles on a baguette. They were my mom's favorite, so at least she'd have a treat while we discussed all the shit going on in her life. I was not one for beating around the bush, so I got right into it.

"Mama, I ran into Antonio downstairs." She gave me a look like she knew where the conversation was going, but she stayed quiet. "Why didn't you tell me about the rent increase?"

She lifted her shoulder and reached for the cigarettes on the counter. "Those cabrones, they're getting subsidies to replace old elevators and fix up hallways and then they pass us the bill." I handed her a glass of passion fruit juice from the fridge and she took a tiny sip before pushing it away. I withheld a sigh.

"They're increasing my rent by eighty dollars for each room." I did quick math in my head and my stomach sank. "I have two bedrooms. With the kitchen, living room and bathroom that's four hundred dollars more every month. How am I going to pay for that? I've been in this building for twenty-one years and haven't been late with my rent once. Not even when we were really struggling that first year we came up from Florida, and I was paying back all those credit cards that man took out in my name."

I winced at the mention of Ramon, because whenever we had a difficult conversation, that fucker always had to come up.

"I'm just so tired, Milito." She sighed and closed her eyes. "I requested an unpaid leave at work, for right after the New Year. It's been so stressful there," she said, rubbing her temples. "I haven't been doing great emotionally either. I felt like I was going to lose my mind if I didn't take some time off. I was hoping to maybe go see someone, or try one of the groups for real this time."

The relief I felt from hearing her actually say it made me weak.

"I know I need some help. It's like these shadows have been slowly creeping in, and now they've been with me too long. I need to let some sunshine in." She looked up at me then. "It bothers me that I'm so down all the time. I can't even be with friends." She looked over at the wedding photo of her and my dad she had on the mantel.

I left the food on the counter and came to put my arm around her, when I saw her eyes fill with tears. "Oh, Mama."

"Your daddy would have turned sixty-five this coming March." She smiled as a fat tear rolled down her face. "He always said as soon as he turned sixty-five and retired he was going to take me on a trip up the coast, and bring me to New York City. Who would have thought I'd end up here without him? So far from where we started our family." Her voice gave out after that and I wiped her eyes, pulling her closer. I just listened, letting her finally say the things she hadn't been able to in so long.

"I haven't seen his grave in twenty-one years. That man robbed me of so much time, and I'm weary, Milito." She looked up at me. "I was hoping to go down and see him during my leave, maybe take the train down there."

Shit.

There was no way I could take time off to go with my mom to Florida until the renovation at the shelter was done and that wouldn't be until March. I had to be here until everything was finished, for the off chance that something could go wrong. I also couldn't risk my super inappropriate relationship with Tom coming out in the wash.

"Mama, I'll go with you if you want to see Dad's grave. But I can't take time off until the shelter's done. We can go later in the spring."

She shook her head. "You don't need to do that. I can do it on my own. You're always watching out for me, papi, protecting me. I'm the parent here, aren't I?"

She was trying for humor, but I could tell she was back to feeling guilty.

"Mama, you have always loved me unconditionally. Even when you couldn't love yourself, you loved me. Please don't say things like that okay? We're a team, tu y yo, Mama."

She touched my face and smiled. "You're so strong and happy these days. Tom is good for you. You look like a man who's well loved."

I kissed my mom on the cheek. "He's a good man, but don't change the subject, Mama."

She pursed her lips like she was about to complain, but I pushed through.

"No no no. En serio. I think you taking leave is great and about time. I can call up my friend who did the intake with you and ask if they have any groups starting in January. I also know a few therapists who would be awesome for you. I'm one hundred percent in support of this plan."

I placed our sandwiches on the counter and came around to sit with her. "Between our savings we can probably take care of some of the balance for the rent increase, and I can pay your rent while you're off. The rest we'll figure out together." She was about to protest, but I held up my hand. "No, mujer, don't you shake your head at me. You deserve this and I'll make it happen for you. You've done so much for me. Please, Mama, let me do this for you."

I knew I'd worn her down when she sagged against the chair and threw her hands up.

"Esta bien. How did you get so stubborn?" I made a face at her, and we both laughed.

"Ma, I'm so happy you're doing this." I squeezed

her hand, feeling hopeful about her taking some time to take care of herself for a change.

"I need it. I hope I can make the best of it."

"I know you will." I smiled, knowing she would love the next part of the conversation.

"So your favorite Dominican millionaire asked if you would like to join him and his child for Christmas brunch tomorrow." She perked right up at that. "Since I was already planning to go there, he asked if you'd like to come too. It'll be pretty low-key, just the four of us, and maybe a short visit with his best friend and his wife who live next door."

By the time I finished my mom was beaming and nodding like crazy, then she clutched her head. "I have to go wash my hair and you need to help me blow dry it if we're going to Tom's for brunch. What should I wear?"

I laughed at her sudden burst of energy. "Calmate, mujer, it's just brunch at my boyfriend's house."

She waved me off and put her sandwich down. "Come on, help me pick out something."

"Why don't we eat first and then we can work on your makeover?" She smiled then and grabbed her sandwich, taking a big bite.

"Milito, hijo, these are so nice. You make them just like I taught you."

Her mood was already turning and I felt like I had a ton of bricks lifted off my shoulders.

I was determined to make sure she could have the time she needed to heal, no matter what I had to do to make it happen.

Chapter Twenty-Four

Tom

"I'll get it! I'll get it!"

I heard little feet running down the stairs and prayed Libe didn't break her neck rushing to open the door for Camilo and his mom. She'd been pacing in front of the Christmas tree downstairs like a crazed chipmunk for hours, waiting until we were all together and she could open the rest of her presents. She'd gotten to open a couple right after she woke up, but a few others had been sitting under the tree for the past two hours, and she was about to blow a gasket.

"Mi Milo is here, Daddy!" she yelled, as she saw me coming down the stairs. She'd started calling him "My Milo" a couple of weeks ago. If I hadn't already been absolutely sure Camilo was the one, the way my kid looked at him whenever he was around would have sealed the deal.

I came down the stairs and saw Camilo and Dinorah walking in. He was wearing a burgundy sweater with his usual skinny jeans and ankle boots. He had his hair in a French braid and looked relaxed walking in with a shopping bag packed with gifts.

Dinorah took off her parka and I saw she was wearing a green sweater to match Camilo's red one. He looked at her outfit and rolled his eyes. Like I couldn't tell he thought she was adorable.

Libe was standing back, trying to figure out how to approach the new adult in her space, but Dinorah immediately knelt down and extended her hand. She held a little Chewbacca toy.

"Hi, Libertad. I'm so happy to meet you, I'm Milo's mom." She looked up at me and winked, as Libe took the small plush doll and squeezed it against her chest. "He told me all about you. He said you're a big fan of Star Wars." Libertad was nodding so hard I thought she was going to snap her neck.

"Yes! I love Star Wars. I was Yoda for Halloween this year and I have a purple lightsaber. You want to see it?" She ran over to me, started to show me the Chewbacca then revised the plan and ran back to Dinorah.

"Do you want to come to my playroom? I have my toys there and I can show you." Then she widened her eyes, ran back to me, and signaled for me to bend down, so she could tell me something. "Daddy, we need to hurry up this presents time, because Dinorah said she needs to go and play with me *right now*." She whispered the last two words with such urgency that none of us could keep a straight face.

I nodded as seriously as I could. "Well we don't want to keep Dinorah from her playtime." I signaled for them to follow us to the study and as we walked I grabbed Camilo by the waist and bent down to kiss him. He beamed at me.

"Feliz Navidad, Tom."

I smiled right back, my heart so full I had to take a moment just to look at him. "Feliz Navidad, amor."

As soon as we sat down, Libe started dragging the gifts out from under the tree.

"Okay I got your gift, Camilo," she said, out of breath as she ran back for another box. "Daddy! Yours is littler because I ran out of the white stuff." She gave me a thumbs-up at this. "But don't worry, it's really great."

Camilo and Dinorah could barely hold in their amusement. She got the last two presents from under the tree in one run then slumped next to where I was sitting and whispered, "Did we get something for Camilo's mom?"

My answer was as stern as I could manage. "Si, Libertad. Sientate." She sat down in the center of the circle of gifts she'd made. "Okay you can start opening yours and then we can each open ours." That was all she needed to hear, and immediately she started ripping into those gifts like she was being timed.

We oohed and ahhed as she showed us her presents, and then gave Camilo and I each some homemade thing that was supposed to be a coaster. I gave Dinorah a gift certificate for a spa which she loved, and then Libe grabbed her by the hand and pulled her upstairs to the playroom. They left the room with Libe chattering about what they would build with the magnetic blocks she'd gotten from Camilo.

As soon as they were out of earshot I reached over to the table to grab my gift for Camilo, and he shyly pulled out his from the bag he'd brought.

He handed it to me and snapped, "You first, let's get this over with, because I'm nervous and think you're going to hate it."

It was almost comical how unaware Camilo was of

the fact that I was crazy about him. "Why would I hate a gift from you?" I asked incredulously, but he did look nervous. I tried to tease him by opening it as slowly as I could and after a minute of me taking each piece of tape off individually he ripped it from my hand and unwrapped it.

"Oh my god. Here!" I chuckled as I took it back from him.

It was a picture frame with the selfie of Libe, him and I we'd taken at the zoo. The three of us were smiling wide at the camera, with the blue sky behind us. My arm was around his shoulder and Libe's little hand was on the side of his face.

We looked happy, like we belonged together.

"Camilo." He made me breathless. "This is amazing." I leaned in to kiss him and when I touched his lips with mine, I finally had to say it.

"Te amo."

His lips turned up to match mine. "And I love you."

He said it so naturally, like it made all the sense in the world. It felt like that too.

I went in for another kiss to seal it. To keep those words between us for a bit. When we pulled back he looked impish, and the anticipation I felt for whatever utterly Camilo thing he would say made me giddy. "Of course I reserve the right to take it back if your gift sucks."

"I wouldn't expect any less," I said very solemnly.

I handed him the present, and he opened it in the same fashion as Libe had attacked hers. I held my breath because I'd taken a chance on this one, and hoped my suspicion was right.

He looked at the cover and gasped. "How did you even get this? I've never been able to find any of his work in print."

It was an anthology by José Ángel Buesa, a Cuban poet who he'd mentioned a few times. I'd had my mom do a little digging in the DR since he'd lived there before he died. She came through with this copy and mailed it.

"There's no way you stayed within the budget."

I might have felt just slightly smug then. "Actually I did, the book wasn't too much at all. My mom got it in the DR, the shipping cost more than the book."

He leafed through it with a big smile on his face.

"This is amazing. Thank you."

"You're welcome."

We sat there for a bit, while he read and I admired the photo. After a while, I pulled him closer. "How was the night with your mom?"

He sighed and looked up to where they'd gone, but I could hear Libe talking a mile a minute.

"Well my mom decided she needs to take some time off work, which is amazing. She says she's been really struggling with her depression and she wants to work on her mental health. The leave is unpaid, and I just discovered yesterday her rent was increased." He grimaced at that, glancing upstairs again. "She needs to take care of the balance soon. I still encouraged her to take the time, because she needs it." He sounded so relieved, even though it seemed like things were not exactly resolved.

"She's upset my dad's sixty-fifth birthday is in March and she hasn't been to see his grave since we left Miami. So she wants to go while she's on leave. I wish I could take her, but she doesn't fly," he said, voice weighed down by the obvious strain all this was putting on him. "It would involve driving there and I can't take time off until I'm done with the renovation." He looked at me with a tired smile. "But I'm still happy because she's finally taking her depression seriously."

I knew I was going into some dangerous territory, but I had to ask. "I know you probably will say no, but can I help with some of the expenses I—"

As I anticipated, he stopped me before I could finish.

"No. Thank you for offering. But we can take care of it. Really, babe. It would make me uncomfortable."

I withheld my frustrated sigh, because pushing Camilo on this was not the right course of action. "Okay, but please, Camilo. If you do feel like you need my help. Nothing would make me happier."

He gave me a terse nod and said, "I know." He didn't have to say he was going to do anything and everything he could to make sure his mom got her time off, even if he had to run himself into the ground doing it. I already knew that.

It was unchartered territory to be the "emotional support." I was usually the one expected to take care of things, but Camilo not only didn't expect me to take care of him, he was decidedly not interested.

"It's hard to sit here knowing how much you're about to take on and not be able to make it easier for you," I said as I tightened my arms around him.

He clicked his tongue and kissed my cheek. "You being here makes it better. I don't need you to fix anything for me, Tom. You loving me is more than enough."

The urge to try and convince him that there was nothing I wanted more than to help was hard to restrain, but I managed. I hoped that if things got hard enough Camilo would let me help, because I didn't know if I could just sit idly by watching him struggle.

Chapter Twenty-Five

Camilo

"I can only have one drink before I take off," I regret-fully told Ayako as we walked out of our dance class into the icy Midtown Manhattan sidewalk. As per usual these days I was rushing from one thing to the next. I was supposed to go over to Tom's place for the night after my class, but I hadn't been able to catch up with Ayako in a while. It was already February and the first few weeks of the year seemed to have flown by.

Ayako just waved a hand in my direction as we hur-ried to the warmth of the bar up the street. "Don't worry. I'm glad you can stay for one, you're always running lately."

I gave her another guilty look. "I know. I can't be-lieve it's already February and it's the first dance class we've been able to do together since before Christmas."

She frowned as she pushed the door for the bar. "Well you've been a busy bee, friend. Between kicking ass with the renovation and taking all that extra work to help your mom with the bills, you've been grinding pretty fucking hard."

"And trying to spend time with Tom," I offered as we hopped onto our stools.

She grinned at my mention of Tom. "Yeah but that one comes with *lots* of perks."

I chuckled at her suggestive tone. "True that. I'm tired as fuck though. *But* my mom has been doing so much better since she started her leave. She loves the support group she joined, and she's going to Zumba classes." It was hard not to smile when I thought how much better my mom looked, it made the lack of sleep and perpetual exhaustion worth it.

Ayako looked genuinely pleased to hear about my mom which was why I loved her. "I'm so glad to hear that, babe."

I sighed, thinking that I wished my mom could take even more time off. "I think the stress from the hospital was making it worse for her depression and anxiety. I'm worried about her going back to work, but I can't keep supporting her and me. I'm barely keeping up and it's only been a few weeks."

Ayako held up her finger when her phone started buzzing. "Shit, give me a sec. On-call week is so fun." I nodded, feeling her pain, and went back to fretting about all the things I needed to do, which was my permanent state these days.

I'd started taking freelance translation work right after Christmas, which helped with my mom, but it was like another thirty hours of work a week, on top of my job. I felt drained and barely had time for anything else. I tried to see Tom as much as I could, but I'd cancelled on him a few times or had to bring work with me to his house.

I knew he was frustrated, because he had more than

enough money to make this whole thing go away for me, and I refused to let him help me, even just a little bit. Rationally I knew I was letting things that happened long ago affect my present. But I couldn't get past the memories of how awful things got with my mom and Ramon once he started helping her with money. The way he felt entitled to tell her what to do, or put her down, was something I never wanted to experience. Even though I was sure Tom wouldn't do that. I still wasn't ready to ask.

Ayako ended the call she'd been on and looked at me. "Why so serious, friend? You still thinking about your mom?"

I stopped talking to order our drinks and then turned to fill her in. "I'm just fucking exhausted, and I've barely made a dent with my mom's back rent. I miss having more time to hang out with Tom and Libe."

She narrowed her eyes at me at the mention of my boyfriend and his daughter, and I knew she would get on my case about not letting Tom help.

"I know what you're going to say, and I'm just not ready to ask Tom for money, Ayako." She opened her mouth, but I held up my hand. "We've only been dating for a bit over four months and miraculously the fact that he's giving our agency literally millions of dollars has not become an issue. I won't add another thing that could potentially mess up our relationship to the mix." She nodded as she sipped her wine, but I could tell she was barely able to contain whatever she wanted to say.

When she finally spoke it was pretty obvious from the way she was *literally* biting her tongue that she was trying hard to see things from my perspective, but not totally getting there. "Okay that makes sense, especially because I know how stressed you've been, making sure the renovation goes without a hitch. Just don't torture yourself too much, when you know you have a man that loves you with money to burn. Who is not only able to, but is actually desperate to help you."

I nodded, conceding her point. "As I told Tom, I'm aware the offer is there and I will ask if I feel like I need to."

"Are you doing that 'oasis' shit again?"

I once again regretted telling Ayako about the oasis thing. This was definitely not what was happening with Tom.

I scoffed at her raised eyebrow. "I won't ever tell you another one of my deep dark secrets, Ayako Russell. Also how does that even make sense? I'm being the opposite of the oasis, since I won't take his money and he's dying to be my sugar daddy. Which, oh my God. Saying that just made my skin crawl." I legit shuddered.

She just closed her eyes and drank deeply from her glass. "You're doing too much, Camilo."

"Seriously though. I'm one-hundred-percent real with Tom at all times. It's incredible really, because he's totally into it," I said unable to hide my genuine bafflement.

"Fuck, you're straight up disgustingly in love." She stuck her tongue out at me.

I waved her off and tried to redirect towards something less mushy. "Okay, now let's talk about how amazing the class was and what you're doing for Valentine's."

She cut her eyes at my change of topic suggestions, but conceded. "I assume this year I'm on my own in our traditional boycott of Hallmark holidays?"

"Yes, but not for the reason you think! I told Tom I

refused to engage in any sort of romantic bullshit on a made up holiday."

I got a chuckle for that. "Of course you did."

"But Libe asked me to come over and help her prepare Valentine's gifts for her classmates. They can bring a little gift for each kid and she wants to make them homemade cards. I've been recruited to help select and apply stickers."

"Okay that's completely adorable and you're clearly gunning for boyfriend/future stepdad of the year award." She smiled wide then and squeezed my knee. "Have I told you how fucking happy I am for you, babe?"

"Yes." I didn't even have to try hard at sounding exasperated. Because there wasn't a single person in my life who wasn't stanning Tom to an unhealthy degree. "My love life is the stuff of legend and fairytale. I love Tom and his kid so much it scares me, and I continue to be deeply obsessed with his enormous dick."

That got us a few looks from the other bar patrons which I ignored, then tried to steer the convo away from me for a bit. "Let's talk about you. What's the word on you and Henock?"

Her eyes got shifty as fuck and she took a big gulp of wine before answering. "Nada. I told you we're friends. There's nothing there. He's really cool and we have a lot of things in common, but that's all." I gave her some side-eye, because I wasn't buying it, but I let her get away with her bullshit story for now. I looked down at my phone and saw I had a text from Tom, which of course had me cheesing, because I was that person now.

Ayako looked at me like I was a lost cause.

Tom: Hey, amor. I just got home from my meeting. Are we still on for tonight? Are you done with your mysterious dance class?

I fired back a text right away.

Camilo: Yes and yes. I'm having a quick drink and catch up with Ayako and after I'll head up to yours. Also my classes are not mysterious, Thomas. I've told you about them a million times.

Tom: But I've never SEEN them. I've got to sneak into one of them sometime, so I can see what you two get up to over there.

He was ridiculous.

Camilo: You can come anytime. *eyeroll emoji* These classes are at the New York Bodies studio, not at the shelter. None of the clients come to this one, so there are no confidentiality issues. Anyone can come, and that includes nosy ass boyfriends!

He responded with a gif of a dude leering.

I laughed and showed the phone to Ayako. She grinned when she read his texts and then perked up. "Send him the video! We signed waivers for this one, so they're probably putting the clips up on Vimeo. They usually upload them right away. Here, let me look." She grabbed my phone and pulled up the studio's Vimeo account. "Oh man he's going to flip when he sees it. Tonight's class was lit."

I was one-hundred-percent into this idea. We'd danced to "Dangerous Woman" for the class and the choreography was super sexy. Ayako and I had taken it a few times because we loved it so much. I knew the video of the group doing it together would be fire.

I nodded enthusiastically as she tapped on my phone screen like she was on a mission. "Okay that's a fantastic idea. I'm running the risk of getting mauled in the hallway of Tom's house. But I can live with the consequences of that."

Ayako smacked my arm, her eyes still focused on what she was doing. "Don't brag about the hot sex you're going to get while I go home to watch Netflix with my cat."

I laughed at her grumbling. "It's not a guarantee it'll be hot."

"Nobody likes a show-off, Camilo," she protested as she opened the link and we watched it in silence. The video was basically a full minute and a half of the entire class writhing, gyrating, straddling chairs, hair whipping and eye-fucking the camera with complete abandon.

We looked pretty fucking hot.

Ayako gave a husky chuckle when the video ended. "Prepare to be attacked as soon as you get to his house if you send him this thing."

I took my phone back from her, and proceeded to do exactly that. "Oh I'm sending it *right now*. Then I'm finishing my drink to give him time to really work up a thirst before getting my ass in a Lyft. I'm broke as fuck right now, but the fifteen bucks will be worth it."

Ayako dipped her head in agreement. "You'll want to get there as soon as possible."

I opened the texting app again after copying the link for the video and sent it off.

Camilo: Here's the link to a video the studio posted from the class. See you soon!

Ayako grinned again. "I give him three minutes before he's asking you when you'll be there."

"He can wait," I said primly, before sipping my glass of wine.

The text came after two. It was only the one word.

FUUUUUUUUUUUUUUUUUUUUUUUCK.

My feelings exactly.

Tom

Camilo Briggs was going to be the death of me. I'd watched the video he'd sent of his dance class three times already and was now sitting downstairs hard as a rock waiting for him. He'd texted he was on his way like ten minutes ago, but I was so revved up I was afraid I'd come before I had a chance to get my hands on him. Still, I played the video again.

Jesus.

It opened with Camilo and the other dancers standing against the back wall of the studio. He was wearing the same type of outfit he usually did for his classes. Tight black yoga pants and a tank top, but on his feet he was wearing ankle boots with a slightly taller heel than usual. His hair was loose, and with his head down, his face was hidden as he slid his back slowly up and down the wall. Seeing that body I knew so well, that I'd run my hands over so many times, without getting a glimpse of his face was entrancing. I literally could not look away.

After a few seconds, he whipped his head up and started making his way slowly to the front of the room. All the while looking intently at something in the distance. His hips undulating as he went, until he stopped in front of one of the chairs that were arranged around the room. He sank into it with both his arms above his head. I sucked in my teeth and gripped myself, entranced. I was so focused on his body and how he moved I was barely blinking.

There were other people in the shot, and Ayako might've been in there too. But I couldn't take my eyes off Camilo. As soon as his ass hit the chair he started running his hands up and down his body, his neck, chest and thighs until he placed them on his knees. He spread his legs wide with his hands, dipping his torso towards the floor.

Those gray eyes were looking straight at me, and all I could think was, *I'm going to fuck him blind the second he walks through that door.*

I gritted my teeth, watching as he turned his body to one side and then the other. His hips turning in a slow circle as he fisted his hair. My breath was coming in short pants and I had to grip my cock harder. The video ended with him standing up and walking to the back of the studio in that sexy as fuck slow strut.

I was sitting there panting and clenching my fists when I heard the doorbell ring. I instantly dropped my phone on the couch and rushed to the door, tearing off my t-shirt as I went, and hoping to God it wasn't a Jehovah's Witness or someone from the cable company. Because my cock was literally sticking out of my sweats, and I had the tube of lube I ran upstairs to get in my hand.

We'd decided to get tested a couple of weeks ago, but with his schedule, we'd had little chance to see each other since then. So, this would be the first time we went without condoms. By the time I opened the door, I was so eager to get at him, my entire body was vibrating.

"Hey—"

I didn't let him finish. I just grabbed him by the arm and pulled him inside. I took his bag off his shoulder and threw it on the table by the door before turning him around, so he was shoved up against the wall. Within seconds I was all over him, pushing my cock against his ass, my hands everywhere.

Camilo's laugh was breathless when he managed to speak.

"Damn, if I knew those videos were going to have this effect on you, I would've started sending them sooner."

I shook my head while trying to unzip his parka with one hand and used the other to take his hat off so I could get at his neck.

"What did you think would happen if you sent me a video with two full minutes of you shaking this ass and looking at the camera like that?" Apparently I didn't speak anymore, I growled.

"Uh, I was hoping for exactly this reaction actually." He tried to laugh but it got caught in his throat when I lifted his hair and sucked on the back of his neck. I was thrusting my erection against him, one hand at the base of his neck as the other one went inside his yoga pants. No underwear again.

"Camilo, for fuck's sake, I'm going to come before we even get naked."

His breath was coming in pants, but I could hear the humor in his voice. "I love that you're this worked up. I didn't take you for an Ariana Grande fan."

I had no idea who he was talking about. I lifted his shirt off and then ran my teeth all the way down his back. Until I was kneeling with my face at eye level with his ass. I bit one cheek and grabbed his erection again, making him gasp before I asked distractedly, "Who?"

I started tugging on his pants impatiently as he kicked off his shoes and turned his head around to look at me, one eyebrow raised. "The song from the video?"

I shook my head confused, because focusing on anything that wasn't getting my dick in him, was practically impossible at the moment. "I had the sound off."

He let out a husky laugh as I frantically tugged his tights below his ass and worked on getting us to the fucking part of the evening.

"You had the sound off, huh?"

"Yes." I kept it short since I was having trouble with the English language in general. Besides I had other priorities, like getting some lube on my fingers and getting at his ass. I used one hand to spread his cheeks and ran the pads of my fingers over his hole, then ran my tongue over the same spot, making him shiver.

"Tom." It was more a moan than anything, but it only worked to get me even more revved up.

I worked a finger in slowly and sucked in my teeth, trying to breathe through the lust-filled fog that had taken over my brain. "I'm going to rail you as soon as I get you ready."

"Damn, that video did leave you feeling some type of way. You came downstairs with lube?" When I looked up at him, his face was completely flushed.

"Si por que te voy a coger aqui mismo," I said, adding another finger.

"Oohh Spanish smashing today." He panted as he pushed his ass out and stretched his arms on the wall.

"Si." That was all I could get out.

He looked back at me and his pupils were blown out, his mouth red and swollen from his own teeth. "Then get inside, baby," he said, breathlessly.

I tugged hard on my balls and took another bite out of that ass. He moaned as I thrust my fingers in, looking for his gland. After a moment he gasped. "Ungh that feels so good."

I was dizzy from wanting him.

After a few more thrusts of my fingers we were both groaning. When I couldn't take it any longer, I pulled them out and stood up fast, pressing my chest against his back. Running my hands over him. He turned his head so I could kiss him and we tangled our tongues, mouths open, teeth clashing. Camilo pulled back, then leaned against me again.

"I don't know if I can stand for this."

Without a word I picked him up and walked us to the couch in the next room. I sat down and started stroking my dick as I watched him take his tank top off and toss it across the room. Within seconds he was straddling me and had the tip of my dick at his entrance. We were face-to-face and the look in his eyes was pure ecstasy as I slowly pushed in. He put one hand on my shoulder for balance and sank down.

"Fuck that's good. God I love your cock." He shook his head, his mouth going slack, and his breaths were coming in short spurts. "And bare. Ahh."

I shook my head and gritted my teeth, trying to keep it together. It felt too good, too tight. I was going to come in seconds with his ass gripping me so hard.

I smacked his ass then and pinched his nipple, making him gasp. "Como mueves ese culo, Camilo." Those circles he was making with his hips were driving me out of my mind. "God this ass. Me vuelves loco."

His smile was absolutely filthy when he answered. "I like making you crazy." He wrapped his arms around my neck and went in for a kiss as we both started thrusting harder.

We were feeding each other our moans and gasps as we moved hard and fast, our bodies locked together so tightly. I grabbed Camilo's cock and started stroking him when I felt my orgasm coming. My stomach tightened and that feeling like all my limbs were turning liquid spread through my body.

"Oh shit, Tom, don't stop—" His words were cut off by a shudder.

After a few seconds Camilo's mouth opened and he threw his head back as a loud moan escaped his lips, ribbons of come bursting out of him. His ass clamping down on my cock sent me right over with him.

I was so blissed out I lost time for a moment. As I came to, I heard Camilo's muffled voice against my ear.

"I'm sending you every video of every class I've ever been in stat."

Chapter Twenty-Six

Camilo

We were on the couch with one of the seemingly dozens of decadently soft and fluffy blankets in Tom's house covering us. He'd been in rare form when I'd gotten to his place after my class, and now almost an hour later he still couldn't keep his hands off my ass. It was the first time we'd gone without a condom, and he was really feeling himself. He grabbed and stroked me so possessively, all I could do was shiver in his arms.

I felt owned by Tom, but not perilously or in a stifling way. More like words were superfluous because we were under each other's skin. I pulled my head off his chest and kissed him, slow and deep as he grabbed me, his hands gripping me hard, his touch grounding. Making me feel at ease for the first time in days.

These past few weeks had been so stressful and busy. I was worried about my mom and money, but here with Tom I felt so good. When I put my head back on his chest, he let out a long exhale and kissed my hand.

"How's Dinorah?"

I looked up at him and smiled. I loved how well Tom

and my mom got on. He genuinely liked her and the feeling was mutual and then some.

"Better. She's still liking the group and her therapist, and is going to the community center for the Zumba classes. She's even talking about volunteering there." I sighed again, not sure if I wanted to get into this next part, but decided to say it anyways. Because dammit, he was my fucking boyfriend and he needed to learn to just listen without feeling like he needed to solve my problems.

"I think part of her issues lately were related to how much she hates her job," I said thinking of how much better she looked now that she wasn't dealing with the constant stress of the hospital. "I'm concerned about her going back. I've talked to her about doing something different, but she's been in this job for so long. I don't know if she'll even consider looking for something else." Tom's face was unreadable, but I could see that he wanted to say something, but was holding it in.

"In any case that's what it is for now. Hopefully we can come up with a plan before her leave is finished, because I can't pay double rent for much longer." Tom grunted at this and I felt him tense. I sighed, knowing what was coming next.

"Mi amor—"

I didn't let him finish, but tried for a conciliatory tone, because I didn't want to ruin the first moment of peace I'd had all week. "Babe, I can't let you support my mom. You must understand why I can't accept money from you like that."

His lips thinned and I knew he was working hard on not pushing. "I wasn't going to suggest it because I already know the answer. I just hate seeing you killing yourself, taking extra work on top of your already very stressful job when money is the only issue."

We'd been over this like ten times, but I'd repeat it another hundred until it took. "But money isn't the only issue, Tom. The issue is me relying on my boyfriend to support my mother. That's crossing so many boundaries and setting us up for all kinds of bad dynamics." I sagged, annoyed at this afterglow-killing conversation. "I know it's hard for you to feel like you're not helping. But I'm just not in a place where I can be okay with that level of financial help from you."

He gave me a sharp nod, and I hated how cold the room felt. But the thought of being beholden to anyone, even Tom, gave me pause and especially when it wasn't just me. This was about my mom too. I attempted to pivot to a less contentious topic.

"So things are really coming together for the reception."

Tom lifted an eyebrow like he knew what I was doing, but after a second gave me a small smile. "Oh so you're still on schedule for three weeks?"

I nodded feeling excited. "Yeah all the big jobs are done. At this point what's left is just surface stuff like painting and finishing some of the flooring. The contractor said we should be able to do the photographs soon."

Since the shelter was a confidential location as a safety measure for adults and children who were there fleeing from dangerous situations, we couldn't have the dedication ceremony on-site. Instead, we were doing it at the Schomburg Center for Research in Black Culture which was close to our offices in East Harlem. Since the guests wouldn't be able to visit the shelter to see the new space, I'd gotten in touch with a photographer to go and capture the new renovated spaces, as well as some of the survivors using the facilities, with their permission of course.

Tom smiled at the mention of the photos. "Your idea of showing the new space through a photography exhibit is amazing. I can't wait to see them. My mom called me today and said she and my dad might come."

I widened my eyes at that and croaked out, "Your parents?"

My horror amused him apparently, because the bastard laughed at me. "Don't tell me you're scared of meeting my mom and dad? Libe's the tough one."

"Libe's bae. I love that kid."

The smile he gave me lit me up inside. "She loves you too. We both do."

I leaned in for another kiss, my heart racing. He made me feel *so much.* "Te amo, Tom, even when you annoy me by trying to give my mom rent money."

He huffed an embarrassed laugh and shook his head. "Y yo a ti, even when you shut me down." I could tell he was trying hard to keep the tone light. "So do I get you all to myself until Sunday?"

I nodded, a bit reluctantly. "I think so. I do have a couple of translations I promised to get done this weekend. But I can wake up early and work on them from here."

"Good. Let me get my sweats on and I'll go make us a snack." He leaned in and sucked on my lip before standing up, making my belly go all liquid with want again. "We need to keep your energy up. I want a live performance later, and I'm hiding all your clothes first," he said grabbing my tank top off the floor and hiding it behind his back, a dirty smile on his lips. "I'm keeping that ass bare and ready for me all weekend," he said as he smacked me on said body part.

"Why does your filthy mouth turn me on so much?"

He leaned down, eyes full of mischief. "Por que si."

"So fucking arrogant." I wasn't even close to sounding like I meant it. He just grinned and grabbed my ass one last time before walking out of the room.

His laugh was too fucking smug, but there was no question, he had me thirsting for him at all times. I watched him walk up the stairs to the kitchen and hoped this thing with money and my mom didn't mess with what we had, because I was completely gone for Tom Hughes.

Chapter Twenty-Seven

Tom

"Hey." Camilo sounded completely worn out, which was his permanent state lately. We'd barely seen each other in the past two weeks. Even Libe was starting to worry about him, since the last times he'd been over to the house he'd been so obviously exhausted, all I wanted was to let him rest. When he'd come over on Valentine's he'd barely been able to stay awake helping Libe with her class gifts. Afterwards he'd fallen asleep within seconds of getting into bed and had run off at 5:00 a.m. to go do more work.

I was worried about him, but he refused to accept any help for his mom's rent, or for anything else for that matter. He'd cancelled twice on me in the last week, and I was starting to feel desperate.

"How are you, amor?"

"Tired," he answered, but I could hear a smile under the weariness in his voice. At least he was still happy to hear from me. "What's up, baby? Talk to me." I heard a long exhale and I could barely hold back the need to go to his office, carry him out and take him to a beach somewhere for a week, so he could fucking sleep. But

I couldn't even suggest it, because that would just get me shut out. Not that what I was about to tell him would likely go over any better.

"Are you slammed today?"

He let out an exhausted laugh. "Always."

Lately I felt like any request I made felt like an imposition. Camilo constantly told me that being with me was the only time he felt like he could relax, but it was getting harder to keep quiet while I saw him struggle. "So, I have a favor to ask." I paused, hoping this didn't freak him out. "My mom is here."

"What? How?" The tiredness in his voice was quickly replaced with panic. "I thought they were coming for the launch."

I felt like shit for asking, but he was the contact for the renovation and he'd told me again and again that he didn't want our relationship interfering with his job. "That was the plan, but she ended up coming for a few days to help a friend who needed to have a check-up with her oncologist."

Camilo sighed and I grimaced, feeling weary of how everything felt so strained lately. "She got in yesterday morning and is leaving tomorrow night. She'd like to go see the renovation before she goes, because she may not be able to make it here for the event."

The silence on the other line was heavy.

"This is really last minute, Tom." He sounded like he was about to cry, and again I felt like shit. Because in the end this was also me being a selfish asshole and trying to find an excuse to see him.

When the silence stretched without a word from Camilo I decided to cut my losses. "It's okay. I'll let my mom know it's not possible," I said, hoping I'd been able to hide my disappointment.

"No, Tom, this is my job." He sighed again. "It's not an issue at all. The main reason I was even put on this project was so that I could communicate with your mother."

We both knew that was bullshit, and I'd just manipulated the situation to see more of him, sort of like I was doing now. I was about to call the whole thing off when he spoke again.

"I can take you guys there today. It would be my pleasure to give her a tour." His cordial, "all business" tone was even more concerning than the weary one before, because this sounded like a different person.

"You know what, mi amor? We can just do it at another time." I forced myself to come up with a lighter tone. "The shelter isn't going anywhere," I said, hating myself for starting this shit.

"Don't be silly, Tom. I just need to let the shelter managers know we're coming, so they can get ready. What time works for you?"

I cleared my throat, but when I spoke I sounded off. "She's taking Libe out to get mani/pedis or something after school."

"I bet my boo's excited for that." For the first time in the conversation, I felt like I was talking to Camilo.

"You know how she is," I said with a real smile on my lips this time.

Camilo exhaled, but he sounded better. "I feel like I'm talking to my long-distance boyfriend. I miss you, baby." I shuddered, feeling the same need deep in my gut.

"And I miss you." There was no hiding the bone deep want in my voice.

"Why don't you guys come around eleven a.m., I'll let you know where to go." He was back to business, but the tone changed, we were *us* again.

"Also...we need to keep things professional between us." He sounded a little mortified, and I rushed to let him know he did not need to worry.

"I understand, whatever you need, mi amor." Simple as that. "I totally get it. Thanks for doing this, mi vida."

As I ended the call I reminded myself once again this was temporary, if I could just be patient and let Camilo do what he needed to do for his mother, we'd have forever waiting on the other side.

"You look at him like he's water after a long day in the sun, m'ijo."

I shook my head at my mother and her mushiness, my eyes still zeroed in on Camilo.

"Behave, Mamí, remember—"

She chuckled, squeezing my elbow. "I know, no 'boyfriend' talk, I'm aware that you went and got yourself caught up in a secret affair." Her eyes twinkled when she looked at me. "This man keeps bringing out new sides of you." She shot me the look that was usually followed by some kind of anecdote illustrating how I was a perfect child.

"You were always so self-contained, not a word out of place, but fierce." She ran a hand over my shoulder, her eyes on Camilo as he approached. "You were always impatient when it came to going after what you wanted. I'm glad someone is finally making you wait."

I pursed my lips at my mom's smug expression. "Not nice, Mamí." She just laughed, tipping her chin at the object of our conversation.

I straightened as Camilo got closer, my body primed to take him in my arms, kiss him. Look him over to see how he was doing. Since we were standing across the street from his place of work, I extended a hand to him instead.

"Camilo, good to see you." He looked frayed, but his smile was warm, and he stood just a bit closer than necessary.

"Tom," he said gripping my hand, then turned to look at my mother. "Señora Gomez. ¿Come esta?"

She waved his hand away and went in for a tight hug and a kiss right there on the busy sidewalk, then told him in a low voice, "Please call me Esperanza. I've been wanting to meet the man who's made my son so happy in the last few months."

"Mamí," I protested.

She turned her head up to look at me and whispered. "I know. I can't make a fuss. I just wanted to give him a proper hello, m'ijo."

She stepped back from him but kept his hand in hers. I looked down at him and saw the emotion on his face, he still hadn't spoken and his lip quivered. I knew he was working hard on keeping it together. I would've given anything to be able to hold him. To have a redo.

I should've known with how close Camilo was to his mother, meeting mine would be monumental. We should've been somewhere he could've been himself with her, where they could talk and hit it off like I knew they would. Instead we were on a sidewalk acting like we didn't know each other.

Finally, he pulled her hand and went in for a second hug. "It's so good to meet you too, Esperanza."

After a moment they separated and my mom gave

me a sympathetic look as I stood stoically to the side
unable to touch him.

Camilo seemed better though, his eyes looked less
worn. He pointed a finger to the west. "We're walking
in that direction." With that he started walking with us
close behind. He glanced up at me, giving me a small
smile. "I got the confidentiality agreements you guys
sent me this morning, thank you for that."

"Of course."

He lifted a shoulder as we crossed the street. "Some
people feel weird about it, but we need to make sure
anyone going to the shelter knows they can't disclose
the location or names of the people staying there. The
safety of our clients is the most important thing."

My mom nodded in agreement, and moved closer
to Camilo. "I completely understand. You don't know
how I wish my sister could have found a place like New
Beginning when she was here."

Camilo put an arm around her shoulder. "I know."
He looked up at me then, his face serious but so full of
affection. "What your son is doing in her memory is
amazing though. We will be able to help many more,
for a long time, thanks to what he's doing."

"He's a good man." My mother never could miss an
opportunity to brag about her sons.

This time when Camilo looked at me, I could see all
his love there openly on display. "He's *the best* man."

My mom laughed at us and the lovesick faces we
were probably making. "Ay Dios mio, cuanto amor."

I didn't have the energy to feel embarrassed, and
when I opened my mouth I did it looking right into Camilo's eyes. "Todo el amor."

It was the honest truth, he had *all* my love.

Camilo said nothing, but I could see the tension in his shoulders had relaxed somewhat. After a couple of minutes of walking in silence, Camilo hurried up the sidewalk to an unmarked building and tapped a code on a panel by the entrance. The door opened and we walked into a small lobby. He gestured toward the well-lit and freshly painted area, where a shiny gold-plated plaque had been installed on one of the walls.

"Welcome to 'Patria's House.'"

My mother let out a startled sob when she saw my aunt's name, and Camilo and I each took one of her hands. When he spoke his voice was gentle.

"Do you need a minute, Esperanza? Take your time."

She shook her head, her emotions all over her face. "I'm ready."

He gave me a sympathetic look and went to push the elevator button.

"We can start on one of the residential floors and finish where we have the communal areas," he said clearly excited to show us around. "As you know, part of the renovation was to expand the living areas, so now we can shelter more clients. We also fully renovated the kitchen and the wellness center is beautiful." It was hard to tell who was glowing more between Camilo and my mom as he told us about the shelter.

As we stepped in he kept speaking to my mom in Spanish, while she held his hand tightly, hanging on his every word. "We now have three apartments that can lodge families. So, if we have a parent who is coming with children we can put them in their own space. We also have two small studios, for anyone who needs to be in their own private room."

We stepped out of the elevator into a colorful hallway. The walls were painted a light blue and each door was a different color. Each room had a plaque with a name. Camilo came to a stop in front of a yellow door that had a small sign with hand painted sunflowers. After a moment a woman opened the door. She smiled as soon as she saw Camilo.

"Buenos dias."

"Hey," he told her warmly. "We came to see your place if that's okay."

"Claro." She stepped to the side to let us in." It was one of the studios and everything looked brand-new. There were some photos on a corkboard on the wall that looked like they'd been pinned on by the resident. I saw there was a baby in a pack and play in the middle of the room. As soon as he saw Camilo, he started bouncing up and down.

His face lit up and he went over to the baby. "Hey, bud," he said bending down to pick him up. Once the baby was comfortably on his hip he walked over to the woman, who was still looking a little shy.

"Nancy, this is Mr. Hughes and Mrs. Gomez. They are the visitors Mercedes told you about. They helped us with the improvements to the house."

Her face lit up at that and she came to shake both our hands. "Gracias. This place is such a blessing. It saved me and my baby." Her voice trembled as Camilo proudly looked on.

As I shook her hand I heard Camilo talk to her, his voice fierce. "You saved yourself, Nancy, we were just here to catch you." She had a rueful smile on her lips, but she gave him a sharp nod.

In that moment I felt the proudest I'd ever been of what I had been able to accomplish in this country.

To have even a small part of helping survivors get to safety was a dream I'd harbored for years. And to be able to share that with my mother and Camilo felt like an enormous blessing.

"You're welcome, Nancy," I told her sincerely. I looked at Camilo then, and I could see he understood exactly what I was feeling. "I am so grateful I could help."

After that we took a tour through the rest of the building. In addition to the wellness center, with the renovation they'd built a new computer room, a child-care area and a few consultation rooms which were used to provide therapy to the adults and children by licensed clinicians. Just being able to have my mom here seeing what we were able to do was monumental. That combined with seeing Camilo in his element, the way the staff clearly respected and loved him was a beautiful thing.

My mom was chatting with the child therapist when I took a chance to pull Camilo aside, and asked as casually as I could manage, "Can we talk in private?"

He tensed for a moment, but then nodded, gesturing to the door across the hall. "Mercedes, I'm going to take Mr. Hughes in to my office for a minute, we'll be right back."

The therapist nodded, seemingly caught up in whatever she was telling my mother. My mom, of course, shooed us away with a knowing look. I wasn't even sure what I was after, other than I needed a moment alone with him.

He invited me into a small neat office, which I stepped into, and waited until he had closed the door.

He leaned against it, and stood there looking at me with tired eyes. His hands at his side.

"You look so tired, mi amor." He just shrugged in his typical "what else is new" gesture.

I walked up to him, not sure how he would receive this breach to his request, but when I gathered him in my arms, his body sunk into me.

"I'm tired and I missed you," he said, his cheek pressed to my chest.

"Thanks for doing this for us, my mom loved it, and you."

He looked up. "It was good to meet her too." He smiled as he ran his hands over my shoulders possessively, as if making sure his property was all in working order. "You look like her. Same nose and eyes."

I groaned in answer as I pressed against him and bent down for a kiss, just a small touching of lips.

"I love seeing you here in your element. I can't tell you how much it meant to me, to be able to do this and you be the one to carry out this wish. Baby—"

I wanted to beg him once again to let me take care of everything, to give him whatever he needed, but instead I said what I knew wouldn't turn into another argument. "Can you come to lunch with my mom and me?" I asked as he laid his head on my chest.

He looked up and he didn't have to answer. I could read the "no" in his eyes. "I can't. I have so much to do today." He looked miserable, and I felt terrible for pressing him after I'd already made him rearrange his day for this visit.

"I really want to. I'd love to hang out with your mom a bit more, but this week is crazy and we're so close to the opening. I just can't. I'm sorry."

He looked like he was about to fall apart. So, I let it go. I kissed him again and then lifted his chin so he would look at me. "Promise me you'll get some rest soon. I'm worried about you. I never see you and when I do, you look like you can barely stand."

I braced for a bristled remark, but he just nodded and responded with a barely audible "okay," and the fact that he didn't even have the energy to fight me on this, felt like the last straw.

He opened the door and looked up at me. "We should go back to get your mom." Those gray eyes that usually lit me up, were dimmed today, they'd been that way for too long.

Chapter Twenty-Eight

Camilo

I was fucking exhausted. I'd been working eighteen hour days for the last two weeks between work and the freelance translations, and I was feeling close to the breaking point. Since Tom's mom came for a visit, things had gotten even more hectic with the dedication ceremony.

I was constantly running on fumes and it was starting to cause a real strain between Tom and me. A couple of days ago when I'd shown up late for a cookie baking date with Libe, Tom asked again if he could help. When I declined, *again*, for the first time he actually insisted and said he couldn't just watch me run myself into the ground, that it was affecting our relationship. He was right, but I still couldn't bring myself to agree. But this week had me so wrung out I was starting to consider it.

My mom had been off for six weeks now and had two more to go and I felt very proud of myself and her for being able to give her this time, even with how rough it'd been. Still, I worried about what would happen once she went back to work. I even suggested moving back in with her for a while until she found something different, but she'd vetoed that instantly. It was also hard talking to Tom about it, because all he wanted was to pull out his wallet, and I was tired of having the same argument.

The only thing keeping me together at the end of this long ass week was the fact that I finally had a weekend off. I was on my way to Tom's place and the plan was for me to stay until Sunday. It'd been weeks since I'd had a weekend when I didn't have extra work to do, and I was so looking forward to some alone time with Tom.

I also still felt guilty about barely spending any time with his mom when she was in town. He hadn't brought it up, but I knew he'd been upset.

I was running up the stairs of the subway station close to his place, when I got a call. I was surprised when I saw the screen. It was almost 6:30 p.m. on a Friday. A call from my mom's property management office could not be about anything good.

I tried to keep most of the exasperation out of my voice when I answered. "Hello."

"Hi, Camilo, this is Cindy. I tried to call your mom, but she's not answering." The friendly tone in her voice set all my alarms blaring.

"She's at her Zumba class tonight. She probably shut off the phone," I said feeling proud of myself for not cursing her out.

"Oh okay, well I'll just leave the message with you then." I'd been dealing with this woman for the last two months and had never heard her sound this perky. "I just wanted to let her know she's all set. We received the payment for all of her arrears, and for the next six months of rent."

I had to stop and stand to the side on the street, so

I could ask her again what the hell she was talking about. "I'm sorry. I'm not sure I follow. What do you mean she's all set? Did my mom come to pay or something?" There was a chance she could've borrowed from Odette, but I doubted she had fifteen grand in cash to lend my mom.

"Oh no, the payment came from the office of Thomas Hughes. His assistant called this morning and they wired it to our bank this afternoon. They were very prompt, and easy to deal with."

I had to be hearing wrong.

"Listen, Camilo, I'm sorry to cut you off, but we're about to close the office, so I have to go. Have a great weekend."

Funny how happy she sounded now that she'd gotten her money.

I stood there on the street stunned into silence. A few minutes passed before I started walking again, and getting pissed with every step I took to Tom's house.

How fucking dare he?

I couldn't believe Tom had done this shit again. After I'd specifically told him, a million fucking times, I didn't need him to pay for my mom's expenses, he went and did it anyway.

I got to his house within a few minutes and by the time he opened the door, I was in a righteous rage. I felt completely betrayed and disrespected.

I couldn't even *look* at him. He was about to go in for a kiss, but I slunk away from him. Then he tried to lean in again, but took a step back when he saw my face. I wanted to scream at him right there on the street, but before I made a scene I walked into the house. I didn't even bother to take off my backpack.

I was not staying in this house for long.

"What's wrong?"

I scoffed at his question and stepped closer to where he was standing all loose limbed, like he didn't know what he'd done.

"You're really asking me that right now, Tom?"

I could tell he was trying to gauge just how mad he'd made me, but when he opened his mouth I knew he had seriously fucking miscalculated.

"Is this about the rent?"

My head felt so hot I was worried I would give myself a stroke just from what I was having to do not to get in his face.

"The rent?" I asked making air quotes. "It's not about 'the rent,' Tom. It's about you paying fifteen *thousand* dollars for my mother's housing without my consent. Behind my back." I was keeping my voice barely below screaming, while he just stood there with his lips pursued. The calmer he looked the hotter I got.

I was about to lean into my fury and ream Tom out, but my fucking phone rang again. This time it was my mother's ringtone. I thought of just letting it go to voicemail. But my concern for her won out.

I took the call while I glared at Tom who looked like he was starting to realize just how badly he'd fucked up. The terrified look on his face did not mollify my anger in the slightest.

"Hey, Mama," I said, not giving a fuck about how angry I sounded.

"Milito, did Cindy call you?" Excellent, now my mom was all up to date.

"Si." That word came out so laden with frustration, I was surprised I could choke it out. My mom was silent for a few beats as if she was trying to figure out what was going on with me, finally she spoke into the phone.

"Papi, please don't be angry at Tom. I know how much you value your independence, but he was just trying to help. You've been going nonstop for weeks and he could do this for you," she said in a pleading voice. "You need to let people help you, son. It's not always on you to fix everything."

I sighed and avoided looking at Tom. If anything, my mother feeling she needed to intercede for his overbearing behavior only made me angrier.

"Okay, Ma. I'll call you later okay?"

"Are you at Tom's?"

"Mama, *por favor.*" I was hanging on to my patience by the thinnest of threads.

She finally ended the call with a worried, "Okay, Milito."

Before I talked to Tom again I took a moment to breathe, and was still trying to get it together when he started talking.

"Camilo, I—"

So much for calming myself.

I held up my hand at him shaking my head hard. "No. I do *not* want to hear it, Tom."

I took off my backpack then, because I needed to move. "I don't know how, after all the conversations we've had, after the night of the concert, you would think I'd be fine with you doing this. I don't need reasons from you, I *know* the reason. You did it because you knew once it was done, I wouldn't be able to give it back."

His face turned paler with every word out of my mouth.

"No, Camilo. I did it because I wanted to help. Mi

amor, I'm worried about you. You've been running yourself ragged. I've barely seen you in the last few weeks and when you're here you're just so tired." His shoulders sagged as he looked at me with a helpless expression on his face. "And it's just money, baby. That I have. I could make this easier for you."

"Oh no. Do not make this about me, Tom. This is about *you* not getting attention." I scoffed and threw my hands up as I glared at him. "I get it now." I snarled at him. "That's how you managed this perfect act so long. It's easy to be Mr. Compromise as long as you keep getting what you want."

I started listing off things with my fingers as I ranted at him. "You decided you wanted to see me and made those bullshit weekly meetings happen. When you were ready to take the whole thing to the bedroom, I went along with that too. The moment you were ready for me to meet Libe, there I was." I cocked my head at his confused expression. "So now you're not getting your QT and you do what? You throw money at it." I shook my head in disgust. "Compromise is not always getting your way, Tom, that's called *manipulation*."

"Camilo, that's not fair. We were in this together. Things went further with us because we both wanted it. Because we make each other happy. Because we love each other."

I knew I was being unfair and hurtful but I didn't care. He'd taken away my agency with his lazy ass attempt at helping, and I didn't know if I could walk this off.

Tom tried again, this time his voice pleading. "I just wanted to ease things for you. Try to take off some of the burden you're carrying all on your own."

I couldn't *believe* Tom and his bullshit.

"What do you think I'm doing here, Tom?" I asked waving my hand around the room. "Why do you think I came to spend the weekend with you? Because I *am* stressed, I *am* tired, and when I feel like this, relaxing and watching a movie with my boyfriend helps. I'm not here so you can be my fucking sugar daddy and pay my rent like your kept boy." I was screaming and I didn't care.

"Camilo, don't make it about that."

I shook my head in disbelief, because this mother-fucker really was trying me. "Making it about what, Tom? *Money?* You're the one that made this about money. I've never indicated to you in *any* way it was appropriate for you to pay for *anything* on my behalf. I'm not Maxwell, who you can just ignore and then try to appease by getting him shit or letting him do what-ever he wants with your money."

Tom looked desperate and scared, but I could not find it in me to relent. If I folded on this now, I would spend my life giving into him.

"Please tell me how I can make this right, Camilo. I truly thought this would make things easier for you. I just. I don't know." He put both his hands in his hair, pulling hard. "Fuck. Why does everything have to be black and white with you, mi amor? Why can't you ever give an inch?"

Before I knew it I'd rushed up to him, almost crash-ing into his body, until we were standing an inch apart. We were so close I had to look up to see his face, and I let him see mine. I let him take a close look at the hurt and humiliation I was feeling.

"I don't give an inch, Tom? Is that what you just

said to me? I risked my job, the renovation project to be with you. I'm not sure if you've already forgotten this given your financial situation, but some of us can't pay for rent and food if we lose our jobs." I slapped the palm of my hand against my chest as I spoke. Tom just stood there silent.

"I could have lost my employment, messed up my standing with my boss and the agency, which would have been fucking devastating. And I did it anyway, because I wanted to be with you. Because I fell *in love* with you. Because I thought I'd finally found someone who could *see* me."

My voice broke then and I knew tears were not far behind. "Someone who understood me and could be kind to those parts of me other people find so hard to deal with."

Tom shuddered, and looked like he was struggling to get words out. "I could not keep watching you kill yourself, mi vida. You have to understand, I didn't know what else to do."

I shook my head, backing away.

"No, using your money to fix a problem is not showing love. It's a transaction. And you know what hurts the most? I still think you know me and that you do get me, but you did this anyway, because it was easy." I laughed then and it sounded so hollow. "I thought all those times before in relationships when people did or said thoughtless things had been painful, but this—"

I was gasping for air so I could speak.

"Tom, you *chose* to do something you knew would hurt me, hurt *us*."

I closed my eyes for a second and when I opened them I saw Tom's face was streaked with tears. When he pulled me into his arms I just let him hold me. From where I was standing, I could see the painting with the street scene from Ethiopia. Today with the room only lit by a reading lamp, the bodies which always looked so bright and full of energy seemed lifeless, down-trodden. I closed my eyes and tasted salt as I licked my dry lips.

Tom put his mouth on my neck and begged. "Perdoname mi amor, por favor. I'm so sorry."

I stayed there until my breathing went back to normal and just as Tom was trying to hold me tighter, I pushed him away, shaking my head.

"No, no. You can't make this better by kissing me and telling me you love me." I turned around wiping my eyes, then picked up my backpack and started for the door. He made like he was about to follow, but I held up my hand.

"I need you to understand something, Tom. I love you. I would do almost anything to be with you, but I will not tolerate what you did today ever again. You put me in an impossible position and you did it by putting money at the center of our relationship. If you can't see why this would hurt me, then you need to figure it out, or I don't know if we can come back from this."

I walked out of Tom's house feeling skinned. Completely exposed and raw. Flayed by the hurt of knowing in the end Tom had taken everything he knew about me and set it aside. What I'd said to him was the truth, this felt like nothing ever had before. I was scared too, because deep down I knew I wasn't strong enough to stay away from him, even if he didn't fix what he'd broken today.

Tom

Priya, Sanjay and Henock came to my house at some point after Camilo left. I didn't know how long I'd been sitting in my living room, but when they came in, the house was completely dark. I heard someone turn on a lamp, and then Priya came and knelt in front of me, her face full of worry.

"What happened, Tom? Camilo texted me saying we should come and check on you."

I laughed bitterly at that, hating myself. Even after he dumped me for being a thoughtless asshole, Camilo still made sure there was someone there to take care of me.

"Where's Kalyani?" I asked when I didn't see the baby.

Priya waved her hand in the direction of their house. "She's with the nanny. We're finally giving it a try. I'm going back to work in a few weeks, so we need to get her settled with someone, now that my mom went back home."

Sanjay sat down across from me and asked again. "What's wrong, Tom?"

I nodded and opened my mouth, but nothing came out. I tried again and when I spoke I sounded so wooden and flat I could barely recognize my own voice.

"I think Camilo broke up with me."

Priya's eyes widened and she looked around as if trying to figure out if Heni and Sanjay had any idea of what was going on. "What, why?"

I put my head in my hands. "I didn't take your advice." I just sat there not explaining, not wanting to say what happened.

I sighed, feeling so fucking awful. Because Camilo

was right. This whole time he'd been the one taking risks, going out on a limb again and again to move our relationship forward.

What did I have to lose really? And when he really needed my support, when he was at his breaking point, instead of asking him what I could do to make it better. I insisted on doing the one thing he'd asked me not to. I turned to look at Priya who was now sitting down on the couch next to me.

"Remember how I mentioned his mom took unpaid leave from work because she was struggling with her depression and needed some time to take care of herself?"

Priya and the guys nodded.

"Well in the end things got complicated. Her rent was increased a while ago and she'd been accumulating the arrears. Taking care of the rent increase basically ate up all of her and Camilo's savings, and they still needed to figure out rent payments while she was out on leave. Camilo insisted she take the time off and started taking on freelance work to make extra money. This was on top of his job, which is already huge with the renovation project being in the final stages." I closed my eyes for this part, because every minute that passed, I was more and more frightened I'd done something irrevocable.

"I've been asking how I could help, and he kept saying everything was fine. But this week when he was here, he could barely keep his eyes open. He looked so exhausted I was worried for him. So, today I paid the balance for the arrears and covered Dinorah's rent for the next six months."

Priya nodded slowly with her brows furrowed, like

she suspected where I was going, but didn't want to believe I'd be that fucking stupid.

"I didn't tell Camilo before I did it."

I heard both Sanjay and Henock curse from the couch across from us.

Priya took my hand and shook her head. "Oh, Tom. This is going to be a tough one to fix, my friend."

I shook my head at her. "I don't know if it can be fixed."

She waved her hand dismissing what I'd said.

"Oh you can fix it. You just can't fix it with money," she said pointedly. "But you *can* fix it. Camilo is amazing and is so good for you, Tom. I've never in all the years since we've known each other seen you this happy or comfortable in your own skin, as you have been in the months you've been with him. He's worth you leaving your pride behind and doing whatever it takes to get him back."

"I know." I ran my hands over my face again. "I didn't think he'd be this angry."

Priya narrowed her eyes, like I was no longer amusing her.

"Yes you did. If not you would've told him beforehand. Clearly, I don't know Camilo as well as you do, but I know him well enough to know denying or minimizing how bad you messed up are not the way to go."

"I just wanted to help." I looked up at Henock and Sanjay trying to get someone to understand. "I thought once the money was paid we'd be able to sit down a moment and he'd—"

Priya cut me off. "Realize you were right all along?" She scoffed. "No, Thomas, that's not how this works."

She looked up at Sanjay, and then back at me. "Tom,

you took away his agency, his ability to decide for himself what was best for him. That's not easy for a person who's used to getting things done on his own. A man like Camilo doesn't take being undermined like this lightly. You *know* that, Tom." I just nodded, drowning in the misery of my own making.

After that she turned to me again and took my hand. "Tom, you know I love you like a brother. The four of us, we've been through a lot together." She smiled sadly. "From rags to riches. The three of you are family. I tell you this because I don't want you to lose someone you're meant to be with. You acted like an asshole and now you need to get really comfortable with the floor, because you're going to need to grovel."

Priya always managed to get a smile out of me, even at the lowest moments. "I know and I don't care. I'll do whatever I need to do. I just need to figure out what."

"You can figure it out, I know you can. The three of you have made all this money and you've all gotten lazy." The distaste on her face was softened by the gentleness in her voice. "Tom, you are the most thoughtful man I know. You're kind and brilliant. You can do better than just pulling out your wallet when someone you love needs you."

She lifted her shoulders and shook her head as if she was exasperated with me. "I can't speak for Camilo, but I have a feeling he acted the way he did because he felt blindsided and ignored. It's hurtful and frankly *annoying*, to see the men we love be as clueless and shallow as to think they know what we need better than we do."

"I didn't say I knew better, I just didn't know what else to do." She clicked her tongue at me, clearly not buying it.

"Camilo was figuring things out, he had a plan, and even though it was hard, he was doing what he needed to for himself and for his mother. Like he had been *all the years* before you came along."

I sighed, leaning my head against the back of the couch. "He told me I didn't know how to compromise, that I just manipulated situations until I got what I wanted in the end."

All three of them averted their eyes and my heart sank.

"You need to figure out a way to show him you understand what's important for him."

She was right, but how?

Heni spoke next. "I don't think you're intentionally getting what you want all the time, but you do rely a lot on people giving in eventually." He lifted a shoulder. "What is it that you want with Camilo, Tom? Because if you want to be with him for the long term, you're going to have to figure out another way to deal with things."

What did I want with Camilo? I hadn't really asked myself that question, but the answer was instant and clear.

Everything.

I wanted everything and forever with him.

"I want him forever."

They all smiled at me then, and Priya kissed my cheek.

"Great answer. We're all totally happy with this plan. Now, how are you getting him back so this forever thing can get rolling?"

Priya's words about me showing Camilo I knew what was important to him came to mind and I got an idea.

I stood up and walked upstairs to look for my phone.

I had to call Camilo and apologize, to let him know I was going to fight to get him back. Then I would make another call, which would hopefully lead to making amends.

I turned back to my friends, grateful for their presence and their support.

"I have an idea, and I really hope this time I can show him just how much I'm willing to do for him."

Chapter Twenty-Nine

Camilo

The messages and missed call notifications on my phone were out of control, after being off the grid for twenty-four hours, people were getting on edge. I'd turned on my phone about an hour ago and was still listening to voicemails.

I'd gotten back home from my blowout with Tom in a fog. I called my mom to tell her I was fine, but that I needed some time to myself. I begged her not to come over or have any of my friends come over until I had time to think. After that I'd just lain in bed, completely numb. Not crying, not angry, just…empty.

I kept playing the fight over and over in my head, how scared Tom looked and how fucked up I'd felt. I knew I needed to talk to him, to give him a chance to at least properly apologize. But I wasn't ready, not yet. I heard the intercom buzz and got up to answer, dreading having to deal with my friends' concerned questions.

"Yeah?"

"It's us, babe. We have wine and other supplies."

"I don't know if I'm up to company yet, Ayako."

Before she had time to answer, Juan Pablo's loud
voice suddenly came over the speaker.

"Camilo Santiago, it's fucking freezing out here, and
this pizza is getting cold. Let us in so we can make
you feel better and figure out how you can get back together with this rich douchebag. Come on, pa. My feet
are going numb."

I grumbled pushing the buzzer. "Fine, but I'm not
in the mood to talk."

I left my door open for them before getting back in
bed. I hit play on my iPhone again and went back to
staring at my wall. After a minute Ayako and Juanpa
stormed into my tiny apartment.

"Oh my god, why are all the lights off, Camilo? I'm
going to kill myself."

That was Ayako. She flipped the kitchen light on,
causing me to yelp and pull the covers over my head.

"Ugh, that's too bright, Ayako." She totally ignored
my complaint and came over to the bed instead. She
immediately started trying to pull me up and hug me
at the same time.

"How are you doing, hon? You had us so worried."
Her forehead was all wrinkled as she pulled back to take
a good look at me. "Where are we at right now? Are we
cursing his name and burning the shit he bought, or are
we just retreating to figure things out?"

I shrugged her off grumpily. "Ayako, chill. I'm getting up in a minute. I'm just cold. And no, we're not
burning anything just yet, but we're definitely not doing
well." She squeezed my shoulder in sympathy.

"We got you, friend. We brought everything we need
to figure this out." She started listing things. "Wine,
pizza, emergency pack of Camel lights—"

She stopped and tilted her head to listen to the music that was playing. "Oh damn, is that 'Ex-Factor'?" She straightened like she was girding her loins. I rolled my eyes at her clowning. "Okay, so we're rolling deep tonight." She looked over at Juanpa like they needed to revise the game plan and he nodded solemnly. They were so extra, but I really was glad to have them here.

"This shit is serious if we're throwing back to The Miseducation," Juanpa said, pulling a pint of some kind of artisanal gelato from the paper bag he was holding. "Good thing we stopped at the boujie bodega down the street and got this."

She gave us both a thumbs-up, and went to the kitchen. Immediately she started putting wine in the fridge and getting plates out, as I stared at their takeover of my apartment.

Juanpa the dirtbag was already eating a slice of pizza out of the box without even taking his coat off. He gestured to the box as if asking if I wanted a slice. I shook my head.

"I'm not hungry."

Ayako scoffed at my rejection. "Well you're going to eat and tell us what happened! Dinorah's worried about you too. She asked us to tell you to call her."

"I called her already. She's at Odette's at a dinner party. I told her I'd come over tomorrow."

Juanpa finished inhaling his slice of pizza and walked over to me after finally taking his Tims and coat off. "Have you talked to Tom?"

I turned my head away and lay back on my side, so I was back to staring at my new favorite spot on the wall. "No, I have like four messages from him, but I didn't call him back. The first couple were right after

I left his house. They were just desperate, and begging me to call him. The last one was from this morning. He said he knew how much he'd hurt me and if I could just give him a little bit of time, he would show me how much he loves me."

I stopped to take a deep breath, feeling like I was going to cry. "Because he never wants to lose me." I sighed as Ayako passed me a slice of pizza. I glanced up at her with a hopeful look. "Vino?"

She just wagged her finger at me. "Not until you eat. *Then* we can get intoxicated."

I frowned and took a bite as she watched me eat. "Fine."

I worked on my pizza for a few minutes as the other two got settled. By the time I'd finished my slice Ayako had gotten in the bed with me, and Juanpa was in a chair next to the bed.

He leaned in, his handsome face serious. "So give us the details, because the eight word text you sent out last night was pretty vague."

After I'd hung up with my mom, I texted the guys and Ayako to let them know what happened. I didn't have the energy to explain, so I'd just sent them a super cryptic message.

I broke up with T. Will call tomorrow.

Then shut off my phone before any of them could respond.

"I need wine first." Ayako passed me the glass she brought me from the kitchen, and I started to speak when Juanpa held up a hand while he pulled his phone out of his pocket.

"Wait, let me FaceTime P and Nesto. They told me to call them when we came over." He talked while tapping on the screen. "They almost drove down here today while you were still MIA. We were too scared of you to show up unannounced after you asked us not to, but it was discussed."

I chuckled helplessly at Juanpa's attempt to make me laugh. "You're not funny."

"I'm not trying to be, you scared us." I still felt like shit, but it was good to have my friends with me right now.

A few seconds later I heard Patrice's voice come over the speaker. "How's it going?" Juanpa just shook his head and moved his chair so Ayako and I could see the screen. Nesto, Jude and Patrice were all sitting on a couch with worried looks on their faces.

Nesto leaned forward, so he was staring right at me. His brows furrowed. "How we doing, brother?"

I lifted a shoulder in response. "Not great, but at least I don't feel like my heart got ripped out of my chest like I did yesterday."

Patrice leaned in too, but Nesto spoke again before he got a chance. "Do you need us to come down? Just say the word and we're there." Both Jude and Patrice nodded furiously at Nesto's offer. "You were here to hold me down when shit got real last year with Jude." He turned his head then and smiled at his blond lover, who stared up at him with such tenderness, it made my heart ache.

After a second Nesto turned back to look at me. "I know things seem completely fucked up now, but I know they'll work out, Camilo. He just got mad extra on you, but you can come back from that." He gave me a cheeky smile then. "Just like the rest of us he had to learn the hard way to take your grumpy ass seriously when you ask for something."

I closed my eyes, feeling the tears starting to well up. There was too much happening in the feelings department. I took another gulp of wine and handed the glass to Ayako, so I could make a time-out sign with my hands.

"You motherfuckers need to stop it with this lovefest. I'm already a fucking wreck, so please keep your shit together for a minute, so I can tell you what happened."

After about two seconds of everyone trying to hold it in, Nesto and Juanpa busted up and for the first time in the last twenty-four hours I felt like maybe things would be okay. When we all stopped laughing, I took my glass back from Ayako and started talking.

"I love him, there's no doubt and I'm certain he loves me. The issue is he broke my trust. And I'm scared if I let him get away with this now, I'll be having to overlook overbearing and, frankly, disrespectful shit forever. The worst part is I know I'll get back together with him if he shows up, even if he does nothing to make amends."

Ayako put her arm around my shoulder after my grim prediction. "Hon, you said he asked you for time in his message and that he said he would show you he understood where he'd gone wrong. Maybe he's thinking of a way of repairing things. He knows where you live and he hasn't come around yet." I got another squeeze of the shoulder and nods all around. "He's a good guy. Clearly he's not perfect and is a little too reliant on his bank account to do his work for him, but he loves you and he makes you happy."

I sipped my wine, thinking about what she said. "Maybe. I hope so. Because I know if we just get back together without fixing this, it will be the beginning of the end. I won't be able to live with myself if I just take him back, after what he pulled."

They all gave me matching sympathetic faces, but didn't offer any more platitudes, clearly there was no quick, easy fix for where things had gone wrong for Tom and I. "Thanks for coming to sit vigil with me," I said to Ayako, then waved at the screen. "And for offering to drive down."

Ayako shook her head at me like I was being ridiculous. "Nothing died, babe."

Juanpa, Nesto, P and Jude gave their own enthusiastic nods, then J spoke. "We'll be here with you until the bitter end, unless you start playing that band with those dudes who sound like whiny cats. You know I can't go there with you, pa."

Fucking Juan Pablo had to make me laugh again. "Shut up, MCR don't sound like whiny cats, and don't even front like you don't have Helena in one of your Spotify playlists. I know what you get up to."

He just ignored me and stood up.

"I'm getting more wine."

Jude balked at Juanpa's derision. "I like My Chemical Romance."

Nesto put his arm around him shaking his head. "Damn, babe, you just said that and I'm still obsessed with you." He waved his hand between the two of them, the smile on his face was pure mischief. "This shit *must* be real."

Jude turned red then pinched him hard on the arm, and Nesto glared in my direction. "Ow, shit. See, Camilo, he's pinching people now too. You're a bad influence."

Ayako and I sat on the bed chuckling while J got us more drinks and the other three messed around on the screen. I felt grateful for my friends and hoped Tom had someone with him tonight. I wondered if we really would be alright. If we could move past this.

I hoped so, I did, but now the seed of doubt had been planted. I feared maybe he *didn't* know me as well as I thought. That he didn't get which were the things that really mattered most to me. I didn't know if there was anything Tom could do to make me fully trust him again.

Chapter Thirty

Tom

"We'll see you Sunday then?"

I nodded as I passed Maxwell Libe's backpack. "Yes, I may get back Saturday. I'll let you know."

He waved his hand at me as he balanced Libe on his hip. "You'll probably be tired, let's say Sunday night. We'll be fine." He smiled at Libe, who had nodded along to every word he said, her thumb stuck in her mouth. "We have lots of plans with nana and grandpa. Right, sweetheart?" he said, nuzzling her hair.

"Daddy, we're going to go ice-skating!" Libe told me excitedly.

"You'll have a great time. I can't wait to hear about it. I'll call you every day while I'm gone, okay?" I leaned to give her a kiss on the cheek.

"Okay, Daddy," Libe mumbled around her thumb as Maxwell strapped her into the booster seat in his car, passing her a book to entertain her a couple of minutes while we talked.

Maxwell looked at me intensely, like he was trying to work something out.

"Thanks for doing this, Maxwell. I know it's very last minute."

It was the Monday after my big fight with Camilo. I hadn't spoken to him since Friday, and in that time I'd come up with a plan I hoped would show him how much I cared for him. It involved leaving town for a few days, however. So, I'd asked Maxwell for help and he'd agreed to take Libe while I was gone.

"It's fine, Tom. It's the least I could do, after all my very poorly timed interruptions." The corner of his mouth lifted then, and in that moment we both probably felt a pang of regret. For us and what we lost. "I'm glad you've found someone you're willing to make changes for. I hope it works out for you."

I shrugged, trying to convey an ease I did *not* feel.

"I'm not sure if this will change things for Camilo and me, but I want to do this for him anyway. Not so he'll take me back, but because I know it's important to him."

Maxwell's smile was bigger this time, even though his eyes were still a little sad. "Well even if it wasn't me, I'm glad someone finally made you learn to pay attention."

That was an understatement. "Oh, Camilo has my attention. That and more," I said, determined to prove just that to him in the next few days.

With that Maxwell started moving, getting into the driver's seat. I waved at them as they drove off and then crossed the street to the garage to get my car. Within minutes I headed up to the Bronx to pick up Dinorah.

Friday night, as I thought of all the things Camilo had been trying to manage in the past couple of months,

I remembered him talking about how much Dinorah wanted to go down to Miami during her leave. Camilo couldn't make the trip with her with everything he had going on, but *I* could. I had the time and the means to do it. And once the idea got in my head, I went with it.

On Saturday morning I'd woken up with a plan in my head. I called Dinorah to ask her if she was up for it, and she'd immediately said yes. She was convinced things would be okay with Camilo and me, but I told her I wanted to do this for her no matter what, and that once we came back I would try to fix what I'd broken. I didn't know if there was anything I could do to make Camilo trust me again, but I could at least do this one thing that would mean so much to him and Dinorah.

The plan was to take her down there so she could get some closure, get a chance to say goodbye properly. Camilo had talked to me about how much Dinorah regretted the way they'd left Miami. How that last year had tainted all the happy years she's had there. I was hoping on this trip she'd be able to at least get a chance to reconnect with the memories she'd made there.

I pulled up in front of Dinorah's building and saw her waiting on the sidewalk with a big smile on her face and a little suitcase next to her. I had only seen her once since she started her leave, but could see why Camilo had worked so hard to make sure she was able to take the time off. She looked like a different person, her eyes were bright and her back straight.

She looked *stronger.* Once again I felt a pang of regret, for messing with what Camilo had been doing for his mother. I now understood why he'd been so determined to do it, and why my interference had cut him so deeply.

I quickly got out of the car and went around to grab her bag. As soon as I got there she started talking excitedly. "Tom, thank you again for doing this. Milito is going to have a heart attack when I call him to tell him." She laughed.

I didn't find it as funny. "How pissed do you think he'll be? Because Milo doesn't like it when I do things without asking and this is a big one, Dinorah," I said as we got into the car. "He's not going to like being kept in the dark again." I was legitimately worried about how he'd take this.

Dinorah patted my cheek and smiled reassuringly. "He'll be surprised. Especially because he's not part of the plan. You know he doesn't like to feel left out. But he'll be okay and he's very busy with the renovation. I talked with Ayako and Juan Pablo too. They'll make sure to keep an eye on him while we're away. My son is strong," she said with a fire in her voice. "The strongest. He just needs time to calm down, and think things through. So do you, Tom."

"I hope I'm doing the right thing."

She squeezed my shoulder and gave me an understanding look. "I hope so too, but even as stubborn as Milito is, he's smart and is not one to be wasteful. He knows what you have is special. He's hurt and disappointed, and a little scared, but he loves you."

"And I love him." I stared straight ahead as I maneuvered the car through the busy streets of the South Bronx, getting us out of the city.

Dinorah scoffed as if to say, "Well no shit."

"I know. From the first time he talked to me about you, I had a feeling you two were like his daddy and me. Meant to be."

I was trying to figure out how to respond to her words without making a fool of myself when she jumped in her seat, and started looking through her purse. "I need to call him before we leave the city, to let him know." She laughed nervously, and I felt her pain. Camilo's temper was nothing to take lightly.

She tapped her phone, and soon it was ringing on speakerphone. She winked at me as we waited.

"Hey, Mama." He sounded so weary, and my heart lurched at the sound of his voice.

"Hola, hijo, so, I want you to know everything is fine."

"Okaaaay," he answered bemusedly.

"I'm on my way to Miami, to go see your daddy's grave. I'll be back on Saturday."

Camilo's shriek echoed in the car. "What?" He spluttered. "How?"

"I'm driving with a friend. Someone totally safe. I'm one-hundred-percent alright." She sighed as we listened to his string of protests.

"I've been wanting to do this for a long time. This month he would have turned sixty-five, this is the right time. I want to go down there and see the places that were special to the two of us. I know we talked about doing it in the summer, but I've got the time *now*. Besides, I didn't want you to have to take time off. I can do this on my own."

"Mama, what if something happens to you?"

She laughed at that and shook her head. "I don't know if you remember this, but I came from Cuba in a boat on my own. I can do this."

"I know." His tone changed then, like he remembered he needed to reassure his mom he believed in her. "You can do anything. I'm just surprised, and a little worried. This is so sudden." After a pause he asked, "Can I talk to the person?"

Dinorah and I shared a look at Camilo's overprotectiveness. "No, you may not, Camilo Santiago Briggs. You just need to trust me. I'll call you every night, and I'll be posting on my Facebook account. You're always pestering me to use it."

He chuckled at that, but when he spoke he still didn't sound very convinced. "Okay, Mama, but text, okay? This is so unexpected, but you sound happy and that's all I want. You, happy."

"I know, papi. Don't worry about me, esta bien?"

"Si. Te quiero, Mama."

"Y yo a ti."

She ended the call and we sat there in silence for a few seconds, then Dinorah laughed. "Well that went better than I thought it would. He's going to fall over when he realizes who my travel companion is."

I smiled with a lot less confidence in this whole plan than I'd initially had, now that I'd heard Camilo's apprehensiveness. "No matter what happens, like Camilo says, what's important is that you're happy."

She smiled and squeezed my shoulder again. "You two will be fine."

I really hoped she was right.

Camilo

I heard my phone's voicemail alert as I got out of the shower. It sounded like Tom's nightly message had arrived.

I sighed and sat on my bed as I tapped the screen to listen. It was Thursday, almost a week since our fight, and we still hadn't seen each other. On Sunday after calling me like ten times, he'd finally texted asking me if I wanted him to stop calling. I responded with one word.

Never.

He'd asked if he could just leave messages. I'd texted back a yes, and asked him not to give up on us, that I just needed time.

So every night since then, he'd been leaving me these heart wrenching messages telling me all the ways in which I made his life better. The plans he had for the future, which all seemed to include me. It was not easy to resist, but I was glad I'd taken some time to think about what I wanted.

By now I was certain I wanted to try again, but I still felt like I needed something, some proof Tom understood why what he did hurt me. He'd apologized, he'd made all kinds of promises. But I still didn't know if he really got that I didn't want someone who was lazy with what mattered to me.

I played the voicemail, anxious to hear him. His deep voice on the speaker made my whole body shudder.

"Hola, mi amor. Today's message will be short, but I just wanted to say that I love you, I miss you and I hope I can see you very soon. Te amo, Camilo."

I almost called him then, because I was getting close to the point where my fortress of solitude was making almost no sense. Needing a distraction, I opened the Facebook app on my phone to check if my mom had posted anything new about her mysterious road trip. I had no idea who she was on this trip with, but she'd looked happy as hell on every picture she'd posted.

On the first day she'd uploaded photos from Virginia

Beach where they stopped, and since yesterday she'd been posting a few from her old haunts in Miami. She even wrote little captions about why each place was meaningful. There were so many places that were special to her and my dad, many of which I didn't remember or hadn't been to.

When she called me last night she'd said she was going to visit his grave today. I knew it would be emotional and hard, and I told her I was nervous for her. But she sounded calm on the phone, and said she was looking forward to it. I expected some photos to be on Facebook already.

As I opened the feed I saw she'd uploaded a few of the cemetery, which was a little creepy. My mom, like everyone else these days, seemed to lack a filter when it came to posting personal stuff on social media.

There were some photos of the flowers she'd brought for my dad, and another one of her later in the day with two people who looked familiar. In the caption she said they were her old coworkers from the hospital she'd worked for when we lived there. She was smiling big in every picture, and she looked better than she had in years.

Suddenly, I felt enormous gratitude for whomever had done this for her. It was clearly the right time for her to take this trip after all.

I kept scrolling and when I saw the most recent post my heart stopped. I blinked and brought the phone closer, to make sure I wasn't seeing things.

It was a photo of my mom at a restaurant, with a group of about five people. The post she'd written said:

At Versailles Restaurant on our last night. They still have

the best Cuban food in Miami. These last few days have been a dream come true. It's been wonderful to revisit all the places that were so special to me and my family after more than twenty years away. This has been a trip of healing, and I am so grateful for getting a chance to do it. I can't wait to get back home and tell Camilo about everything he missed.

She actually inserted a smiley face next, because I was in bizzaro world right now. The three words with which she ended the message were what almost gave me a cardiac episode.

Thank you, Tom.

There he was, my slippery as hell boyfriend sitting next to my mom and some random old people in Miami, holding up mojitos for the camera.

That sneaky fucker.

He'd driven my mother down to Florida. I should have been pissed he *once again* did something behind my back, but the only thing I felt was gratitude, and so much love.

This was not just sending a check.

Tom had driven for two days with my freaking mother in his car, and taken her to Miami so she could see my dad's grave for the first time in twenty years. And tomorrow was going to get in the car and drive another two days to bring her back. That was not light work.

That was *love*.

Shit. I was so screwed.

I quickly opened the text app and sent him a message.

Camilo: You sneaky fucker.

After a few seconds, I saw the three dots pop up and waited.

Tom: Am I your boyfriend the sneaky fucker, or just plain old sneaky fucker?

A laugh escaped my lips and I tapped another text right away.

Camilo: Just get yourself and my freaking mother back here in one piece, and we'll see about your status. You stubborn, insufferable man.

I could feel my heart in my temples, and if I probed just a little I knew I'd find I was feeling stupid levels of happiness.

Tom: You're still texting, so it must mean I'm not at the very top of your shit list anymore.

He thought he was hilarious.

Camilo: Where's Libe?

Tom: With Maxwell. He felt bad for all the interruptions...

Camilo: He should. Nosy asshole.

Tom: LOL

Camilo: When will you be back?

Tom: Saturday, early evening most likely.

Camilo: Okay.

I really needed to say this.

Camilo: And thank you.

Tom: Not necessary, but you're welcome. Will I see you when we get back?

Camilo: Maybe. I'm calling my mom now and you better not be listening to what I say to her!

Tom: You're the boss, mi amor. I love you.

Camilo: I love you too, you greasy bastard.

Tom

"It's about damn time! I've been waiting here for hours." My heart almost beat out of my chest when I saw Camilo waiting in the doorway of Dinorah's apartment. It was almost 9:00 p.m. and we'd been on the road for over twelve hours. I was exhausted from all the driving I'd done in the last week. But every ache and pain evaporated when I saw him with his hands on his hips, trying his best to look pissed and failing completely.

"Milito, papi, don't yell at us, we're tired."

He was not mollified in the slightest by Dinorah, and just kept glaring at us.

"Of course you're tired, who drives to Miami and back in a week?" he said, throwing his arms up, as he came up to us. "Do you think you're still twenty-two, Dinorah? You're sixty years old, woman." He grabbed her as she made it to the door and hugged her hard. Closing his eyes as he put his nose in her neck. "I missed you, Mama."

"I missed you too, papi, but it was a very nice trip." She looked over at me and Camilo pulled back from her to turn his attention my way, then pointed in the direction of my face.

"You look like you're about to collapse. Leave it to your slithery ass to figure out a way to get out of me yelling at you for yet again doing some sneaky shit." He griped, as I stood there silently reveling in Camilo's moody litany. "Of course you had to go and do something so fucking perfect and amazing. I now have no other choice but to take your shifty ass back."

This last part he said softly as he grabbed my hand and dragged me into the apartment. I was still pulling Dinorah's suitcase. He took it out of my hands and out of the way, so he could put his arms around my waist.

I looked down at his face, losing myself in those gray eyes that came into my life to light up my world.

"Are you taking pity on me then? Because, baby, I'm ready to keep groveling. I was always in for the long game with you, Camilo. From day one." His eyes softened and his mouth fell open like he was trying to breathe through what he was feeling.

He looked over his shoulder when he heard his mom's suitcase rolling down the hallway to the bedroom.

"Mama." She stopped and walked back over to give us each a kiss on the cheek.

"We'll talk tomorrow, papi," she told Camilo then looked up at me with a fond smile on her face. "Take this poor man home, he's exhausted. Thank you again, Tom. I can't tell you what these last few days have meant to me."

I looked at her, feeling so much for this woman. We'd spent hours talking while we drove and I'd learned so much about her and her strength. The things she'd lived through to come to this country, and those she'd experienced after.

The love she had for her son.

We were similar in so many ways, Dinorah and I. We'd come to this country clutching hard to our dreams, and we'd made the best of what we'd found here.

"Yo se, Dinorah. It was an honor and a pleasure." She gave me a kiss and tight hug, before pinching Camilo on the cheek. "Next time we'll have to bring this one with us."

I turned to look at him and saw the emotion on his face as he whispered in agreement. "Next time."

She walked off again and closed the door of her bedroom behind herself.

"So now you're my mom's favorite?"

"Am I *your* favorite though? That's what I want to know."

He pushed up, putting his arms around my neck and kissed me. I felt his smile as our lips met. We stayed there for a while, our bodies swaying as we touched and stroked. Feeling each other again after so many days apart. After all that hurt and silence.

"I missed you so much, Camilo. It scared me so much to think I could have lost you. I'm sorry. I will never take the easy way out in our relationship again."

He nodded with his head pressed tight against my chest.

"I know."

When we pulled apart, Camilo grabbed my hand, and started moving. "Come on, let's get you home. I'll drive because you look like you're about to fall over."

I nodded tiredly and smiled as he pulled me to the door and out of the apartment.

The world felt just as it should be with Camilo, once again, taking my hand and leading the way.

Epilogue

Camilo

"The next time you suggest Christmas in the DR and I hesitate, please smack me upside the head."

I was living my best life right now with the windows down feeling the sea breeze touching my face. The road from the Santo Domingo airport was so close to the ocean that the water splashing against the rocks almost hit our car. It was seventy-eight degrees and sunny on December twenty-third, and I was having trouble remembering why I hadn't agreed to coming a week earlier like Tom suggested.

Tom smiled and shook his head, his eyes focused on the road.

"How about I remind you we could be lounging on the beach in eighty degree weather, drinking beer, instead of freezing in East Coast winter hell?"

I gave an enthusiastic nod at his brilliant suggestion as I lowered the car window all the way down. "Deal," I said as I lifted my face to the warmth of the sun.

The last nine months had been incredible.

Tom and I were solid. After he and my mom got back from their trip to Miami, we took our time coming together again. We talked and made plans. There was a lot of figuring out to do, because we knew we were building something to last forever.

My mother was doing great too. She'd ended up quitting her job at the hospital only a couple of months after her leave, when the agency she'd been going to for her support group offered her a job as an office manager. She loved it there and was a lot less stressed.

She still had her struggles and bad days, but in general was doing much better. So much better in fact, she'd actually finally been up to getting on a plane to come on this trip. I looked at the rearview mirror and saw her and Libe chatting quietly. I assumed my mom was listening to all the instructions Libe had for what they would get up to once we got to the house. Those two were thick as thieves these days.

There were still a lot of working parts to manage though. Work had been hectic for both Tom and I. Once the renovation in Harlem was done I finally had to come clean to Melissa about just how greatly I'd crossed boundaries with Tom. She'd been gracious and understanding, especially since I had done my job and then some, but I'd felt compelled to prove to her she could still count on me. And of course, I'd taken too much on. So now I was overseeing renovations on our other shelter.

I'd also been consulting with a social services agency for LGBT survivors here in the DR, which Tom was funding fully from the ground up. His mom and some of her friends were heading the project, and they'd asked me to help them with the programs they would implement. I was planning to visit while I was here, and could not wait to meet the staff and see the space. Tom on his end had a few things in the works with Henock and Sanjay here in the DR and in East Africa. His semi-retirement was slowly coming to an end, but he was trying very hard to maintain the work-life balance which eluded him before.

I turned around to look at him, and had to hold back from running my hands all over him. He was all business driving the humongous Range Rover which had been waiting for us at the airport parking lot. His parents left it for him there this morning, so we'd just walked to it and driven away in it.

No big deal.

One of the biggest challenges for me in the last year was learning to let the over-the-top shit that happened with Tom roll off my back. His money, the way he lived, and the things he could afford were just a part of who he was. He was so generous and low-key about it all the time, I'd had to let it go a bit. I was also getting better at allowing myself to enjoy some of the many perks. Like spending a week at my boyfriend's beachfront penthouse in the DR.

God, he was so fucking hot.

How did he still turn me on this much after a year? He looked so sexy today with a little salt-and-pepper scruff and his aviator glasses. We'd taken off our New York City winter gear after we got out of the airport, so right now he was wearing jeans, a tight t-shirt and leather flip-flops on his feet. I wanted to climb on his lap and have my way with him right here in this damn car.

My thoughts must have shown on my face, because he ran his hand along my thigh, and gave me one of those low filthy chuckles that got me so worked up.

"My folks are waiting for Libe and Dinorah to take them down to the beach as soon as we get in." He turned his face towards me and licked his lips while I sat there shivering. "So we can, umm, take a nap while they're gone." His fingers were running along the inside of my thighs in a manner suggesting there would be no such thing as napping once we were alone.

I had absolutely no problem with that.

I cleared my throat and looked at the backseat again, and saw the scheming to take over the world back there was still going strong.

"A nap sounds nice. Then you'll take me to your private beach, Mr. Hughes?"

Another dirty grin. "I have some spots I can show you."

"I bet you do." I cut my eyes at him, like I didn't know exactly what he was up to. "I'm here to get to know the rest of your family, not be your personal entertainment, Thomas Caonabo."

"I promise you'll like it."

So fucking smug.

I was about to tell him so when Libe yelled as Tom took a right turn off the highway onto a small road.

"Abuela's house!"

The road we turned onto was literally feet from the ocean. We drove past villas and houses while Libe frantically pointed at an apartment building at the end of the street. Tom's dad had retired the same year he sold his company. As a gift Tom bought some land in a beach town right outside of Santo Domingo, and built four condos for the family.

As people do.

So now his parents lived there full time. The other

three were there for Tom, his brother and any friends who wanted to come to the beach. It was completely over the top, but like I said, I was rolling with it.

As Tom parked the car in one of the spaces on the gated lot in front of the building, I heard my mom exclaim from the back.

"Tom, this is gorgeous."

I looked up at the building myself and yeah, she was right. It looked like something out of a celebrity lifestyles magazine.

It had four floors and there was glass on all sides, so you could see the ocean from any spot in the building. From where we parked we could see the white sandy beach just a few yards away. I turned to Tom with my jaw on the floor and saw him nodding as he maneuvered the car.

"We were lucky to get this land. My parents love it here, and it's nice to be able to have a place at the beach when we're home."

He jumped out of the car as his parents came out of the lobby and walked to the car. Libe was in the back taking off her seat belt, and launched herself at her abuela when she opened the door.

"Abuela! We're here!"

Tom opened the door for me and I got out to greet his parents. I'd met his dad at the shelter dedication ceremony back in the spring, and they'd both come back in the fall for a weekend. They'd met my mom then too, of course they all got along great. I also loved Tom's mom.

Like he'd predicted, when I finally got a chance to get to know her more, we realized we had a lot in common.

"Camilo, bienvenido," she said as she walked over to me with her arms wide open.

"Gracias. It's so good to be here and not freezing in New York."

She laughed as she came in for a kiss, then turned to do the same to my mom. "Hola, Dinorah. This is the best time to come. No mosquitos and no humidity. Weather is perfect all the time."

I turned around to give Tom's dad a hug.

"Hey, Richard."

"Camilo, good to see you." Then he turned to give Tom a bear hug. "Son, so happy to have you here with the family."

I spluttered at that and Tom laughed.

He turned to look at me with that lopsided smile he was usually sporting when we were deeply immersed in "family time."

"Amor, you want to go up with my folks. I'll find someone to help bring up the bags." Then he looked at his mom. "Mamí, you're taking Dinorah and Libe to the beach right?" Esperanza gave him a wink and a very enthusiastic yes as she herded us inside.

I had the suspicion Tom was up to something, but I was on vacation and not going to get worked up about him doing his usual sneaky shit.

Tom

This was it.

I was doing this *right now*. I closed the door to the apartment and heard my parents, Libe and Dinorah chatting in the hallway as they walked down one floor to their place.

Camilo and I were finally alone after almost an hour

of catching up with my family, and I was desperate to get my plan in gear.

I walked in the master bedroom and saw him standing on the balcony, his hair fluttering in the breeze.

There wasn't a cloud in the sky and the water below was a blinding blue, the rays of the sun sparkling on the surface like diamonds. Just below us the palm trees lining the beach swayed in the breeze. It was a perfect island day, and to have Camilo here with me felt like a reward I would spend the rest of my life being grateful for.

I walked up to him and put my arms around his waist, my chin on top of his head.

"Hey, amor."

He lifted his head for a kiss and I pressed our lips together.

When we pulled back Camilo sighed happily, his eyes bright. "This view is amazing, Tom. I'm having a pretty intense 'How is this my life?' moment again. I'm so happy to be here right now."

I nodded and kissed him again, once again feeling too full of feelings to speak.

"It feels so right to be on my island, with my love." His face turned soft and he pushed his head back against my chest as I spoke. "Sometimes it's like I don't have the words in English or Spanish to explain how I feel about you—"

He smiled as I moved, so we were face-to-face. "To tell you how much you've brought to my life. You've opened my eyes and my heart. You humble me with your strength. I don't deserve you."

He put his hand up as if he was about to protest, and before I lost my nerve I pulled the red and gold box out of my pocket. I'd debated on whether to do the kneeling thing and decided Camilo might just laugh at me for being corny.

I opened it to show him the two bands inside, grinning at Camilo's yelp.

"Tom?" he gasped, but a smile was already forming on his lips.

I moved to push our foreheads together.

"Camilo, mi amor. You're the one. From the very first moment I saw you, you've been changing my life. I want us to wake up together every day. You're my forever, Camilo."

I closed my eyes then, and could feel Camilo's cheeks popping while I asked what felt like the most important question of my life. "Will you marry me?"

I opened my eyes and found him nodding, as he pushed on his tiptoes to kiss me hard. He nipped at my lips as I fumbled with getting the rings on our fingers. When we pulled back he had a pissed off look on his face.

I couldn't help laughing. "You're mad at me now?"

He put his hand up to look at the ring and then pulled my head back down, so he could kiss me again. "Like you had to ask me? I've *been* ready, Tom."

I threw my head back, laughing again, and picked him up. I was so ready to be done with all this, and move on to the real celebration. But just as he wrapped his legs around my waist and I turned for the bedroom, we heard a chorus of voices coming from my parents' balcony on the floor below.

"Did he say yes?"

I could hear Libe's excited little voice over the rest. Camilo laughed with his lips against my neck, as I walked us back close enough to look down at my parents' balcony.

When we could see them, we both leaned over and answered together.

"*Si!*"

* * * * *

Reviews are an invaluable tool when it comes to spreading the word about great reads. Please consider leaving an honest review for this or any of Carina Press's other titles that you've read on your favorite retailer or review site.

To purchase and read more books by Adriana Herrera, please visit her website: adrianaherreraromance.com.

Or sign up for her newsletter: adrianaherreraromance.com/newsletter.

Acknowledgments

Somewhere in the middle of writing Camilo and Thomas's book, I realized that I was not only writing love stories centering Afro-Latinx life, food, culture and queer communities— I was also writing a love letter to Latina mothers. The strength, resilience and fierce love of immigrant women, are at the center of what make our communities push forward. They continue to be the place where we come to find our strength and to rest our heads. I'm so honored that my stories can offer a glimpse of how mighty Latina women are.

Getting a book ready for the world can be quite a journey, but I have been so lucky to have so many amazing people with me along the way.

I am so grateful for:

Kerri Buckley, my editor, for helping me get these stories to exactly where I need to take them. We continue to be an awesome team!

The Carina PR and Marketing team, for all your support getting my stories out there.

Linda Camacho, my agent, for everything and especially for your book naming prowess. Camilo, Tom and I thank you. I can't even remember what titles I came up with, but your suggestions were perfect.

My writing community. Alexis, Harper, Kate, La-Quette, JN, Tere and Rayna. I can't even imagine what my writing journey would be without you guys.

My partner and my girl. The love, support and enthusiasm I receive from you both is *everything.*

Thank you to my beta readers—Tina and Elsa—for your encouragement and your generosity.

To JC Lillis and Lydia San Andres for your kind words and sound advice. Camilo and Tom's story is that much stronger because of you.

Finally, thank you to Harlem and the Bronx. I always dreamed of writing a love story that took place in the parts of New York City that gave me and my people a home in New York. The Bronx was the place that harbored my aunts when they left DR in the sixties to come to the States, and the place I spent summers growing up. After I'd made my own passage from the island thirty-five years later, Harlem was the first place in New York City that made me feel like I'd landed in my forever home. I hope I did them justice.

Author's Note

New Beginning is not completely fictional and neither is the work that Camilo and his coworkers do. Domestic Violence is considered a public health issue by the Center for Disease control.

No matter where you live or who you are, there are people in your community, people you know, who are experiencing this type of violence. In those same communities there are organizations working tirelessly to support survivors on their journey to safety.

If you'd like to support your local domestic violence social services agency, here are a few places where you can learn how to do so.

https://www.domesticshelters.org/
https://www.thehotline.org/

*And coming soon from Carina Press and
Adriana Herrera*

*Haitian-born professor Patrice Denis is not here for
distractions that will veer him off the path he's worked
so hard for. One particular distraction: Easton Archer.
The goldenboy prosecutor who last summer gave Patrice some of the most intense nights of his life...and is
still on his mind over a year later.*

*Read on for a sneak preview of
American Love Story,
the next book in
Adriana Herrera's Dreamers series.*

Chapter One

Easton

He made my heart stop.

Over a year had passed since I'd seen Patrice Denis for the first time, and still, he was the most beautiful man I'd ever seen. Too bad I was so inconsequential to him that he'd been in Ithaca for over a month and was yet to send me a text with as much as a "fuck you."

I stood there observing him from a distance. He had his locs coiled on top of his head, and was wearing glasses that I'd never seen before, distractedly talking to a man who seemed a lot more invested in the conversation than Patrice was. As I watched the guy lean in close enough to brush against Patrice's shopping cart, I gripped the handle of mine so tight it squeaked. An unexpected flare of jealousy, coming out of nowhere, just from seeing someone in his space. I shook my head, amazed at the feeling. I'd spent my entire adulthood thinking I just was not the jealous type.

That was before Patrice Denis walked into my life.

I was still trying to decide whether I should just keep moving or go say hello when the man he'd been talking to walked away. Patrice looked after him, his face stony. The relief loosening my chest did not go unnoticed.

I headed towards him, knowing there was a good chance I'd get the same icy reception the other guy got, but I wasn't strong enough to stay away. When my cart was only a few feet from him, he turned around and the smile he gave me was...everything. After a second, he must have realized he was beaming at me and schooled his expression.

But it was too late. I'd seen it.

He'd been happy to see me. I was certain of it, and it gave me the last push I needed to jump back in. I leaned on the handle of my shopping cart and smiled up at him while he held a shiny red apple in his hands.

"Professor."

He turned fully towards me and just having his body so close made a shiver run down my spine. He had on a Cornell sweatshirt with some cutoffs and leather flip-flops on his feet. I noticed he'd switched the stud in his nose for a small silver hoop. That big body as imposing and powerful as ever. An image of that carved chest looming over me flashed through my head and it was all I could do not to whimper.

I was staring. I knew that, but I couldn't help it. At least he seemed a bit flustered too; he shook his head as if trying to clear his thoughts before answering.

"Easton. Good to see you," he said with a sheepish look, such a contrast from the serious one from a few minutes earlier. "So is this place like a major hangout in town? It's eight on a Sunday and I've already ran into like three of Nesto's relatives and half of my department."

Banter then, I could banter. "To be fair, his uncle and his sister do work here."

He conceded my point with another smile.

"Philmans is pretty busy most days, and everyone shops here. It's actually pretty calm compared to how it is during the day on the weekend. That's why I come here at this time. Get my shopping done faster."

He gave me a cheeky look and suddenly the man I'd been pining over for the last year was right in front of me. "Is that why you come here so late, avoiding disgruntled customers?"

I scoffed at the jab. "For your information, Professor Denis, I happen to have one of the best conviction records in the state."

He raised an eyebrow about a hundredth of a centimeter which I guess was his version of acknowledgement, then spoke in a more serious tone than I was hoping for. "I'm aware, counselor."

I nodded, feeling unsure of how heavy this conversation was about to get and desperate to come up with something to make the conversation lighter.

I brought out my grievances instead.

"I was wondering if you'd made it up here," I offered, lifting a shoulder, the unsaid *since I never heard from you again after you fucked me on every flat surface in my apartment* hanging in the air. "Welcome to the Finger Lakes."

He bowed his head and started to look uncomfortable, but before I could interject, he opened his mouth.

"Sorry I didn't get in touch. Things have been a little crazy this year. The job market was hectic and unpredictable and I didn't decide on this position until late in the game. It's been an adjustment, to say the least."

I dipped my head in response, not sure how to proceed. All I could think was *I want to touch him so badly.*

I had no right to it though, on that at least I was very
clear. Patrice's lack of interest was not exactly subtle.
Last summer we'd been incendiary, coming together
over and over again. From that first day when I'd seen
him helping out at the truck the attraction had been undeniable. We'd see each other by chance while he was
here helping his best friend with his food truck, and in-
evitably we'd be back at my place tearing each other's
clothes off. But in the year after, his silence had been
almost complete.

Despite our connection, once he was gone *he was
gone.*

I knew he'd been back over the winter to visit Nesto,
but he never made any efforts to get in touch or let me
know he was in town. So when I heard from a friend
in common he'd taken a job at Cornell, I was elated,
thinking we'd be able to reconnect. A part of me even
foolishly thinking his decision to take a job here had
something to do with me. I'd texted him to congratulate
him, but he'd responded with a Thank you, and never
contacted me again.

Patrice cleared his throat and I realized I had been
spacing out.

So smooth.

"No worries. I know how it is. Never thought you'd
end up here. It's a nice surprise." I dearly wished I could
sound neutral when I was around Patrice, but thirsty
and parched were my only settings when it came to him.

This time he averted his eyes before answering me.
I wondered if he was a bit more affected by me than

he let on. "Hard to say no to a job offer from an Ivy League school."

Okay, not exactly a romantic revelation. I barely contained a frustrated sigh before I nodded. "Sure. Congratulations on that. It's a big deal. How are you getting on? Did you find a place?"

He pursed his lips at the mention of his living situation. "Yeah, but I won't move in there for another week or so. I'm staying with Nesto and Jude until then." His best friend Nesto was coupled off with Jude, the local hottie librarian, and living in pre-marital bliss.

"Is your place in town?" I had no shame.

He gave me a funny look like he wasn't sure why I was asking, but after a second he nodded. "Yeah. It's that old building behind the co-op, I rented the apartment on the top floor."

I kept my expression neutral, but was surprised, that place catered more to students than faculty. He didn't look very excited about the apartment, and I didn't blame him. "I signed the lease months ago, but they've been delaying the move-in date for weeks now." He scowled. "They seem to have some issues with the building. I'm starting to think I may need to look for something else. But housing here is such a hassle. I'm not sure I'll be able to find something close to campus this late in the game. Classes already started."

I should have left it alone, but the temptation was too strong and before I knew it, I was blurting it out. "Landlords in Ithaca can be a pain in the ass. If you do want to look for other options let me know." This time I was the one clearing my throat and feeling awkward, but I pushed through. "My building has a couple of units open."

He perked up at that but almost immediately went back to his calm, cool and collected demeanor. I could tell he was interested though. He'd been to my place a few times last summer and knew it was in a nice location and that the apartments were pristine. Still, I was bracing for him to turn me down when he nodded and mumbled an *okay*.

In the interest of not coming off like a full-on creepy asshole, I decided not to offer up the fact that I owned the building. I fidgeted with the kale I had in my cart as I figured out how to proceed. I was afraid Patrice would judge me if I said it and I didn't want that. So I kept my mouth shut, and grinned at him like an idiot while he considered my offer.

He thought about it for another minute and then nodded. "I might call you up to ask for the landlord's info. If I can't move in this week, I'm looking for another place."

"Sounds good. Listen—"

I was about to take my shamelessness to the next level when I saw him jump and then pull his phone out of his pocket. He smiled when he looked at the screen, and spoke before I could. He held up his phone. "It's my mom. We're supposed to Skype tonight. I should get going," he said, giving me another smile, but this one was not at all inviting.

"It was good seeing you, Easton."

Then he walked away without so much as a backward glance. I stood there wondering if I really could read people as well as I thought. Because from the first moment with Patrice, I thought we'd shared something big, something worth exploring. I could lie to myself when he was a few hundred miles away, but maybe it was time for me to accept I was the only one who'd felt that way.

Patrice

"Well look who finally made it into town."

I heard Nesto call out as I walked into his restaurant. It was 8:00a.m. on Monday morning, and he'd run out the house at 7:00 a.m., so he could be here to receive and order. He'd left Jude, his partner, and me home to take our time before we each headed to work. But he'd forgotten his iPad which he apparently needed. So I stopped by on my way up to campus to drop it off. As I handed it to him, I saw Ari, one of Nesto's employees, walk out of the kitchen and wave at him.

"Did you drive in, P?" Nesto asked with amusement. I was not fond of driving and had only bought the black Audi SUV I now owned after much prodding from my friends.

"Yes." He laughed at my very unenthusiastic answer.

"Did you get my man to work in one piece?" His humorous tone fully masked that he actually wanted to know if I'd safely delivered his lover to work.

I'd lived most of my life in New York City and never had a need for a car. It was a big milestone to now be someone who needed to drive everywhere. Only my friend Camilo was sympathetic to my dilemma, but even he told me to face the fact I would need one if I was living in Ithaca. Juan Pablo and Nesto just told me to get over it.

My mom, on the other hand, had been very reluctant about the car purchase. She was usually all for the flex, but me driving a car upstate was not sitting well with her. She kept saying it made her nervous. I tried to temper her uneasiness by reminding her that I wasn't going to be driving in the city and would most likely not get into a head-on collision with a yellow cab going eighty on the wrong side of a one way street. As one would on any given day in Manhattan.

She acquiesced, begging me to be careful. I usually joked around with her whenever she got overprotective—I was her only child and sometimes that meant she was a bit more in my business than necessary. But this time I didn't push, because I knew what she worried about was not me getting into a fender bender. She worried about what the mother of every black man who got behind a wheel of a car in this country worried about.

Hell, I worried about it too, and it pissed me off, because I refused to live in fear. But I wasn't delusional either, and still spent the night before I picked up my car watching YouTube videos on what to do if you got stopped by the police. I also made sure I kept my license and registration on the visor above the driver seat where it was fully visible and easy to get. I hated having to do that, and how paranoid it made me feel, but I wasn't a fool. I was pretty good at avoiding things I didn't want to deal with, but some things you ignored at your own peril.

Nesto stood there tapping on the iPad I'd just handed him and shot me the occasional glance as I brooded on his question about Jude. Which only made me think of Easton.

I knew I'd run into him eventually. This was a small town and we knew a lot of the same people. And no matter how many times I told myself I was here because no one could say no to a tenure track position at an Ivy

League school, I couldn't lie to myself. The fact that Easton lived here *had* been on my mind in a big way while I was deciding to take this job.

I'd gotten other good offers, including the one which I'd told myself when I applied to it that I would take over any other, UC Berkeley. From the beginning of my search I'd said I wanted an urban area. That living in a rural area as an out black gay man would involve too much low grade stress to justify the move, even if it was a prestigious school.

And yet, here I was.

I sighed again, my lips still sealed while Nesto kept doing shit on his iPad giving me the time he knew I needed. I wondered if he suspected my mind was stuck on Easton Archer.

He was so fucking fine; seeing him last night was sobering. Everything inside of me seemed to realign when I was around him. Easton made me feel like I was the center of the universe, like I could be however I wanted and he'd be into it.

Being myself in front of people I didn't know was not easy for me. Even with my friends I was closed off and guarded at times. I was always on the lookout for what was up, mindful of the space I was taking. Aware of all the different ways people were looking at me. How I was coming off, and the assumptions people were making about me.

A black man had to always think about the space he was in.

Most of the time it seemed like people were looking right through me. Not Easton. He looked at me, like my friends and my mother looked at me. Like he could see *all* of me. The me on the outside and the me on the inside, and that fucking scared me. There was too much I didn't want to be seen so clearly. That the zen thing I tried to go for, the slow movements and the soft voice, were just my way of keeping the almost overpowering frustration I constantly felt from coming out.

Easton was so lighthearted, like he'd never known pain. The guy's job was to prosecute SVU cases, I knew he saw heinous shit day in and day out, and yet his face was always as open as a blue sky. No hurt, no bitterness. Such certainty everything would be alright. That if you fought the good fight you'd take the day. Like he could show what he felt and didn't fear anyone would come back later and use it against him.

I didn't know what to do with that.

Me, I was painfully aware of what it took for me to get the job I had. What I'd had to do, ignore, let go of, overlook or just bury down until it burned out in my gut. I could work ten times as hard as anyone else, get as far ahead as possible, and the feeling like it could all be taken away was ever present.

That was a heavy burden, one that I never seemed to shake off. Which was why I didn't let my emotions get the best of me. Closeness was not something I could do easily. I'd practically given up on getting it from anyone other than my best friends and the few family members who continued to speak to me after I came out.

Until last summer and Easton. As soon as I set eyes on him walking towards Nesto's truck, those impish green eyes and that perfect smile lured me in. I was still trying to let go. With Easton it was like my heart and my body were working together to override my entire approach to life.

"Dude, you look mad emo right now." Nesto's reproachful tone pulled me out of my fretting. "I've been standing here for five minutes waiting for you to talk. The fuck, Patrice?"

"Sorry. Just got distracted. Yeah, I gave Jude a ride, so he needs one of us to drive him back home." At the mention of his partner, Nesto's face lit up.

Jude had changed Nesto in so many ways. He and I had always been the intense ones in our foursome. Nesto, Camilo, Juanpa and me. Like me, Nesto had never made time for romance or indulged in situations that could end up messy. But here he was, he'd taken huge chances when he'd left the city to come here. He'd put it all on the line with his business *and* his heart, but it had paid off. Here he was living with a man he loved. His whole life on a different track.

I wanted to talk with Nesto about seeing Easton. I knew I needed some advice, but still couldn't make myself open my mouth. Why was is it so hard for me to talk about this stuff? Nesto was like my brother, we'd seen each other through everything. Why couldn't I open up to him about this?

Before I talked myself out of it, I did it. "I ran into Easton last night."

Nesto just shook his head at me like I confused the fuck out of him. "Oh. How's he?"

I knew the smile on Nesto's face when I mentioned Easton was genuine. Easton had been a good friend to Nesto since he'd arrived in Ithaca. My friend looked out the window, his eyes trained in the direction of the county courthouse where the District Attorney's office was. "He's been busy since he started the interim DA gig. Hasn't stopped by as often. He usually comes here for lunch a few times a week."

I shrugged, feeling stupid, because I wanted to spill my feelings all over this floor and that was very far from the norm for me.

"He was fine. It's not like we had a heart-to-heart," I said, lifting a shoulder like an asshole. "I was getting some snacks to bring to the office and he stopped by and said hello. We only chatted for like five minutes."

Nesto just stared at me, unbothered, waiting for whatever else I was going to say to come out of my mouth. After fidgeting with my pocket square and generally acting like a preschooler, I finally said it. "He said his building had some vacancies when I told him I was still waiting to move into my rental."

Nesto's eyes widened at that. Like I'd just told him the best news he'd heard in a while.

"I actually thought about him, he told me he'd been fixing up those two units after the tenants left. He wanted to do something to the floors."

He must have noticed the confused look on my face, because he angled his head before asking cautiously, "He didn't tell you he owns the building?"

Why would Easton "forget" to mention that?

"No, he sure as fuck did not tell me he'd be my landlord! You know what, forget it."

Nesto was not done, though, he flipped his hand and pointed two fingers at me. "He probably didn't mention it because you would have told him no and pulled that judgmental stank face you're rocking right now at him." Nesto twisted his mouth to the side before really going in.

"P, what the fuck is your deal, dude? I mean I know why you may be all cagey with him, but why are you doing this shit with me? Come on, son. Even if you won't admit to your damn self, I know your ass is up here at least partly because you're thirsting after his dick. Don't deny, because I know the jobs you turned down to take this one. Not that I'm not fucking elated to have you here, because you know I am."

I frowned as he spoke because he was telling the absolute truth.

"Okay let's say it's true. Let's say I do like him, what am I going to do with that, Nesto? I have literally spent the last ten years of my life thinking about how the system that Easton works every day to uphold is weaponized to keep people like me in chains. How do I reconcile that? I mean really, I'm asking, because I have no fucking clue how to do that."

Nesto sighed and looked at me like I was too fucking difficult to deal with this early on a Monday.

"I don't know, pa. I got no pearls of wisdom to bestow upon you," he said wearily. "All I know is, life is too fucking short—and frankly fucked up—to dismiss someone who makes you happy out of hand, just because your jobs put you at odds. I mean what do you really even know about Easton? Other than he's fine as fuck and a generally pleasant guy." He was ticking his fingers at this point. "And that he can obviously work his dick in a way that totally does it for you."

I rolled my eyes at that and Nesto chuckled holding up his hands to concede some kind of point.

"I know you're gonna keep agonizing over this, and I understand it's more than your jobs being at odds. Being with a man like Eason feels like compromising. *I get that.* I know it's not anything to take lightly or minimize. So take your time and do what you need to. But just chill out a little, okay? Let your guard down for once. Some people are worth sacrificing certain things for."

The beatific look on his face let me know Nesto was probably talking about Jude. They'd worked hard at their relationship and their devotion for each other was plain to see. Getting together hadn't been easy for them either. Jude had a hard past which had made the early stages in their relationship complicated, and Nesto almost let his workaholic ways ruin things for them, but they'd powered through it. Nesto had the life he always dreamed of.

He knew what he was talking about.

I dipped my head, acknowledging he had a point. "I know certain people are. I appreciate you understanding that things are complicated and I will try to take your advice and let my guard down a bit. At the moment, I'm not feeling ready though. I need more time to get my bearings here, get a feel for my department, and the fuckery I'm sure is happening there. So Easton will just have to be on hold for now."

He threw his hands up again, like he knew I wasn't going to budge an inch.

"You do you, P. We here if you need us. Let me throw you a bone by changing the subject."

I laughed. "Sure."

He looked back towards the kitchen to where Ari, who was now an assistant manager at the restaurant, was standing.

"Ari wants to ask you if you would be his mentor. Nothing too deep, just some advice on school and what to do after he's done."

The warmth in my chest at what Nesto said was a surprise. I'd never really done that before, and had no clue anyone would consider me as someone they could get mentoring from.

"Really? I thought he wanted to be a lawyer? I'm an economics and public policy guy."

Nesto shook his head. "That's the thing, he's getting interested in the stuff you do. He read your dissertation paper on distributive justice and he's been all over it. Also he's obsessed with your Twitter game." He shook his head with a baffled look on his face, like he was talking about a deep and dark world that he had no clue why anyone wanted any part of. Nesto was not the political one in our foursome.

"Ari's deep into black Twitter now, follows all the dudes you're on there pontificating with. It doesn't matter though. Whatever he ends up doing, I think it'll be good for him to have someone he can talk about stuff with." He flattened his lips, worry furrowing his brow. "He's on his own out here. All his family is still in the Congo, other than his uncle, who as far as I can tell is a raging homophobe. And that's a problem, since he's been making noise about coming out to him."

He looked towards the kitchen again. "No pressure man, of course."

I shook my head, already feeling really compelled to do this for Ari. He was such an impressive young man, and had overcome so much. He'd come to the States as a refugee from the Congo and ended up in an immigrant detention center for almost two years, before they let him go without ever giving him a reason for why they detained him in the first place. It would be an honor to support him. I nodded at Nesto and lifted my hand towards where Ari was busy checking things off from a clipboard.

"I would be happy to. I'm not sure how useful I'll be, but I'm willing to give it a shot."

I noticed that Yin, who like Ari had been one of Nesto's original employees, was standing a lot closer to Ari than a coworker would. Yin was petite, his delicate features serious as he worked with Ari.

Ari was a lot taller and bulkier than Yin. His ebony skin a contrast to Yin's milky complexion. Their bodies were comfortable next to each other though. Like lovers. Nesto must have been able to tell what I was thinking because he just glanced at them and shook his head with a fond smile on his face.

After a moment Nesto hollered for Ari. As soon as he was within reach Nesto slapped him on the back. Ari looked at him like he was his hero.

"Ari, come and talk to Patrice. He's down with mentoring you."

The young man's face lit up before looking a little embarrassed.

"Boss man, I asked you not to say anything."

Nesto shook his head and laughed. "Why, man? How's he going to know you want him to mentor you if we never say anything?"

I intervened before Nesto embarrassed the kid any more. "I'd be honored to, Ari. I'm not sure how much I can actually mentor you on, you seem to have your shit more than together. But whatever you need, let me know."

"Thank you, Patrice. That would be great. I have a lot of questions."

"Sure. I have to get going, but Nesto has my number. Send me a text and we can set up a time to talk.

I'm interested in hearing your plans, Ari. Nesto said you enrolled at Cornell this semester. Good for you."

He nodded enthusiastically. "Yes, I'm only taking two classes, but it's going well."

"Great." I waved at Nesto, who had gone behind the counter to do some work. "Catch you at home, Nes." He nodded with his eyes focused on the screen as he waved his hand over his head. I moved in to give Ari dap and then made my way out onto the street.

I walked to my car feeling lighter than I'd been a half hour before, Nesto's words about giving things with Easton a chance floating in my head.

Don't miss
American Love Story
by Adriana Herrera,
available October 2019 wherever
Carina Press books are sold.
www.CarinaPress.com

About the Author

Adriana Herrera was born and raised in the Caribbean, but for the last fifteen years has let her job (and her spouse) take her all over the world. She loves writing stories about people who look and sound like her people, getting unapologetic happy endings.

When she's not dreaming up love stories, planning logistically complex vacations with her family or hunting for discount Broadway tickets, she's a social worker in New York City, working with survivors of domestic and sexual violence.

You can find her here:
Twitter: www.Twitter.com/ladrianaherrera
Instagram: www.Instagram.com/ladriana_herrera
Facebook: www.Facebook.com/laura.adriana.94801
Website: AdrianaHerreraRomance.com
Newsletter: adrianaherreraromance.com/newsletter/